PRAISE F...

1632:
"A rich complex alte... ...and vivid action. A great ... ...ake

" ... gripping and expertly detailed ... a treat for lovers of action-SF or alternate history ... battle scenes depicted with power ... distinguishes Flint as an SF author of particular note...." —*Publishers Weekly* (in a starred review)

1633:
"[T]thoughtful and exciting ... highly recommended."
—*Publishers Weekly*

"[Readers] of Flint's 1632 will see its strengths in its sequel right from the beginning ... The same formidable historiography, wit, balance ... [readers] will turn every page and cry for more, which the authors intend to provide."
—*Booklist*

" ... take[s] historic speculation to a new level in a tale that combines accurate historical research with bold leaps of the imagination ... [a] rousing tale of adventure and intrigue."
—*Library Journal*

1634: The Galileo Affair:
"In many ways this reads like a Tom Clancy techno-thriller set in the age of the Medicis with the Three Stooges thrown in for seasoning.... The closing chase sequence is literally a riot." —*Publishers Weekly*

" ... *1634* is long on political intrigue and romance ... [and] an attempt to free Galileo from his trial and house arrest by the Inquisition. That Galileo turns out to be crotchety and unpleasant instead of a noble defender of truth only adds to the mix. This is a good choice for fans of alternative history...." —*Library Journal*

BAEN BOOKS by ERIC FLINT

Ring of Fire series:
1632 by Eric Flint
1633 by Eric Flint & David Weber
Ring of Fire edited by Eric Flint
1634: The Galileo Affair by Eric Flint & Andrew Dennis
Grantville Gazette edited by Eric Flint

Joe's World series:
The Philosophical Strangler
Forward the Mage (with Richard Roach)

Pyramid Scheme
(with Dave Freer)

Mother of Demons

Crown of Slaves
(with David Weber)

The Course of Empire
(with K.D. Wentworth)

The Warmasters (with David
Weber & David Drake)

The Shadow of the Lion
(with Mercedes Lackey
& Dave Freer)

This Rough Magic
(with Mercedes Lackey
& Dave Freer)
The Wizard of Karres
(with Mercedes Lackey
& Dave Freer)

Rats, Bats & Vats
(with Dave Freer)
*The Rats, the Vats,
& the Ugly*
(with Dave Freer)

Mountain Magic
(with David Drake, Ryk E.
Spoor & Henry Kuttner)

*The World Turned
Upside Down*
(edited with David Drake
& Jim Baen)

The Bellisarius series, with
David Drake:
An Oblique Approach
In the Heart of Darkness
Destiny's Shield
Fortune's Stroke
The Tide of Victory

The General series, with
David Drake:
The Tyrant

Grantville Gazette

volume 1

edited by
Eric Flint

GRANTVILLE GAZETTE

A Baen Books Original

Baen Publishing Enterprises
P.O. Box 1403
Riverdale, NY 10471
www.baen.com

ISBN: 0-07434-8860-1

Cover art by Thomas Kidd

First printing, November 2004
Second printing, April 2005

Distributed by Simon & Schuster
1230 Avenue of the Americas
New York, NY 10020

Produced & designed by Windhaven Press, Auburn, NH
Printed in the United States of America

Contents

Preface for the paperback edition,
   by Eric Flint...1

FICTION:

Portraits, by Eric Flint 5
Anna's Story, by Loren Jones 17
Curio and Relic, by Tom Van Natta 77
The Sewing Circle, by Gorg Huff 115
The Rudolstadt Colloquy, by Virginia De Marce 233

FACT:

Radio in the 1632 Universe, by Rick Boatright 297
*They've Got Bread Mold, So Why Can't
   They Make Penicillin?* by Robert Gottlief 319
Horse Power, by Karen Bergstralh 335

Afterword, by Eric Flint..361

❧ To Cheryl Daetwyler ❧

Baen's Bar

Throughout this book you will see references to Baen's Bar and a conference there devoted to the 1632 universe ("1632 Tech Manual" conference). The Bar is an Internet website, a virtual bar, if you will, where readers and fans of Baen Books hang out, chat, and take part in some serious (and not-so-serious) discussions, including Baen books.

How do you get there?

1. Go online and open up your web browser. Type (without quotes): "http://bar.baen.com" into the Address/Location bar in your browser & hit the Go radio button.
2. Sign up for the Bar at the WebBoard sign-in page.
3. Log into the WebBoard and you will see a listing of all the conferences at the Bar.
4. Be sure to read the FAQs conference, especially the "Newbies FAQ" before posting for the first time in the Bar.
5. See you there!

Editor's Preface

Eric Flint

The *Grantville Gazette* originated as a by-product of the ongoing and very active discussions which take place concerning the 1632 universe I created in the novels *1632, 1633* and *1634: The Galileo Affair* (the latter two books co-authored by David Weber and Andrew Dennis, respectively). This discussion is centered in one of the conferences in Baen's Bar, the discussion area of Baen Books' web site (www.baen.com). The conference is entitled "1632 Tech Manual" and has been in operation for almost five years now, during which time over one hundred thousand posts have been made by hundreds of participants.

Soon enough, the discussion began generating so-called "fanfic," stories written in the setting by fans of the series. A number of these, in my opinion, were good enough to be published professionally. And, indeed, a number of them were—as part of the anthology *Ring of Fire*, which was published by Baen Books in January, 2004. (*Ring of Fire* also includes stories written by established authors such as myself, David Weber, Mercedes Lackey, Dave Freer, K.D. Wentworth and S.L. Viehl.)

The decision to publish the *Ring of Fire* anthology triggered the writing of still more fanfic, even after submissions to the anthology were closed. *Ring of Fire* has been selling quite well since it came out, and I'm putting together a second anthology similar to it which will also contain stories written by new writers. But, in the meantime . . . the fanfic kept getting written, and people kept nudging me—okay, pestering me, but I try to be polite about these things—to give them my feedback on their stories. The problem, from my point of view, was that that involved work for me with no clear end result I could see.

Hence . . . the *Grantville Gazette*. Once I realized how many stories were being written—a number of them of publishable quality—I raised with Jim Baen the idea of producing an online magazine which would pay for fiction and factual articles set in the 1632 universe and would be sold through Baen Books' Webscriptions service. Jim was willing to try it, to see what happens.

In the event, the first issue of the electronic magazine sold well enough to make continuing the magazine a financially self-sustaining operation. Since then, a second volume has come out and we're in the process of putting together the third and fourth volumes.

So, Jim decided to try a new experiment: this volume, which is a paperback edition of the first electronic issue, with a new story by me included in the mix. It's an experiment, because we don't know yet whether we'll do the same thing with later volumes of the magazine.

There are four stories in this issue, in addition to the one I wrote for it. Two of them—Loren Jones' "Anna's Story" and Tom Van Natta's "Curio and Relic"—were originally submitted for the anthology *Ring of Fire*. Both of them were stories I would have included in the anthology, except that I ran out of space and, for one reason or another—none of which involved the actual quality of the writing—I decided to accept other stories instead. Loren does have a story appearing in *Ring of Fire,* by the way, entitled "Power to the People."

Virginia DeMarce, the author of another story contained here ("The Rudoldstadt Colloquy"), is another of the authors with a story in *Ring of Fire.* She is also my co-author in an upcoming novel in the 1632 series, *1634: The Austrian Princess.* Finally, her story here introduces a character—Cavriani—who will figure in later stories in the series. (Indirectly he already has, in fact, in the form of another member of the Cavriani family, in *1634: The Galileo Affair.*)

Gorg Huff's "The Sewing Circle" was submitted for the magazine. Gorg is a new writer in the setting, who has not previously been published. He does have other stories coming out in later volumes of the magazine, including a sequel to the one in this book.

All three factual articles in this issue were written at my request. Rick Boatright was the radio expert whom David Weber and I leaned on for advice while writing *1633*, and his article fleshes out the background for the radio material contained in that novel (as well as future novels in the series). The same is true for Bob Gottlieb's expertise with regard to disease and antibiotics. Karen Bergstralh is an experienced horsewoman and an expert on horses, a subject which I find is routinely mishandled in fiction. (Especially the movies—the downhill charge in the recent movie *The Two Towers* is admittedly a lot of fun. It is also preposterous.)

—Eric Flint
April 16, 2004

Portraits

Eric Flint

"I still can't believe I did that," said Anne Jefferson, studying the painting. It was obvious that she was struggling not to erupt in a fit of giggles.

Pieter Paul Rubens looked at her, smiling faintly, but said nothing. He'd gotten a better sense of the way the woman's mind worked, in the days he'd spent doing a portrait of the American nurse, even to the point of understanding that for her the menial term "nurse" was a source of considerable personal pride. But he still didn't fool himself that he really understood all the subtleties involved. There was a chasm of three and half centuries separating them, after all, even leaving aside the fact that they were—at least officially—enemies in time of war. If not, admittedly, actual combatants.

The sound of siege cannons firing outside reminded

him of that enmity. For a moment, the big guns firing at distant Amsterdam caused the windows in the house to rattle.

The Jefferson woman heard them also, clearly enough. Her grin was replaced by a momentary grimace. "And back to the real world . . ." he heard her mutter.

But the grin was back, almost immediately. "It's the pom-poms and the baton," Jefferson said. "Ridiculous! I never even tried out for the cheerleading squad."

Rubens examined the objects referred to. His depiction of them, rather. The objects themselves were now lying on a nearby table. They weren't really genuine American paraphernalia, just the best imitations that Rubens' assistants had been able to design based on the American nurse's description. But she'd told him earlier than he'd managed to capture the essence of the things in the portrait.

"Coupled with the American flag!" she half-choked. "If anybody back home ever sees this, I'll be lucky if I don't get strung up."

The English term *strung up* eluded Rubens, since his command of that language was rudimentary. He'd spent some months in England as an envoy for King Philip IV of Spain, true, during which time he'd also begun painting the ceiling of the Royal Banqueting House at Whitehall Palace. But he'd spent most of his time there in the entourage of the English queen, who generally spoke in her native French.

However, he understood the gist of it. Jefferson had spoken the rest of the sentence in the German which they'd been using as their common tongue. Jefferson's German was quite good, for someone who'd only first spoken the language three years ago. Rubens' own German was fluent, as was his French, Italian, Latin and Spanish. Not surprising, of course, for a man who was—and had been for several decades now—recognized by everyone as the premier court artist for Europe's Roman Catholic dynasties, as well as being a frequently used diplomat for those same dynasties.

"Do you really think they will be offended?" he asked mildly.

Jefferson rolled her eyes. "Well, if anyone ever sees it I'll probably get away with it just because it was done by Rubens. You know, *the* Rubens. But they don't call them 'hillbillies' for nothing. Seeing me half-naked, wrapped in an American flag and holding pom-poms and a cheerleader's baton . . ." She brought her eyes back to the portrait, and shook her head ruefully. "I still don't know what possessed me to agree to this."

"Indulging a confused old artist, shall we say?" Rubens smiled crookedly. "You have no idea what a quandary your books from the future pose to an artist. If you can see a painting you *would* have done, do you still do it? When every instinct in you rebels at the notion? On the other hand . . ."

He glanced over his shoulder. His young wife Hélèna Fourment was sitting on a chair nearby, looking out the window. "Who knows? I may still do the original portrait, with her as the model as she would have been. But this seemed to me an interesting compromise. Besides . . ."

His eyes moved to the portrait, then to the young American model. "I was trying to capture something different here. Hard to know whether I succeeded or not, of course. You are such a peculiar people, in many ways."

Hearing a small commotion in the corridor outside his studio, the artist cocked his head. "Ah. Apparently the day's negotiations are concluded. Your escort is here to return you to Amsterdam. It has been a pleasure, Miss Jefferson. Will I see you again some day?"

Anne went over to a side table and began gathering up her things. "Who knows, Master Rubens? We might none of us survive this war."

"True enough. Even for those of us not soldiers, there is always disease to carry us away. So—please. Take the portrait with you."

She stared back at him over her shoulder. Then, stared at the painting.

"You've got to be kidding. That's . . . a *Rubens.*" For a moment, her mouth worked like a fish gasping out of water. "The only place you find those in the world I came from is in museums. Each one of them is worth millions."

"You are no longer in that world," Rubens pointed out. "Please. In this world of mine, you will do me the favor. And—who knows?—perhaps the portrait will somehow help shorten the war."

He took it off the easel and presented it to her. Hesitantly, Anne took it.

"You're sure?"

"Oh, yes. Quite sure."

After Jefferson left, Rubens turned to his wife. "A pity she is such a skinny thing," he murmured. "Of course, she wouldn't let me portray her breasts properly anyway. Odd, the way their American modesty works."

Fourment simply smiled. It was a rather self-satisfied smile. She was even younger than Jefferson, had a bosom that no-one would describe as "skinny," and there was nothing at all odd about the way her modesty worked. In her world, she was a proper wife and always properly attired as such. In her husband's world, she was whatever he needed her to be.

"When are you going to do *The Three Graces*?" she asked. "Or *The Judgment of Paris*?"

He shrugged. "Perhaps never."

Fourment pouted. "I thought I looked *good* in those paintings!"

Rubens didn't know whether to laugh or scowl. In another universe, those paintings would have been done in the year 1638. Bad enough for an artist to be confronted with illustrations of his future work. Worse still, when the wife who served as the model for them began wheedling him about it!

In the end, he laughed.

Another man was scowling.

"I still don't like the idea," Jeff Higgins grumbled, as he and Anne Jefferson brought up the rear of the Dutch delegation returning from the parlay to Amsterdam. "And Gretchen'll be having a pure fit."

"She'll get over it," Anne said firmly. "Look, I had orders. So there's an end to it."

She gave Jeff a none-too-admiring sidelong glance. "How is it, three years after the Ring of Fire, that you *still* can't ride a horse?"

Jeff gave the horse he was mounted on a look that was even less admiring. "I don't *like* horses, dammit. I'm a country boy. The only breed of horse I recognize is Harley-Davidson."

"You own a Yamaha."

"Fine. I'm a traitor too."

"Give it a rest, Jeff!" Now Anne was scowling. "I had *orders*."

"Mike Stearns is too damn clever for his good," Jeff muttered.

"So run against him, the next election."

Jeff ignored the suggestion. His head was now turned to his left, where the Spanish batteries were located.

"Well, at least it looks like they've stopped firing. I guess we'll get back into the city after all."

"Like we have every other time. You're paranoid. And what are you complaining about, anyway? *I'm* the one who has to ride a horse carrying a great big portrait. The only thing that's saved me so far is that he didn't have it framed."

Jeff looked at the portrait Anne was balancing precariously on her hip. He couldn't see the actual image, because it was wrapped in cloth.

"I can't believe it. A *Rubens*. When are you going to show it to us?"

Jefferson looked very uncomfortable. "Maybe never. I haven't decided yet."

"Like that, huh?" Jeff's scowl finally vanished, replaced by a grin. "Gretchen won't let you keep it under wraps, you know that. She'll insist on that much, at least."

When Rubens was ushered into the small salon which the Cardinal-Infante used for private interviews, Don Fernando rose to greet him. The courtesy was unusual, to say the least. The Cardinal-Infante was the younger brother of the King of Spain, in addition to being the prince in all but name who now ruled the Spanish Netherlands. People rose for him, not the other way around.

But he was a courteous young man, by temperament— and, even for him, Rubens was . . . Rubens.

"What is it, Pieter?" asked Don Fernando.

"Thank you for responding to my request so quickly, Your Highness." Rubens reached into his cloak and drew forth several folded pieces of paper. "After Miss Jefferson departed my studio and returned to Amsterdam, we discovered that she had left this behind. It was lying on the side table near the entrance."

The Cardinal-Infante frowned. "You wish me to have it returned to her? Forgive me, Pieter, but I'm very busy and this hardly seems important enough—"

"Your Highness—please. I would not pester you over a simple matter of formalities. Besides, I'm quite certain she left it behind deliberately." He gestured toward a desk in the corner. "May I show you?"

The Spanish prince nodded. Rubens strode over to the desk and flattened the papers onto it, spreading out the sheets as he did so.

"She is a nurse, you know—a term which, for the Americans, refers to someone very skilled in medical matters. But I'm quite sure she didn't draw these diagrams. That was done by a superb draftsman. Not to mention that the text is in Latin, a language I know she is unfamiliar with."

The Cardinal-Infante had come to his side, and was now bent over examining the papers. As was to be expected of a royal scion of Spain, Don Fernando's own Latin was quite good.

"God in Heaven," he whispered, after his eyes finished scanning the first page.

"Indeed," murmured Rubens. "It contains everything, Your Highness. The ingredients, the formulas, the steps by which to make it—even these marvelous diagrams showing the apparatus required."

The Cardinal-Infante's eyes went back to the lettering which served as a title for the papers. *How to Make Chloramphenicol.*

"But can we trust it?" he wondered.

Rubens tugged at his reddish beard. "Oh, I don't doubt it, Your Highness. I realize now that was why she agreed to pose for me, even though it obviously made her uncomfortable. That strange American modesty, you know. Scandalous clothing combined with peculiar fetishes regarding nudity."

The Spanish prince cocked his head. With his narrow face, the gesture was somehow birdlike. "I am not following you."

Rubens shrugged. "Over the days of a sitting, an artist gets to know his model rather well. Well enough, at least, to be able to tell the difference between a healer and a poisoner." He pointed to the papers on the desk. "You can trust this, Your Highness. And, in any event, what do you have to lose?"

"Nothing," grunted Don Fernando. "I'm losing a dozen men a day to disease now. Mostly typhus. We can test it on a few of them first. If we can make the stuff at all, that is."

"That's no problem, I assure you." Rubens hesitated a moment. "We're in the Low Countries, you know. Not—ah—"

"Benighted Spain?" The Cardinal-Infante laughed. "True enough. Outside of Grantville itself—maybe Magdeburg too, now—there is probably no place in Europe better supplied with craftsmen and artisans and workshops."

The two men fell silent, looking down at the papers.

"Why?" the Cardinal-Infante finally asked. "From what you're saying, she could hardly have done this on her own."

The continent's greatest artist pondered the matter for a moment. Then, shrugged. "Perhaps we should just tell ourselves they also have peculiar notions of war. And leave it at that."

"That won't be good enough, I'm afraid." Don Fernando sighed. "I have no choice but to use it. But . . . why do I have the feeling I'm looking at a Trojan Horse here?"

Rubens' eyes widened. "It's just medicine, Your Highness."

The Spanish prince shook his head. "Horses come in many shapes."

Gretchen was, indeed, still in a steaming fury. "Why don't we hand them ammunition as well?" she demanded.

Anne was tired of the argument. "Take it up with Mike, dammit! I was just doing what he told me to do, if I ever got the chance."

Gretchen stalked over to the window of the house in Amsterdam where the American delegation was headquartered. Along the way, she took the time to glare at the wife of the man in question.

Rebecca just smiled. Diplomatic, as always. "It's not just the soldiers, you know."

Diplomacy was wasted on Gretchen. "You propose to tell *me* that? I am the one who was once a camp follower, not you!"

Gretchen was at the window now, and slapped her hand against the pane. Not, fortunately, quite hard enough to break it. "Yes, I know that three women and children die from disease in a siege, for every soldier who does. So what? It's the soldiers who do the fighting."

Rebecca said nothing. Eventually, Gretchen turned away from the window. To the relief of everyone else in the room, her foul humor seemed to be fading. If nothing else, Gretchen could always be relied upon to accept facts as given.

"Enough," she stated. "What's done is done. And now, Anne, show us this famous portrait."

Anne fidgeted. Not for long.

"Do it!" Gretchen bellowed. "I will have *that* much satisfaction!"

After the portrait was unveiled and everyone stopped laughing, Gretchen shook her head.

"You coward," she pronounced. "If we're to play at this posing game, let us do it properly. I will show you."

The next morning, Rubens was summoned by the Cardinal-Infante to that area of the siegeworks where the Spanish prince was positioned every day.

Once he arrived atop the platform, the prince handed him an eyeglass and pointed toward Amsterdam.

"This, you will want to see."

After peering through the eyeglass for a moment, Rubens burst out laughing. "That must be the famous Richter."

He lowered the eyeglass. "No odd modesty there. What a brazen woman! And I see she's read the same books I have. One of them, at least."

Don Fernando cocked his head. "Meaning?"

Rubens pointed toward the distant figure of Gretchen Richter, posed atop the ramparts of the besieged city. "That's a painting that will be done—would have been done—two hundred years from now. By a French artist named Eugène Delacroix. It's called *Liberty Leading the People*. And now, Your Highness, with your permission, I *must* gather my materials. The opportunity is impossible to resist. What magnificent breasts!"

The Cardinal-Infante's eyes widened. "You will *not* give it the same title!" The words were half a command, half a protest. "Damnation, I don't care if she's naked from the waist up and waving a flag. She's still a rebel against my lawful authority!"

"Oh, certainly not, Your Highness. I'll think of something suitably archaic."

A moment later, Rubens was scampering off the platform, moving in quite a spry manner for a man in his mid-fifties.

The prince sighed, and gave in to the inevitable. "Tell the batteries not to fire on that portion of the city's defenses, until I say otherwise," he told one of his officers. He smiled ruefully. "Hell hath no fury like an artist thwarted."

After the officer left, Don Fernando went back to studying the distant tableau through the eyeglass. A magnificent pair of breasts, indeed.

By the time Rubens returned, with his needed paraphernalia, the prince of Spain had made his decision.

"You will call it *The Trojan Horsewoman*," he proclaimed. "That seems a suitable title, for a portrait depicting what has become the most peculiar siege in history."

Anna's Story

❧

Loren Jones

Anna ran for all she was worth as the mercenaries chased her, fleeing her father's farm with no destination in mind except away. Two of the mercenaries followed her, shouting as she ran for her life and virtue. She didn't notice the change in the landscape until she ran over the edge of a small cliff and collided with a strange man.

Another scream ripped from her throat as she looked around. Strange men in strange black clothes were all around her, surrounding her and the man she had collided with. She looked down and saw some sort of medal on his chest. That medal proclaimed him the leader, and her fear redoubled as she imagined the punishment he would inflict for her seeming attack upon his person. Again instinct sent her surging to her feet and running away, down the hill and across a stream that shouldn't be there.

17

Behind her she heard the *boom, boom* of two arquebuses being fired in rapid succession, followed by several sharp cracks that sounded like pitch-bubbles snapping in the hearth. She didn't look back. If the new men were fighting Tilly's bastards, all the better. It gave her more time to escape and hide.

1

George Blanton was spending his Sunday in the same way he had spent every Sunday for over twenty years: watching sports on TV. It didn't matter what sport was on. Football, baseball, basketball, hockey, soccer, horse races, car races, even golf: if it was a sport, he watched it. He was watching his favorite "all sports" channel when the world suddenly went white. Tremendous thunder roared through his house, making his ears ring.

George sat stunned as the world around him returned to normal, except that the TV was off. Looking at the clock, he saw that the second hand had stopped. *Power failure?* he asked himself, nodding as he saw that even the VCR's incessantly flashing clock was blank. *Yep, power failure. Shit. But what was that flash and boom?* Standing, he walked to the pantry and opened the breaker panel. A quick inspection showed that nothing was tripped, and the tattletale on his incoming power was off. It was the line again.

Anger and disappointment roiled in his belly, making him clench his teeth. He had been complaining for more than a year about the lines into his farm, and the power company still hadn't done anything. Walking over to the window, he looked outside as he angrily picked up the phone. He knew the number by heart, and started dialing before he noticed that there was no dial tone either. Power and phone? Lovely. Well, he had a solution to one of his problems. Dave's generator was already hooked up and ready to start. Slamming the phone back onto the hook, he stomped out to the back porch, turning the main breaker off as he passed the pantry.

He paused before starting the generator to say a quick prayer for his son, Dave. Dave had gotten divorced a few years after George and Mary had retired and moved to the farm. The place was big: fifty acres of pasture and a ten-acre garden that Mary had adored, and the farmhouse had six bedrooms. There had been more than enough room for their only child to join them.

That was before Mary had gotten sick. She had played it down, refusing to go to a doctor. She had sworn that it was just her misspent youth catching up to her. Three months later she was gone. Cancer had taken the love of his life.

Dave had taken his mother's death hard. He'd been working at the mine, bringing home decent wages, but he had become eccentric. That's what his friends called it; George called it bonkers. Dave had decided that the end of civilization was near, and had begun hoarding things: guns, ammo, food, water purifiers, survival books, assorted other weapons, and clothing. And booze. The hayloft out in the barn was packed with his stuff—cheap department store footlockers full of it.

The union contract had allowed Dave to list his parents as his beneficiaries, rather than his ex-wife, and George had become financially independent on the same night that he'd lost his will to live. Dave had been driving home after drinking with his buddies, and had died when his truck hit a tree.

George shook off his momentary grief. Mary had been gone for seven years, and Dave for three. The generator had been one of Dave's better ideas. It was a good one, commercial quality, and it was tied directly into the house. So long as the main breaker was off, it would power the house and barn. The flick of a switch turned George's power back on.

George went back in to watch TV again, dismissing the flash and thunder as figments of his imagination. He was drifting these days, and figured that he had drifted off in a doze until something happened to wake him up. Probably whatever it was that knocked out the phone and electricity.

He spent fifteen minutes fiddling with the satellite receiver, but couldn't locate a signal. Now he was really getting mad. Sports had become the only thing that he looked forward to anymore. Stomping over to the phone, he grabbed it to check for a dial tone, but it was still dead. Then a flicker of movement drew his attention outside. Someone had just run into his barn.

His eyes narrowed even further. He didn't like his neighbors. They knew it, and didn't like him either. None of the kids in the area even cut across his land any more. He had seen to that by having a few of them arrested for trespassing. Now someone was in his barn.

His anger at the power company transferred to whoever was out there, but now it had become a quiet fury that bore little resemblance to his earlier boisterous rage. He walked silently out of his door and crossed the yard. The barn doors were open wide, and his Dodge Ram pickup was sitting right where he had left it. Looking around, he couldn't spot anyone, so he yelled, "Who's in here? This is private property! Get out!" Nothing moved. Then he heard a scraping sound from the loft, and something that sounded like a stifled sob.

"Come down from there!" he shouted, but there was no response. Climbing the ladder, he carefully looked around. He didn't want to be surprised and lose his grip. When he didn't see anyone, he climbed the rest of the way up into the loft. There was a trail of sorts in the dust that had blown in since the last time he had been up there, and he followed it to the back corner. As he drew near, he saw a flicker of movement. Moving closer, he grabbed the top locker in the stack that whoever was up there was hiding behind, and pulled it toward him.

A shriek pierced his ears as he spotted the disheveled young girl in the dirty dress. She was plainly terrified, and he quickly backed away. It didn't do much good. She continued to shriek as he held his hands over his ears. "Stop that noise!" he roared, almost drowning out the girl's shrieks.

Something about his shout silenced the girl. When his ears were no longer being assaulted, he took a step forward, but she shouted, *"Nein! Nein! Geh weg! Geh weg!"* George stopped. He didn't understand everything that she said, but he understood *"Nein! Nein!"* Anyone who had ever seen a WWII movie knew what that meant. "No! No!" In German.

German? *What the hell?*

George looked at the girl for a moment, and then started to put two and two together. Power and phone dead. Loud noise. Messy, frightened girl who speaks German hiding in his barn. Nodding to himself, he figured out exactly what had happened. A car or busload of German tourists had crashed and taken out a telephone pole.

Now that he knew what was going on, he calmed down. Looking at her, he saw that her dress was torn and she was covered with dirt. Well, that explained some of her fear. She'd probably heard all sorts of horror stories about the sexual habits of hillbillies. Chuckling to himself, he looked around. There were a few things in the loft that weren't part of Dave's hoard, and a box of them was right where he needed it to be. Opening the box, he brought out the old bathrobe that Mary had given him one Christmas. He hated the thing, but it was from her, so . . .

He walked back over to the girl and tried to hand it to her, but she shrank away from him, still frightened. George was getting annoyed now and stepped back to glare at her for a moment before sighing deeply. *Take it easy, you old fool. She's frightened and doesn't understand,* he silently said to himself before deciding on a plan. He put the robe on to show her what it was, and almost cursed when it stopped short of closing with six inches of his belly still exposed. Mary had given him the robe a *long* time ago. Taking it off, he again tried to hand it to the girl, but she still cried out when he stepped closer. He finally gave up and threw it at her.

"There. Put it on or don't, I don't care. Come down to the house when you feel like it." He pointed over to the house as he spoke, but the girl just sat there staring at him. He decided to try some of the pidgin German that he had picked up from the movies and said, "Comen see to da housen, ya?" The girl still just stared at him, so he gave up and left.

George returned to the house and tried the phone again. Still dead. Taking a deep breath, he looked around. Nothing seemed to be out of the ordinary. Looking back out at the barn, he nodded to himself. That girl came from somewhere. The power and phone were out for some reason. That left only one thing to do: drive to town.

The keys to his truck were hanging near the door. That had been Mary's idea when they first moved here, to hang the vehicle keys by the door like her parents had done. Now there were only two sets hanging there: the truck and the tractor. Grabbing the truck keys, he left, carefully locking the door behind him. No telling if anyone else was going to follow the girl to his farm.

He got into the truck and started it, then looked up at the loft. There was no sign of the girl, so he backed out and headed to town. He drove slowly, watching for pedestrians or any sign of a wreck, but there was still nothing out of the ordinary. He made the turn off of his road and headed toward town, but slowed and stopped in the middle of the road as his mind finally registered the countryside. There was something very wrong with what he was seeing. There was supposed to be a hill off to his left, but it wasn't there. A column of smoke was rising into the air off to the south, but there should have been trees in the way.

Cautiously driving on, he kept his eyes open for any other signs of trouble. He made it into town and found people milling about, lining the streets. Whatever the problem was, it was widespread.

An old woman in her Sunday dress waved him down and immediately climbed into the truck. "George, take me out to Jimmy's house. I have to get to the children."

"Beth, what the hell's going on here? I don't have power or phones at my place, and there's a little girl in my barn shouting German at me."

"I don't know, George. No one does. But the word we got was that Dan Frost has been shot, and there's lunatics on the loose with antique rifles, shooting at whatever moves. Now, move, damn it! I have to get to the children." Elizabeth glared at George as he put his truck in gear.

"All right, Beth, all right. If there isn't any help here in town I may as well go home, too. Damn, I wish I knew what was going on around here." He started driving back out the way that he had come, then slammed on the brakes. Looking closely at Elizabeth, he lifted one eyebrow. "You said the police chief has been shot? Who's in charge, that fool Dreeson?"

"Drive, George. No, not Henry Dreeson. Mike Stearns has taken charge. Dan deputized him and the UMWA before he passed out. Now go. You said that there's a girl in your barn? Ken Hobbs said a girl ran over the side of some cliff and collided with Dan just before he was shot. The men that shot Dan was chasin' her. That might be her. It happened out your way. I'm surprised that you didn't hear any gunshots."

"Men were chasing her? With antique rifles? God Almighty! That would explain why she's so afraid, but why's she shouting in German? And it still doesn't explain where she's from." He shrugged. "As to hearing anything, I've got the generator going. It's quieter than most, but it's still noisy as a lawn mower. Can't hear much over it if I'm close." George drove on, thinking about what he was going to do when he got home. Men with antique guns running around shooting folks. A girl in a torn dress in his barn. He almost missed the turn into Jim Reardon's place, but managed to make it without getting off of the gravel.

Elizabeth gave him a sour look, but didn't say anything until he stopped in front of the house. "Go home, George, and lock your doors. And get out a shotgun. Just ain't safe 'round here right now." She hurried up the steps and was met by Jim's wife. Once the door had closed behind them, he drove off.

George pulled into the barn and climbed out of the truck, carefully locking it behind him. It was the first time that he had ever locked his truck at home. He started to climb the ladder to the loft, but decided that he should listen to Beth and get a gun first, so he turned toward the house.

The doors were still closed and locked, and there were no broken windows. Unlocking the door, he started to put the keys back on the hook, then thought better of it and put them into his pocket instead. Then he went to his gun cabinet.

The guns were mostly sporting rifles and light shotguns, but not all of them. Nestled inconspicuously in the corner was the M-14 that Dave had been so proud of. *Antiques my ass,* he thought as he quickly loaded the rifle. Then he went to the barn again.

At first he couldn't find the girl, then he heard her on the other side of the loft. Walking carefully over to her, he smiled and held his hands open out to the sides. "Young lady, you don't need to be afraid. I'm not going to hurt you. What's your name? I'm George. George Blanton." He patted himself on the chest and said his name several more times, just like in the movies. The girl continued to stare at him.

"Are you hungry?" he suddenly asked, desperately trying to get some reaction out of her. He took a step forward and reached out his hand.

The girl shrank away from him, shouting, *"Fass mich nicht an!"* She was trying to crowd herself farther into the corner, and her eyes were so wide that he could see the whites all around.

He still didn't understand what she was saying, but the way that she was acting made her meaning clear. She was still frightened. "Okay, I'll just stay over here," George replied softly, taking a step back. "Are you hungry?" he asked, pantomiming eating. The girl didn't say anything, but she swallowed and licked her lips. George nodded and backed away.

The footlockers in the loft were all labeled, and he picked one marked READY TO EAT. In it he found vacuum-packed beef jerky, crackers that might still be edible, and an assortment of Army MREs. Where Dave had gotten *them*, he had never asked. And after asking to try one once, he had never asked that again either. *Sheesh! The things they feed to soldiers.* Grabbing some jerky strips, he turned back to the girl. She was watching him intently, and he tossed two strips to her.

She picked them up and looked at them with wide eyes and a confused expression on her face. George cleared his throat to get her attention, and, when she looked up, tore one of the packages open and took a bite of the jerky. Or at least he tried. The tough meat gave his dentures a real workout.

The girl looked carefully at the package in her hand, then followed George's example. The plastic clearly confused her, but it was when she took a bite of the meat that she finally showed some sign of life. The first piece disappeared in seconds, and the second quickly followed. And after a few moments she had the reaction that George had been waiting for. She began swallowing and trying to clear her throat. Whatever else you wanted to say about jerky, it was dry as a bone.

George smiled and waved for her to follow him as he climbed down from the loft. There was a sink in the barn, and he always kept a cup or two handy. Now he made a big show of getting something to drink as the girl watched over the edge of the loft.

She finally gathered her courage and her skirts and climbed down, nervously watching over her shoulder to make sure that George didn't try anything while her back was turned. Once her bare feet were on the ground, she carefully walked toward him. George put an old coffee mug on the side of the sink and left the water running as he stepped back.

The girl came forward cautiously, watching George all of the time. When she reached the sink, she picked up the old red and white checked mug and looked it over carefully, then got some water. She seemed to find the running water fascinating, and trailed her fingers through it as she drank. After three mugs of water, she put the cup down.

George was watching her carefully, and moved over to the side of the barn, staying in her field of vision, and picked up a scrap of cloth. He tossed it to her, but she just caught it and stood there. He pantomimed washing his face, and she dropped the cloth and backed away. Then her eyes opened wide and she looked past him down the road.

George spun around, unslinging the rifle and bringing it up to his shoulder fairly quickly. Scanning the area carefully, he turned back when there was a sound behind him. He glanced back just in time to see her disappear into the loft again.

George was torn between anger and amusement, but the amusement won out in the end. "Why, you little scamp! You suckered me," he said, turning his face up toward the loft. A chuckle rumbled in his chest, and he felt himself grinning. Girls: born to deceive. Shaking his head, he went to the house and left her to her own devices for a while. The jerky had awakened his appetite, and he intended to deal with it properly.

His mother had taught him to cook when he was a child so that he could help with his brothers and sisters. During his more than seventy years he had almost always cooked. Not everything, mind you. It had been part of Mary's pride that she held a job and kept up her household as well, but there were times when she had needed his help. When Dave had been born he had been given a choice of cook or change diapers, so he had immediately gone to the kitchen. Now that Mary and Dave were both gone, he tended to himself. And his unasked-for guest.

He thought about the girl as he rummaged around in his pantry. She looked to be about fourteen, maybe a little older. Wracking his brain for a moment, he finally remembered what Dave had eaten most when he was a teenager: macaroni and cheese. Fortunately, he had a ready supply and years of experience fixing it. He quickly filled a pan with water, salted it lightly, and set it on the stove to boil. Then he grabbed a box of mac-and-cheese and a measuring cup.

He caught himself humming a merry tune as he worked, and paused to wonder why he was so happy. When he finally realized what he was so happy about, he had to stop and sit down. He had been lonely for so long, and he had always driven off everyone who tried to befriend him. Now a stranger, a frightened little girl, was forcing her company on him. And he loved it.

The hiss of water splattering over the rim of the pot brought him back into the real world, and he quickly added the noodles to the water and prepared the rest of the fixin's. Ten minutes later he had a pot of prime teenager chow ready to go.

Two bowls balanced nicely on top of the pot, and he grabbed two spoons and a serving spoon. No sense in being a barbarian about things. Then he returned to the barn and stopped in his tracks. How was he supposed to get the food up to the loft? An idea occurred to him immediately. Setting down his burden, he walked over and grabbed his stepladder.

Setting it up beside the loft ladder, he put the pot on top, climbed halfway up the loft ladder, then reached down and put the pot up on the loft floor. Then he climbed the rest of the way up.

The girl was peeking out from behind a stack of footlockers as he heaved himself up the last step. "Well, there you are," he said, slightly out of breath. "You could have helped a little, you know." He bent over and picked up the pan and bowls, groaning a little as he straightened back up. "And don't you dare giggle." He glared at the girl, and she immediately vanished.

George spent a few minutes arranging a picnic area. Two stacked footlockers made a table, and two more, one on each side, made benches. Then he placed the bowls and served the mac-and-cheese. "Come on," he said gently, waving to the pair of eyes that was peeking at him over a pile of lockers. She came forward shyly, like a kitten, and he swore to himself that if she'd had whiskers they would've been twitching. George sat with his hands in his lap, waiting. When she was seated across from him, he bowed his head and said Grace. He really didn't care if she joined him or not. He had been saying Grace and a lonely prayer for Mary and Dave for years. When he looked up, she was sitting with her head bowed, her lips moving silently. Then she crossed herself and looked up into his eyes. "Ladies first," George said softly, indicating that she should take a bowl.

The girl looked at him, then slowly took the bowl that was closer to her. He nodded and took the other bowl. She waited until he had taken a few bites before she started eating, but she was done long before he was. He smiled as he remembered that Dave had been much the same at that age. She was all but licking the bowl, and kept glancing at the pot, so he chuckled and waved for her to help herself. There wasn't much left, but it was gone entirely before he finished his. They sat there staring at one another for a few moments, and she seemed about to say something when there was the sound of a car horn honking on his road, coming closer by the minute. She was up and hiding in a flash, and George felt his annoyance growing again. Damn it all, the girl was acting like she had never heard a horn before.

Leaving the dishes where they were, he climbed down and waited at the tailgate of his pickup. A sedan soon pulled to a dusty stop in front of him, and Beth Reardon climbed out. "George, is that girl still here?"

"Yes. I was just about to get her talking when you drove in, honking like a flock of geese."

"Harrumph! Not likely. George, Jimmy just came back from the high school. Seems that there was more trouble than we thought." She quickly related the story of the firefight at the farm. "That girl the miners rescued claims that we're in Germany, Year of Our Lord 1631."

George stared at her for a moment, then looked back over his shoulder. "Bullshit." WHACK! He stared at Elizabeth as if she had grown horns and rubbed the suddenly sore spot on his chest.

"Don't you curse on the Sabbath, George Blanton." Elizabeth glared at him, and he felt surprisingly contrite. "Haven't you ever read any time travel stories?"

George eased away from her a little. "When I was younger, and didn't know any better. In the fifties. Even TV has given up on real time travel."

"Well, TV didn't come up with this, George. Those men who were chasing her raped her Ma and damn near killed her Pa. She doesn't speak German by accident, and she doesn't speak *English* at all. And she's never seen anything like us before." Elizabeth stopped talking and looked up into the barn. Sure enough, there was a dirty face with wide eyes staring down at her.

Walking over to where she was just below the girl, she held out her hand. "Come down, child. You're safe here." Reaching into her pocket, she pulled out a book. George looked over her shoulder and saw that it was a English-German dictionary. Looking up words as she spoke, she said, *"Kommen,"* flipped a few pages, *"Unten,"* flip flip, *"Mädchen."* "Come down, girl."

The girl had set straight up when Elizabeth spoke, and looked confused. Elizabeth pointed to the girl, then to the ground at her feet and repeated the three German words. *"Kommen unten, mädchen."*

The girl was looking perplexed, but she climbed down the ladder. She shyly stepped up to Elizabeth and said, *"Wer sind sie?"*

That was the first calm thing that George had heard her say, and he almost knocked Elizabeth down reaching for the dictionary. "What'd she say?"

"Hold your horses, George," Elizabeth snapped. "Let me look. *Ver sind zee.*" She looked, but couldn't find the word *"ver."* Then she looked at the pronunciation guide. "W is pronounced V. *Wer*, translates as 'Who.' *Sind* translates as 'are.' *Zee* translates as—see. Ocean or Sea. That can't be right. Let's try sea. Nope, that ain't it either. *Sei*. Looks like 'be.' *Sie* could be 'she,' 'them,' or 'they.' Who are they?" George and Elizabeth looked at one another and shrugged.

"How about 'Who are you?'" George suggested, and Elizabeth nodded.

"As good a question as any." Turning to the girl, she patted her chest. "Elizabeth. Elizabeth." Then she turned to George and patted his chest. "George.

George." Looking at the book, she flipped a few pages. "*Was*. Was? Oh, I forgot. *Vas*," flip, "*ist*," flip, "*euer*," flip, "*name. Was ist euer name, mädchen?*"

"Anna. *Ich heisse Anna.*"

"Glory be," George muttered as he rolled his eyes toward the sky. "Her name is Anna." Looking at Elizabeth, he grinned. "Ask her where she's from."

During the next hour they learned that she was from, "over there." The men who were chasing her were, "mercenary pigs." If they had caught her she would have been, "raped and killed." George grew angry at that and looked back toward the south. Then the girl whispered something to Elizabeth that he didn't catch.

"What did she say?"

Elizabeth started to open the dictionary to look it up, but stopped. She hadn't raised three daughters and ten granddaughters without seeing that facial expression and posture hundreds of times. "George, get out."

"Why?"

"Because there are some things that a gentleman leaves a lady to do in private." Elizabeth glared at him and he backed away.

"Well, all right, you don't have to get nasty about it," he muttered as he walked away. "Bossy females."

Elizabeth knew the Blanton farm well. She and Mary had spent many an afternoon in the garden complaining about their menfolk. She knew exactly where the toilet in the barn was, and she quickly led Anna to it. She had banished George because the toilet stall was just that: a horse stall with a toilet in it. It had been built that way because there was normally only one, or at most two people in the barn at any given time. And since it was mostly men, they usually had their backs to the rest of the barn anyway.

Anna looked at the white porcelain fixture with a mixture of awe and confusion written clearly across her face. Elizabeth almost laughed. "What did you expect, a board with a hole in it over a hole in the ground?" It didn't bother her at all that Anna couldn't understand her. She walked forward and lifted her skirt, then took care of her own needs first. Then she flushed the toilet and waved Anna toward it.

The girl was clearly unsure, but also clearly about to burst. The feel of the smooth, cool plastic seat was a surprise from the look on her face. When she was done, she pushed the handle and watched the water swirl away. Her eyes were wide as she turned back to Elizabeth.

Elizabeth had been busy with the dictionary while Anna had been occupied, and said, "*Kommen mit mir.*" She hoped that it really meant, "Come with me." From Anna's reaction, it did, and the two of them walked up to the house. George opened the door as they climbed the steps and ushered them through, closing and locking the door behind them. "Phone's working, Beth."

"Oh, good. I have to call Jimmy." Elizabeth quickly grabbed the phone and called her son. She related the details of what they had found out about the girl, chattering a mile a minute.

George glanced over and saw the girl watching Elizabeth talk on the phone. The look on her face said clearly enough what she was thinking. Mad. She was trapped by people who were totally mad. It was more than he could stand, and he burst out laughing. That earned him an even more troubled look from Anna, and a reprimand from Beth.

"George, what's gotten into you?"

"Her," he gasped, waving at Anna. "The look on her face, seeing you talking to yourself like a loony."

"I was *not* talking to myself, George Blanton." Elizabeth planted her fists on her hips and glared at him while he continued laughing.

"She doesn't know that. She really doesn't know that Jim was on the other end of the phone. She was just standing there, watching you have a conversation with no one. I swear, she was about to run back out of the house."

Elizabeth stopped snapping at George and looked at Anna. Sure enough, Anna looked like she was about to run away. Quickly grabbing her dictionary, Elizabeth looked up some words. "That; *das*. Is; *ist*. Our; *unser*. Way; *weg*. To; *zu*. Speak: oh, this is better. To speak to; *ansprechen*. Someone; *irgendeiner*. Far away; *weit weg*."

Anna looked at her as if she had grown horns.

"That book ain't going to do us much good for explaining things like phones or radio or TV. The girl doesn't have the background to understand. Hell, Beth, you and I both remember when TV first came out. Movies in the home. What a wonder, and we had had radio all our lives. If what you tell me is true, then she doesn't know what radio is or even that sound propagates in waves. If you showed her, she would probably think it was a demon." He paused and smiled. "Been known to think of the phone as a demon myself now and again."

Elizabeth gave him a sour look, but nodded. *"Kommen mit mir, Anna,"* she said softly. She led Anna into the kitchen and flipped on the light. Anna's reaction to that was almost comical, but Elizabeth didn't laugh. "Sit," she commanded, waving toward a chair, and Anna obeyed. George suspected that Anna hadn't understood the word, but had understood the gesture.

Over the next hour Elizabeth tried to explain a little of what they knew, fumbling through the dictionary over and over again when Anna clearly didn't understand what she meant. It was only the ringing of the phone that finally distracted her.

George answered the phone while Elizabeth and Anna looked at him. After saying "hello," George just nodded and occasionally grunted his agreement with whoever was on the other end. Then he hung up.

"Beth, that was Jim. He wants you to stay here tonight."

"Why didn't you let me talk to him?" Elizabeth asked angrily.

George stopped and looked puzzled for a moment, then shrugged. "Didn't think to. Anyway, I agree with his reasoning. It's getting dark, and he doesn't want you to drive home alone. I'd like you to stay and help with Anna. She seems to have taken a shine to you."

Elizabeth nodded and said, "All right." Then she looked at Anna. "The first thing that we need to do is to get you cleaned up." Nodding sharply once, she stood and grabbed Anna's hand, and led her to the bathroom.

What followed would forever be a mystery to George. There was a lot of shouting in German, more shouting in English, some splashing and banging, and finally silence. The door opened a crack and Elizabeth looked out. Her hair looked like she had been in a tornado. She was splattered with water, and there were flecks of soap foam liberally dispersed around her face. And her dress was in her hand with a wad of other clothes. "Go wash and dry these, George, and get us some robes."

George raised an eyebrow, but took the bundle. Robes? The only robe that he had was his own. He got to thinking and went to the linen closet. No robes, but there were those huge bath sheets that Dave had gotten. They would have to do. He handed them to Elizabeth and went to the laundry room.

Anna's clothes felt like linen and wool, and he wondered which cycle he should use. Then he looked closer and shrugged. Her dress was already badly torn. Beth's dress was good cotton, so he just threw them all in together and pressed start.

Anna and Elizabeth were sitting in the living room when he came back. Elizabeth was brushing her hair and looking smug. Anna was pouting and looked as angry as a wet kitten. George wisely kept his mouth shut.

He looked at the TV and the satellite receiver and shrugged. No sports tonight. Or maybe ever again, for that matter. He sighed and looked at the video collection on the shelves to his left. He looked at Anna and Elizabeth, then back to the tapes, and nodded to himself. They needed a distraction, and so did he. And he knew just what he wanted to see.

Anna sat up straight when the TV came on and looked startled and frightened when the pictures started flickering across its face, and then mesmerized when the movie began. *The Sound of Music* rang through the house, and Anna seemed to be fascinated by it in spite of the language difference. She listened to the singing and hummed along, much to George's annoyance. She gasped when the wonders of another world were displayed for her. And fell asleep on the couch before the second tape.

George and Elizabeth noticed and shared a smile. When the washing machine buzzed, Elizabeth went to put the clothes in the dryer. And when the dryer buzzed near the end of the second tape, she smiled and waited until the end before getting up. "That was nice, George," she said as she went to get her clothes.

George nodded and turned off the TV and VCR and put the tapes away. Anna was curled up like a kitten on the couch, and was showing far more leg than he could ignore. She was a pretty little thing, and just thinking of what had almost happened to her made his blood boil. There was a quilt over the back of the couch, and he gently pulled it over her, tucking her in carefully to avoid waking her.

Elizabeth said good night and headed to the guest room while George made sure the doors were locked and the generator had plenty of fuel. Then he went to his room, propping the M-14 beside his bed.

Morning was heralded by the arrival of Jim Reardon and his family. All seven of them. Anna stared as the group of lunatics swarmed around her asking questions, clearly not understanding what was happening. Elizabeth's bellow was rewarded by total silence.

"Marge, Lizzy, Melody, fix something to eat. Jimmy, sit down. You boys go perch somewhere. Honestly, you have no manners."

George was standing by the stairs, watching with wide eyes as Elizabeth corralled her herd. Once things had settled down, he went to the kitchen. The tattletale on his incoming line was on, and he breathed a sigh of relief. Going to the porch, he shut down the generator, then switched on the main breaker. The lights flickered a little, but hardly anyone noticed. They were all focused on Anna, who was still seated on the couch, wrapped in the quilt.

"Beth, I think the boys and I ought to excuse ourselves while you women see to Anna. If I'm not mistaken, that's her towel there on the floor."

Elizabeth looked startled for a moment, then embarrassed. "Boys, outside. Right now."

There wasn't even one objection to her order and

George was soon out at the barn with Jimmy, Jim III, Bill and Alex.

Jimmy looked at him as he leaned against the truck. "George, what have you heard?"

"Only what you and Beth have told me."

Jimmy nodded and propped himself against the door. "That's about all anyone knows right now. Dad's history books hardly mention this era. It wasn't one of his interests. The encyclopedia says that we're smack-dab in the center of the Thirty Years War." He paused when Melody ran out of the house, opened the trunk of the car, then ran back inside. "Mom said that Anna's dress was torn, so we brought some of the girls' stuff with us. She looks to be about Mel's size. Anyway, the teachers are researching what they can. All we know is that there are a bunch of mercenaries led by someone called Count Tilly raping and pillaging their way across Europe. And we are in their path." Jimmy paused for a moment, then cleared his throat. "Uh, George, do you still have Dave's stash?"

George nodded. "Up in the loft. Why?"

"We may need it."

Elizabeth shouted from the porch, stopping their conversation as she called them back into the house. George almost didn't recognize Anna at first. She was dressed in a modest blue dress that he had seen Melody wear to church a few times, and her hair had been brushed out and tied up in a simple ponytail. Little Jim, Bill and Alex immediately went silent, but their wide eyes said volumes. Volumes that their mother and grandmother could read immediately.

"Boys, go set the table," Elizabeth ordered, and they reluctantly obeyed, looking back at the pretty girl until the kitchen wall got in the way.

George really couldn't blame the boys. She was a beautiful girl, a stranger, and fit right in between them in age. As the old saying went, "I saw her first." He felt a chuckle building and finally let it loose.

Jimmy looked at him and grinned. "Yeah."

Elizabeth almost snarled at them both. "That's enough. Anna, come here," she commanded, waving to her side, and Anna obeyed. "After we eat, we have to go to the high school and see how her parents are doing. Marge says that her father is in bad shape."

Jimmy looked around. "It's going to be a tight fit in the car."

"I can take the boys with me in the truck, Jim."

"That'll be fine," Elizabeth agreed, and the boys immediately got excited.

"I call shotgun," Bill immediately shouted, and there ensued a fast and furious argument which George ended with a shouted, "Shaddup!"

Everyone looked at him with wide eyes. "Little Jim has shotgun. Literally. Jim, grab the Ithica 12-gauge out of the cabinet. I've got the M-14. Jimmy, you and Marge grab a gun too. If we're driving around these parts, we're going armed."

Jimmy looked at him and nodded. "We've got two 12-gauges in the car."

George looked at him and nodded, not needing to say anything else. Melody came out of the kitchen just then and announced that breakfast was ready. Soon everyone was eating, sitting at the little table or standing in the kitchen, and Anna was timidly trying the strange food but apparently liking what she tried.

The boys did the dishes automatically, just like at home, and soon they were sorting themselves out in the vehicles. Bill and Alex were wedged tightly between George and Little Jim in the truck seat, but it wasn't too crowded. The two younger boys together weren't as wide as George, and Little Jim wasn't much bigger than his little brothers. Anna was wedged into

the back seat of the Reardon's car between Elizabeth
and Melody, with Jimmy and Marge bracketing Lizzy
in the front.

Jimmy led off, with George close behind them. It
was a fair drive to the school, and George was watching everything as they passed. Everything seemed to
be normal, except there were hills missing from the
distance.

Mike Stearns and a beautiful woman with dark hair
met them at the school. Elizabeth had explained where
they were going to Anna, and she immediately looked
around. *"Wo ist Mutti? Wo ist mein Vater?"*

The woman with Mike smiled and said, *"Komm'
mit,"* then took Anna by the hand and led her into
the school, talking every step of the way. George and
the Reardons followed along in their wake, with Mike
bringing up the rear.

In the makeshift hospital, Anna was led to her
father first. The dark-haired woman explained what
the doctor said, and comforted her as the seriousness
of his situation became clear. Then they led her to
her mother.

Anna spoke, but the woman on the cot hardly
noticed. Then Anna cried, and collapsed, begging her
mother to look at her, to speak to her. Finally, the
woman on the cot seemed to realize who was there
and burst into tears. She grabbed Anna in a fierce
hug, crying and talking all the while.

George and the others stayed back, giving them as
much time and privacy as they could. Finally Anna's
mother pushed her away as she drifted off to sleep.
Anna sat on the floor, staring at her mother, until
Elizabeth went and collected her and led her from
the room.

Mike Stearns was waiting for them when they came
out. "Mr. Blanton, thank you for taking care of her.

None of us had any idea where she went after she knocked Dan down and ran off. We'll see if we can find a place for her to stay until her parents are ready to go home."

George looked at Anna, then at Elizabeth, and back to Mike. "She has a place to stay, Mike. And her mother, too, when she's ready."

"I thought you liked living alone, George," Elizabeth said softly. "That you didn't want any company."

"I thought so too, Beth. But I guess that I was wrong." Smiling at Anna, he held out his hand. "*Kommen*, Anna. Let's go home."

2

The drive back to George's farm was silent. Neither of them could speak the other's language beyond a few words.

Anna didn't want to risk annoying the old man. She was getting a sense of him, of his personality. He wasn't really a mean old man. He was just set in his ways. That, at least, she understood. Grandfather Steffan was like that about some things. He had his own ways, and no one could change him. That thought steadied her.

She looked out at the scenery as it sped by, amazed by how fast they seemed to be going, and how smooth the ride was. The farm wagon was nothing like this. Soon they were driving into the barn.

George opened his door and got out, but Anna just sat staring at the door.

"Well, what are you waiting for? Expect me to open the door for you like you were some lady?" he asked harshly.

Anna looked at him in confusion. She didn't understand him, and she couldn't see how to open the door.

The expression on her face finally registered, and George sighed. "Here, like this," he said, tapping on the door and pulling the handle.

Anna watched him carefully, then tried it. There was a click, but nothing happened. George said, "Push," and she looked to see him pushing the door with his other hand. Her hand came up and the door opened. She turned a radiant smile on him that stopped George in his tracks as she climbed out. She followed the example that the Reardons had set at the school and pushed the door closed behind her, then walked around the truck and stood waiting for him.

"All right, Anna, let's go inside and get you settled," George said, motioning toward the house. Anna walked beside him, watching him closely as he brought out the bundle of keys. Once the two were inside, George was at a loss as to what he should do. Elizabeth had taken her dictionary with her, and the five or six German words that he knew just weren't enough.

George finally sighed and shook his head. "What did you do that for, Blanton? Take on a foundling that you can't even talk to." He looked at Anna and saw her puzzled expression, and smiled. "Don't mind me, Anna. I've been the only person that listens to me for years. Living alone can do that." He smiled and saw her smile in return.

"Well, the first thing to do is get you settled in a room. The only rooms with beds are mine, the guest room that Beth used and . . . and Dave's room." He paused as a wave of grief and sadness washed over him. "I think Dave's room has been empty long enough," he said softly to himself. To Anna, he simply said, *"Kommen."*

Dave's room was at the far end of the house. That had been Mary's idea, to give him some privacy from his parents' prying ears. After all, he had been thirty-three when he had moved back in with them. And a handsome man as well, if the women that he attracted were any indication. He had kept his affairs light and quiet during the years that he had been there, and seldom woke his parents late at night.

The room was musty and dusty. George hadn't really kept it up after Dave's death. He hadn't really cleaned it after Dave's death. Now he sighed deeply.

"This place needs a through cleaning." Looking at Anna, he said, "Stay here," and motioned with both hands for her to stay while he went back downstairs to the laundry room.

Window cleaner, furniture polish, and a roll of paper towels were handy in a cupboard, and he returned to find Anna exactly where he had left her. "Anna, it's time to clean this mess up." Handing her the window cleaner, he tore off a paper towel, then laughed at her startled expression. "Here you go. Start on the windows."

Anna just looked at him, then at the strange bottle and stranger cloth in her hands.

George was almost annoyed again, but caught himself. *Of course she's confused. Did they even have window cleaner or spray bottles here?* Gently taking the bottle from her, he led her to the window and showed her how it worked. Her surprise gave way to an almost comical joy as he demonstrated how to wipe the windows, then handed her back the bottle. He watched as she cleaned the next window before returning to his own task.

The bookshelves in Dave's room were mostly full, and George absentmindedly glanced at the titles as he dusted. Gunsmithing, cabinet making, herbal medicine, how-to encyclopedias, explosives . . . Explosives? What the hell was Dave doing with a book about explosives? *The Anarchist's Cookbook?* Yikes. Dave really had been bonkers. He was just finishing the fifth shelf when he became aware of Anna standing at his side.

"Done are you? Well, let's move on then. The bathroom next." Dave's room shared a bathroom with the next room over. That had been another reason that he had been given this room. George led Anna to the bathroom and opened the door, then quickly shut it. Dave's collection of magazines was still there. Turning to Anna, he motioned toward the bed. "Let's make up the bed instead."

George simply stripped the bed by grabbing comforter, blanket and sheets all at once and pulling. Anna stared as the good quilted mattress was revealed, and George grinned.

"Never seen anything like that before, have you?" he asked rhetorically. He knew that she hadn't, and that she couldn't understand him anyway. "Let's get these washing, and get fresh linen." He turned and left the room, pausing only once to look back and jerk his head in an effort to get her to follow.

The laundry room was big by most standards. It had a large-capacity washer and dryer, along with a large, three-by-eight foot table for folding clothes. That had been installed at Mary's insistence. Three of the four walls had cabinets mounted on them, and George grabbed a bottle of liquid laundry detergent from the one above the washer.

"Comforter first," he said over his shoulder to a curious Anna. "I have sheets and blankets enough, but no more comforters." He stuffed the comforter into the washer and turned on the water, smiling at Anna's surprise. "You may think I'm crazy, Anna, but this beats the hell out of a washtub." He added a capful of detergent and led her back out into the house.

"This is the linen closet," he said as he opened a door. Shelves of neatly folded sheets, pillowcases, towels and blankets were arrayed in order from top to bottom. He grabbed a set of sheets and matching pillowcases and handed them to Anna. Then he grabbed a bright yellow blanket and headed back upstairs with Anna in tow.

Anna was delighted with the sheets, and her surprise at seeing the way the fitted sheet wrapped the mattress was enough to make George chuckle. He started to spread the blanket, but stopped and motioned for Anna to do it. When her fingers encountered the velvety material of the blanket she stopped and rubbed her cheek on it in sensuous pleasure.

George used her fascination with the blanket as an opportunity to slip into the bathroom and pick up Dave's "collection." The boy had had some . . . strange tastes. Things that his mother and father never would have dreamed of. But he had been an adult, and could make his own decisions. Quickly bundling the magazines together, he went into the next room and stashed them in a convenient box.

Anna had finished the bed, even the pillowcases, by the time he returned. She was standing with her hands clasped in front of her and her eyes lowered as he walked up to her. "Smart girl. Saw me take the others off and figured it out yourself. Now we can clean the bathroom." Waving for her to follow, he led the way back and handed her the window cleaner again. He tapped the mirror, counter, window, and shower. The toilet bowl was dry after so long, and he flushed once to get it filled again. Rust-colored water flowed down fitfully, and he flushed three more times to get it to clear up. The bowl, however, was still badly stained.

Sighing, George headed back down to the laundry room cupboards. Even the best toilet-bowl cleaner on the market was going to have trouble with that mess. Anna was still working when he returned and came over to watch curiously as he poured the crystals into the bowl. She reached out to touch the foam as the crystals began their task, but George caught her wrist. "Not a good idea, Anna. That stuff burns."

The two continued cleaning for an hour more before George was satisfied. "Well, Anna, your room is ready. And I'm ready for lunch." He smiled and walked out of the room with Anna following close behind.

Like many of his neighbors, George ran his stove, water heater, dryer and furnace on gas from under his own land. The wellhead and compressor were out in the barn. The old O'Keefe & Merritt range in the kitchen was left over from the first occupants of the house, and he and Mary had loved it. All done up in white enamel, it was sturdy, simple to use, and heavy as hell. It had real pilot lights, none of those fancy piezoelectric igniters. Four burners shared the top with a built-in griddle. The oven was side-by-side with a broiler below, and there were drawers for storage below them. A back plate was behind the burners, and built-in salt and pepper shakers bracketed a clock at the top of it. There was also a cover that folded down over the burners and griddle or folded up into a shelf.

George considered Anna for a moment, then shrugged. She was already suffering from culture shock, and a little more was inevitable. George had traveled all over the world when he was in the Navy. He had been stationed in nine states in his six years, but only one of them had made a lasting impression on him. California. Specifically, California cuisine. California cuisine was a mix of so many different ethnic bases that it couldn't rightly be called anything else.

"Anna, have you ever had a burrito?" he asked, grinning. He went to the refrigerator and grabbed a pound of ground chuck, some sharp cheddar, lettuce, tomatoes, and onions. Smiling at Anna's intensely curious stare, he put everything on the table except the meat, then went to the stove. His old cast-iron frying pan was on a hook beside the stove and he put it on the stove beside a burner. "Watch this, kiddo," he said with a smile, then turned the burner on.

Anna jumped back when the blue flames erupted into being, then came forward. She extended her hand slowly toward the flames, and pulled back when she felt the heat. Her questioning gaze made George chuckle again.

"You'll learn soon enough." He put the pan over the flames and dumped the meat into it. An assortment of large wooden spoons was in a drawer beside the stove, and he used one to break the lump of meat up and stir it around as the pan heated. Motioning Anna forward, he pulled a hot pad from the rack and wrapped it around the handle. "You take over here," he said, stepping back and handing her the spoon. "I'll cut up the rest of the stuff." He smiled and went to the table where he had left everything. He brought over a small cutting board and was soon slicing and dicing away. He glanced back at Anna, then quickly stood and moved to her side. "Stir it, girl, don't let it burn." He grabbed the hand that held the spoon and stirred the meat, turning it to get it browning evenly. "Keep stirring," he instructed, stepping back as Anna complied.

George quickly chopped the lettuce and onion and sliced the cheese and tomatoes, then turned back to the stove. "Time for salt and pepper," he said softly. He lightly salted the meat and then grabbed the pepper, but hesitated. He liked his meat peppery hot, but both Mary and Dave had accused him of trying to kill them. Sighing, he lightly peppered the meat. He could always add more to his own later. He took the spoon from Anna and stirred it some more, then shut off the burner and moved the pan over to the griddle and propped it up on the spoon to drain the meat.

Anna had taken advantage of his momentary distraction and picked up the salt and pepper shakers. Salt she knew, of course, but the pepper was something that she didn't recognize. George turned around in time to see her make a huge mistake, but not soon enough to stop her from making it. Not being able to identify the gray powder by sight, she lifted the pepper to her nose and sniffed.

Anna's eyes began to water as she was wracked by a series of intense sneezes that almost lifted her from her feet. George managed to catch the pepper shaker before it hit the floor, but there was nothing that he could do for Anna except let nature run its course. After about twenty rapid-fire sneezes she got control of herself and gave George such a bewildered look that he had to laugh. That earned him an all too eloquent glare.

"Don't sniff things that you can't identify, Anna," he finally managed to say as he gasped for breath. He put the pepper on the table and waved her to a seat on the other side. There was a Ziploc bag of large flour tortillas beside the stove and he placed two on each of the plates that he had laid out. Then he put on some cheese and onions, layered on a little meat, and added the lettuce and tomatoes. He almost added more pepper, but Anna's reaction was still making him chuckle, so he let it be. Placing a plate in front of Anna, he took his to the opposite chair and sat down. Clearing his throat to get her attention, he showed her how to roll the tortilla and picked one up, then began eating.

Anna copied George, and soon found that, whatever else could be said about her host, he was a good cook. The meat had a bite that she identified after a few moments as pepper. *So that's what the gray powder is*, she thought to herself. She kept looking at George, glancing up when he moved to see if he wanted her to do anything. The dark-haired woman at the place where her parents were being helped had said that these people had many strange customs, but that they were good people. She was finally beginning to really believe it.

After they had eaten, George introduced her to the concept of a dishwasher.

The two spent the rest of the day trying to work out some signals that they both could understand. George was astute enough that he could read her body language in many cases, like when lunch caught up with her and she needed to use the toilet, but didn't know how to excuse herself. He sent her on her way and busied himself with his video collection. The only thing that he had that was in German was the subtitled version of *Das Boot*. She might understand the language, but what she would think of a U-boat and the war he didn't even want to consider.

He wanted something light and happy. Something that could bridge the language barrier. Something like a slow smile crossed his face as he found the tape that he wanted. Language would still be hard, but the situation would be something that she could relate to. Hell, she might even know the story.

Errol Flynn swung across the screen, his green hunter's tights and feathered hat displayed in brilliant

Technicolor green. Anna clapped her hands as the wondrous story unfolded, occasionally shouting at the actors when she could see what they didn't. George sat back and relaxed. Far from being frightened by the movie, Anna seemed to be enthralled. The story of Robin Hood was, after all, set in medieval England, a land not that much different than medieval Germany.

After the movie, George led Anna back to the kitchen. He spoke over his shoulder while he started dinner. "I hope that you don't mind a light dinner, Anna. I don't usually eat much late in the day. Gives me indigestion no matter what it is." He had been washing two large russet potatoes as he spoke and then walked over to the microwave oven. He poked each potato with a fork several times and placed them on a paper towel, then turned the oven on for twelve minutes.

Anna looked carefully at the glowing box with the tubers in it, then looked at George. *"Was ist?"* she asked, and he was surprised to realize that he understood her.

"That is a microwave oven, Anna. It cooks food using radio waves to excite the water molecules in the food—oh, what am I saying? You don't understand any of it. Just wait until they're done and you'll see." George smiled and patted her on the shoulder as he walked back into the other room.

Anna followed him, wondering what wonders he was going to reveal to her next. What he revealed was a tendency to sit quietly while his dinner cooked. He sat in a glider-rocker and looked out the window as the sun set in the wrong place.

He began to speak softly, more to himself than to her. Anna realized that he was talking to her about her parents, but didn't understand what he was saying. She thought that it was probably something about getting rid of her, or keeping her as his servant. After all, he was a rich man with a huge mansion, yet he didn't have servants. Just look at the room that he had had her clean. That was obviously meant for someone special. Especially that wonderfully soft and smooth blanket. She could only imagine royalty sleeping under something like that.

A bell chimed from the kitchen and George immediately went to get the potatoes. Anna, as always, trailed right behind him. He pointed to the cupboard to the left of the sink and said. "Get two plates," while he checked the tenderness of the potatoes with a fork. They were done, and done just right. Anna handed him two plates and he used the fork to lift a potato onto each, then handed one to Anna and nodded toward the table.

Anna stared suspiciously at the steaming brown tuber on her plate while George got the butter from the refrigerator. She watched even closer when he used his fork to open it up, and quickly followed his example. She found the white interior to be just as hot as it looked, and sucked a burnt finger as she glared at it.

George chuckled and buttered his potato before sliding the butter over to Anna. She watched as he spread the butter and salted his potato before eating, and she copied him. Like just about everything else, she found the potato delicious.

When they had finished eating, George allowed Anna to see to the dishes herself, smiling encouragingly as she rinsed the plates and loaded them into the dishwasher. It was getting late and he had decided that even if she wasn't tired, they were going to bed.

He pantomimed going to sleep by putting his hands together and laying his head on them with his eyes closed, and she nodded her understanding. She immediately went to the couch that she had slept on the night before, but George caught her elbow before she could lie down. "Upstairs, Anna. Your room."

Anna looked at him with questions and uncertainty clear in her face, and he guided her to the stairs. Her breath came just a little quicker as he led her up the stairs, but seemed to ease a little when they walked past his room. She was shocked when he opened the door of the room that they had cleaned and said, "Your room, Anna. For as long as you stay."

Anna looked at him with wide eyes. George was tired and getting irritated, so he put a hand in the small of her back and pushed her into the room. "You, sleep, there," he said, pantomiming by pointing at her, putting his hands under his head, then pointing at the bed. Then he turned out the lights and closed the door, muttering under his breath the whole time.

Anna waited until she heard the door down the hall shut, then turned the lights back on. She looked around the room, warily checking every corner, before walking over to the bed. She touched the wonderful blanket again, trailing her fingers across it, and a deep sigh escaped her lips. It was so soft, and so much too fine for her. Could George really mean for her to stay here, to sleep in this soft bed under that wondrous blanket?

A tear, unbidden and unwanted, trickled down her cheek. It was all too much. How could she be here? She was a poor girl, a farmer's daughter, yet here she stood in a room fit for a lady, beside a bed fit for a queen. She finally took a long, shuddering breath and nodded to herself. Ever-fickle fortune had smiled upon her when she hid in that barn. She would not examine her good fortune too closely, just in case it was illusion.

Quickly slipping out of the dress that she had all but been forced into that morning, she used the amazing toilet and scrubbed her teeth with a finger at the sink before turning out the lights once again and slipping between the smooth sheets on the heavenly soft mattress, under that oh-so-wonderful blanket. Sleep came as she smiled softly, content to let God watch over her.

George awoke early and contemplated his situation. Here he was, a grumpy old man, with a teenage girl as a houseguest. That was how he had decided to look at it. She was his guest, not an interloper.

He rose quietly and got dressed. His clothes were old and worn, but he doubted that Anna would comment on his fashion sense, or lack thereof. Thinking of her, he again shook his head. The first thing to do was to get her up and dressed, then go see her parents. He was unsure of exactly how badly her mother had been hurt, beyond the horror of the gang rape. Maybe he could talk to the doctor. Doctor Adams hadn't been his doctor, but that fellow and his associates were elsewhere. That was another thing that he had to start worrying about. His own health was not the best, and there was going to be a shortage of his medications unless another source could be found.

George shook it off and said, "First things first, old man." He finished dressing and walked down the hall, but Anna's door opened before he reached it. "Up early, are you? That's good. Let's go see your parents first and talk to the doctor." Anna obviously didn't understand him, but nodded when he finished talking and followed him downstairs and out the door.

George opened the truck door for her, making sure that she saw how it was done. Once he was seated, he had a few moments of trouble convincing her to buckle up, and finally just reached over her and strapped her in himself while she just looked startled.

The ride to the high school was quiet. Normally George listened to a country station on the radio, but that station wasn't on the air here, so he left it off. Anna, of course, didn't know what she was missing.

When they arrived at the school, Anna immediately took off toward the clinic. George strolled slowly behind her, looking around as he walked. The place was busy. People who hadn't had anything to do with high school in decades were coming and going from every direction. He walked to the clinic and found Anna seated on the floor beside her mother's bed.

The two were talking rapidly in German. Anna kept nodding her head while her mother kept shaking hers. When Anna noticed him, she stood and grabbed his hand, dragging him to the side of the bed and talking a mile a minute again.

The woman on the bed fixed George with a bleak stare. There was something in her eyes that he couldn't describe, and was pretty sure he wouldn't like if he could. She whispered something to Anna, and the girl took his hand.

"Anna is safe with me, ma'am. I don't mess with children." A movement at the corner of his vision caused him to turn away, and he found himself facing a strange black man in a white doctor's coat.

"Mr. Blanton, I presume," the doctor said with a smile. "I'm James Nichols. My daughter and I were in town for the wedding, and got caught here."

"Wedding?" George asked.

"Uh-huh. Rita Stearns and Tom Simpson."

"Didn't hear about it. How is she?" he asked, looking down at Anna's mother.

"As well as can be expected under the circumstances. Physically, she only has some scrapes, bruises and two broken ribs. Mentally . . . mentally she's fragile. Seeing the men who did it to her dead may have helped a little, but she's still a rape victim. She also saw what happened to her husband, and that can't help." Doctor Nichols walked away, motioning for George to follow.

"He lost a lot of blood before we got to him. That, plus the shock and other things that were done to him makes me wonder how he survived. He's going to be in danger for quite a while, and he's in for a long recovery."

George nodded his understanding. "I have plenty of room at my place when they're ready to go. Anna is settling in, but I wish I spoke German or she spoke English. It's hard to not be able to understand one another."

"Learn German, Mr. Blanton," Doctor Nichols instructed. "From what I've been hearing, there aren't many people in this area that speak English."

George gave him an intense look. "What have you heard? I've just been getting bits and pieces."

Doctor Nichols gave George a quick verbal sketch of their predicament. "So, here we are, a bunch of Americans in southern Germany. Unless some bright boy comes up with a miracle, we don't have anywhere else to go, and no way to get there."

George shook his head slowly back and forth, then returned to Anna and her mother. "I'm going to go talk to some people, Anna. You stay here, okay? Stay here with your mother." George motioned with both hands for Anna to remain where she was, then walked away.

Doctor Adams was also at the clinic, and George asked to see him in private. The doctor nodded and led the way to an empty classroom. "Yes, Mr. Blanton, what can I do for you?"

"Well, Doc, I don't know. I'm on several medications, but the ones that worry me are the blood thinners and blood pressure meds. What's going to happen when I run out?"

Doctor Adams rubbed his chin as he considered his answer. "This is something that we've already run into. One of the people that was rescued yesterday—day before yesterday?—time goes so fast sometimes. Anyway, one of the people that was rescued was having a heart attack at the time. Doctor Nichols managed to stabilize him, but we don't have the facilities to handle that sort of thing. I'm afraid that you and the rest of our elderly are in for a rough time. We can manage some control of your blood pressure with diet, and aspirin can be substituted for your blood thinners to some extent. I hate to say it, but you're in trouble."

George gave Doctor Adams a sour look. "That's not the answer that I wanted to hear."

Doctor Adams simply shrugged. "It isn't the answer that I wanted to give, but it's the best I've got right now."

George nodded and went to collect Anna. She was sitting beside her mother's bed, holding her hand as she slept. She looked up when George arrived and stood, tucking her mother's hand gently under the blanket. George simply nodded and walked away, and Anna followed him.

The walk out to the truck was silent as each of them considered their situation. George was watching Anna carefully, and the girl was watching the floor beneath her feet. She glanced up and caught him watching her and smiled a sad little smile. Seeing that, George smiled in return and patted her shoulder.

Boys and girls who he assumed were students were rushing about the school, moving chairs and desks from room to room with seeming purpose. A woman passed by and George stopped her to ask what was going on.

"It's for the meeting tomorrow. Weren't you informed?" the woman asked, looking at him closely. "I don't recognize you, or this young lady. Were you just passing through?"

George gave the woman a sour look. "No, I live here. Name's George Blanton. I live out south of town. This girl here is Anna. Don't know her last name. She's from that farm where the miners rescued the family."

The woman was nodding as she listened. "Now I know who you are. Well, there's a meeting for all residents who care to attend here in the auditorium tomorrow morning. That's when the science types are going to announce what they have found out about how we got here, and how to get back."

George nodded and led Anna outside and put her in the truck. "Well, Anna," he said as he got in, "I think that we need to go see Beth and Jimmy." Anna's expression brightened at the mention of Beth's name, and he chuckled. "I'm going to get that dictionary so we can communicate better."

Little Jim was out front when George and Anna drove up, and he hurried inside to announce their arrival. Elizabeth and Marge met them on the porch and took them inside. "Beth, I need to borrow that dictionary of yours."

"Talking to her is harder than you expected, isn't it, George?" Elizabeth asked as she walked across the living room.

"Yep. There are a lot of concepts that I just don't know how to convey to her."

"Such as?"

"Well, such as who we are and where we're from. America doesn't even seem to register as a country to her."

Elizabeth stopped and looked over her shoulder at him. "If what we're hearing is true, America isn't a country yet, George. Just some English and Spanish colonies in the new world. I don't even know if they call it North America yet."

That stopped George in his tracks. "Not even America yet? Oh, God in Heaven, how could I have forgotten that?"

"Because it hasn't really sunk in yet. You know it in your head, but you don't really *know* it in your heart."

"No, you're probably right. I keep expecting something to happen, something that will make everything the way it was. It's almost like . . . it's almost like when Mary died." George looked at the floor and slowly shook his head.

Elizabeth nodded and stepped closer, putting her hand on his arm. "And when Jim died. I know. It's surreal now. We're still in shock. But the reality is going to set in soon enough."

George nodded. "They're having a meeting about it tomorrow at the high school."

"Jimmy told us," Elizabeth said softly. "He was talking to Mr. Ferrara, Lizzy's science teacher. He doesn't think that there's any way to get back."

George nodded and looked at Anna, but she was gone. He whipped his head around, scanning the room, but there was no sign of the girl. Marge saw his look and smiled. "She's with Liz and Mel. I think that they're trying on dresses in their room."

George sighed. He didn't have the experience for handling Anna. Not really. Dave had been his only child, and boys were easier than girls. "Well, since we're alone now, I have a favor to ask."

"Ask away," Elizabeth answered.

"Well, Anna is a teenager. I'm sure her mother took care of the basics, but, well, things have changed. I'm just not comfortable with the idea of trying to discuss it with her."

"Discuss what?"

"Well . . . her period," George answered somewhat sheepishly. He had been married for over thirty-five years, but that was part of Mary's life that he hadn't intruded on.

Elizabeth shook her head. "Men. Jim never wanted anything to do with the girls when they were going through puberty either. I'll take care of it. Or we will." She glanced at Marge and received a nod of agreement.

"Thank you. It's just something that I never wanted to learn anything about."

Elizabeth led George into the kitchen and poured two cups of coffee. "She's a pretty girl, George. You may have other problems as well."

"How so?" George was seated at the kitchen table and accepted the cup that Elizabeth handed him.

"You saw how the boys reacted to her."

"Oh, no! Not my problem. That's for her daddy to deal with."

Elizabeth reached over and touched his hand. "He may not be able to, George. The doctors aren't sure that he'll make it. That leaves you so long as she's living under your roof."

George looked startled for a moment, then shrugged. "We'll deal with that when the time comes. I'm hoping to get her mother home with us soon. Ken Hobbs said that their farm is still standing, but it's damaged pretty badly. It'll take a lot of work to get it livable again. Besides, I really don't think that she should be on her own for a while. I can take care of all of us with Dave's stash."

Elizabeth nodded. "We talked about that last night. Dave's guns and stuff may be needed. We may have to defend ourselves against one of the largest armies in history."

George closed his eyes for a moment. "There's more than guns up there, Beth. Lots more."

"Keep it there for now, George. That stash may be your salvation."

George chuckled and shook his head. "If Dave was here he'd probably be crowing like a spring rooster about being right."

Anna reappeared in a different dress and a smile a mile wide. Melody and Lizzy were grinning just as hard, and occasionally giggling. Melody finally had to say it. "Anna thinks Jim is cute."

George immediately put his head in his hand and just said, "Oh, lord."

Marge laughed and shook her head. "Are you ready to negotiate a dowry, George?"

George gaped at her while the rest of the women laughed, including Anna. Then Elizabeth and Marge gathered all of the girls and went toward the back of the house.

George walked outside and watched the boys as they did their chores around the farm. They had apparently been allowed to skip school. That made sense to George. Not much point in going to school when there weren't going to be any classes.

It was more than an hour later when the women reappeared, and Anna walked over to George's side with a slightly dazed expression. Elizabeth was shaking her head, but she had an amused smile on her face. "She'll be all right, George. She's just a little shocked by us."

"Oh, gee, can't imagine why," George said sarcastically. "Come along, Anna. Let's go home." Turning back to Elizabeth, he gave her a little bow. "Ladies, I thank you. I'm going to see about bringing her mother home after the meeting tomorrow. I may need some more help."

"We're only a phone call away, George," Elizabeth answered, smiling at both of them.

George and Anna spent another quiet night, each lost in thoughts of their own. In the morning they returned to the school to find Anna's mother sitting up and sipping tea. Anna immediately dropped to her knees and started talking. George didn't understand a word of it, but her tone was joyous and light. Then she stood and motioned George forward. "George, *diese Frau ist meine Mutti*, Tilda Braun."

George was more surprised that he understood her meaning than the introduction. He shook off his surprise and bowed deeply at the waist, then said, "I am pleased to meet you, Missus Braun." He was also surprised to find that he had not learned Anna's last name until now.

Tilda looked at him with her haunted eyes, but there was something more in them than there had been. Surprise warred with fear and despair, and there was just a glimmer of what could be hope. "You *ist gut*, good man, George. Tank, thank you," she said in halting English, much to George and Anna's surprise.

"You are welcome. I wish I had that book." He smiled at Anna and Tilda, then shrugged. "When you are ready, we will take you home. You have a room of your own for as long as you need it." He smiled, hoping that she understood, then nodded at Anna. "You stay here, Anna. I'm going to the meeting, and I'll be back for you when it's done." He smiled and motioned for Anna to stay where she was, then turned and left. Anna and Tilda's voices were a constant buzz of strange words behind him as he walked away.

The meeting in the gymnasium was not the tedious affair that George had feared. The information was mostly a rehash of what he already knew. They were stuck in 1631 Germany. It was spring. There was a huge war raging around them. And some ass from out of town thought that they ought to chase Anna and her people away. George was on his feet, shouting at the top of his lungs as John Simpson referred to his little Anna as a disease carrier. He hadn't been this angry since—well, he couldn't remember when he had ever been this angry.

Mike Stearns took the podium next and expressed his own displeasure with Simpson's comments, and George felt his admiration of the boy growing. Damn it all, now he understood why Dave had thought the world of Mike's leadership abilities. And of Mike as a person. The boy had what it took to lead a mob of hillbillies like these.

When the vote came, George added his voice to those for Mike and his agenda. Screw that stuffed suit. His kind had been why George had retired at age fifty-five, even though he could have continued on for another eight years. The stuffed suits had driven him out.

George left the gym with a definite feeling of unease, but a sense of purpose as well. Stuck here and on their own, he knew one thing for certain: they needed to plant crops. Food, as it had been pointed out, was going to be a priority. No arable land could be left fallow, and he had—well, he had Mary's garden. He hadn't planted it in years since her death, but it was good land. Maybe better now for having been left alone for a while.

George returned to the clinic and found both Anna and Tilda ready to go. Doctor Adams was there as well, slowly shaking his head. "Mr. Blanton, I'm glad to see you. It seems that my patient wants to leave."

"Already?" George asked, looking at Tilda.

"I go. Not gut to *Aufenthault*, to stay. Go *zu Hause*. Go home." Tilda nodded sharply at her last remark and stood.

"Well, home is my house for now. I'm sure Anna has told you that you have a place with me. Your house is . . . damaged." George looked away, saddened by the memories that were going to be part of that house for years to come.

Anna and her mother shared a sharp exchange of words, with Anna stamping her foot and saying something that needed no translation. George interrupted, earning a nasty glare from both of them.

"If you want to go back to your farm, I'll take you, but I really think that you'd be better off with me."

Again Tilda looked him in the eye and said, "Go *zu Hause*."

George sighed and nodded, then led the way out of the clinic and school with a loudly chattering Anna and Tilda right behind him. At the truck it took all of Anna's powers of persuasion to get her mother into the cab and belted in. Tilda still took the ride in white-knuckled silence with an indescribable expression on her face.

The end of the road was where the three first saw the true extent of the Ring of Fire. The cliff had crumbled due to the traffic over it that first day, but it was still a mighty testimony that something tremendous had happened. George let Anna help her mother up the bank while he struggled up on his own. His balance was hampered by the M-14 in his hands, but there was nothing that could have convinced him not to take it.

At the farm they saw the evidence of the firefight and its aftermath. The house stood, but the interior was a wreck. A fly-infested stain near the barn told of spilled blood. George stood outside, scanning the area carefully while the two women searched the house.

Anna was the first to come out, her face tear-streaked and puffy. Tilda was not far behind. Her eyes were bleak with despair. All that they'd had was ruined, ravaged by the same men who had ravished her. Now she looked at George with pleading in her eyes. With the farm so thoroughly despoiled, they had only one hope.

George smiled sadly and put an arm around Anna and said, *"Kommen."* He added a little pressure and turned back the way they had come, leading them back toward the home that awaited them.

3

George spent most of the next day convincing Tilda and Anna that he was not making servants of them. It was an uphill battle. Tilda was just not willing to accept that good fortune had finally come her way.

George left the two women alone in the house while he checked out the tractor. It was a good little John Deere utility tractor that had been modified to run on natural gas. That plus the farm implements that were rusting beside the barn were his main concern. He and Mary had purchased the tractor new when they had bought the farm, and had bought all of the attachments that they could afford to go with it. Harrow, plow, mower, reaper, loader and backhoe attachments were a hefty investment, but one that had paid off more than once.

He made several trips into town to buy penetrating oil, motor oil, hydraulic fluid and seed. The seed was the most important purchase. It was going fast now that the people of Grantville had awakened to their plight. Food, the emergency committee had decreed, was among their top priorities. The army was *the* top priority, and George graciously donated most of Dave's weapons and ammunition to the cause, only keeping the M-14 and a shotgun for his own use. And the Colt Python .357 magnum that was nestled under his mattress. That was a gun that no one knew about, and he intended to keep it that way.

Once Anna and Tilda understood that he was going to plant, they joined in wholeheartedly. George looked up from his work on the tractor to see the two women walking the field pulling weeds. He tried to stop them, but all he got for his trouble was a lecture in German and broken English about the state of his field and their duty to help. He finally gave up and concentrated on fixing the recalcitrant tractor.

When George finally got everything working, he hooked up the harrow and pulled it into the field. Anna and Tilda stood in openmouthed amazement as he plowed the weeds and old plants under, leaving behind bare earth when he was done. Where they had taken a half a day to clear less than an acre, George did all ten in just a few hours.

He smiled as he drove back to the barn. Tilda was a good woman, but just a touch on the stubborn side. She and Anna were waiting for him at the barn and he used the hydraulics to detach the harrow before shutting off the tractor. Once he climbed down he faced off with Tilda. "You see?" he asked, smiling slightly. When Tilda answered with one sharp nod, he smiled and continued with his work. He took the opportunity to fuel the tractor up, topping-off both of the gas bottles before moving on.

George's next task was to attach the plow. It was only a four-row plow, but it would take care of the garden in just a few more hours. Tilda and Anna walked the field behind him, amazed at how easily he was able to plow, and pleased by how rich the soil was. By nightfall, the field was ready to plant.

George and Tilda sat at the kitchen table with the dictionary late into the night, trying to find a way to discuss their living arrangement. Tilda was absolutely convinced that she and Anna should share a servant's room, and George was just as convinced that each of them should have their own room. After all, he repeatedly pointed out, her husband would eventually join them. Every time he said that he saw hope flicker and die in her eyes. Tilda was convinced that her husband was never leaving the clinic except in a box. George and Tilda finally decided that each was the most stubborn person that the other had ever met. Tilda slept with Anna while George shook his head in despair.

Another week passed before the emergency committee contacted George again.

Three men drove up to George's house in a battered old pickup with a natural gas tank in the bed. They parked at the bottom of the steps and got out, but only one of them climbed the steps. He didn't get a chance to knock.

George opened the door and stood facing his visitor through the screen door. "Hi, Willie Ray. What's up?"

The man looked at him uncertainly. "George, the emergency committee put me in charge of food production. I see you've already started your plot, but we need that tractor of yours working pretty much nonstop, not just sitting in your barn until you need it."

George stared at Willie Ray for a moment, then crossed his arms over his chest. "You're not taking my tractor."

Willie Ray took in the stubborn set of George's face and tried again. "George, we've got to—"

"You're not taking my tractor," George said sternly, interrupting Willie Ray. "Have you given the emergency committee *your* tractor?"

"Well, no, but . . ."

"No buts, Willie Ray," George snarled. "I'll fight you if you try. You should know I didn't give the army all my guns. I gave them everything I could do without. All my son's stuff. All his guns, ammo, and supplies. I need that tractor for myself and my guests."

Willie Ray was puzzled for a moment, then seemed to remember about Anna and her family. "Well, we still need that tractor producing. If you won't give it up, you'll have to run it yourself."

"I can do that," George agreed with a single nod.

Willie Ray nodded back. "Good. We've been contacting everyone who has any land at all and making arrangements to get crops planted. We'll be contacting you when we need your equipment."

George said, "That'll do," and watched Willie Ray leave with his helpers.

That'll do. George Blanton, you're a fool," George said aloud as he drove the tractor to yet another job. "Should'a known I'd get stuck plowing every backyard garden in the county."

The emergency committee had convinced just about everyone in Grantville to plant what land they had, but that wasn't really all that much. The real farmers, like Willie Ray and a few others, who had larger tractors and plows were off in the German countryside in well-armed groups making sure that every farm in the immediate vicinity of the Ring of Fire was planted.

George's destination today was the Reardon house. They only had five acres, but they were going to plant every inch of it that they could. Jimmy came out of the house as he pulled up.

"George, how are you?" he asked, smiling broadly.

"Sick and tired of plowing," George answered.

Jimmy laughed. "Then why don't you climb down and let me handle it for a while. Mom wants to talk to you anyway."

George left the tractor idling as he climbed stiffly down. "Thank you, Jim. Times like this I wish I'd let Willie Ray take the damn thing."

Jimmy laughed again and agilely climbed up to the seat, then drove into his yard and started plowing.

George sighed and limped up to the door, rubbing his back with one hand as he did. The suspension on the tractor just wasn't meant to be sat on for days on end. His knock was immediately answered by Elizabeth.

"Come in, George," she said, stepping aside. "What can I get for you?"

"Some strong muscles and a few new vertebrae, if you have them on hand," George answered with a little laugh. "If not, then I guess some iced tea will have to do."

Elizabeth smiled and guided him to a chair, then went to get some drinks. She returned to find him seated with his legs stretched out. "Here you are. Let me get you a footstool." She nudged a padded footstool over to him and he carefully put his feet up on it. "You look tired, George."

"I am tired, Beth. Tilda and Anna are taking care of my garden without me since I'm always out and about. The good news is that it shouldn't go on much longer. We'll have every bit of arable land planted by the end of the month, and then I can relax a little."

Elizabeth nodded. "I was over to see them yesterday. We've been going through the girls' things and we had some more dresses for them."

George nodded and looked out the window to where Jimmy was plowing. "I heard. Tilda is finally adjusting to the situation and starting to really take charge. I haven't had to actually do anything except run the plow for a week. She's doing everything."

"She's worried about her husband. And you," Elizabeth said softly. "She told me that you were overdoing it."

"I'm not overdoing it, Beth. I'm just doing what I can to keep what's mine."

Elizabeth frowned, but nodded. "Just don't kill yourself, George. Those people need you."

"I know, Beth. And you know what? It's a good feeling. A very good feeling."

George's health problems were a secret that he carefully kept from Anna and Tilda. He made regular trips into town, riding the tractor since the gas for his truck had been siphoned off by that pirate Stearns and his men for the army. Doctor Adams kept track of his blood pressure and coagulation factors, substituting one medicine or another when his prescribed medications ran out.

Anna's father hovered near death for weeks. The

damage that had been done to him was slow to heal, but eventually it did, and George was introduced to Jurgen Braun.

Jurgen listened in silence to what his wife and daughter had to say about the man who had taken them in. He was reluctant to stay in George's house, fearing the debt that his family was accumulating with the obviously rich man, but found that he had little choice in the matter. He was free of the doctors, but still so weak that he could hardly stand on his own.

The planting was done long before Jurgen joined them. Seedlings were sprouting and George joined Tilda and Anna in the fields, hand weeding the tender young plants. It was a chore for George's back, and as often as not he spent his evenings cuddled up with a heating pad.

Jurgen was in the guest room that George had tried to get Tilda into, and Tilda had finally moved in with him. That still left just three of the six bedrooms occupied, and George soon had other boarders as well.

After the Battle of Badenburg, or the Battle of the Crapper as it was irreverently called, he was joined by four more families, and Anna moved in with her parents. The men who joined George and the Brauns were all farmers who had been pressed into service with Tilly's mercenaries. The women were their families and camp followers. George shook his head at that, but kept his peace. Strange times made for strange arrangements. The big farmhouse that George and Mary had rattled around in started to seem mighty small with eleven adults and thirteen children crowding it.

George's pastureland was also pressed into service. The army had captured horses and oxen along with the men, and an assortment of other farm animals that ranged from chickens to goats and pigs. The chickens were scrawny things compared to the birds that had come through the Ring of Fire with the Americans. The pigs and goats were, well, pigs and goats. George's new boarders quickly cobbled together pens and a chicken coop from supplies that had been lying around the barn since before George and Mary had bought the place.

The barn was cleared of its decades-long accumulation of junk, often yielding odd treasures. The people who had owned the farm before George and Mary had been real farmers. Buried among the clutter and junk were farm implements that the Germans understood. Good steel shovels. Steel rakes and hoes. A scythe with a broken handle. Old tack, with its leather brittle from age and neglect. The men and women *tsk*-ed at the state of George's tools, but kept their mouths closed. Tilda and Anna had told them of the wonderful machine that could plow a whole field in half a day. If George could let good tools rust this way, it must be a wonderful machine indeed.

The Brauns' farm was also being tended now that there were enough hands to tend it, and soon George found himself not being allowed to do anything but drive the tractor. It was still his chore because he was the only one who knew how all of the attachments worked, but the men and women who were living in his house insisted that it was more than he should have to do. After all, he was their host, and they saw it as their duty to tend to his lands while they lived under his roof. He was also just about the oldest person that any of them had ever met, and they were genuinely concerned about him.

The newcomers found George every bit as strange as Anna had in the beginning, and Anna took great pleasure in showing them all of the modern conveniences that George's home had to offer.

George and the Reardons learned bits and pieces of the German language as the year progressed, and the Germans learned English as well, so that by fall and the harvest the babble in George's house would confuse just about anyone. Still, they communicated well enough, and George found himself relegated more and more to the roll of Grandfather to All.

Little Jim was serving with the army now, and it was a source of constant worry for all of the Reardons and for one German girl in particular. Anna had a crush on Little Jim, and waited impatiently for his visits. Little Jim, fortunately, had just as big a crush on her and visited as often as he could. This made for some interesting times as the two negotiated. It didn't help that Jim's sisters, mother and grandmother were all on Anna's side.

The time finally came as winter gripped the land that Little Jim, all six feet three inches of him, came hemming and hawing to stand in front of Jurgen Braun.

"Well, Mister Braun, I, well, I would like to have Anna's hand in marriage," he finally managed to say, swallowing hard to fight down his nervousness.

Jurgen looked at Jim closely and shook his head. "Anna *ist* too younk. She *ist* only *sechzehn*. Zixteen. And you, younk man. You are but a boy. Too younk. You haff no land or trade off you own."

Little Jim looked at Jurgen with evident confusion. "Sir, I'm eighteen. I'm legally a man now, and I'm old enough for the army. And as for a trade, I've been working for Uncle Ollie in his machine shop off and on for years. The only reason that I wasn't working there this year was that he didn't have enough business to keep me busy. But now, with him starting to talk about making cannons and rifled muskets, he's going to have more business than he can handle."

Jurgen looked at Jim carefully. The boy was big enough, obviously strong, and even good looking in an overfed, American way. And he was financially well off. His father's eldest son, he would have land of his own one day.

There was a flicker of sadness at that last thought. His son, born when Anna was three, hadn't lived through his first year, and Tilda hadn't quickened again in spite of all of their prayers and efforts. To have this boy as his son, even by marriage—it was a thing worth considering. But still, was he really interested in Anna, or did he wish to marry her to acquire more lands for himself? After all, Anna was his only child, and would one day inherit the farm. There was one way to find out. "You unterstand, younk man, dat Anna hass no *mitgift*."

Jim was perplexed by the German word. He had never heard it before, but Grandma Beth quickly looked it up and showed him the page in the dictionary. "If you mean dowry, yes sir, I understand. It don't bother me none. We can live with my parents until I can get a place of my own."

Tilda looked at Jim as if she were measuring him for a coffin. "Anna ist a goot girl. Sturdy and strong. She vill make goot wife for ju, even if she ist too younk and comes wit no lands yet."

"Missus Braun, you've got a lovely daughter, and when the time comes I'm sure that we'll have as much land as we'll need. As I said, I'll probably be working in Uncle Ollie's machine shop rather than farming anyway, so land isn't a big issue for me."

Elizabeth entered into the negotiations in earnest now that Little Jim had gotten things rolling. "Jurgen, Tilda, Little Jim is a fine young man. He is a skilled machinist, and has been working during his summers since he was twelve. That's quite a while by our standards. And please remember that we have different assumptions about when it is proper to marry."

She looked at Little Jim with a definite frown on her face. "Sixteen is too young, by most standards. Well, today's standards. I was sixteen when I married your grandfather. He was nineteen then. But that makes no difference as far as these two are concerned." She looked smiled at Little Jim. "What makes a difference to me is that they seem to be truly in love. They can wait a bit before the actual ceremony, but I, and his parents, wouldn't be against an engagement." She looked in the dictionary and came up with the German word for betrothal. "A *verlobung.*"

Jurgen and Tilda consulted quietly for a few moments before Jurgen answered. "Ve ist not in goot times. Dis var ist not to end zoon. Ze school, they say it ist many years to come before it ist end. But ve are Americans now. Ve vill liff like Americans, ja? Zo we decide. She may be *verlobung*. Engage. But not to marry until she *ist achtzehn*. Eighteen."

Tilda continued at her husband's nod. "Anna *ist* not rich girl, but not beggar. In tee years ahead she vill make her *mitgift*. She vill not come to altar vith empty hands."

Elizabeth nodded and stepped aside to let Little Jim speak again. "Mister Braun, I am willing to accept these conditions. As a token, I offer Anna this ring. It's Grandma's engagement ring that Grandpa gave her." He smiled broadly at Elizabeth, then at Anna.

Anna stepped forward at her father's nod, and Little Jim went to one knee. "Anna, will you marry me?"

Anna looked confused for a moment. "I haf already say yes."

George smiled at her. "It's kind of tradition, Anna. He proposes on one knee and you say yes, then he gives you the engagement ring. That makes it official."

Anna looked slightly confused, but said, "Yes, my Jim, I vill marry you." Jim put his grandmother's ring on the ring finger of her left hand, then stood and took her gently into his arms.

Elizabeth and George stood to the side, smiling at the scene. She smiled at the proud smile on his face and patted his arm, then went to hug her grandson and his future bride.

George continued to secretly see Doctor Adams as his health, once propped up by modern medicine, continued to decline. As the medications that were stocked in the town pharmacies ran out, herbal remedies were tried. But as the winter wore on, even the herbs could not control his blood pressure.

George awoke in the middle of the night. He was gripped by a crushing pain that was driving the breath from his chest as he struggled to reach the few nitroglycerin pills that Doctor Adams had managed to find for him. They were there on the nightstand, he could see them, but they were out of reach. The pain eased slightly as his sight dimmed, and he managed to whisper one word with his last breath. "Mary."

Anna found George the next morning. With the cold weather they had all taken to sleeping in late, snuggling under blankets until the sun was well above the horizon. George was usually the last one up, but when he hadn't appeared by ten she went to find him.

"George? Ist you goink to sleep all day?" she asked playfully. Then she saw his face. There wasn't anything obviously wrong, but she knew before she touched his cool cheek. A choked sob escaped her lips as she backed away, and she finally turned to scream, "MUTTI!" before she collapsed beside his bed.

Tilda and everyone else in the house crowded into

George's room. The old man looked so peaceful, but there was no question about his death. One of the elder boys was sent to town to inform the authorities, and soon Doctor Adams and Chief Frost were driving up in a natural-gas-powered police cruiser.

Doctor Adams looked at George and took his pulse for form's sake, but he knew it was far too late. "He went quietly," the doctor said, as he noted the pills still on the nightstand. "He has been expecting something like this. Ever since his medications ran out he has known that he was living on borrowed time."

Dan nodded. "He told me, and swore me to secrecy. He didn't want anyone fussing over him. Now I'll have to tell everyone. Did he tell you who was to see to his affairs?"

The doctor nodded. "I am. He didn't have much of a will, and I brought it with me. We wrote it up about three months ago when the last of the blood thinners ran out. Here." The doctor handed over a single sheet of paper, notarized and witnessed as was proper, and the chief read the single sentence.

"I, George Armstrong Blanton, being of sound mind and failing health, upon my death do bequeath all of my worldly belongings to my adopted granddaughter, Anna Braun."

Curio and Relic

❧

Tom Van Natta

May 1631

"Hello? Anybody there?"

Paul Santee took off the holstered .45 when he heard the call. It came again, nearer. "Hello, the house!" No sense in scaring someone who probably meant well. He tucked the .45 behind his belt in the small of his back. No sense in being stupid, either. Stupid tends to kill people, and he was still alive. Something *strange* had happened last weekend, and he didn't know what it was. It was good to hear another voice, especially one that seemed friendly.

"Hello! Mr. Santee?" The caller turned out to be a kid, a gangly blond teenager who stood at his gate. Santee stepped out on his porch and waved the boy in.

Eddie Cantrell carefully closed the gate behind him. He wasn't too happy about finding this cabin—he'd secretly hoped it was outside the Ring of Fire—but when Mike Stearns asked about war veterans, Santee's name had come up, and Eddie had been asked to go see if his backwoods cabin was inside the Ring, and if he was still alive. Obviously, yes to both. Eddie walked up the path carefully, slowly, trying to figure out how to explain things. He'd heard that Paul Santee was a survivalist, a loner, mean as hell. The man in front of him was small and wiry, grizzled, graying. He didn't look particularly mean, or particularly anything, except for his piercing eyes.

Santee stared at the kid appraisingly. "What can I do for you?" he said gruffly. The kid looked alarmed. *Should have made some small talk first,* Santee thought. *That was a bit abrupt. I'm sure out of practice.*

"Mr. Santee, do you know what happened?"

That was what Santee wanted to know. Give the kid some minimum information and see how he responds. "Well . . . Five days ago, thunder and a big flash of lighting from the clear blue sky. Path to the road disappeared about a hundred feet down the way. Weather's been strange. Phone is dead. My bedroom window faced south, but not any more—maybe the earth's axis of rotation shifted. There's a big wall of dirt that seems to go on and on." A long pause there, as he looked at Eddie. "And some damn bird was out there yesterday that sounded exactly like a cuckoo clock. Do *you* know what happened?"

"Uh, well, Mr. Ferrara—he's my science teacher— says we were moved to Germany, in the year 1631. And that there's a war on, with us in the middle of it."

Santee looked hard at the kid, trying to find some sign of repressed mirth that would indicate a joker.

He saw none of it, just an anxious teenager repeating what he'd been told.

"Who is 'we'?"

Eddie was confused at first, then figured it out and responded. "About a six-mile circle around Grantville. Everybody inside—everything inside—moved here. Gas wells, coal mine, power plant, everything." He looked up the path on the other side of the house. "I guess your driveway leads off to Butterchurn Road. That didn't make it."

"Oh. Okay. Damn. Shit. Take some thinking on." That story was totally unbelievable, but so were the plain facts all around him. Goddamn it. The kid clearly had more information, but it would take a while to get it, and Santee didn't like standing for long stretches. "Would you like something to drink? I just have water, but it's clean and cold."

Eddie nodded. "Thanks. That sounds good, but then I've got to get back." Santee still scared him a little. "Mike Stearns is the head of the committee. He said if you were here inside the Ring, he'd, uh, like to meet you."

"What's your name, son?"

"Eddie Cantrell." He paused, wondering if he should add "sir" to it, but it was too late.

Santee held his door open. "Come on in, Eddie. My name is Paul, but everybody just calls me Santee. It's real neighborly of you to come out here to tell me." He wondered if that sounded as hokey as it felt saying it.

They sat at Santee's table and drank cold spring water. Eddie told about the tumultuous day of the Event, and the town meeting and what the people were doing to cope with the war they found themselves in. They were going to fight, of course. They'd sent him here, he said, because they were trying to find every American within the Ring and gather them in Grantville to help with defense. Santee didn't betray any surprise, just kept listening and asking occasional questions. After a while Eddie relaxed a bit and decided Santee was just trying to be nice, even if sociable chitchat came hard to him. At Santee's subtle probing, Eddie explained that he was on his own now, since he was on a different side of the Ring of Fire from his home, including his father (who he said was "okay, when he had the time") and stepmother (who he admitted he wouldn't miss much).

The talk returned to more immediate matters. "How did you get here?" Santee asked him.

"I rode my dirt bike up that hill"—he pointed across the canyon—"and saw your smoke, and then your cabin. Lots of Germans running from the war around here, but they don't make smokestacks like that. No way to ride here, so I just walked. Brush got thick in places, but no problem."

"Good job. You must move pretty quiet when you want to." Santee even gave him a brief, crooked smile. "None of my business, but what are you going to do? I don't mean the town, I mean you."

"Well, I've been drafted, I guess. Frank Jackson's running the army; I'll do what he tells me to. He's a Vietnam vet." Eddie sounded a little impressed at that. Then he looked at his watch and quickly stood up. "Uh, I have to get back. I'm late now. Thanks for the water and all. Hope to see you in Grantville. . . ."

On impulse, Santee said, "Just a second, Eddie. You say there are armed Germans out there. Do you have a gun?"

"Uh, no. I had a .22 and a shotgun, but now . . ."

"Just a sec then. Be right back."

Santee disappeared through a side door and came

back in a few minutes with a pistol in a fully enclosed holster.

"This is a Russian Nagant revolver. Seven shooter, not the usual six shots. Damn ammo costs forty bucks a box, so the pistols are cheap. Uh, 'were.' Damn."

Eddie smiled. "Everybody's doing that. Weird for everyone."

"Yeah. I suppose so. You know about gun safety?"

"It's loaded. Don't point it at anybody. Know what you're shooting at." Eddie repeated it mechanically; it had been drilled into his head a thousand times.

Santee nodded and handed the pistol to Eddie. "You know it; just remember it. Take this outside and dry-fire it a few times. Trigger pull is god-awful. Cylinder moves back and forth front to back; that's normal. I'll go round up the ammo."

Eddie did as he was told and found that Santee was right. His forefinger got tired right away, the sights were terrible, and the gun was uncomfortable in his hand. But he was fascinated by the various moving parts and was peering closely at the mechanism when Santee rejoined him with the ammunition. Santee showed him how to load and unload the gun, then opened a box and took out some ear muffs and safety glasses.

"Ready to try it?" Eddie nodded. "Shoot at that metal gong by the woodpile over there. The hill will catch anything that misses the woodpile."

Eddie shot seven times, and missed all but the last. The ringing gong made them both smile. "You'll do," was all Santee said to Eddie as they moved back toward the cabin.

Santee briefly showed him how to clean the revolver, and Eddie said again that he had to get back. It was going to be dark soon. "Thanks for letting me borrow this gun, Mr. Santee."

"Not borrow. It's yours to keep. I don't need the damn thing. I was going to trade it off for something else, and I'm glad to see it go to someone who can use it. Just keep it clean and it'll last a long time. Ruskie guns are butt-ugly but hell-for-strong."

Eddie thanked him awkwardly but profusely, then headed off through the brush, leaving Santee alone with his thoughts.

He lit a fire in the wood stove and found a pan to heat up some canned stew. He normally tried to cook dinner, but tonight was a night for thinking, not cooking. He had moved to this small cabin in 1990, and hardly ever left it. It had a spring on the hill above, so it had running cold water, and a septic system, but no power. The power company would have been happy to bring him power at two dollars a foot from the road, but he didn't have the five thousand or so dollars that would take, nor really need the power. But he did have a friend with the phone company who'd made a "mistake" and got him telephone installation for sixty bucks. A generator provided power when he needed it—mostly to run power tools and check his e-mail daily—and his jeep took him on monthly trips into Fairmont or Wheeling or Charlottesville to get supplies. He had a garden, his hunting, his pension, his collection of old guns, and plenty of time. Most of his old friends were dead or had gone all domesticated, and most of his new friends he'd never met except online. He'd been fairly happy, semi-retired, living the life every ex-sergeant says he dreams of . . .

He'd rarely been to Grantville. It had been out of his way from the roads he could reach, and too small a town for good prices, but now it was the only town he could get to. And from what Eddie had told him, it was at *war*, for chrissake. He'd left the war back in Vietnam, and it had taken him quite a few years to get it out of his mind and sleep soundly again. Ever since then, he'd tried hard to never let any of that mindset back into his life. That kind of thinking, war thinking, really fucked you up for living in the real world.

But the real world had just changed, hadn't it? *Snap to*, he told himself. Good survivors don't waste time trying to play the old game when all bets are off. If he'd been dealt a new hand, he'd better take a close look at the cards.

Eddie had said that Mike Stearns, the head honcho, wanted to meet him. *Like I'm going to go take tea with the fucking governor! Who I need to talk to is—what was his name, Frank Jackson?—the guy who's running the army.*

The next morning, Santee walked into Grantville. There was no real path, just some game trails, so it had taken him two hours to go down the hill and into the town and would probably take him three hours to get back. Far from the sleepy town he vaguely remembered, the town seemed to be buzzing with activity. No cars, though; people were walking everywhere. *Smart, save the gasoline for the army.* The thought came to him with surprising ease, worrying him a bit. *Damn it, I'm a civilian now. Have been for twenty years.* No need to examine everything as if he was still a platoon sergeant. But he couldn't help noticing that lots of the men were wearing pistols, perhaps even most of them. The .45 on his own hip fit in nicely.

Asking around, he found out that the new army commander, Frank Jackson, was big in the Mine Workers union. Eddie had said he was a 'Nam vet; if he hadn't been just a desk jockey, he might do. Santee headed for the cafeteria where people said Jackson usually had lunch. Lunch sounded good after his long walk, and he was pleasantly surprised to find the food abundant and free. After eating, he found Jackson surrounded by a dozen miners, deep in a spirited discussion. *No time like the present.*

"Frank Jackson? Can I talk to you after lunch? Alone?"

Frank looked up, annoyed. "And you are . . . ?" His tone said "Who the hell are you?"

"Paul Santee. Tunnel rat. We ate some of the same bananas." He kept his tone flat, almost careless.

One of the miners next to him started to say something blustery, "Well, you can just . . ." but stopped when Frank interrupted. "Sure. I'll be with you in, say, five minutes?" Santee nodded and moved away to wait.

Frank held up a hand to the questions that came from all sides. "Vietnam. The tunnel rats went down into those little VC tunnels with just a knife and a flashlight, maybe a small pistol. There were booby traps, and spiders and scorpions and snakes, and a bunch of gooks who wanted them dead. Anyone who did it has twice the guts I ever had, and anyone who made it back has twice the luck I have, and was very, very good at it. Think about it." He wolfed down the last of his food. "I've got to go talk to this guy. Keep on trying to figure out what sort of problems we'll have once we open the second shaft, and then figure out what to do about it. I'll talk to you when I get back." Still chewing, he walked away from the miners, who were buzzing in low tones.

He and Santee stepped outside. Frank said, "Before yesterday I thought I knew all the vets around here. And you being a Rat, well, if this was a bar I'd buy you a drink. So what can I do for you?" His tone was affable and open; Santee relaxed a little.

"Oh, I've lived here for years; up in the hills west off of Butterchurn Road. I guess my mailbox is still back in West Virginia, but my cabin's on this side. I haven't been to this town in five or six years, because my road used to go off toward Fairmont."

"And now it doesn't go anywhere?"

"Right. The kid you sent to hunt for me told me what happened, so I came to see what's going on here—since it looks like we're all in the same little boat together."

"Yeah, Eddie told me he'd found you yesterday. We'd be glad to have you join us. We're putting together an army of self-defense, or the nearest thing to it we can manage. We need everybody we can get, and it would really help a lot to have somebody else with combat experience." He looked at Santee expectantly.

He thinks I'm going to re-up right here on the spot! Fuck him. "I'll think about it. I need to know more. What are the chances, what are the plans, who's supposed to be in charge, who's really in charge."

Frank nodded. "Sure. Sensible questions. Listen, I've got to get back to my Mine Workers committee right now, but I want to talk to you some more. And to get your questions answered, you probably need to see Mike Stearns—he's the guy we elected to run things for now. Mike's easy to talk to. How about if I make you an appointment with him this afternoon, and then I meet you for a beer after work?"

Santee nodded warily. Frank seemed decent, he thought, but so what. He'd go meet Stearns, and then talk to Frank again, and then maybe decide what to do. He followed Frank back toward the building.

∽   ∽   ∽

That evening, working on their third beer, Santee and Frank had gotten through discussing Grantville's defenses and started talking about the war—the old one. Frank had talked about what he'd done in Vietnam, and Santee closed his eyes and let some of the memories flood back. "Let's see," he said, "I got out in '79. Twelve years and I was back at corporal, and lucky not to be in the fucking stir. We cleaned out some tunnels out by Dim Noc, then just sat there for three days while the surface troops tore us up. After a while, I just melted into the jungle. I don't know if I was the only one alive at that point or not, and I've still got shrapnel in my hip. I sat there and watched my buddies get shot, and there wasn't a fucking thing I could do about it. I got back to our camp two weeks later. I found the motherfucking full-bird who ordered the choppers away from the pickup area and busted his jaw and both elbows."

He glared at Frank, who passed the unspoken test when he nodded emphatically. Bad officers were common enough in 'Nam; good men died when they did stupid things. "I'd just made E-7 and was breaking in some new guys. 'Piece of cake,' I told them—the tunnels weren't big and we went through them fast . . . Bastards." The last was said almost under his breath.

Santee took a deep breath, let it out, and started again. "Anyways, I don't talk about it 'cause it just pisses me off. I get—got—some disability and some money from some stocks and such. I do okay. I live up on the hill, and I hunt and fish and garden . . ." He paused a moment. *So, am I going to tell him? Yeah, he's going to find out anyway.* "And for fun, I have an Oh-Three FFL." Frank looked puzzled and he explained. "I'm a licensed collector of Curio and Relic Firearms. I can get guns in the mail, legally, if they're over fifty years old or on the special list. So I buy 'em and trade 'em, and keep a few I like."

Frank sat up with renewed interest. "Uh, if you don't mind my asking . . . how many guns do you have?"

"Oh, say fifty or sixty or so long guns, and maybe twenty pistols." The actual count was higher, but you didn't lay all your cards face up. "The thing is, lots of them are oddballs." At Frank's quizzical look, he went on. "I got German and French and British rifles from World War One—they all have different calibers, and they keep changing calibers too. For instance, I went hunting last year with a Turkish Forestry Carbine in 8mm Lebel. It started life as a French Berthier infantry rifle from World War One, and the Turks cut it down to a carbine in the forties. I'll bet I have the last boxes of 8mm Lebel ammo in . . . hell, in the whole world." Of course, *the world* had a different meaning now. "And some old rolling-block rifles, and Mausers, and Carcanos . . ." He stopped at Frank's lack of recognition and waved his hand dismissively. "A bunch of 'em, anyway. I gave Eddie Cantrell an old Russian revolver. I figured he'd be safer with it."

Frank grinned. "Yeah, he showed it to me. He was real proud of it. I'm glad you did that; Eddie's basically a good kid." Frank closed his eyes and tipped his head back a moment, thinking. "Your arsenal may be screwy, but most of what we've got is screwy, and the whole Ring of Fire is screwy. If you'd be willing to contribute some of it, it could make a huge difference in our war effort."

So here it was. Santee had to make up his mind now. He kind of liked Frank Jackson, and Mike Stearns had seemed competent during their brief meeting that afternoon, but he still didn't like the choices—come join their army and give them all his guns, or tell them to fuck themselves and go back and defend his cabin and guns by himself. He decided on compromise: give them some of his guns and help them out a little but stay independent. He'd long ago promised himself he wasn't going to take orders ever again, and that still held.

"I'll tell you what," he said slowly. "I'll do an inventory and see what I have that I don't need and you guys could use, and I'll let you know."

Frank looked deflated, but he said, "Thanks a lot. We'll appreciate any help you can give us."

They talked on for a while, but it was getting late. Too late and too dark for Santee to walk back to his cabin, even if there hadn't been marauding Germans around. He warily accepted the spare bed Frank offered him for the night, but he left early the next morning and chewed over his choices all the way back.

It was a cold shock to see his front door half broken, hanging open on its hinges. Santee froze, then stepped silently back behind some brush, drew his .45, and listened intently. Nothing. From where he stood he could see tracks in the dirt, coming and then going—big odd-looking, flat footprints. *Germans!* Three of them, he decided; two tall and one short. He waited a long while, then flicked a pebble onto the porch. Nothing happened. Very quietly, very stealthily, he crept up on the porch and entered the cabin.

He was shocked at the devastation. It seemed as if everything that could be broken was broken, and everything loose was on the floor. Dishes, books, lamps, pieces of computer equipment, food. Even the stovepipe had been knocked loose, and greasy black soot had fallen all over the mess. A few papers rustled forlornly in the breeze from the open door. But he gave the scene in the front room only a glance. Sick with apprehension, he stepped quickly over the piles of debris and through the open side door into the spare room. The storage boxes there were dumped and things were thrown around, but the floor seemed unbroken. With a huge sigh of relief, he pushed aside an overturned box and flipped an almost invisible catch that released an almost invisible hatch cover in the floor . . . Thank God they hadn't found the guns!

Later, after he'd tacked up plastic sheeting over the broken door and windows, unearthed his futon from the mess to sleep on, and found enough food still intact for a cold supper, Santee was still shaking, but hot rage had turned into simmering anger. *If I knew who did this I'd kill 'em—with my bare hands!* Stealing his stuff would have been bad enough; trashing it was pure malice. But if the culprits had been a party of Germans, as seemed likely from their tracks, killing them bare-handed was a tall order for a little guy in his fifties with shrapnel in his hip. If they decided to come back, he'd have a tough time with them even if he was well armed, even if they didn't bring any friends along. And he'd have to stay up nights pulling his own sentry duty. And eat what? Most of his food stores had been trashed. They hadn't found his Jeep, but there were no roads he could take now to replenish any supplies. . . .

Suddenly he realized just how alone he really was. He shook his head, almost in despair. He'd been wondering if he really needed to get involved with the people in Grantville. Obviously the choice had been made for him. Goddamn it.

Santee found Frank Jackson again the next day, in the office that had been created for him in one of downtown Grantville's vacant buildings. "I told you I'd bring you a list of the guns I could spare for the army," Santee said, "but I've got a problem. Two problems."

"Shoot," Frank said.

Santee told him what had happened to his cabin.

"Oh, God," Frank said. "I was afraid that kind of thing might start happening. Single isolated cabins are just too tempting a target. Can we send a squad out to help you chase them down? We can spare—"

"No need," Santee interrupted, rather bitterly. "Much as I hate to have the decision made for me, I've decided I can't live out there any more. Not just dangerous; no way to get supplied. Got to move."

Frank looked sympathetic. "Shit. I'm sorry. Do you want me to see about finding you a place to stay here in town?" Santee nodded. "And will you have a lot of stuff to move?"

Santee fidgeted. "Well, that's the other problem. The personal stuff that I can salvage probably won't amount to much—two or three backpack loads ought to do it. But then there's the guns . . ." He fished out a rather crumpled handwritten list and handed it to Frank.

Frank quickly scanned the list. "Pretty impressive looking. I don't know half these names, though." He looked up at Santee. "You mean you're donating these to the army?"

"What the hell else am I going to do with 'em? Can't sell 'em, can't shoot 'em all myself, sure as hell can't eat 'em. Maybe your guys will go out and kill the bastards who trashed my cabin with 'em."

"This is quite a list. They're going to be a big help . . ." He stopped, seeing Santee's sardonic expression. "But first we've got to get them here, right?"

"Yep."

"How long do you think we have before the Germans find them first?"

"Oh, they're pretty well hidden. If the bastards didn't find them when they tromped all through the cabin,

I doubt if they're going to find them now. Unless we advertise they're there by making constant little trips carrying two guns at a time."

"Yeah, I see what you mean. Since we don't have to rush, let's think about how we can get them here more or less safely." Frank thought a moment. "Are you going to be around this afternoon, like three-thirty or four?"

"I could be."

"Good. I have to go to a meeting now, but why don't you come back then and I can spend more time with you?"

"Okay, I'll be here," Santee said. *Busy man*, he thought as he left, *but he was real smooth in getting rid of me*.

Santee was back a little before four, and Frank seemed more relaxed. He said, "I've found a place for you to stay, if you want it, a guest cottage a block from the big church. Small, but Ruth Tippett will be happy to let you use it. Her husband was a Korean veteran, and she told me to specifically say she'd be proud to have you."

Santee grinned at him. "Maybe she wouldn't be if she knew some of the shit I pulled."

They talked briefly about the arrangements for Mrs. Tippett's cottage, and then Frank changed the subject. "Listen, I've been thinking. The army's growing. We've been getting more and more raw recruits in, and I mean raw—they don't even know how to stand in line. It would sure be a big help if we could find somebody with military experience who could show them the basics and—"

"No!" Santee snapped. "I can see where you're heading, and the answer is no! I appreciate the help finding a house and all, but I'm not going to be a goddamn training instructor for anybody. Keep me out

of the fucking chain of command! Remember, when I
was in the army I broke a colonel's jaw. And the last
time I had a job, I was unloading a truck and the
driver about run over me and I whupped his ass. Big
sucker, he was, and I'm a little shit, so they believed
me when I said he started it, but I still had to go.
And the time before that . . . well, I made sergeant
three different times. Never mind." He took a deep
breath. "I guess I'm saying I'm not cut out for taking
orders any more. I just get pissed off when they turn
stupid." He glared defiantly.

"Okay," Frank said in a flat tone, "message
received."

Santee felt a little bad. "It's not that I don't want to
help. Maybe I can do something else. Reload ammo or
something. I do know guns—well, rifles and handguns
anyway . . ." He trailed off.

"I'll think about it," Frank said.

A week later, Santee had settled into Mrs. Tippett's
cottage and Frank dropped by with a proposal.

"Chief Weapons Scrounger? Hell of a title," Santee
said.

"Yeah, but we need one. Mike and I were talking.
Lots of folks around here probably have hunting guns
they aren't using. And there are the gun nuts, too;
who knows what they have. Between them there'll be
guns in all sorts of different calibers and conditions.
So your job would be asking people for their spare
weapons and then sorting them out, and the ammo,
too. We don't have an armorer or anything."

"Hmm," Santee said slowly. "You said this is an
army job? Who would I report to?"

"Just me, if you want to call it reporting. No chain
of command—let's just say Mike and I tell you the
job we want done and you do it."

Santee closed his eyes and thought a long moment. "Okay. All right. I can do that." *Have to do something; I'll go crazy here otherwise.* "When would you want me to start? I still need to make one last trip to the cabin."

"You can start when you're ready," Frank said, looking relieved. "Welcome to the U.S. Army."

"I'll need some help if I'm going to scrounge weapons. Someone who knows the town, and maybe Eddie Cantrell; he seems sharp enough to pick up the job without a month of training."

"There's a map of the town on the wall at the hardware store. Or you might still be able to buy one for two bucks at the mayor's office if they still have any left. Eddie can help you, but we can't spare anyone else. All the adults around here are already trying to do a thousand things at once.

Santee sighed. "Okay. Pass the word, or give me a badge, or whatever."

"Will do. One thing though . . . you'll be dealing with civilians, ladies and such, and your language is . . . uh, colorful."

Santee tried to look prim. "Golly gosh, to think that one of our fighting soldiers might actually say naughty words."

Frank grinned at him. "Mike said, 'Tell him to keep it down in front of the ladies, but teach it to the youngsters. It's part of their military training.'"

"Well, that's one thing I'm expert enough to teach, anyhow."

"We hope you can talk people out of their 12-gauge pumps, and rifles in .308 and .30-06 and .223—those are going to be our standard military calibers. And if you can, spend some time teaching anyone who's rusty, or inherited something. Redistribute the nonstandard ammo as best you can; try to make sure everyone has at least a hundred rounds." Santee nodded. "And one last thing: Mike wanted me to emphasize that handing over their weapons is voluntary—really voluntary—and even if someone offers to give up their last gun, make sure they don't. We need armed civilians as much as an army, and the Second Amendment still stands."

"Absolutely! Couldn't agree more." *At least these guys have the right idea.* "Okay. I'll not only collect extra weapons, I'll try to make sure every house has at least one gun and some ammo and knows how to use it."

Two days later, after Santee's last trip to his cabin, they talked again. Frank had managed to scrounge up an extra map of Grantville somewhere. It was one of the full-sized maps the town had kept a few copies of in stock, and Santee was glad to get it. The detail was much better than on the computer-generated map he'd been using. Frank also said he'd talked to Eddie, who was proud to be the new Assistant Weapons Scrounger.

Santee said he was ready to start the job tomorrow, after he rested. "I brought down the last of my stuff, plus two rifles, and I'm beat."

"Mrs. Tippett says, until we can get an armory, we can use her front room to store all the guns and ammo you round up. That should make things handy for you. I already know some people who have shotguns to contribute, and pretty soon I guess we're going to have to figure out how to get your guns down here."

"Yeah, I've been worrying about that. When I was up there yesterday I didn't see signs that anybody but me had been there, but we can't be lucky forever. I figure those guns are worth a fortune these days, and we sure as hell don't want any of them shooting back at us."

"You said you've got, what, sixty rifles, plus how much ammo? We could round up some pack horses, I guess, or try to get your jeep through . . ." He trailed off.

"You guys got the kids doing basic? How about a nice Recon run?" That was a long trip in full packs. Army recruits have hated them since the dawn of time.

Frank's face lit up. "I like it! We can get sixty rifles in one trip."

"Uh, I counted," Santee said, a little sheepishly. "It's more like eighty. Plus some pistols."

"Okay, two Recon runs. We can send some armed scouts with them for protection."

"Uh . . ."

"Three?"

"Four. Maybe five. Bullets are heavy." Santee shrugged.

"You're going to be 'That bastard on the hill' to those boys." Frank grinned.

"Won't be the first time privates have cussed me. Do 'em some good, in the end."

"If it's any compensation, remember that Mike says you're allowed to teach them to swear."

"Go up and down that fucking hill enough, I do believe they'll learn all by their lonesome."

"Yes ma'am, I'm sure you should keep your shotgun. You wouldn't want some mo— uh, evil person to get past our sentries and into your house without some way of fu— uh, sending him to meet his maker. Are you sure you know how to use it?"

"Son, I was shootin' pheasants when you were in diapers, and you ain't a young man. Don't you worry about me none. But my husband's rifles you're welcome to; we lost him back in '93. I'm happy to help out the country."

Eddie spoke up. "Do you have plenty of shells for the shotgun? Sixteen-gauge is a bit out of style, but I'm sure I can round up some more in town."

She pointed to the closet. "Twelve boxes should be more than enough, plenty of buckshot and slugs, too. Now you get along, take those back to the army, then go visit the Bradleys next door. Owen used to brag over his hunting rifle something fierce, and Grace won't know what to do with it."

Santee practically bowed his way out of the house, followed by Eddie. "Yes ma'am. Thank you, ma'am."

As the door closed, Santee wiped his brow, though it wasn't a warm day. This was as hard a job as he'd had in twenty years. *Talk sweet and mind your tongue around the ladies—enough to drive a fucking* preacher *to swearing!*

"That went well." Eddie said. "She's a little old-fashioned, isn't she?"

"Yeah. Nice, though. Let's hope they're all that easy." They carried the rifles back to Mrs. Tippett's front room (now an arms depot) and planned their next sortie.

Santee said stiffly, "Well, okay, Mr. Jones. We're only supposed to pick up what guns there are to spare."

"Fine. I got none to spare." Bobby Jones was a loud, fat, redneck-looking man in a dirty T-shirt who (according to Eddie's friend Jeff) worked as a mechanic and handyman and was the person to call if you wanted it cheap and didn't care if it was done right.

Eddie was absolutely sure that Jones was lying. "Okay," he said, turning as if to leave. "Say, when did you shoot that deer? Nice rack on him." He pointed to the stuffed head on the wall.

Thus primed, Jones went into a long, boring description of the hunt. " . . . Anyways, Coop and me and Doug went there the year before, scouting around for sign . . ."

Santee looked impatient, but Eddie listened attentively. Once, when Jones was looking away, he signaled Santee to stay quiet.

" . . . Anyways, I finally got him down to the car and got old Dickey Estes to stuff him for me."

Eddie nodded. "Great. Thanks. Well, we gotta go now . . ."

Santee and Eddie stepped outside, and as Jones stood in the doorway, Eddie turned and said to him, "I think we'll go talk to Coop and Doug next. Is Dickey Estes still around?"

Jones suddenly stopped as he was closing the door on the Chief Weapons Scrounger and his young assistant. He realized what Eddie had done and tried to think of a way around it. Mild panic washed over his face as he looked at Eddie.

Eddie carefully kept his face blank, showing nothing that could directly challenge the large man. Jones' hunting buddies would surely tell them about the guy's guns—and Eddie was sure he had several to spare. That's why he'd put up with the long story, of course. Now that the trap was sprung, Jones could only admit he had some rifles to donate, or be disrespected as a hoarder by his friends.

Jones looked at Eddie, then slumped his shoulders. "Wait a minute," was all he said as he went.

Ten minutes later Santee and his assistant were struggling back to Mrs. Tippett's with eight rifles and assorted ammo. "Slick, Eddie! Good job. I didn't see how you could really be interested in that stupid long-winded story of his. . . . We've got to get a wagon or something!" He'd almost dropped a box of shells and had to reposition his load. "So, what made you think of that?"

Eddie grinned bashfully "I learned it playing Dungeons and Dragons. We had a similar problem back in Bloomtree, but it was with one of the Elven blacksmiths. Worked out about the same, except for the cursed gauntlets we got stuck with."

Santee chuckled. "Well, we better check these rifles. I bet some of them don't work. From the look of that guy's house he knows nothing about cleaning."

"So we have a total mishmash." Santee had just handed his written report to Mike Stearns and Frank Jackson, who were standing in Mrs. Tippett's crowded front room among piles of firearms and ammo. "A bunch of deer rifles in, by my count, fifteen different civilian calibers, and no more than a few hundred rounds of ammo for most of them. A bunch of foreign military rifles, mostly German 8mm. The thing we have the most loaded ammo for is the SKS—everyone who bought a rifle bought a case or two when it was cheap, but we only have a half dozen of the rifles and they're under-powered for long-range shooting. And that ammo isn't reloadable; it's mostly Chinese military surplus crap from the nineties and the cases are steel, not brass. So when that ammo's gone, the damn rifles are useless."

"Shotguns?" asked Mike.

"Those we have, mostly pumps. And three shotgun shell reloading machines." Santee liked how Mike didn't ask stupid questions like "Are you sure?" or "Where did you look?" Let the pros do their job and get out of the way. "The military calibers you asked me to look for, we have more of those than I thought. Mostly hunting rifles, .30-06 and .308. Also some .223 for the mouse guns."

Frank murmured "Civilian M-16" to Mike, who nodded.

Santee continued. "Problem with the .223 is it's a wimpy caliber, made to wound instead of kill, and we've only got a few of the rifles. Some miner got a couple of cases of .308 for his M-14, but he'd loaned the rifle to his brother in Pennsylvania, so we have an extra twenty-four hundred rounds for, well, anything that takes .308." Santee didn't *know* about Frank's M-60 machine gun, possession of which was a felony (or would be in a few hundred years), but he suspected it from hints Frank had dropped. He'd let Frank handle that his own way.

"A bunch of .22 rimfire—rifles, pistols, and ammo. Maybe thirty thousand rounds. Still a drop in the bucket, and .22s won't punch through any armor— good for small game, though. And then there's one real oddball . . ."

He paused, and Mike and Frank looked at him expectantly. "You know that big, huge, ugly house those rich assholes own, out off the highway?" They nodded; the owners lived in Washington D.C. and had only visited occasionally. The house was scheduled to become public property when they had the time.

"Well, I had a hunch, and I got Eddie to sneak in through an upstairs window. They must have been planning one hell of a safari. I found this big motherfucker there." He hauled out a gigantic bolt-action rifle, inlaid with gold leaf, with fancy hunting scenes engraved in the metal. "It's in .577 T-Rex, which is another way of saying 'You didn't need that shoulder.' It throws almost two ounces of bullet real fast. It's meant to stop charging elephants. This sucker probably cost him twenty thousand bucks. He had over a hundred rounds of ammo, too. What the hell he expected to shoot in West Virginia is anyone's guess."

They looked over the rifle and its exquisite

workmanship. Frank said, "Dude must have had a small peter," which drew smiles from Mike and Santee.

"I don't suppose we'll have much use for it," Santee said, shaking his head, "but it sure is something to behold."

They discussed which guns to assign to various groups in the army and which to keep in reserve. It wasn't much of a discussion because there weren't all that many guns and most of their army was still unorganized and untrained.

Finally, Santee summed up. "Bottom line, here's what we can do. We can shoot up all our ammo. We can also reload for most of the center-fire calibers we have. Only enough powder for twenty or thirty thousand rounds of rifle, and maybe that much pistol. Sounds like a lot, but you'll have a lot of shooters, and you can only do so much with dry-fire practice. Then we go to the local black powder, if we can get it." Frank and Mike nodded, they had thought of that themselves. "We lucked out with primers, I found a couple of cases of old ones in the back room at the hardware store, and they store pretty well. There are about fifty thousand there, and lots more in basements and workshops all around town. A bunch of folks around here reload; I'm trying to get all the spare equipment brought together so we can set up a reloading workshop. Bullets we can make from lead if we have to. But once those primers run out, that's it. Flintlocks, if we live that long." He looked disgusted. "I played with flintlocks once. They fired about eight, maybe nine times out of ten. Not good enough. Not fucking good enough."

The others nodded soberly. He knew his report wasn't too encouraging, but they'd have to make do. The alternative . . . well, there was none.

July 5, 1631

Eddie Cantrell was in the reloading shed, carefully pouring powder into brass rifle cases. It was a tedious, fussy job. Santee had been with him most of the afternoon but had gone outside to talk to Mike Stearns and Frank Jackson. The three were now standing in the shade outside the window, talking loudly.

Like most of the town, Santee was hung over, but was nonetheless close to yelling. "No fucking way. Uh-uh. Not me, Frank, not me. I'd shoot one of the stupid bastards, and then where would we be?"

"Come on, Santee. Those young recruits need to be trained by the folks who know what they're doing."

Santee looked tense and nervous, the opposite of his blithe confidence at the Battle of the Crapper, where he hardly got to fire a shot. "Frank, I'm an old, crotchety bastard. I know it. I have no patience for fools. I don't speak any German and I don't think my whorehouse Japanese will help. I'm an old relic. Find some other stupid fucking idiot about twenty years younger than me. I'm going to go get me some aspirin and then I'm going back to the reloading shed. Shoot me if you want. No." He turned and stomped off.

Mike and Frank stood there, watching the receding Chief Weapons Scrounger. Frank shook his head. "He's a relic, all right, and a curio, too. Fits that damn gun license of his."

Mike was philosophical. "Some people will either work alone or not at all. You can't push a rope."

"Yeah, I suppose. He's happy and productive in a job the army needs doing. I guess it's better to just leave him alone."

∾   ∾   ∾

Ten minutes later Santee joined Eddie in the reloading shed. "Stupid fuckers still want me to be a drill sergeant!" he said. "Can you imagine me teaching a bunch of stupid pissant kids? Shee-it. How are you doing there?"

By now, Eddie knew Santee well enough to kid him, just a little. "Mr. Santee? You're teaching *me*. Does that mean I'm not a stupid pissant?"

Santee barked laughter. "You can't be all that bright or you wouldn't be here. Humph. Now how much powder are you putting in those cases? And where are the bullets we'll be using?" Eddie showed him both, to Santee's approval.

"Say Eddie, I noticed you had to go help with Driscoll's computer when all the other privates were policing up the fired brass. How did you swing that?"

Eddie trusted Santee enough by this time to let some of the truth out. "Well, I'd been asked to help them when I had the time. I just sort of decided having the time then was the best way of not freezing my fingers and getting torn up by the briars." Eddie glanced up a little apprehensively, checking for Santee's reaction. He needn't have worried.

"Good thinking. A smart soldier avoids the grunt work if he can—as long as you're there at the fight, I mean. And you were. I saw you do some stupid things in that battle, but Jeff did 'em even stupider, and you have to back up your friends sometimes."

Eddie just nodded. He didn't like to think of how close it had come to a bloodbath, down there by that outhouse. If the converted coal truck hadn't come in when it did, he wasn't at all sure he'd still be alive.

"Fight when you need to," Santee said, "just don't be a hero. They die too quick."

"Not me. Idiot—I mean Jeff—can be the hero." He

turned back to the loading bench. "Get us all killed next time," he muttered.

The next day, Santee heard voices inside the reloading shed. He hesitated, then stood outside to listen. It sounded as if Eddie had two younger boys there and was showing them around. "We're keeping the loads down to minimum levels so the brass will last longer and we use less powder. We can't do that for the machine gun, and we're loading Julie's ammo specially."

"Cool!" said one of the younger boys. "Can we try it sometime?"

"Well, I don't know . . . Mr. Santee is in charge of things here."

"Pleeease?" came the wheedling reply.

Santee had heard enough, and walked in the door. He said sternly, "Hello, Eddie. Hello, boys. Eddie, can I see you a minute?"

The "uh-oh" looks among the boys were priceless. Santee managed to keep his face straight.

"Uh, sure." said Eddie. "Don't touch *anything*," he said to the boys.

Outside, the two walked far enough away from the shed to be out of earshot.

Santee finally let loose the grin he'd been hiding. "So, it's not every day you get to whitewash a fence, eh, Tom Sawyer?"

Eddie beamed, relieved that he wasn't in trouble and rather pleased that Santee realized what he was doing. "Yeah."

"Okay then, time for a command lesson. If one of those kids double-charges a round and blows up a rifle, or worse yet a person, who's to blame?"

Eddie thought a second, and his face got serious "Me, I guess."

"Yep. So if you want to make this work, you better watch them. Keep the shifts short so they stay interested. Come up with safety checks for each round you load—after you put the powder in, a wood dowel should drop to the same level in each case."

"I'd thought of something like that. One caliber and load at a time, too."

Santee nodded. "Make a schedule. That shed is too small for a bunch of boys in there. I'll try to get Frank to talk up how important reloading is when he's around any teenaged boys. That should get you all the help you want." Eddie nodded, his face earnest.

"Now I'm going to go back in there and give you and those boys the safety lecture of your life, and read you the riot act on letting anyone in there unsupervised. That should scare them into taking this seriously . . . Tom Sawyer."

Santee picked a beautiful day a few weeks later to try out their hand-loaded ammunition. He and Eddie took two hunting rifles, a .30-06 and a .308, along with a few hundred rounds of ammo loaded to various speeds. The idea was to find a mild but accurate load for each of the two main rifle calibers, and then try some full-power loads for the M-60 and Julie's wickedly accurate sniper rifle. (One of Julie's targets was hanging in the reloading shed, so all the shooters in town knew what it—and she—could do.)

To keep the noise from disturbing the townspeople, they'd picked a shooting area far out of town, down a lane that led past the area of the Battle of the Crapper. They tied the rifles, ammo, and various spotting scopes and shooting gear to a primitive, unsteady cart they'd cobbled together and towed the whole assembly behind Eddie's dirt bike. Eddie rode slowly and carefully, shutting off the motor and coasting downhill whenever possible to save precious gasoline; Santee walked alongside.

On the far edge of the battle site they passed a small clearing. "Look at that," Eddie said. He stopped the bike and pointed. "Germans have been out here with wood-axes. I wonder how long it took to chop that big tree down?"

"Hard to tell. I had to chop firewood by hand when I was your age, and it was a Pure-D bitch when the wood was tough. I had a good steel axe, too. The natives here probably don't have anything but bronze or iron axes."

"Miz Mailey would know, I guess, or another one of the teachers." Eddie got off the bike to examine the tree. "What I'm wondering is why they did this. It was after the battle—see here where the axe cut through this bullet track—but they just left most of the tree here after they cut it down. I'd only go to all that effort if I wanted that wood."

Santee was puzzled too, and scouted around the area. "Can't really tell, I guess. Maybe something scared them off? There are wolves around here; I've heard them at night. Or boars; I know wild boars are pretty mean and run in packs. Still, it doesn't make sense—there are at least four sets of footprints around here, and four people with axes should be able to take care of themselves. Weird."

They shrugged and went on toward their shooting area, which Eddie's friends had helped scout out for them. It was in a valley formed by a small creek, pointing up a gentle slope so stray shots wouldn't escape. They didn't expect this first set of ammunition to be particularly accurate.

Assuming that the point of aim with their lower power ammo would be off, they'd brought large sheets of cardboard with targets at the top, and now they set them up at one hundred yards. Then they put on earmuffs and safety glasses and started systematically testing the ammo, one load for one target, not adjusting for aim, just to see where the bullets were hitting and how they were grouping together.

After the second set of shots Santee squinted into the spotting scope. "Pretty good group there, Eddie. What load is that?"

"What?" Eddie took off his earmuffs, and Santee repeated the question while he took off his own. "Uh, number fourteen. I left the details back in town."

"Not a problem, just keep notes like we talked about."

Eddie scribbled. "Okay, got it. Let's go get the targets so we can measure . . . What was that?"

"What was what?"

"I heard something, like a scream. A long ways off." They paused, making no noise, waiting.

"There!" Eddie said. "You hear it?"

"No, but if you heard a scream, I believe you. I don't have young ears. Where'd it come from?"

"Can't tell. Maybe over that way." He pointed vaguely off to the left.

Santee quickly reloaded the two rifles and gave one to Eddie. Grabbing the spotting scope with one hand, he started up the side of the small valley, in the direction where Eddie had pointed, motioning for him to follow.

When they got to the top of the slope, they could see a farmstead about a half mile away; smoke was coming from one of the buildings. Santee quickly dropped prone and set up the spotting scope, peered through it, and stiffened. "Damn. Shit. There's some bastards down there sacking that farm. The house is on fire, and I just saw a half-naked woman being chased by three guys. Shit."

"I'll go get the ammo." Eddie said, and rushed off before Santee could say anything. In a few minutes he was back with the canvas bag that held all their bullets, and had thought to throw in the canteens full of water. Santee had moved over to a low spot beside a fallen tree. Eddie dropped the bag beside him and began sorting out the ammo, which had gotten jumbled. He found a box of .30-06 for himself and handed a box of .308 to Santee.

"Eddie, put on your muffs. I'm going to try a Julie and at least scare 'em good. They're bringing up a horse and wagon, I guess to haul away their booty."

The first shot wasn't close, but it kicked up dirt where he could see. By the time he'd fired the fifth shot and the magazine was empty, he was hitting near the wagon, and he'd definitely provoked a reaction. The marauders turned the wagon to face him and started whipping the horse. He saw six or eight men run to the wagon as it started across the field toward them.

"They must know there aren't many of us by our rate of fire, and they must want modern guns real bad. We've got to take out that horse." Eddie looked stricken, and he said, "Can't help it. Shame to waste a good animal, but he's their motor. Try that load number fourteen if you have any more. I can't seem to hit the fucker."

They both kept firing at the wagon as it came slowly across the field. It was obviously heavy, and they didn't seem to be having any effect on it. Finally, as it got to the edge of the field where a lane ran in their direction, the horse suddenly dropped in its traces.

"Got the sombitch!" Eddie could barely hear him because of his earmuffs, but understood. He had rolled over and begun fishing for more ammo in the bag when Santee suddenly jumped up and swung his rifle around. Two shots rang out, the second one a deep boom that didn't come from Santee's gun. When Eddie turned to look, he saw a man with a wheel-lock slowly folding, blood on his chest. When he turned back to congratulate Santee, he saw him lying on the ground, on his side, writhing in pain. The gun Santee had been shooting was lying next to him demolished, the stock splintered.

Eddie dropped to his side. A continuous stream of quiet profanity now came out of Santee. "Motherfucker shot my rifle. Shit. I think it broke my fucking leg. Shit. See any blood?"

Eddie looked at Santee's right leg, which was already swelling. "No blood. Maybe just a bruise?

"I can feel the bone grating," Santee's said tightly. His face was white with pain. "Okay, here's what we do. Take a quick look at that wagon."

Eddie poked his head up and quickly ducked back down. "They cut the horse loose. It looks like they're about to get the wagon onto the lane."

"Okay, quick three-sixty and see if you see any movement."

Eddie looked. "I don't see anything. Probably they sent a guy ahead when they first heard us shooting, and you got him."

"What's the range to that wagon?"

Eddie took another quick look. "Three hundred yards, a little downhill. They've turned the wagon around, and I think they're pushing it this way."

"Sight in, bear down, and use the Julie loads. Aim for the center of the wagon. You should be able to punch right through it at this distance."

Eddie did as he was told, while Santee tried to fish through the bag of ammo for the .30-06 cartridges that would fit the remaining rifle.

Eddie had fired all five rounds in the rifle when he ducked down again.

"Santee? My turn to cuss. Shit. I just figured out why they chopped that tree down. They know how to stop our bullets: it just takes enough wood, and the bullet track in that tree they cut down told them how thick it had to be. They put a couple of feet of green wood planks on that wagon, and they go almost down to the ground. Without the horse they only have people to push it, so they're moving slow, but it's coming this way."

Santee handed Eddie some more bullets. "Shoot low, try to bounce one under the wagon."

Eddie shot again, then dropped back. "I think it worked. I saw one fall. I think they put him in the wagon. They stopped moving, for now at least."

"Okay. Now do as I say. Help me get up to the top of this ridge, and put the ammo next to me." Moving was clearly painful for him, and it took them a minute or two to get him set up in a good position, ammo and canteen within easy reach.

"Eddie. Get on your bike and go pick up that big motherfucking safari rifle. Then get your ass back here and blow the shit out of that wagon." Eddie started to open his mouth, but Santee stopped him. "No arguments. This is an order, Eddie. Last lesson in soldiering: sometimes you gotta suck it up and do what you're told."

Eddie swallowed hard, and nodded.

"I'll wait for you here." Eddie nodded again and ran down the hill.

Eddie ran into Mrs. Tippett's house without knocking, running for the parlor where some of the guns were still stored.

"Young man, what are you doing?" she said, indignant at the intrusion, and followed him.

Eddie pushed the stacks of rifles aside, searching for

the big safari rifle. "Santee's been shot. He's holding off the bastards by himself. I gotta get the big rifle and get back there."

He found the rifle, tore it out of its case and slung it over his shoulder, then stuffed his pockets with the big bullets. Mrs. Tippett asked what she could do to help.

"Call the cops and tell them it's out past the Crapper where the battle was—Jeff and Larry and Jimmy Andersen will know where. Sorry about this"—he pointed to the mess he'd made—"I gotta go. You call them right now, okay?" He ran out the door and jumped on the still-running dirt bike.

The trip back to Santee was the longest of Eddie's life. He was no motorcycle racer, and the little dirt bike just couldn't go fast enough. He almost wrecked it once, when the big rifle slung across his back shifted, so he slowed down some, but kept speeding up again whenever the track was straight.

As he got close to the shooting area he heard a shot, which made him speed up even more. He'd only been gone a half hour or so, but the shot meant that someone—hopefully Santee—was still alive. He rode the bike up the slope but dumped it when it got too steep. He ran the rest of the way up to Santee, who was still there, shooting over the rise.

Santee turned and grinned. He had a trickle of blood running down the side of his face, and some splinters in his hair. "Good time," he said, a little weakly. "Good timing too. I think they were getting ready to rush me, but they heard your bike. That damned wagon's only fifty yards away now."

Eddie was panting. He didn't answer, just loaded the hotdog-sized cartridges into the big bolt-action rifle. It held only two in the magazine and one in the chamber.

"They're shooting from the back right side of the wagon. I think there are six of them left; they're reloading fast enough to make me keep my head down. I've only got twelve rounds left, but they don't know that."

Eddie crawled up next to Santee with the big rifle and got ready to shoot over the hill, but Santee stopped him. "No, you'll break your collarbone. You have to stand up to shoot that monster. Stand below the ridge bent over, then stand up and shoot right after I do."

"Okay . . . ready."

At Santee's shot, Eddie stood and sighted in on the lower right side of the wagon. When he pulled the trigger on the .577 T-Rex rifle, his world exploded. It felt like he'd been kicked by a mule in his right shoulder. He went blind for a second, and the rifle flew out of his hands. He had no earmuffs this time, and his ears started ringing painfully, but he could faintly hear *Mein Gott!* from the wagon. In pain, he picked up the rifle again and worked the bolt.

Santee was now aiming over the top of the ridge, hoping the attackers would break cover. Eddie's next shot did some damage to one of them, either directly or from flying splinters, because a loud scream of pain came from the wagon. This time Eddie didn't drop the rifle, but his shoulder was so bruised by the recoil he could barely work the bolt. Just the same, he readied his third shot.

"Got the fuckers scared now, Eddie. One more time."

At the third shot, there were more screams from the wagon, and the rest of the marauders broke and started running the other way. There were only four now, and one was limping. One took off uphill into the forest, but the other three ran straight down the lane. Not being used to the Americans' long-range rifles, they thought adding distance was the most important thing to keep them from being shot. They'd made several mistakes that day, starting with raiding a farm near American territory, but this was their last. Santee fired and missed; then with his last shot, two fell down—either one bullet hit two of them, or the limping man couldn't run any further. The last man ran away weaving down the road, then off through some trees, moving away from Santee and Eddie as fast as he could.

Though Eddie's ears were ringing, he still heard the horn from the pickup full of men from the town as it raced up the hill. Santee was now lying on his back with his eyes closed, and Eddie dropped to his side in worry, but then quickly relaxed. Dead men don't alternately grimace with pain and grin.

September 1631

Santee limped into the downtown office that served as Army headquarters, and with his cane at his side, lowered himself carefully to a chair by Frank Jackson's desk.

"Hey!" Frank said, "Good to see you up and around. Eddie thought they wouldn't let you out for another week."

"Oh, I sweet-talked 'em. How's Eddie doing?"

"He's okay. His hearing's fully back now, and he's been drilling with the other soldiers. And he's started a regular little program, showing the younger teenaged boys how to reload. So, how's the leg?"

"It's healing fine. But I sure had to lie in that

goddamn bed a long time. I'd have gone nuts if I hadn't had so many visitors."

"Well, after all, you're a bona fide hero."

"You mean I'm a bona fide dumbass. I got shot. If I hadn't lowered my rifle to see what I shot, like a greenhorn, I'd be called Stumpy."

"Heroes get shot too, you know."

"Bullshit. Heroes get dead. I got lucky."

"No, really. You and Eddie accounted for seven bandits, plus you saved a farmstead. That's not just luck." Santee grunted. "Mike and I think you deserve a promotion."

Santee looked alarmed. "Oh, Jesus!" he said in emphatic disgust. "No, I don't. You'll want me to take on some new job I'll hate. I like what I'm doing! Leave me alone."

"Look, you're wasted just making lists of guns and pouring powder into little shell cases. You know so much more than that." Frank looked him straight in the eye. "Please, Santee, we really do need you. Your experience is just too valuable for us not to tap into. What'll it take to get you to say yes?"

Santee closed his eyes and thought for a long time. "Okay," he said finally. "Here's what I could do. You guys are going to have shavetails, right? Wet-behind-the-ears second lieutenants in your new army, right? Eddie going to be one?"

Frank nodded, silent.

"Well, I could talk to them. Not all the time, not every day, my patience would go, but I'll talk to them. Everyone else is going to be teaching them how to give orders. I'll talk to them about what it's like to *get* orders, and what happens when they fuck up. Maybe, just maybe, one of them won't get their jaw busted by a sergeant."

Frank sat back and beamed at him. "That's one of

the best things you could do! From what they tell me, those kids in our officer candidate class really need it, the Americans and Germans both. Half of them want to be their unit's best friend, and the other half want to be their lord and master. Neither way works worth a damn, and someone's got to teach them that."

They talked a while longer and worked out the details. Santee still refused any official army title, so he'd continue as the Chief Weapons Scrounger, even though most of the actual scrounging was now done. He'd still manage the inventory and oversee the reloading program, but for most practical purposes he'd be a roving instructor for the new officers they'd be training.

"Maybe I'll call the course 'Command Is a Loaded Gun,'" Santee said, thinking about what he was agreeing to.

Frank grinned at him. "I think the Army will still want to call it 'Principles of Leadership' or some such boring thing. Not *that* much has changed."

After Santee had said good-bye and limped out onto the street, he stopped and shook his head with a rueful grin. "Damn, they roped me in again. I'm lucky to make it out of there without them making *me* a goddamn officer," he said to nobody in particular, and headed home.

The Sewing Circle

Gorg Huff

Delia Ruggles Higgins was five foot nine, whipcord thin, and a self-described packrat. As of the Ring of Fire, she was fifty-nine and had been a widow for seven years. She had graying hair and black eyes. She figured she had "gracefully surrendered the things of youth." Not without regret, but with what she hoped was grace.

These days she ran the storage lot that had been her living with her late husband Ray, and still was now that he was gone. For the last four years she had also managed her daughter Ramona, who had a true knack for picking Mr. Wrong. Ramona and her boys David and Donny had moved back in with her a few months after Donny's dad had dumped her and gone back to his wife. David was small for his age, skinny with brown hair. Delia was expecting a growth spurt anytime now. Donny was thin too, but his growth spurt was still probably some years away.

Ramona did most of the routine work at the storage lot, and since the house was next door, Delia was available if something came up that Ramona couldn't handle. Which happened all too often. She took after her father physically. She was plump and short with light brown hair and pale blue eyes.

Delia had a big doll collection. It was not, she would cheerfully acknowledge, a great doll collection. It was almost entirely cheap plastic dolls bought at the Goodwill in Fairmont, the local thrift shops, and Valuemart, whenever they had something cheap. She had, for example, five Michael Jordan dolls: three ten-inch ones, and two eighteen-inch ones she had found still in the box at a clearance sale. She had lots of fashion dolls, Barbies, Sandies and others. Some she had posed with members of the *Enterprise* crew. She liked Star Trek. There were also baby dolls, and Santas, which you could get really cheap right after Christmas.

It wasn't, with the exception of a few gifts, an expensive collection, but it was a big one, collected over the last twenty years or so. Ray had not commented when she started collecting dolls. He just shook his head and from then on bought her dolls for Christmas, birthdays, and whenever the mood struck. She used her grandmother's old Singer sewing machine to make doll clothing and to repair and fit people clothing she got at Goodwill and other thrift stores in the area.

She gardened quite a bit, growing both vegetables and flowers. She grew vegetables in the back yard, which was larger than the front by a considerable margin. Not enough for a truck garden, but enough to add fresh fruit and vegetables to the larder in spring and summer. The front yard was devoted to flowers.

They were just for fun. She had roses and daffodils, and a variety of others. She had even planted flowerbeds outside the mobile home that served as an office for the storage lot.

Then came the Ring of Fire. Delia came home from the town meeting three days after the Ring of Fire in a state of shock, which was replacing her previous state of denial. She had not believed the rumors. In spite of everything, she had not wanted to believe the stories. Now they were confirmed.

She still had the storage lot, but it wasn't the steady income it had been. The circumstances had changed. She had no idea how the change would affect the storage rental business. *Hell, with Mike Stearns running things, we might get nationalized,* she thought half seriously. Delia had never been fond of unions, or union bosses. There was some money in the bank—though what, if anything, it was worth now, she had no idea. Things had been tight before the disaster. Now?

She looked over at her daughter. Ramona was not taking things well. Then again, Ramona never had taken changes well, not even as a child. Right now she was going though the pantry, picking things up and putting them down, with little rhyme or reason. David, Ramona's elder son, was doing better. He had taken his younger brother Donny to their room as soon as they got home, but David had been better than his mother in emergencies, even when he was ten. Delia sighed.

June 8, 1631: Delia Higgins' House

The house had clearly needed cleaning, and it helped keep Ramona busy. Delia made an inventory of everything they found. About the only exceptional things in the house were her dolls and the sheer amount of unfinished sewing. She had obviously gotten behind in her sewing.

Then there was The Storage Lot. About three acres of their five acre lot were devoted to the collection of used metal shipping containers that made up the storage lot. Before the Ring of Fire it had provided the family with a living. Three quarters of the containers had been rented, about half of them to people outside the Ring of Fire. Since the Ring of Fire, though, she was left with only a third of the containers rented—and things were only getting worse as people emptied their containers for items to sell to the merchants in Rudolstadt and Badenburg.

There were two ways of looking at the property in the storage containers rented by people outside the Ring of Fire. One theory was that it now belonged to her, since it was on her land and in her containers. The other was that it belonged to Grantville, like the land that was owned by people outside the Ring of Fire.

Delia was not sure which way the powers-that-be would come down on the issue. She understood that they might feel that the needs of the many outweighed the needs of the few. She even agreed, in theory, but she had Ramona and the boys to consider. So, for now, she was keeping a fairly low profile, trying to figure out which way things were going to go. She had not opened any of the containers that were rented by people left behind because if she waited till their rent was overdue she would have up-time legal precedent on her side. Meanwhile, her income had gone down by over fifty percent, and any gain represented by the stuff in the containers was both iffy and short term.

They needed another source of income. There was all the old clothing, quite a bit in the sewing room, and still more in a storage container. One good thing about owning a storage lot: you generally had a place to put your stuff. *It was the perfect job for a pack rat*, Delia thought, grinning reminiscently. She would look into repairing and selling some of the old clothing.

June 12, 1631: The Wendell House

Dinner that night was venison steaks, well done, with salad, both bought at the grocery store for about what beef steaks and salad would have cost before the Ring of Fire. The venison was cheaper than the beef would have been, but the salad was more expensive. Bread for the moment was priced through the roof. The table was set with a silver plate candelabra and light for dinner was provided by candles rather then light bulbs, not to make dinner more romantic, but because the Wendells had figured out that light bulbs were going to be expensive and hard to replace. Still it lent an elegance to the family dinner. At the head of the table sat Fletcher Wendell, a tall gangly man with dark brown hair and hornrimmed glasses. He was not a particularly handsome man but his face was rendered charming by animation. Across from him sat his wife Judy, statuesque rather than gangly, with mahogany hair and blue eyes. Recessive genes had played in making their daughters. Sarah was a carrottop with rather too many freckles distracting from the evenness of her features. Which left Judy the Younger, twelve and so pretty as to border on the beautiful. Rich auburn hair and a pale complexion with only the lightest sprinkling of freckles.

Judy the Younger asked: "Mom, Hayley says that money is worth more now than it was before the Ring of Fire, but Vicky says it's not worth anything cuz there ain't no United States no more. So who's right?"

Judy the Elder stalled while she thought about her daughter's question. "Because, not 'cuz,' dear. And 'isn't,' not ain't."

Fletcher Wendell came to his wife's rescue, sort of. "Back before the Ring of Fire, there was a bank in Washington that had a bunch of fairies with magic wands. They made new money when they were happy, and made it disappear when they were sad. Apparently, when the Ring of Fire happened, one of those fairies was in town, and it now resides in the Grantville bank."

"Daaad!" Judy the Younger complained, while her older sister Sarah smirked.

"I take it," said Daaad, "that you don't believe in Federal Reserve Fairies? That's just the problem, don't you see? Neither do the down-timers, at least not yet. Part of my new job with the finance subcommittee is to keep the Federal Reserve Fairies happy. Another part is to convince the Germans and all the other down-timers that they are real, because they perform a very important function and it only works really well if most people believe in them."

Judy the Younger looked disgusted. Sarah didn't even try to hide her smirk. Judy the Elder was moderately successful at disguising her laugh with a cough, then she gave Fletcher the "look." At which point Fletcher held up his hands in mock surrender.

"All right, I surrender," he said, which no one believed for a moment.

Judy the Elder gave her husband one more severe look then spoke again. "Your father's subcommittee recommended to the cabinet that they declare that money on deposit in the bank and the credit union is still there, that debts owed to people or institutions inside the Ring of Fire are still valid, but debts or accounts in places left up-time are gone. Just common sense, but some people argued about it. Some wanted accounts in other banks honored. Sort of transferred to the local bank. Others wanted all debts to the bank erased."

Fletcher grimaced. "Well . . . pretty much—except there's still a big argument about mortgages. People who owe their mortgage to the local bank are raising a fuss because they think they're being discriminated against. They think the out-of-area mortgages should be assumed by the new government. Truth to tell, they've got a point—and Lord knows the government could use the money."

Judy the Elder plowed on. "Leave that aside, for the moment. Right now, wages paid by the city government or the emergency committee are being kept the same as they were before the Ring of Fire. Dan Frost is still paid the same. The coal miners are getting paid according to their pre-Ring of Fire contract, as are the people at the power plant. The difference is that now the emergency committee, which is receiving the income from coal sales and electric bills, is paying them. As will whatever government follows it. Unless it divests itself of the businesses. What that does is provide a stable point in the money supply which, hopefully, will help keep the money from increasing or decreasing in value too quickly, but no one wants wage and price freezes to last any longer or be any more widespread than absolutely necessary. So the owner of the grocery store sets the prices at the grocery store, with suggestions by the emergency committee. Now back to your question, how much is a dollar worth? If you're talking about paying the electric bill, or the house payment, it's worth exactly what it was worth before the Ring of Fire. If you're talking about buying groceries, it's fairly close to what it was before. For a Barbie doll, it's worth a lot less, because no one is making Barbie dolls any more, and the down-timers are buying them up. So take care of your Barbies, they are going to be worth a lot one day."

"Ah, but the down-timers don't have any money," Fletcher put in with a grin. "At least, not American money. So right now, everyone is trying to figure out how much of our money their money is worth, and vici verci. Which is where the Federal Reserve Fair—" Fletcher paused, casting an overdone look of meek submission at his wife. "Ah, the bank comes in."

"Oh, go ahead Fletcher," Judy the Elder put in, with an equally overdone, long-suffering sigh. "You won't be satisfied till you've run those poor fairies into the ground."

"Not at all. I'm very fond of the Federal Reserve Fairies. They do the kind of magic we need done." He smiled cheerfully at his daughters. "The thing about the Fed Fairies is they hate it when prices go up too fast. It makes them very sad, and they wave their magic wands, and make the bank have less money. Then the bank charges more interest when it loans out what money it does have. What makes the Fed Fairies really happy, is when prices stay the same, or go down. When that happens, they can't help themselves, they just have to wave their magic wands to make more money. As a matter of fact, they look into their crystal balls to see what the prices will be like months or even years in the future, and wave their magic wands in response to what they see. At least they did before the Ring of Fire. I think the crystal ball must have gotten bumped or something cuz the predictions we're hearing at the subcommittee meetings are bouncing all over the place. So one of the things we're working on is trying to determine the 'real' value of all the goods and services within the Ring of Fire, measured in up-time money, so we can help the Fed Fairies figure out which way to wave their wands."

His face grew comically lugubrious. "Now, when people don't believe in the Fed Fairies, they have to come up with some other explanation for where the money comes from. Like, 'The Government.' The problem is, governments always need money, and if they can make it themselves, well, people are afraid they will. And that they will keep on making more of it until it takes thousands of dollars to buy a ham sandwich. So, an important part of my new job is to convince the down-timers that Mike Stearns can't just make more money whenever he wants to. That, instead of the government making the decisions, the Fed Fairies will decide how much American money there is, so they can trust American money to hold its value."

Sarah was always happy to play along with her father's teasing of her little sister. "How are you going to make the fairies happy so they will make more money and we can all be rich?"

"The more stuff there is to buy, the more money you can have without the prices going up too much. We brought quite a bit of stuff with us through the Ring of Fire, but to make the Fed Fairies really happy, we need to find stuff that we can make here."

The rest of the evening was spent in discussion of production and levels of usage. In spite of the dry subject matter, or perhaps because it isn't quite so dry as most people think when presented right, it was an enjoyable conversation, and even Judy the Younger had fun.

June 13, 1631: A Creek Inside the Ring of Fire

David Bartley had a crush on Sarah Wendell; which he of course, would never admit to. This was bad enough. What made it worse, was that Sarah had a crush on Brent Partow; which, of course, she would never admit to. Brent and his twin brother Trent were David's best friends, and had been since his family moved to Grantville in ninety-six.

Brent didn't have a crush on Sarah. He was the second largest boy in the ninth grade. He was interested in football, all things mechanical, and recently all things military. Girls, as Girls, had been creeping into his awareness, but only creeping, and the Ring of Fire had pushed them back several steps. He was good looking, and enthusiastic in his interests, willing to share them with others and listen to their views, so far without regard to their gender. Which may explain Sarah's crush.

His brother Trent, the largest boy in the ninth grade by about a millimeter and maybe a half a pound, acted as a governor for his exuberant fascinations. Brent would come up with a plan to make or do something, and Trent would come up with all the reasons it wouldn't work. Then they would argue it out, using David, and lately Sarah, to act as referee and deciding vote.

The upshot of all these social interconnections was that the four hung out together, and talked about football, all things mechanical, and recently, all things military. All things military focused on the Ring of Fire, and the changes it had and would bring about.

Where the kids sat, near a small creek, the buildings of Grantville were hidden by steep tree-topped hills, as well as quite a bit of the sky. "Flat," around here, meant any angle less than thirty degrees. If there wasn't a building right next to you, it seemed as though you were in virgin forest never touched by men.

Sarah was talking about her dad's new job at the finance subcommittee, and its importance to all things military. "Dad says that we're going to be in trouble if we don't come up with stuff to trade with the Germans."

Trent argued almost by reflex. "We have plenty to trade, TV and radio, cars and microwaves. All sorts of stuff." It was, after all, obvious that people from the end of the twentieth century must be rich in comparison to people of the first half of the seventeenth.

Sarah was not impressed. "Can you build a TV? What about a TV station? My Dad says 'We have to buy food, and we are gonna keep right on needing food.' We're not gonna keep having TVs and so on to sell. Once they're sold, they're gone."

Sarah, an astute observer might note, was a bit pedantic on the subject of *My Dad Said*. She might have a crush on Brent, but she loved and respected her father. That last part, had he known it, would have come as quite a shock to Fletcher Wendell. He was convinced that his daughter's youthful admiration had gone the way of the dodo a year and a half hence.

Before the Ring of Fire, that youthful admiration had indeed been on the decline. When his job disappeared with the Ring of Fire, Sarah was naturally concerned with how that would affect her. This entailed a certain amount of resentment; youthful admiration had gone almost comatose. What use after all, is an insurance salesman in the Dark Ages? Then, with his new job with the finance subcommittee, Fletcher Wendell suddenly had an important role in the survival of Grantville. His older daughter's admiration for Dad had popped right out of its sickbed as if it had never even been asleep. Which fact she had gone to some length to hide—admiration for one's dad being damaging to fourteen-year-old dignity.

"There're things we can build," David said, "We have the machine shops." This comment had less to do with defending Trent, than the fact that David, for all intents and purposes, didn't have a dad and sort of resented Sarah's harping on hers.

"What?" Sarah asked.

Alas, David had no ready answer, so he had to make do with a disgruntled shrug and a vague "Lots of stuff." Not nearly impressive enough. Shortly after that the gathering broke up and the kids went home.

David was bothered by that shrug, and the lack of knowledge it represented, much more than anyone else in the group. Partly that was because it's always less pleasant to taste your foot than to see someone put theirs in their mouth. But mostly it was because the grim reality of Sarah's comments hit a bit closer to home for him than for the others. He remembered some bad times from before they moved back to Grantville after "Uncle" Donovan left. David's world had come apart before, and it showed all the signs of doing so again. There was a sort of directionless tension in the air. As if the grownups around him knew something had to be done, but didn't really know what. And there were major money concerns, always a bad sign. Worse, unlike last time, it seemed to cover the whole town, not just his family.

David started actively looking for something to make. Something for people to spend their energy on. Something that would bring in money. Something, anything, to make the uncertainty go away.

Brent Partow spent the night thinking about what Sarah had said as well. He wasn't worried, he was interested. Brent spent his life in search of the next interesting thing to do. To Brent, Sarah's concerns about saleable products simply meant a fun game of *what can we build?* By the next day he had a plan. He talked it over with Trent, who only had minor objections. Trent was afraid that if the grownups found out they might like the idea. Which, of course, meant they would take the thing over, put it in a class, suck all the fun out of it, and turn it into work. Trent was also afraid that if the grownups found out they might be displeased. Which, of course, meant they would forbid the kids the game, and just to make sure, assign them something boring to do. So his sole restriction was: *no grownups*.

June 14, 1631: A Creek Inside the Ring of Fire

David was the first to arrive. Then Brent and Trent arrived together. By the time Sarah got there, the issue was decided.

Sarah, feeling somewhat left out, initially scoffed at the plan. But then David pointed out that, if what her father said was true, it was their duty to Grantville to do something. That ended that. David was a dedicated and marginally astute observer of Sarah Wendell.

So the four began their search for the right thing to make. First they compiled lists of things. Guns, airplanes, hovercraft, cars, electric engines, nails, pliers . . .

The lists got very long because Brent had declared that the first winner would be the person who came up with the most possibilities, whether they turned out to be possible or not. So the first list included such practical and easy to make things as phasers, space shuttles, nuclear submarines, and cruise missiles. Each of which was greeted with raspberries and giggles, but each of which gained the originator a point marked down by Trent. A number of the suggestions that were to eventually be made by one or another group of up-timers were greeted with the above accolade. After about an hour the kids were starting to get a little bored. Trent's suggestion that they adjourn, and each make a separate list over the next couple of days, met with general approval.

June 16, 1631: The Grantville High School Library

Sarah won by fifteen entries. There was some debate as to whether all her entries were indeed separate items. In a number of cases she had included the final item along with several component parts. Among the four lists there were close to a thousand separate items. If you eliminated duplicates, there were still over five hundred. When you eliminated the utterly impossible, matter transmitters and the like, there were still over three hundred.

Then they tried to eliminate the impractical. But what makes the difference between practical and impractical? That is not so easy a thing to determine, and each kid came at the question from a different angle. To Brent and Trent it was still very much a game, so their version of practical had more to do with interesting than anything else. Sarah imagined presenting her parents with a list of things that could be sold and gaining their respect, so her version paid much attention to what would be saleable. David was the only one who was actually looking for something that would make a good investment for his family. His problem was, he really wasn't sure what that meant.

All in all, the whole thing was a lot of fun. Some things—nails, for example—were eliminated when Sarah informed them someone else was already working on them. The finance subcommittee was apparently keeping track of that sort of thing. Other things, such as airplanes, were marked as practical but not for them. A number of things were marked as practical for them; but they didn't stop at the first of these, since they had agreed to go through the whole list.

Then they reached the sewing machine. Brent, who had little interest in sewing, proclaimed that it was impractical because it needed an electric motor—and they had already determined that for them, the electric motor was impractical.

David remembered his grandmother's old Singer and that it had been converted from treadle power. This was not actually true, merely a family rumor, but David didn't know that. So he pointed out that a sewing machine did not need an electric motor, which was true.

Sarah, who recognized the root motive of Brent's rejection of the sewing machine—sexism, pure and simple—naturally took a firm position in favor of the sewing machine.

Poor Trent didn't know which way to turn. Arguing with Brent was dear to his heart, as was tearing down impossible schemes, but sewing machines were for girls.

"They're too complicated," he claimed, "we could never make one from an encyclopedia entry. We would need a design or a model or something."

"We have one!" David was well pleased to be on Sarah's side against Brent. "At least my grandma has one, and it's old. It was converted from treadle or pedal power to electric sometime, but all they did was put on an electric motor to replace the pedals."

What are you going to do when faced with such intransigence? You just have to show them. Trent and Brent were going to show that it could not be done. David and Sarah, that it could.

June 16, 1631: Delia Higgins' House

Delia was sewing when the kids arrived. She had been sewing quite a bit lately. She had worked out a deal with the Valuemart, and she had been patching, hemming, and seaming ever since. It was now providing a fair chunk of the family income. Still, she was pleased enough to hear the pounding hooves of a herd of teens to take a break. Such herds had been in short supply since the Ring of Fire.

She was a bit surprised when the kids wanted to look at her old Singer. Kids took an interest in the oddest things. She showed it off readily enough. She was rather proud of it; almost a hundred years old, and still worked well.

Brent was converted. There were all sorts of gadgets and doohickeys, and neat ways of doing things. Figuring out what did what and why, and what they could make, and what they could replace with something else would be loads of fun.

Trent resisted for a while, but not long. A sewing machine really is a neat piece of equipment.

June 16, 1631: Evening, Delia Higgins' House

As Delia watched David at the dining room table, his dark eyes studying some papers with an intensity rarely lavished on schoolwork, she thought about the incursion of the small herd of teens. David was up to something, she could tell.

She remembered a phone call she had gotten four years ago, from a ten-year-old David, explaining the hitherto unknown facts that Ramona had lost her job two months before, that they were about to be thrown out of their apartment, and there was no food in it anyway.

"Could we come live with you Grandma? Mom can help you out with the storage lot."

"Where is your mother?" Delia has asked.

"She's out looking for work. 'Cept she ain't. She goes to the park and sits." David hastened to add: "She looked at first, she really did. But Mom don't like it when things don't work. After a while she just quits."

They had worked it out between them. It was mostly David's plan. She had called that night and asked if Ramona could come home and work at the storage lot, to give her a bit more time with her garden.

It had been a while after they got back to Grantville before David had gone back to being just a kid. There had been a certain watchfulness about him. A waiting for the other shoe to drop, so he could catch it before things got even more busted. The watchfulness had slowly faded. Ramona had never been aware of it. Any more than she had ever known about the plot to bring them home. But Delia remembered that watchfulness, and it was back. Subtler than before, more calculating, but there. David had decided that he needed to save his world again, and was trying to figure out how.

This time Delia would not wait for a phone call.

She finished dressing the Barbie in her version of a 1630's peasant outfit. "David, come give me a hand in the garden. I just remembered some lifting I need you to do for me."

Delia kept a compost heap for her garden. This occasionally involved David, Donny or Ramona with a wheelbarrow. In this instance, it made a good excuse to get David alone for a quiet talk.

David, deep in the process of determining which parts of a sewing machine might best be made by a 1630's blacksmith, grumbled a bit; but did as he was told.

It took all of five minutes, and more importantly a promise not to interfere without good reason, to get David talking. This didn't reflect a lack of honor on David's part, but trust in his grandmother. Once he started talking it took a couple of hours for him to run down. During those two hours, Delia was again reminded that kids understand more and listen more than people generally gave them credit for. Or than they want credit for, mostly.

The economics of the Ring of Fire were made clear. Well, a little clearer. She learned about Brent and Trent's talent for making things, how they worked off one another. She learned about Sarah's understanding of money, and the financial situation of Grantville as a whole, and how Delia's family's situation was a smaller version of the same thing. That they had lots of capital in the form of goods, but nothing to invest it in. That what were needed were products that they could make the machines to make. David had to explain that part twice to make it clear. He used the sewing machine as an example.

"It works like this, Grandma. We have a sewing machine. If we sell it, it's gone. Mr. Marcantonio's machine shop could make sewing machines if we didn't need it to make other stuff, but eventually it's going to have breakdowns, and it won't be able to make sewing machines any more. Especially if all it's making is sewing machine parts and not machine shop parts to keep the machine shop running. But if Mr. Marcantonio's shop makes some machines that make sewing machine parts, then when those machines break down we have some place to go to get more of them. Every step away from just taking what we have and selling it costs more, but means it takes longer for us to run out of stuff to sell. The machines that make the sewing machine parts don't have to be as complicated as those in Mr. Marcantonio's shop, because they don't need to be as flexible. 'Almost tools,' Brent says."

Sarah Wendell and the Partow twins made a new friend that evening; their parents, even more so. Delia was impressed by the kids and the parents who had given them the knowledge they had.

She was also impressed with David. She promised not to interfere unless asked, but made him promise to ask for her help if needed. She added her vote to the sewing machine because it was a machine itself, so in a way it added yet another level to the levels he had talked about. She gave permission to disassemble her Singer if it was needed. She also promised backing if the kids came up with a plan that they convinced her could work.

"We'll find the money to do it, David. You and your friends come up with a plan that has a good shot of working and I'll find the money."

David Bartley went to bed that night at peace with the world. For the first time since the town meeting after the Ring of Fire, his stomach didn't bother him at all.

That is, until he remembered that grownups weren't to be involved. How was he going to tell the others? He had to tell them. Grandma could help a lot.

June 19, 1631: Grantville High School

David had admitted his breach of confidence three
days before. After being shunned for a day and a
half, he had been invited conditionally to rejoin
the group. They wanted to know what his grandmother had said, and they wanted assurances that
she would not call in their parents or try to take
over the project. He had provided the assurances,
and added that she thought the sewing machine
was a good idea.

After much enjoyable debate, they had narrowed
the list of things down. The sewing machine was now
top of the list because they had permission to take
apart the Singer. Before that it had been fairly low
on the list because of its complexity.

Besides, Sarah had noticed a trend. Sewing machines
were renting as fast as people could find them, and
the price was going up. After some obscure conversation with her parents she had realized that meant
there was a ready market for a fairly large number of
sewing machines. Brent had thought of several places
where a single machine could make up to three or
four parts. You would make a bunch of one part, then
change an attached tool and make another kind of
part. If they could get a good start, they would be
ahead of local competitors.

Trent felt it would be better in the long run to
make separate machines for each part. "You're making
them too complicated Brent, you always do." Lots of
really fun arguments in the offing.

The sewing machine was starting to look like a
really good product, if they could build it—and just
maybe they could. They had an incomplete list of
the parts involved, most of which could be produced

manually, and now they were in a position to get a complete parts list.

June 20, 1631: Delia Higgins' House

The Great Sewing Machine Disassembly took most of the morning and reassembly was scheduled for the afternoon. Since Delia was now in on the secret and Ramona and Donny were at the storage lot, the kids could talk freely about what they were actually doing.

The sewing machine was carefully disassembled. As each part was removed it was placed on an old sheet spread on the floor. Its outline was traced on the sheet and it was numbered. Trent made a list describing each part and where it came from. Sarah had brought a digital camera from home.

Each step in the process was explained to Delia, which added to the fun. There is something very gratifying in explaining something to a grownup when you're fourteen and in charge of it. It remains gratifying, of course, only so long as the grownup listens and does not try to take over. Delia listened. Delia offered no more than words of encouragement and the occasional leading question. In this way Delia managed to get her suggestions listened to. Not many were needed. Brent and Trent were knowledgeable, and Trent was meticulous. A born bean counter, Delia thought, but carefully did not say.

A part would come off the sewing machine and be placed on the sheet. While Trent recorded its function, Brent would suggest ways it might be made, with only a little regard for how practical those ways might be.

When Sarah got bored with the mechanics Delia engaged her in discussions of salability versus cost. This involved several repetitions of "My Dad said" and some of "My Mom said" as well. All of which Delia listened to with unfeigned interest. She was noting the differences between David's version and Sarah's. Sarah's version had more detail and quite a bit more references to what the finance subcommittee was doing. They were working to establish American money as an accepted local currency with surprisingly good success.

Surprising because American dollars, being paper, did not at first appear to be worth anything. But the down-timers were familiar with several forms of monetary notes. Sarah wasn't familiar with all of the mechanisms the down-timers used to transfer value through paper notes, but she had been told that they did, especially for large sums. The tricky part was, what was backing the American dollar? It was not gold or silver in a vault somewhere, but a calculation of goods and services. The Germans, at least some of them, saw the potential value of such a system. But they also saw how the system could be abused, and their experience had not taught them to have faith in governments. On the up side, Grantville had a lot of stuff the down-timers wanted to buy, and there was nowhere else for them to get it. Unfortunately, too much of that stuff was irreplaceable. It wasn't stuff made in Grantville, but stuff bought from elsewhere up-time.

David took his own notes on the various subjects, trying to follow both conversations. His notes were a bit chaotic, but then again, so was the situation. David was beginning to develop something approaching a management style. It consisted of finding out as much as he could about everything he could, and then keeping his trap shut till there was a deadlock, or bottleneck of some sort, and giving credit for the idea to someone else. "Brent suggested," "Sarah said" or "Trent said"—sometimes even "Grandma said." David did his best to properly attribute credit, but sometimes he got it wrong. Sometimes there was no one to attribute the idea to. In those cases David fibbed. He went ahead and attributed it to the person he figured most likely to have said it if he hadn't.

It was getting close to noon and David, as the least essential person, was assigned to make lunch. No hardship. David liked to cook. They had some jars of homemade spaghetti sauce in the icebox and plenty for a salad in the garden. Delia called the parents and arranged for the gang to have lunch with Delia and family.

Lunch was a quiet meal. The kids didn't want to add to the list of who was in the know, and for now, neither did Delia. Ramona was unwilling or unable to admit that David could think for himself. To the extent it was possible, Ramona handled the fact of her children growing up by ignoring it. As soon as the sewing machine project came out into the open, Ramona was going to have to face some things.

After lunch they went back to it. The sewing machine was going back together with only a little trouble, but it meant a lot to Delia and each sticking screw bothered her. So she concentrated on continuing her conversation with Sarah.

About three that afternoon, Delia brought the whole question of whether this was a game or for real to a head.

"How do you form a company, Sarah?" she asked. "When Ray set up the storage lot all it amounted to was registering at the county courthouse and getting a tax number. But the county courthouse is three hundred years away in another universe. So how do we do it in the here and now?"

Somewhat to the surprise of the group, each member had decided that they really wanted to do this. Most of the hesitation had been the belief that they would not be allowed to—that the project would be declared frivolous, and they would be told not to waste time. Or that it would be declared too important to be left in the hands of children, and taken away from them.

Brent and Trent wanted to do it because really making sewing machines offered a more concrete outlet for their creative urges. Sarah, because this was the sort of thing that Grantville needed. David and Delia, because the family needed a source of steady income and neither had that much confidence in the longterm outlook of the storage lot. It was running at a loss at the moment and might well go broke within the next year or so. A storage container is, in its way, a luxury—and one that people apparently could not afford, at least for now.

"To form a company," Sarah said, after they got back to the question, "is pretty standard. I think. I'd have to check with Mom, but I think it's just a contract between someone and the government, or several people and the government. That is what the registering Mr. Higgins did at the county courthouse was. A corporation is more complex. I don't know which we need but I can find out. What we need to do, is work out how much everyone is putting in, in labor and money. Then figure out who owns how much of the company and register it that way. The thing is, this is going to take a lot of money."

At that point every one got quiet. The kids because they didn't have any money to speak of; Delia, because she wanted the kids to realize that they really weren't in a position to just build the sewing machines in their back yard, that the game was starting to get real. Delia wanted to give them a chance to back away without losing face. So she waited a bit, to let it sink in, watching.

Then, liking what she saw: "How much money?"

"I don't know. Mom says that it's a law of nature that every thing costs more and takes longer than you expect."

"We have around a hundred parts," Trent interjected. "Some can be hand-made, some will take special tools, and some will take machines. Some must be finely tooled. I have the numbers right here."

"But that doesn't tell us what we need to know," Sarah pointed out. "At least, not all of it. How long will it a take a blacksmith to make a part, how much will it cost? The only real way to find out is to go find a blacksmith and ask him, and you know some are gonna lie, and others are gonna get it wrong, because they think it needs fancy work, or because they don't understand how precise it needs to be. So the only real way to find out for sure how much it will cost to make a sewing machine part, is to make one. Actually, to make several. Until then we're guessing."

"Well, a guess is better than nothing," said Delia. "What if we go through Trent's list one item at a time and make our best guess at the cost of each item?"

The rest of the afternoon, as Brent put the sewing machine back together, the others went though the list of parts and guessed.

When they were getting ready to go home Delia asked: "Have you kids looked at the museum on Elm Street?"

This was met with blank looks. Then Trent hit his head. "Oh. I remember, they have lots of old sewing machines."

The light came on. They had all been there on school trips. *On your mark. Get set . . .*

Delia held up a hand. "Not tonight. You're expected at home. We'll work something out tomorrow."

That's the trouble with grownups—they don't understand urgency.

June 21, 1631: Delia Higgins' House

Ramona was at the lot, but Donny was home, wanting to get in on whatever the older kids were doing. So when the twins and Sarah arrived there was a certain amount of awkwardness. Which brought up the problem of keeping this a secret. Delia suggested that David take Donny into the kitchen and make everyone a snack. In other, unsaid words, keep him occupied for a little while. Donny understood the words left unsaid, but a look from Grandma was enough; he went, grumbling.

Once Donny was out of the room, Delia got right to the point. "Keeping this a secret won't work much longer. Donny already knows something is up. If we want to create a company to make sewing machines. Is that what we want?"

Delia waited, looking at each of the three in turn and received their nods of confirmation. "Well, that isn't something that can be kept from your parents, and even if I could, I wouldn't." *Not without a really good reason, anyway*, she thought to herself. "Up to now, it's been a game. The first step to making it real is to bring your parents into it. I can talk to your parents, if you like. Or you can talk to them and I'll give what support I can. How do you want to handle this?"

Sarah had never been all that concerned about her parents' reaction anyway, so she was in favor of full disclosure. Though she offered the warning that "Mom and Dad will probably make us include Judy."

"Oh no! Rachel!" moaned Trent, referring to their ten-year-old sister.

"Naw," countered his twin brother. "She's been following Heidi around since the Ring of Fire. Heidi might be a problem though. She's pretty pissed."

Brent paused with a nervous glance at Mrs. Higgins. Delia looked back with a raised eyebrow.

"Uh, upset with guys right now," Brent continued. "Might try to get back by horning in."

Brent was referring to their older sister, who was sixteen—but, in the twins' opinion, not at all sweet. Heidi had just gotten her driver's license, and suddenly there was no gas for the car. A pretty blond girl with a good figure, she had expected the boys in school to be mooning over her this year, but the Ring of Fire had focused almost the entire male teen population of Grantville on matters martial. It had all come as an unwelcome shock to Heidi. She was a bit self-centered.

"Maybe. Mom's got her number, but might stick us with her just to get her out of her hair. Which," Trent continued, "is why I'm worried about Rachel. Mom has a lot to do right now, and she is worried about Caleb." The twins' older brother had gone into the newly formed Grantville Army the day after graduating high school. "So we are liable to get Rachel and Heidi, whether they want in or not."

There was a glum silence for a moment, as the kids worried about the prospective interlopers. On the other hand, with the adult backing that Mrs. Higgins had offered to provide, it seemed less likely that the project would be either taken over or cancelled by adults.

Sarah nodded and with dignity made the formal request. "Both my parents are at work right now. Let me talk to them this evening, but if they could call you tonight, Mrs. Higgins, it would probably help."

"Dad's at work, but Mom's home. Maybe we should call her now?" suggested Brent. At Delia's nod, he headed for the phone. There was some discussion, then Delia was called to the phone. More discussion followed while the kids looked on, ending with: "Thanks, we'll see you tomorrow night."

"Boys," Delia said as she hung up the phone, "your mother, and probably your father if he can get away, will be here for dinner tomorrow. I imagine you'll be grilled tonight. If you would care for a little wisdom from the ancient, I suggest you don't try to promote the project but simply answer questions as calmly as possible." The boys nodded respectfully. This confirmation of her status as ancient, while not unexpected, wasn't particularly comforting.

"Sarah, I hope your parents will be able to come too. I think it would be a good idea if we all got together and talked things through before going much further." David and Donny returned with a snack tray.

"Meanwhile why don't you four take Donny and go to the museum. Spend the day, take notes, and explain what is going on to Donny. Take the snacks with you."

Telling Ramona about the sewing machine project was much less difficult than Delia had imagined. Ramona was, after all, the one who had been presiding over the emptying of supply containers. She knew things weren't going well for the lot, and she understood that the Ring of Fire had changed things. What she didn't understand was how things had changed, or what she was expected to do about it. Her biggest concern—terror really—was that as an adult she would be put in charge of something. That Mom was still in charge came as quite a relief.

June 22, 1631: Delia Higgins' House

The Partows had, over some strong objections, left Rachel at home with Heidi. The Wendells had brought Judy the Younger. While there was some discussion of the sewing machine project over dinner, it wasn't till after dinner that the pitch got made.

"You four," said Delia, grinning, "take Donny and Judy into the sewing room, so your parents and I can talk about you behind your backs."

The kids retreated at speed. Which impressed their parents.

It can be uncomfortable, but still gratifying, to have a casual acquaintance spend a couple of hours telling you how great your kids are, and how much they respect you, complete with quotes of things you have said to them while convinced they weren't listening.

Uncomfortable, because it's really easy to remember changing diapers—they make an impression, after all—and forget some of the changes the intervening years have made. They sneak up on you. Are my kids really that bright, hard working, and mature, and why didn't I know about it? Gratifying, because you want to believe they really are what you raised them to be, and it's nice when someone else tells you that you did a good job. With teenagers, it's especially nice when you find out that they actually listen to you.

At least Fletcher and Judy Wendell and Kent and Sylvia Partow found it so, probably because of those concrete examples from Delia:

"I never understood how the federal reserve worked till I heard Sarah's discussion of the Fed Fairies."

And:

"My family has owned that Singer since before I was born. I have repaired it countless times, and I have learned more about the how and the why of its inner workings in the last few days than I had learned in the preceding fifty-nine years, mostly from Brent and Trent. I've watched Brent sketch out a machine to build a part of the Singer—one that I am sure will work—and then seen Trent tear apart the design and add or change details that make it work better. It's been a privilege to watch the kids work."

For the next four days, as the parents had time to look them over, the kids showed their parts of the proposal to their parents.

Kent Partow, a tallish heavyset man with sandy brown hair and brown eyes, was impressed by the work and the skill his twin sons had put into the designs. He told them so, briefly: "Basically a good job, boys."

He then spent the rest of the four days when not busy at work or sleeping telling them in detail each and every place where their designs fell short. The focus of his criticisms didn't have much to do with things that would actually keep the designs from working. He readily admitted there weren't many of those. No, he dealt with ways that their designs made extra work for the person making the machine, or the person who would be using it.

Mr. and Mrs. Wendell lavished their praise rather more generously, almost uncomfortably so. Certainly enough to produce resentment in Judy the Younger. Well, more resentment. The real focus of Judy's resentment was that she wasn't getting to play.

They did suggest several small changes, and one monster.

The monster was this: Normally, in a project like this, you would make your estimate and add say, twenty percent for the unforeseen. In this case, because of the fluidity of the situation, and the large number of unknowns, they suggested a fudge factor of one hundred to two hundred percent of the original estimate.

June 26, 1631: Delia Higgins' House

They met again for a formal presentation of the whole package. David was the primary presenter.

"The first and most important point, I guess, is that we're not trying to just build sewing machines, not anymore. That's sort of what we started out with. But Sarah pretty much put paid to that notion even before we were firmly settled on sewing machines. What we want to build is a company that will build sewing machines. The company will have two major branches. Outsourcing for parts that can be made by the down-time craftsmen, and a factory that will have an internal technological level somewhere between 1850 and 1920. With a few gadgets from later.

"We decided on outsourcing rather than hiring down-time workers . . ."

And they were off. Over the next three hours David went through the organizational chart, cost analysis, machines and tools needed, potential market, the works. He called upon Sarah, Brent and Trent as needed, to explain details and answer questions.

Their parents were genuinely impressed. The Wendells had seen the money end, but not really the technical end. The Partows had seen the technical end, but not the money end. And neither had seen how it all fit together. There was room in the plan for mistakes, and ways to handle it if things went wrong.

While the Wendells and the Partows had jobs, they didn't have much in the way of available capital. Both their houses were primarily owned by the bank, and regardless of the kids' good work, it had to be acknowledged that this was a risky venture.

They would allow their kids to participate, but could offer little more than that. Delia had been prepared for that response and was willing to support the project. She would attempt to get a loan. Fletcher Wendell would support the loan to the extent he could, but he could not offer too much hope.

June 30, 1631: Delia Higgins' House

David was sitting at the dinner table. "They're going to fight a battle, Grandma," he said, "Not ten miles from here. At that nearby town called Badenburg."

"Well, are you upset or pleased?" Delia wasn't criticizing, she was just helping him figure it out. It was one of the things about Grandma that David liked. She let him feel about things the way he felt about them, not the way he was "supposed" to feel about them.

"I don't really know." He gave the matter some thought. "I figure, the battle itself will be a cakewalk, and it's kind of exciting. What it means, though, that bugs me some. We're in the middle of a war! I worry about Mom. She's not good at tough situations."

Delia suddenly realized that he was right. War! With

refugees, armies and bandits, and generally desperate people. "These are the times that try men's morals," when the rules get forgotten. They had a house full of things of value and a storage rental lot with lots of steel containers. People would want what was in the containers—for that matter, they would want the containers for the steel. How could she have gone a month without realizing it?

Before the Ring of Fire, Grantville had been a low crime area. They had been able to get by with a chain link fence and a padlock. But now the value of much that was in those storage buildings had gone up immeasurably, and as for crime, they might as well be in the Wild West, or next door to a crack house. It had been pure dumb luck that they had not already been looted and Ramona killed in the bargain.

Or so it seemed to Delia. In fact, the luck had a large modicum of fear in it. To the people outside the Ring of Fire, it was a matter of dangerous and unknown powers. Who knew what might be protecting the storage lot, or any other property inside the Ring of Fire for that matter.

Almost, Delia rushed out to find guards right then, but not quite. Today wasn't the day to go out hunting new employees, not on the day of the battle. Not when she had no way to pay them. Della worried the problem the rest of the day.

Up to now the storage lot had been a reliable source of income. A small source, true, but it had very little in the way of expenses attached to it. The lot was paid off when Ray died, and the only bills were electric, telephone, and taxes once a year, but with a guard or guards, that would change. With most of the containers not rented, it would cost more every month than she got in rent. Still, there was really no choice.

June 30, 1631: Partow House

For once even Heidi was quiet. Everyone was quiet. Caleb would be in a battle today. Brent tried to work on the gearing for the sewing machine, but he couldn't keep his mind focused. It kept veering off to the battle. Logic said that it would be an easy victory. The good guys even had a machine gun, but people would be shooting at his brother, and Brent's traitorous mind seemed insistent on pulling up every nasty thing he had ever said to, or thought about Caleb, and wishing he could take them back. Brent looked at his twin. Trent was probably doing the same thing, only more so. Trent worried more.

July 1, 1631: Police Station

Dan Frost was not expecting Delia Higgins to appear in his office the day after a battle; when he spotted her, his first thought was to wonder how she had heard about Jeff proposing to the German girl. She hadn't, and Dan did not enlighten her. It really wasn't her business and he wasn't sure how she would take the news.

Delia wanted to know about hiring a security guard. It turned out that the battle had finally brought home to her just how dangerous the situation was. Dan had reached the same conclusion over a month ago, while he recovered from a gunshot wound. Experience is a hell of a teacher.

What Dan desperately needed was more officers, but every business that had someone to take care of the small stuff, and to call his people for the big stuff, would take a little of the pressure off his over-stretched police force. Providing they could tell the difference, something he was not at all confident about. Still, even a presence could sometimes stop trouble before it started. After a little consideration, he found he was in favor of the idea.

Delia was concerned about the cost and figured that a down-timer might work cheaper. But she didn't want to hire someone to rob her storage lot, and since she didn't speak German, she would like someone that had at least a little English. She wondered if he had any suggestions?

Dan asked for a few days to look around and see what he could find.

July 3, 1631: Grantville P.O.W. Holding Area

Johan Kipper had been scared before each and every battle he had ever fought, and there had been many, but this was different. For one thing, this was after the battle, and he wasn't waiting to fight, he was waiting to be judged. He was to be judged by a camp follower. He didn't know the Gretchen girl well. Hardly at all, but she was the one to judge him, and that was scary. Johan was not a very good man and he knew it. He was a mean drunk and he knew that too.

There weren't many people who were held in more contempt than soldiers, but camp followers were. They had been the only safe outlet for the anger he felt at the way his life had turned out. At least they had seemed to be. Johan was scared now, in a way that he had never been scared before.

What made Johan a little different than some of

his fellow soldiers was that he realized what scared him. Not that he would be treated unfairly, but that he would be treated as he deserved.

He had started out as a soldier forty years ago at the age of fifteen. Absolutely sure he would become a captain. Ten years later, he had hoped to become a sergeant. Now, he didn't even want to be a soldier any more, but he didn't know anything else. His family had been in service. Servants to a wealthy merchant in Amsterdam. He had run off to be a soldier.

Johan was fifty-four years old, and spoke a smattering of half a dozen languages. He was five feet six inches tall, had graying brown hair and six teeth, four uppers and two lowers. He had the typical pockmarks that denoted a survivor of smallpox, a scar running down the left side of his face, and he was tired. Tired of fighting, tired of killing, and scared of dying.

He was surprised that he wasn't one of the ones that got his picture on a piece of paper and told to get out of the USA. He was less surprised, almost comforted, by the lecture he got about getting drunk and hitting people. The lecture amounted to "Don't Do It. We can always take another picture if we need to."

When offered a place in the army he respectfully declined. When asked what he was qualified to do he said he had been in service once. He had to explain what he meant. "My family were servants in Amsterdam." He was assigned to a labor gang.

July 3, 1631: Wendell House

Sarah knew it was bad news as soon as her parents came through the door. Her father had talked to the bank. No loan would be forthcoming. He wanted her to know that he was very proud of the work she and the others had done. That it was a good proposal, and probably would have been granted if they were older. Even with Delia as the primary applicant, just the fact that the kids were involved had killed it. He apologized for not being able to really push it. He was in a tough situation. Her being his daughter made it harder for him to argue for something she was involved in.

It all just sort of rolled over her. She understood the words. Her parents had tried to prepare her for the probability that the loan application would be rejected, and she had thought they had succeeded. In a way, it wasn't the loan being rejected that shocked her so much. It was that it mattered. That was what she hadn't been prepared for. How very, very, much it mattered, and not just to her.

The hardest thing was knowing how it would affect the others. In the last month she had gotten to know them better than in years of friendship, and she had been able to read a bit between the lines. The four of them had all been more worried about the Ring of Fire and what it meant than they had let on. Doing this, something that would help make Grantville self-sustaining, had helped. That was the hardest thing about being a kid, especially in a situation like this, not being able to really help. No! It was being able to help but not being allowed to.

July 3, 1631: Delia Higgins' House

She had been expecting the call. Nothing ever goes the easy way. She had hoped, but not really expected, that the loan would come through. She still wasn't

sure about the storage containers. She wasn't sure
how the emergency committee would come down.
At this point, she wasn't even sure how she would
come down. She might just decide to give whatever
was in them to Grantville, but they weren't her only
resource.

Most people didn't really understand about her doll
collection. They assumed it was much more important
to her than it really was. She collected dolls because
she liked to, no more or less than that. There were a
few, gifts and memories, that were important to her.
But mostly they were just nice to have and fiddle
with, now and then.

Important? Important was David working on something rather than casting about like a rat in a maze
with no exit. Seeing excitement rather than despera-
tion in his eyes, and the eyes of the other kids as
well. Important was keeping the promise that she had
made when she told him that, if they came up with
a workable plan, she would find the money.

Important was the kids not feeling helpless. Delia
knew helpless. She remembered when she had realized
that Ramona would never be quite so bright as the
other kids. Not retarded, no, but not as bright as she
should have been.

Dolls weren't important.

Of course Delia was lying to herself. She really
did care about her dolls, and it really would hurt to
give them up. Just not as much as she cared about
other things. So maybe it wasn't a lie. Or if it was,
it was a good lie.

Still she had no notion of how to go about selling
them.

July 4, 1631: Grantville

The parade was great fun. It let them all forget, for a little while, that the loan had been rejected. The wedding was less fun, but not bad. David, Donny, Ramona and Delia were on the Higgins' side of the wedding, along with Delia's parents. They were probably Jeff Higgins' closest relatives down-time, second cousins twice removed, or something like that. David never could get it quite straight. One thing he never would have expected was cousin Jeff turning out to be a hero. Or getting the girl. And boy, what a girl he had gotten.

July 6, 1631: Police Station

Dan Frost had taken Delia Higgins' request to heart, and not just for her. He now had a list of twenty or so potential security guards. None were what he really wanted, but the best candidates were either going into the armed forces or police training. These would be the equivalent of night watchmen. His primary consideration was that they not be thieves. None of these had that reputation. And three of them had at least a little bit of English.

Well, Delia had asked first, and she wanted someone with at least some English. He'd suggest Johan Kipper, since he had the most English. From the report he was honest enough, and decent enough, unless drunk.

July 6, 1631: Delia Higgins' House

Johan Kipper was literally cap in hand when he was introduced to Delia Higgins. A gray woolen cap, with a short baseball cap style bill. The "Police Chief"—a title that seem to mean a commander of constabulary—had told him of the job. It was a dream job for an old soldier. Not much labor, just walking a post. The police chief had also told him a little of his prospective employer.

"I don't want to hear you've caused Mrs. Higgins any trouble. She's a nice lady, and will treat you right. I expect you to show her respect."

To Dan Frost "lady" was just a polite way of referring to a female. To Johan, "Lady" referred to a person of rank. Johan wanted this job.

Delia Higgins had expected a local, not a soldier in the invading army. The interview was uncomfortable for her.

Delia was looking for more than a night watchman. She needed a link to this time and place. She needed someone who could help her find a buyer for the dolls. Johan's appearance bothered her. First, because by any modern standard he was a remarkably ugly man. Mostly that was because of his bad teeth and the pockmarks. By the standards of his time, he was the low end of average. Second, because part of what she needed was someone who could speak to the down-timers for her. She hired him, but she wasn't happy about it.

The agreement was maintenance and one hundred dollars a month. Really poor pay, but all Delia felt she could afford. As for the job, Johan would live in the "office," and he would be expected to make at least four walking inspections of the lot each night. There would be occasional errands for him to run. Long hours but light work.

For Johan, the interview was much worse. She asked her questions. He answered them in his somewhat broken English. She asked more questions, seeking clarification. This woman looked at him, really looked. She didn't examine him like he was a horse or a dog she was thinking of buying. She really saw him. She acknowledged him like he was a real person. Complex, capable of thought. Like he had value. She was, as the English might say: "Neither fish nor fowl nor good red meat." He could not find a place in his world where she belonged. What made it worse, almost intolerably worse, was that he fully realized that it was her world that mattered now, not his. And if he couldn't even find where she fit, how was he to find where he fit?

She had, as far as he could see, the wealth and power of a prosperous townswoman, but she did not act right. She didn't scorn. Johan was not a stupid man. He had understood better than most what the arrival of a town from the future meant. He realized that the rules had changed. That these people could do things that no one else could do.

For instance, despite the fact that she seemed apologetic about it, the "maintenance" turned out to be much more than Johan expected. To Delia Higgins, "maintenance" included *her* paying for *his* health and dental care. It also included uniforms for work and at least some clothing for off work. It included eating as well as any member of her family did, and his own room, and a bathroom, because they had never removed the bathroom fittings from the home—"mobile home," they called it, whatever that meant—that acted as an office.

Johan was not an evil man, though he often thought he was. For fifty-four years, with one exception, he had kept his place. Knowing full well that stepping out of it could mean his death. That is a lot of habit. The thing about chains is they're secure. They're safe. You get used to them. Then you get to depend on them. Johan had worn the chains of lower-class existence his whole life. He didn't know how to walk without their weight.

July 7, 1631: Storage Lot

David wasn't favorably impressed by the new night watchman Grandma had hired, and he wasn't sure he trusted the man around his mother. So he watched him for half the morning. Why not? The bank had refused the loan. What else was there to do?

David had seen toughs before. When they had lived in Richmond, it had not been in a good part of town. He knew that they were just people. Some had even been friendly in a strange way. Sort of the way a lion will lie down with a lamb, as long as he's not hungry. This guy was a bit on the scary side, but there was something about him. A deference David had never seen before. At least not directed at him. David realized that the night watchman, Johan, was afraid of him. Not physically afraid, but concerned about the problems David might cause him.

It made David wonder how to act. He didn't consider, not seriously anyway, picking on the guy, but it made talking to him seem a less dangerous undertaking. They talked most of the afternoon.

They talked about battles and captains, about work and honor. When it slipped out David almost missed it's importance. "Ye don't act right, ye up-timers," Johan said. Then seemed embarrassed by the lapse.

"How should we act?" asked David.

"Ye don't act yer proper place!" Johan said, then apparently tried to take it back. "Sorry Master David, I spoke out of turn."

But David had an inkling, just an inkling, of what was wrong. With authority he replied, "No. You've said too much, or not enough, and this may be something we need to know."

He watched as Johan fumbled with the words. "Like I said, sir. Ye don't act yer place. One minute ye're one thing and the next another. Ye talk like a banker, or a merchant, or a lord or craftsman, or, oh, I don't know. Ye talk to me the same way ye'd talk to yer president."

David almost popped out with: "Sure, you both work for us." But he didn't, because it wouldn't help. Instead he asked: "How should we act? If you were hired by a lord or a merchant, how would they act?"

David listened as Johan talked about how the nobility, and nobility wannabes, acted toward servants and hired hands in general. There were a lot of things, and when you put them all together they amounted to the most calculated, demeaning, rudeness David had ever heard of in his life. He knew damn well he could never act that way, nor could anyone in Grantville. Well almost no one.

All of which left David in a real quandary, because he had picked up something else in that lecture on proper behavior for the upper classes. Johan didn't just expect him to act that way. Johan wanted him to act that way. Any other behavior on his part felt like a trap. David wondered why anyone would treat someone else that way. And when the answer came to him it was such a surprise that it popped right out of his mouth. "God. They must be terrified of you."

Johan looked at him like he was a dangerous lunatic. Like he might pull a shotgun out of his pants pocket and start shooting. David cracked up. He laughed till he had tears running down his face. Then he laughed some more. All the while Johan was looking more and more upset. Finally David got himself more or less under control. And he apologized. "I'm sorry, Johan, but your face. Looking at me like I was crazy."

David was laughing because, for the first time since he had met Johan he was not afraid of him. He had the key, the approach that would let Johan live among them, and not be a bomb waiting to go off. He didn't know why, but he was sure. Six words spoken clearly and honestly. "I am not afraid of you." David said it clearly, honestly and without the least trace of fear. "I don't have to trap you into doing something that would be an excuse to punish you. I don't need to make you weak, to feel strong, or safe. That's why we act the way we do, Johan! The way that seems so wrong to you. Because we are not afraid. Not the way these German lords are, and because we are not afraid of you, you don't have to be afraid of us.

"Here is how you should act around us. Do your job as well as you can. State your views freely. If you think I am doing something wrong, say so. I may, or may not, follow your advice, but I won't punish you for giving it. I promise you that. Can you do that, Johan? If you can, you will have a place here. For as long as we can make one for you."

David Bartley bought himself a man with those words. An old dog that wanted to learn a new trick. Or if he couldn't learn it, at least to be around it. He wanted to be unafraid like Master David; so very unafraid that he could be kind.

∾   ∾   ∾

After Master David left Johan thought about the afternoon. Of course he had known he was being watched from the beginning, he had approved of the fact. At least they weren't stupid. After a while the young master had seemed to calm a bit. Johan wasn't sure why. They talked for a while and Johan actually started to like the boy. That was when he'd put his foot in it. You don't tell a lord that he's not acting right. Not if you don't want to lose your place. The lad had not been offended, though, just curious, and he had acted the proper young lord. Insisting that Johan tell it all. His blue eyes firm yet kind.

"I am not afraid of you," the young master had said, and Johan had had to believe. *And the lords are*. As he thought about it, Johan believed that too.

July 10, 1631: Storage Lot

Business was picking up at the storage lot since the Battle of the Crapper. Perhaps the hiring of Johan had been lucky.

Johan had had four years of schooling, but nothing beyond that. His family was not wealthy enough for more. From school he had been placed in service to be taught the role of a footman. He had found the position stifling. At fifteen, after a beating he felt he didn't deserve, he had run off to be a soldier. The soldier's life had not turned out to be the path to advancement he had expected. For forty years, Johan had marched and fought in battles all over Europe. Then he had run into Grantville, and the Higgins clan. He had been adopted, unofficially, unconsciously, but adopted all the same. Once David had broken the ice, he brought Donny into the process.

Donny had found himself a part-time teacher, and part-time student of Johan. In the subjects of reading and writing English, and speaking German respectively. Comic books were used, as were other books. It was fun, but had limited results.

July 13, 1631: Thuringen Gardens

That afternoon Johan was talking with some of the other survivors from the ill-fated attempt to take Badenburg. Unlike Johan, most of them had joined the American Army. They had spent the last fifteen minutes telling him how good life was in the American Army with its shotguns.

Johan was having none of it. "Not me, boys, I'm too old for the army life. Besides, I have it better than you lot. Mrs. Higgins made me two new sets of clothes, and bought me underwear with elastic." If he was in a place even a little less public he would have taken down his pants and shown them. He almost did anyway. He was proud of his new clothing. Instead he focused on the clothing he could decently display. "And see my new shoes. I have another pair at home, and three pair of pants and four shirts. I've money for a pint when I want one, good food, and Mrs. Higgins has engaged to get me new teeth, at her expense, mind." Which she had.

Delia Higgins had found Johan's appearance to wander between frightening, disgusting and pitiful, depending on the light. So she had set out to rectify it as best she could. First, she put together some uniforms, so at least he would look like a security guard, rather than a bum. The state of Johan's mouth was one of the more objectionable things about his appearance. So the teeth were next on her list. There was nothing she could do about the pockmarks.

July 15, 1631

For some time the mood among those that had an interest in the Higgins Sewing Machine Company had been subdued. Some work had gotten done, but not much; for a little while the game had become real, and now it lacked appeal as a game.

The news was not all bad. The Battle of the Crapper had been something of a turning point. People were pouring into Grantville and now every nook that had held someone's gear but could house people was needed for housing. People still needed to store their stuff, though. So the luxury of the storage containers had become a necessity again, and every container available was rented.

Which in turn brought to a head the question of the containers whose renters were in another universe. Delia was feeling just a bit guilty about having sat on contents of the storage containers. In the days just following the Ring of Fire, she, like everyone, had been frightened. Her response had been effectively to hide and hope no one noticed what she had. In doing so, she could have left something in the storage containers that Grantville desperately needed; something that might have made the difference between life and death for the up-timers.

The storage containers were opened, and their contents sorted. It turned out that there was little or nothing in them that wasn't duplicated elsewhere.

Those contents that were seriously needed by the emergency committee were turned over freely, to ease Delia's guilty conscience. Most of the rest went to the Valuemart on consignment. A few things were kept, but mostly it brought in some cash, quite a bit of cash, and freed up a third of the containers for renting. It was in the middle of this process that Johan brought them the merchant, Federico Vespucci.

David had discussed what was going on with Johan. What sewing machines were, and why they were so important, both to Grantville, and to his family—and how the lack of a bank loan had probably killed their plan to make sewing machines.

Delia had talked to him too, about the need to find a way to sell her dolls. Johan had put two and two together. He had figured out the reason for selling the dolls. He wasn't sure he approved, not that it was his place to approve or disapprove. Still, that much wealth put into the hands of children . . .

It seemed unwise. On the other hand, there were just the children and two women in the household. Perhaps David and his friends were the best chance they had.

Delia explained that she was looking for a merchant. One that would give her a good price on some of her dolls, but wasn't sure how to find one. Johan knew how to find merchants, and how to deal with them. He had, on several occasions, been dog robber for this or that officer. He could bargain fairly well, especially when he was doing it for someone else.

It took him a week to find the right merchant. Federico Vespucci was getting ready to return to Venice. He had risked the war to come to Badenburg for reasons he preferred not to discuss. He had arrived weeks after the Ring of Fire, and he was desperate to be the first merchant to sell products from Grantville in Venice, so he wanted to buy quickly, and be on his way. Best of all, Vespucci did not speak English. The up-timers were wizards at any number of things, but bargaining, in Johan's view, was not among them.

Well, not his up-timers anyway. Johan was starting to take a somewhat proprietary view of Mistress Delia, Mistress Ramona, and young Masters David and Donny. They knew a tremendous amount to be sure, but they weren't really, well, worldly. Which, he thought, made quite a bit of sense, since they weren't from his world. Having come from a magical future.

Thus, they lacked the simple understanding that all merchants are thieves. It was purely certain that any merchant that had an opportunity to talk directly to them would rob them blind, talking them into selling their valuables for a pittance.

While it might not have been true of all up-timers, Johan was right about his up-timers. They rented their storage containers for a set monthly fee. Bought their groceries at the store where you either bought, or didn't, but didn't haggle over the price. They hadn't even haggled much when buying their car. All in all, they had virtually no experience in the art of the haggle, and haggling is not one of those things you can learn from a book.

Federico had come to dinner to discuss the possibility of buying some of the items that might be had from the storage lot. Then he had seen the dolls. Dolls everywhere. In the living room there was a set of shelves covering an entire wall full of dolls, and they weren't the only ones.

The dolls were unique, with their poseable limbs and inset hair, and made of something called "plastic" which Federico was sure could not be duplicated, even in far off China. Even to approximate them would be the work of a skilled artist working for months using ivory or the finest porcelain.

"And unfortunately, not for sale. Now about the furniture in the storage containers." So Johan said.

Federico was no fool. He knew full well that the storage containers with their furniture, even the fancy comfortable mattresses, were little more than a come-on, a way to get him here to see the dolls. He knew that the scoundrel who had attached himself to these up-timers was a cad and a thief. That he was going to be robbed blind. Federico knew all that, and it didn't matter a bit.

Federico fought the good fight. He was a merchant after all, and a good one.

How did he know that plastic was so hard to make?

They brought out the encyclopedia and read him the passages about the industrial processes involved in making plastic. Which didn't matter, since the dolls were not for sale.

He would need proof that they were authentic up-time dolls.

They could provide certificates of authentication, proof that they not only came from Grantville, but from the personal collection of Delia Ruggles Higgins. Of course, the dolls weren't for sale.

All in all, with Johan's deliberate mistranslations and Delia's enthusiastic discussion of her dolls, it had the making of a remarkably shrewd sales technique.

All of which wouldn't have worked at all, except Federico knew perfectly well what would happen when he reached Venice with the dolls. There would be a bidding war, and the dolls would be shipped to royal courts, wealthy merchants, and everything in between, from one end of the world to the other. All at exorbitant prices. Some, a very few, would actually end up as the prized toy of a very wealthy child. Most would end up in various collectors' collections of rare and valuable knickknacks.

It wasn't quite enough. Federico left that night with no commitments made.

July 16-18, 1631

That might have been the end of it. Not hardly. Johan would have found something. If nothing else, they would have offered a few more dolls. That was what Federico was expecting. Or failing that, Federico would have gone back and made the deal anyway. In spite of the urgent letters he had for delivery in Venice, he was not leaving Grantville without those dolls. But a deal under the current conditions would have meant bad blood. Real resentment, the kind of anger that means the person you're dealing with never wants to deal with you again, and warns their friends away. Says words like "thief" and "miser," not with a half-joking half-respectful tone, but with real intent.

In any event it wasn't necessary. Two weeks earlier, David had given Johan an old *Playboy*. It had happened at the end of a discussion of the fairer sex, in which young lad and old man had agreed that girls were complex and confusing, but sure nice to look at. He figured that the old guy would use it for the same thing he did; to read the articles, of course.

This was still the age when the quality of art was determined primarily by how closely it reflected reality. The photographs in a *Playboy* magazine looked quite real indeed, just somewhat, ah, more, than nature usually provides. This gave the pictures a certain amount of added artistic value. Johan had noted this, and on the morning of the sixteenth, had shown the *Playboy* to Master Vespucci, with the explanation that there were some forms of art that proper Christian ladies didn't appreciate. It was a deal closer. It saved everyone's pride. Several additional images were agreed on and things were settled. Master Vespucci would get his dolls and get to keep his pride. Lady Higgins would be spoken of with respect, and even her scoundrel of a servant, as someone who knew how things worked.

Little did they know, but with Delia's full knowledge, Ray Higgins had been a long time subscriber to *Playboy*. She had been no more upset about Ray's *Playboys* than he had been about her dolls. Well, she didn't buy him *Playboys*, but she did no more than shake her head. In one of the storage containers that was reserved for family use, there was a collection of *Playboys* going back almost to the first issue. Alas, the blockages of communication between the generations and the genders hid this knowledge from those most able to use it. The *Playboys* continued to gather dust.

The final deal was made. A consignment of selected dolls, all sizes and types, each with a signed and sealed certificate of authenticity, and undisclosed sundries, were exchanged for a rather large sum of money. In fact, most of the money that Master Vespucci had available to him in Thuringia. The things he'd been planning to buy in Badenburg would just have to find another buyer. The sundries were David's *Playboys*, all twenty-four of them. And fifty really raunchy color photos downloaded from the internet up-time, that he had used the last of his color ink to print.

Delia got to keep most of her dolls, at least for now. They had asked the bank to loan them rather more money than the sales realized. Almost twice as much in fact. They had asked the bank for the total amount they had estimated plus the hundred percent fudge factor that Mrs. Wendell had suggested. Now, that fudge factor was gone. Federico Vespucci had paid them little more than the minimum they thought they would need. They would have sold more dolls, but Federico Vespucci hadn't had any more money to spend. It was enough to start.

David didn't know whether to laugh or cry over the sale of the dolls. There was a tremendous sense of relief that they would, probably, be able to build the sewing machine factory. On the other hand, Grandma's dolls! Even if it wasn't the whole collection, or even the largest part of the collection, still, Grandma's dolls! And she was effectively committing the rest of the collection, on an as-needed basis. How do you respond when the queen gives you the crown jewels for your wild ass gamble? You can't say: "No thanks, ma'am, it's not worth it."

The others, especially Sarah, felt somewhat the same. Sarah, being a girl, had gotten the tour of the dolls in a bit more detail than the guys. She knew that Mrs. Higgins could tell you precisely where and when she had gotten most of the dolls in her collection. Even if it was just "We were in the Goodwill, and there was the cutest little three-year-old there that day. With her mother's permission, I bought her a baby doll, and these I got for me." They weren't just dolls, they were memories. How do you repay someone who sells their memories to invest in your dream?

July 20, 1631

The sale of the dolls had been finalized. Now the company was legally formed. Since all the start-up capital had come from Delia's dolls, the kids insisted that a majority share go to Delia. Brent, Trent, Sarah, and David each got ten percent, Delia got the rest. Delia turned around and gave Ramona and Dalton five percent each, and her grandchildren David, Donny, Milton, Mark, and Mindy, two percent each. Which meant that David ended up with twelve percent. She also gave Jeff and Gretchen five percent as a belated wedding present. Finally, for his help in finding the buyer for her dolls and negotiating the deal, she gave Johan five percent.

The gifts of shares were not entirely acts of generosity. They were also acts of politics. Dalton and Ramona had never gotten along. Dalton had felt, with some justification, that Ramona got more support from his parents than he did, and resented it. So Delia tried consciously to be somewhat even handed. She also wanted more people to have at least some interest in the success of the sewing machine company. Especially in the case of Jeff and Gretchen. She had figured out that Jeff and Gretchen were playing a much more active part in the political structure of Grantville than she was. Delia almost gave some to her parents, who were retired and living in Grantville, but after the ragging they gave her over the whole project, she didn't. Instead, she gave it to Johan. She had realized he was a valuable resource for them all, and wanted to tie his loyalty to the family in a material way.

There was one other reason for the gifts that Delia thought long and hard about. She figured the thing most likely to kill the company was if the kids gave up on it, and the thing most likely to make them give up, was if they felt they had lost control. That their decisions, their actions, didn't matter. She explained it to the kids as soon as she got them alone. "You know and I know that it's unlikely any of the others will ever vote their shares," she said. "Maybe Johan, but he'll probably vote the way David tells him to.

"I remember the concern you all had, that the grownups would take it away. Well, we won't. As of now, the four of you can outvote me, and nobody can outvote you, without me on their side. This was your project in the beginning and it still is. I want that clear in your minds. You kids thought it up, you did the work, and more importantly, you will still be doing the work. If it is going to work, you're the ones that will make it work. If it's going to fail, well, that's you too." Delia grinned a very nasty grin. "Scary ain't it?" She softened a bit. "I'll be here if you need advice. So will your parents. But this is yours.

Trust can be a heavy load, but it can strengthen even as it weighs you down.

July 23, 1631: Delia Higgins' House

Delia, on balance, liked Sarah's lectures; they had passion. Sarah had just delivered one on the whooshing noise the down-timer money made as it disappeared into Grantville's economy. After the kids left, Delia called the Wendells and asked. She got confirmation, complete with bells and whistles. Judy Wendell said, "If the up-timers don't start spending money pretty soon we're going to end up doing to this economy what the iceberg did to the Titanic."

"But we are spending money! Lots of it. Everyone is worried that we won't have enough to buy food."

"That's food," was Judy Wendell's response. "And while food is more of the local economy than it was up-time, it's still less than half of the total. We're not sure yet how much less, but so far, all our revisions have been down. Most people here aren't full-time farmers, and a lot of the farmers aren't growing food crops. It's the other things where we're hurting the economy. Hardware, clothing, luxuries, and services. We have more and better of most of them, especially the luxuries. Which really suck up the money."

"The dolls you just sold are an excellent example. You cleaned out that Federico Vespucci fellow. Every bit of the money that he was going to spend in the surrounding towns went into the sewing machine company's bank account and most of it is still there. Don't get me wrong, Delia, I am thankful for the faith you have shown in the kids. More thankful than I can say. I agree that the sewing machine project has a fair chance of success, and will be valuable to Grantville and, well, the whole world, whether it works or not. Still, that money, and most of the money that has come from selling off the contents of the up-time renters' storage containers, is sitting in your bank account. Then there is everyone else. The local down-time townspeople are coming to see and buying. Merchants are doing the same, but from farther afield. Money is flowing into Grantville, and for the most part it's staying right here. If it's here, it's not paying craftsmen in Badenburg for their labor and skill.

"We need the down-timers to accept up-time money, because we need to be cash rich enough to spend our money on luxuries and investments. That's not going to happen till we are sure there is enough to spend on necessities. A big part of that is getting the down-timers—and more than a few up-timers—to treat up-time money as real money. There must be enough extra money in the system to make up for the time between when we sell something and when we buy something."

Delia had gone out and hired another guard. Then a few days later she added Dieter, who was accompanied by his wife or perhaps girlfriend. Delia wasn't sure and didn't ask. Her name was Liesel. She had been with him as a camp follower when he was a soldier in Tilly's army and the relationship had held firm. The other new guard was a refugee. Johan had been moved up to guard captain, and was available to the Higgins Sewing Machine Company as German speaking chief bargainer.

Fitting everyone in was a hassle. The mobile home used for an office was a one bedroom. Its living room was used as the office, and until the Ring of Fire the bedroom had been used to store padlocks and dollies and other equipment. The bedroom had been cleared out when Johan was hired. The equipment had been moved into a storage shed. But the living room was still needed as an office during the day. It was also where the guards slept. Three men and one woman in one bedroom was less than comfortable. So Johan had moved into the sewing room in the main house. They had strung up a blanket to give a semblance of privacy, and Ramona had tried to keep the noise down in the office while the guards were sleeping.

The discussions had not been the only reason for the hires. One guard was not enough. People need time off. With the increased crime, Delia figured she needed at least two guards, preferably three. Then there was the fact that setting up the HSMC would, unavoidably, require doing business with people outside the Ring of Fire, and she wanted someone reliable with the kids when they were out there. So Johan, and occasionally one of the other guards, would be needed to accompany the kids. This way, she could provide the kids with Johan's help without charging them for it. The kids were getting to be something of a pain about not taking any more of Delia's money than they absolutely had to.

As for Liesel, she had put herself to work in the house, after checking with Johan to find the location of mops and other cleaning tools. Delia had, after some resistance, given up and put her on the payroll. It wasn't as if she would miss doing the housework; and, truth be told, the house had never been so clean.

It still wasn't all that much of a payroll. All four Higgins employees worked for room, board and clothing, plus a very low salary, more of an allowance really. Oddly enough, they seemed to think her quite generous.

Delia had decided to raise the rates on the storage containers. She called up her renters with the bad news. Explaining that, with the change in circumstances, she had needed to hire added security. She lost a few customers, but by now she had a waiting list.

July 25, 1631: A Smithy in Badenburg

Johan watched quietly as young Master Brent went on, again, telling the blacksmith what the part did and why. "It's really just a lever," Brent said, "but it's clever how it works. This end rests against a rotating cam that makes one complete rotation every two stitches. The cam has a varying radius. As the cam rotates, the short end of the level is moved in and out. That moves the long end of the lever up and down, pulling the thread or loosening it as needed to make the stitch. So it's very important that each end of the lever is the right length and while the major stresses are vertical it needs enough depth to avoid bending. The model and the forms provide you with a system of measuring tools to tell how well the part is within specifications." Then Brent looked at Johan to translate.

Johan did, sort of, his way. "See the pattern drawn on the board with the nails in it?" The board was a piece of one-by-eight about a foot long that Brent and Trent had made. He waited for the nod. Then took the wooden model and placed in on the nails where it fell easily to cover the internal line and leave the external line exposed. He wiggled it. The inside line remained hidden. The outside line remained in view, as there wasn't much wiggle room.

"See the way it covers the inside line and doesn't cover the outside line? This model would pass the first test if it was iron."

He removed the model from the nails and slid it through a slot in the wood. "It's thin enough it would pass the second test." He then tried to slip it through another slot but it wouldn't go. "It's thick enough it would pass the third test. The fourth test is a weight test. But if it's good iron and it passes these it should pass the last as well. So that's the deal. Each one of these that passes the tests, we'll pay you. If it doesn't pass, we don't buy it."

Then the bargaining began in earnest. It took a while, but Johan got a good price. Not quite so good as he wanted, but better than he really expected. With the craftsman's warning, "Mind, all my other work will come first."

And so it went. Over the following days they visited craft shops of several sorts. They ordered finished parts where they could, and blanks where the techniques of the early seventeenth century weren't up to the task. The blanks would be finished by the machines they had designed.

July 26, 1631: Dave Marcantonio's Machine Shop

Dave would soon see the truth for himself. Kent had been bragging on his boys for weeks now. To hear him tell it, he'd fathered Orville and Wilbur Wright as twins. Dave returned the favor by teasing him about being a doting dad. Still, it was a fairly new situation. Before the Ring of Fire, Kent had been alternately pleased and worried about how his kids would turn out. Then, when Caleb had gone into the army, Kent's pride had quadrupled, and most of the worry about how he would turn out had been replaced with worry about him getting hurt.

The real change had happened with Brent and Trent. About a month ago, he had started going on about his twin mechanical geniuses. Practical pragmatic mechanical geniuses, with a plan to build a sewing machine factory, and even somewhat about their friends Sarah and David. Mostly Sarah. In Kent's estimation, David Bartley's major claim to fame was having the right friends. Though he liked the boy's grandmother, Delia Higgins.

Dave had gotten chapter and verse on the idiocy of bankers when the bank loan fell through. Then a week ago, when Delia Higgins had sold the dolls, Kent had conceded that David also had the right grandmother, and offered an almost grudging acknowledgement that Trent and Brent's loyalty to their less competent friend was returned.

The thing that impressed Dave Marcantonio, though, was that the kids got together and insisted that Delia receive the lion's share of the company. Good kids, even if he doubted that they were the mechanical geniuses their father claimed.

The designs were pretty good; not real good, but

not bad. At one point, when he pointed out a place where their designs would need two parts where one slightly more complex part would do for both they gave Kent a look and Kent blushed. Dave had known Kent Partow for years. They were best friends. He knew and even shared Kent's preference for simpler machining jobs. Too darn many people added bells and whistles where they weren't needed, but sometimes Kent took it too far. It wasn't hard for Dave to figure out that Kent had made them change it. He didn't laugh in front of the kids, but Kent was in for some teasing later.

The designs were really quite good, Dave realized, as he continued to examine them. There were a number of places where they managed to have several of the production machines use common parts. And some places where the machines were basically modular. The power transfer for three of the seven machines were effectively the same structure, so with some adjustment, if one machine broke then another could be refitted to take its place. That was a fine bit of work. They hadn't been too ambitious either. The machines were simple, designed to do one or two things and that was it. The thing that had fooled him was that, good or not, they were somewhat amateurish. Not that they were sloppy, but the kids didn't know the tricks of the trade. They didn't know how to make their designs immediately clear. These took more study before you got a real feel for what they were doing.

Okay. Maybe they were mechanical geniuses. At the least, they were clever kids that thought things through. Which was a hell of a lot more than he would expect from a couple of high school freshmen. He figured someone had had an influence on them. Partly Kent, but someone else too. These designs had been gone over before. By someone practical.

Good designs or not, it was still going to cost. He looked at the kids and remembered why he hadn't had any. Let someone else tell the charming little monsters "no." He gave them his best guess as to cost. Told them it was a guess. Made sure that they understood that since the Ring of Fire, defense and power came first. That they were at the back of a fairly long line and it was a safe bet that other projects would come along and cut in front of them.

He told them that they would have to come up with the iron and steel for the parts. Finally: "I'll have to charge you as we go. Let me look at the designs, for a week or so, and see if there is anything I can do to make them cheaper to make."

They took it well. They thanked him and said the week was fine. They had been expecting it to be worse, but Dave, not being as well known as the other two professional shops in town, hadn't been getting quite so flooded with work. Besides, he was discounting his price. Kent was his best friend, after all.

August 3, 1631: Dave Marcantonio's Machine Shop

Dave had spent the evening a week ago looking at the kids' plans. Then, with a strong feeling he was missing something, he had gone to bed. He had slept poorly that night, but the next morning he had it. The reason he hadn't gotten it at first was that it was not an improvement in the machine, not from the kids' point of view. What it was, was an adaptation of one of the kids' machines to do one of the common jobs he used the computer lathe for. It would only do that job, and it wouldn't do it as fast or as well. But if he built the late-nineteenth century style cam and lever lathe the kids had designed, and used it where he could, it would probably add more than a year to the life of the fancy rig.

He spent the next several days trying to figure out what to do about it. In one sense, it was the kid's design, but in another sense it wasn't. None of these designs were really original to the kids. They were adaptations of designs found in books, or even adapted from sections of the sewing machines themselves, just as his was an adaptation of theirs. There weren't any patent laws, so there wasn't any legal reason why he shouldn't just go ahead and build his machine. What if he did the right thing and the kids got greedy? They had reason enough. They had to be desperate for money to get their sewing machine company going. Then he thought about the fact that the kids had gotten together and insisted that Delia Higgins get the lion's share of the sewing machine company. The kids weren't thieves and Dave Marcantonio was no thief either. Never mind facing their dad. If he ripped off a bunch of kids, he wouldn't be able to face himself.

When the kids came in he told them about several minor changes that he had made that would make their production machines a bit easier to build. Then he told them about the adaptation of their machine he was thinking of building. He offered to build the first two machines basically for free, in exchange for the right to use their designs as the basis for production machines to add to his shop. They would still have to provide the metal blanks, but he would machine them for free. They agreed. It would save them a bundle.

Actually they did more than agree. Brent and Trent asked to see the designs for the new machine and offered to help in any way they could. They loved that he liked their designs well enough to use them.

August 10, 1631: Badenburg

Karl Schmidt was a substantial fellow, like his father before him. He was fifty-two and had been recently widowed. He owned a foundry in Badenburg. It was a smallish foundry, with a smithy attached, where they made door hinges, wagon parts, and other things of iron, mostly for local use. He had four surviving children: his son Adolph, a twenty-two year old journeyman blacksmith, and three teenage daughters, Gertrude, Hilda and Marie.

He had known of the Ring of Fire almost from the beginning. At first, it had been a strange and frightening thing, surrounded by dark stories of magic and witchcraft; then miracles, as the stories of who they actually were got around. A whole town full of people from the future, surely God's handiwork. Yet they didn't claim to be angels or saints. Why would God go to the trouble of sending a town from the future if it was filled with normal people? There had been several sermons around then, about the angels that visited Lot in Sodom without announcing their angelic status. Some of the priests had pointed out, that if an angel didn't have to tell you that he was an angel, then certainly a demon or devil didn't have to tell you he was a devil.

It was an enigma. Karl did not like enigmas. They troubled his sleep. His solution at first, was to keep his distance. Then stories about what Tilly's men were doing at a farm outside of Rudolstadt, and more significantly, what happened to them, got around. The ease with which the out-of-timers killed was terrifying. Rumor had it that it had only taken a few of them, half a dozen at most, to kill dozens of solders. Yet the same rumor said that they had done it to save the farmer and that they had, in spite of the fact that he had been nailed to a barn door and was the next best thing to dead when they got there. Some stories said he was dead. Karl didn't believe that, but how much could be believed? Some people visited Grantville, but Karl was not one of them. A few people from Grantville visited Badenburg. Karl didn't meet them, though he could have.

Karl was a slow fellow. Not in the sense of slow witted, he was really quite bright, but he liked to take his time and think things through. Meanwhile he had business to see to.

Adolph, Karl's son, was not quite so substantial a fellow as his father. From what Adolph could tell, his father thought him quite flighty. In fact Adolph was fairly substantial and becoming more so every year. He was a journeyman smith, and ran the smithy part of the business.

Adolph's latest worry had to do with Grantville, and it wasn't the least bit spiritual. Several merchants and more farmers who had been expected to spend their money in Badenburg had instead spent it in Grantville. A number of potential customers from Grantville had taken the attitude that "Grantville dollars are as good as anyone else's money and probably better." In short, business was bad.

Upon receiving his son's complaints, Karl had sought out what contacts might be made with people either from Grantville or people that knew Grantville. He was directed to Uriel Abrabanel, a wealthy Jew he had done business with before. Uriel was, it turned out, surprisingly, no, shockingly well connected with the Grantville elite. His niece was engaged to be married to the leader of Grantville. Karl considered himself a worldly man, and not a bit prejudiced. He, like everyone, knew that Jews cared for money above all else. That most of them were usurers. Karl was an educated man. He knew that those stories about them eating babies, poisoning towns, or bringing on plague were probably nonsense. The Abrabanels were known to be of a good family as Jews counted such things. But still, the leader of what was now perhaps the most powerful town in the area was engaged to a Jew.

Uriel Abrabanel greeted Karl on the ground floor of his two-story home. It was a fairly pleasant room, with a large casement window for light. There were several bookcases along the walls, and comfortable seats for guests.

His guest was apparently not comfortable, but Uriel doubted that it was because of the chair. In Uriel's estimation, Karl Schmidt was a fairly standard local man of business. His prejudice against Jews was about the standard: enough to keep him from socializing, but not enough to keep him from doing business. Nor did he significantly overcharge, which had to be taken in his favor. Still, it cannot be said that Uriel was overly concerned over any shock to the fellow's system that might occur upon learning of Rebecca's upcoming marriage, and all that it implied.

On the other hand, there was no reason to end a generally good working relationship by rubbing Karl's nose in it. Perhaps a more general explanation was needed.

"From what I understand, the future nation from which Grantville comes has some markedly different customs. Religious tolerance is expected. Their attitudes on that and a number of other issues have come as something of a shock to any number of people. For instance, their women dress in what we would consider an immodest manner. This should not be taken as license to show them any lack of respect. That mistake could be very dangerous. They are somewhat casual in their mode of address. They apparently mean no offense by this, it is just their way. I suspect that it is an outgrowth of their attitude toward rank. They are the most aggressively democratic people I have ever encountered."

Master Schmidt was not stupid, and if he liked to think things through, it did not mean that he could not see the writing on the wall if it were writ large enough. To Karl Schmidt this was writing in letters ten feet tall. Uriel Abrabanel's social and political situation was now significantly above his. For all intents and purposes, the man's niece was about to marry into royalty. This United States looked to be something that might grow.

Yet here he was talking to Karl Schmidt just as he had when, as a good Christian, Karl's social position had been the higher. Karl quietly congratulated himself on his temperate and unbiased attitude toward Jews. He really did.

The discussion of the Americans continued. Their technology, and their money. Master Abrabanel expressed solid confidence in both. Occasionally in the course of the conversation, Karl noticed that his attitude toward Master Abrabanel bordered on the deferential. Well that was only proper, considering the change in circumstances.

They talked of business within the Ring of Fire. Karl mentioned that a child, apprentice age, accompanied by a man who was apparently a family retainer, had approached his son with a proposal to make certain parts for something called sewing machines. The deal had fallen through because they preferred to deal in American dollars. They hadn't actually insisted, but had explained that using local coinage meant they had to go to the bank and get it. They expected a reduction in cost to cover the trouble.

Master Abrabanel could not be of much help in terms of the specific business. He had seen sewing machines in Grantville, but he was unaware of any company making them. On the matter of the money, he had had several conversations with members of the Grantville finance committee on the subject of how they intended to maintain consistency in the value of American dollars. Their arguments were clear and persuasive.

Master Abrabanel then expressed a willingness to accept American dollars, just as he would several other currencies, in payment of debts or for goods. Even to exchange them for other currencies. For a reasonable fee.

Karl left Master Abrabanel in a thoughtful mood. His prejudice said that a Jew would not risk money on the basis of an emotional connection. Which, given Master Abrabanel's expressed confidence, made the American dollars seem more sound.

August 12, 1631: Delia Higgins' Place

It had been an unpleasant roundabout trip to the Higgins estate. It was an unusually hot day, and Karl Schmidt was not a good rider. He didn't like to ride. He also didn't like going around in circles, and the Ring of Fire had produced a ring of cliffs facing in or facing out all around itself, with only a few places where it was easy to pass. All this was bad enough, but the things he had seen en route were worse. It was one thing to talk about people from the future, even to consider what powers they might have gained. But to see a road that wide and that flat, and put it together with what they called the "APCs" . . .

These people were rich almost beyond measure. The civilian APCs parked along the way really brought it home. The civilian APCs weren't a special case, they were the norm for these people. Their money worked, that was easy enough to see. The question this left Karl Schmidt with was whether *his* money was good anymore. Karl was not the first to ask that question.

The Higgins estate itself was divided into two parts. One was fenced with a kind of heavy gauge wire fence held up with what appeared to be metal bars. Along the top were strands of a different wire with spikes on it. There was a gate made in a similar manner that was open, and a smallish boxlike building next to the gate that looked like it might be made of painted metal, or perhaps the plastic he had heard about. Farther back, he could see rows of really small buildings: flat topped boxes set side by side, each no larger than a largish outhouse. They too might be made of metal, or perhaps plastic.

The other section had a more familiar, but still somewhat strange house on it. They appeared to have built out, rather than up. It was a single story, with an attic that he wouldn't put a servant in. The roof was flatter than it should have been. From the extension of road that led to the large door, and the APC parked in front of it, one section of the house was for storing APCs. Why wasn't the APC in the room that was clearly designed for it? Was there another APC in it, or was it being used for something else?

There were too many windows and those windows were too large. The more he looked, the stranger it got. The place was short, no more than ten feet from the ground to the eaves. On a day like today, with no airspace, it must be stifling in there. They seemed no more concerned with winter than summer. He could see no chimney, just a little pipe sticking out of the roof.

He sat his horse for a little while, mopped his brow, and thought it out. He finally decided that, since this was a matter of business, he should go to what appeared to be the business part of the estate.

Ramona Higgins had, after her initial start, let the whole Ring of Fire mess sort of slide by. She was fairly good at that, having had quite a bit of practice. Her way of dealing with a world full of complexities that she couldn't quite manage had always been to let them slide by while concentrating on those matters she could handle. Her self-image had never been all that strong, and it was primarily based on what others wanted from her. She wasn't lazy, just easily confused. If what people wanted from her was something Ramona could readily supply, she felt good about herself and liked the person. If not, she felt bad about herself and didn't. The exceptions to that unconscious rule were few and far between: her mother and her sons were about all. But Mom and the boys went to some trouble not to ask things of her she could not readily provide.

From her mid-teens, in addition to a willingness to work hard at anything that didn't confuse her, the other thing that Ramona could provide was sex. She had a tendency to like guys better than girls. She was a moderately attractive woman in her late thirties. There were some lines, but not all that many, nor all that deep. Her figure, by modern standards, floated between lush and overweight. She fully filled her bra, her hair was sandy brown or dirty blond depending on who you asked, and the lighting at the moment. She had good teeth, no pockmarks, and clear light blue eyes.

In short, by the standards of the sixteen-thirties, she was stunningly attractive.

Karl was stunned, not just by her, but also by the environment. When he entered the mobile home that served as an office, it was cool. Karl had never experienced air-conditioning. What was actually Ramona's nervousness at dealing with a down-timer, seemed to him the very epitome of feminine modesty and deferential courtesy. Everything seemed almost magical in nature. He had wandered into a fairy tale, complete with fairy princess. With some difficulty, because he spoke only limited English and she spoke virtually no German, it was determined that the Higgins Sewing Machine Company was handled by her mother; assisted, so Ramona chose to see it, by her son. The place he needed was the main house.

Karl did something then that the solid staid man hadn't done since he was in his twenties. He kissed a lady's hand. She blushed quite prettily.

Karl was not a particularly handsome man, but he was big and strong, and had a certain presence. At least it seemed that way to Ramona. Perhaps it was the unlikely combination of the big, almost ugly man, the polite formality, and the kissing of her hand, but he seemed quite charming.

August 12, 1631: Delia Higgins' House

Karl didn't seem all that charming to Delia. Since the Ring of Fire, strange large men on horseback were not calculated to make her comfortable. Still, when it was made clear that this had to do with the sewing machines, she called Johan. David and Donny were with Brent and Trent, at Dave Marcantonio's shop, while Sarah was watching her little sister at home. So it was left to Delia, with the help of Johan, to deal with Karl.

Her attitude remained reserved. Partly it was because Karl Schmidt seemed wrong to her: shifty and hard at the same time. She didn't realize it, but in a number of important ways he seemed, and was, much like Quinton Underwood, and more than a little like Delia Higgins. They talked about the sewing machine factory. Karl picked up on the what's and the why's of it all more readily than she had. Not the mechanics, since he got to see the sewing machine working but not disassembled; still, he got the part about machines to make machines quite readily.

What he didn't get, was why they had to wait for the kids. It seemed to Karl that it was an excuse, a tool to manipulate him, probably to lower his prices.

It was some days later before a deal was made. The deal was made because the Schmidt family had the best shop for what the kids wanted. Not the only one, but the best. By the time the deal was made Karl was less sure that the kids were a ruse. They actually seemed to know what they were talking about.

August 12, 1631: Dave Marcantonio's Shop

David Bartley, the proud uncle, watched Brent, Trent, their father, and Mr. Marcantonio—new daddies all—gathered around at the birth of their machines. Triplets, but not quite identical. David, as was appropriate for an uncle, was pleased, but not totally enraptured by the appropriate number of fingers and toes, or in this case gears, levers and cutting blades. Donny, on the other hand, was thrilled to be included.

The machines worked, but like many babies were just a bit cranky. There were places where the gears stuck, just a bit. It was hoped that with use they would smooth out. It would take some skill to use them. Not so much as Mr. Marcantonio had, nor so much as the down-time smiths had. These were finishing machines that took a blank provided by a down-time smith or foundry, and fined them up. Trent and Brent would be using them first, and for the moment they would stay in a corner of Mr. Marcantonio's shop.

August 25, 1631

After the initial burst of activity, things slowed to a snail's pace as more urgent jobs claimed more and more of Dave Marcantonio's time. He was fitting in parts of their machines wherever he could, but he didn't have a lot of slack time. They were doing a lot better with the down-time contractors, in spite of the fact that they had to watch every cent, and bargain prices generally don't go with fast delivery.

Still, money-wise they were doing better than expected. Mr. Marcantonio had the blanks he needed to make the next four of the production machines, and at about two-thirds of what they had expected to pay. They also had a small but respectable stock of down-timer made sewing machine parts, at better prices than expected. Partly this was due to Johan's bargaining skills, but mostly it was because the down-time shops had been losing a lot of their normal business to the up-time shops, and they badly needed the work.

Sarah, and especially her parents, were worried about the situation. One of the dangers of introducing a lot of new products into an economy is that it can cause deflation that leads to a depression. Some of the merchants and many of the farming villages around the Ring of Fire were accepting American money, but not all of them. Without the American money, the sudden influx of goods and services could end up ruining everyone within fifty miles of the Ring of Fire.

Which was why they were getting their parts for such low prices. The craft shops in the area were desperate for business, any business. The HSMC's money was buying more than it should have been.

August 27, 1631: Delia Higgins' Garage

"It's still good," said Brent, as they fiddled with one of the five partially completed sewing machines, "it's only about an eighth of an inch shallow."

"I don't know," said Trent. "If the catcher is an eighth of an inch off the other way it'll jam." The catcher was the twins' term for a device that hooked the thread and pulled it around the bobbin every other stitch. Unfortunately, several of the parts to the bobbin assembly were still waiting on finishing machines to come out of Mr. Marcantonio's shop. So, while the needles went up and down, and the "thread puller" pulled the thread at the right time as far as the boys could tell, they were still some distance from actually sewing a single stitch.

September 1, 1631: Grantville High School

"Hey, Brent. Do you really own a company?"

"What are you taking this year?"

"What's this shit about you owning a company?"

"Yea, they make sewing machines so they can have cloths for their dollies."

"Except, they ain't actually made no sewing machines yet, and I hear they never will."

"I don't know. I heard that Mr. Marcantonio said that they designed good machines, and that some of them are going to be used in shop class." Which was the first Brent had heard about that.

The first day as a sophomore in high school is supposed to be different from the first day as a freshman. Well, this was certainly different. People who would not talk to lowly freshmen when they were sophomores and juniors, now as juniors and seniors, seemed quite willing to talk to lowly sophomores, at least if those sophomores owned a company. Others seemed to resent them for not staying in their place.

Then there were their classmates.

A significant percentage thought the whole thing was ridiculous. That Delia and the kids were wasting valuable resources that Grantville needed for other things. That they would never build a working sewing machine, and even if they did, why weren't they using the money for something that mattered? Like weapons or reapers?

"I'll tell you why," said one would-be wit. "Because no one would let the Bill Gates wannabes mess with something that mattered."

Sarah almost got in a fight over that one. "Baby Gates" was the first, but not the most popular of the nicknames the four got. The "Sewing Circle" was the favorite. Then there was the rather convoluted "Barbershop quartet," based on the notion that they were four would-be "singers."

They found a similar range of attitudes, mostly without the name calling, among the teachers. Some were enthusiastic, some concerned, and some sarcastic.

All in all, the change in status made it a difficult and confusing first day, to be followed by a difficult and confusing first week. All of the "Sewing Circle" had some heavy-duty adjustments to make. Over the summer they had been less involved in high school stuff than most of the kids in Grantville. They had after all, been rather busy.

"This too shall pass," and it did. There was altogether too much going on for any but the most obsessive to keep up the teasing for long. It rapidly became just one more thing among many that the sophomores in Grantville High concerned themselves with. There were discussions about the army, about the future of Grantville, and about the German immigrants. Then there were the German students. Who had their own attitudes and beliefs.

The German students were, for the first few weeks, reluctant to put themselves forward. Partly this was because of the language barrier, but not entirely. They also felt a status difference. The up-timers were rich, with rich parents, and the down-timers were refugees. *Don't give offense, study hard, and make friends.* These instructions, often contradictory in practice, were impressed on the down-timer kids by their parents, all too often using a belt or a rod to reinforce the point.

Their attitude toward the "Sewing Circle" was somewhat different. To them, the important point was not whether the sewing machine company would actually succeed. That wasn't unimportant, but the really important point was that the "Sewing Circle" had parents who could afford to start them in a business. Granted, all the up-timers were rich, but there's rich, and then there's *rich*.

Since Delia Higgins was the backer of the enterprise, this attitude focused on David.

Short and skinny for his age, David Bartley had never been one of the popular kids among the up-timers. Mostly, he still wasn't. But among the down-timers he was very popular—especially with the down-timer girls.

The down-time girls took a pragmatic view of romance. David, Brent and Trent—but especially David—looked like they might be wealthy enough to marry years before most other boys in school. Not that the girls were looking to marry right away, but the period between puberty and satisfaction was uncomfortably long for a tailor's daughter.

Unfortunately, or perhaps fortunately, David didn't really know how to handle the situation.

September 10, 1631: Delia Higgins' House

There were extra guests for dinner at Delia Higgins' house the night of the first TV broadcast. Ramona had invited Karl Schmidt and his family. They had been seeing each other since mid-August. Not every day, but once a week or so, Karl would bring in a load of parts and Ramona would take the afternoon off.

Delia was slightly concerned. David wasn't, not anymore. Acculturation works both ways and it works faster on kids. Johan had been acculturating David right along. Besides, it wasn't that much of a jump really, just putting it in terms appropriate to the time.

David had had a conversation with Master Schmidt. Ramona Higgins was a lady of high station, with a family that would take it very badly if she were treated with a lack of respect. Normally such comments from a boy just turned fifteen might be ignored. In this case, however, Johan was sitting a few feet away cleaning a double-barreled shotgun and adding translation and mistranslation as needed. Besides, in the discussions about the sewing machine parts, David had gotten to know Karl a little bit. He was bigoted, but no more than most, and he wasn't a user, unlike some of his mom's previous men.

Karl had not been insulted, or particularly frightened. Just cautioned. After all, Young Master Bartley had not told him to stop seeing Ramona, simply to treat her with respect. It reaffirmed her status, without closing the door in his face. To Karl, the surprising thing was that the door was not closed. David had managed to come off like a young baron allowing a commoner to court his mother because that's what his mother wanted.

Karl knew that David was not titled. He also knew that the President of Grantville was not titled. Titles didn't matter here, power mattered. If Karl played his cards right, he might well be accepted into this new informal nobility, and his family with him.

He had treated her with respect. Perhaps a bit more respect than Ramona really wanted. Certainly enough respect that he had swept her off her feet. Hence the dinner invitation. She wanted to meet his family. She wanted her family to meet his family, and she wanted everything to go well. She had fussed all day.

Normally dinner at the Higgins house was informal. The "servants" ate with the family. Not this time. Liesel would have none of it, and neither would Johan. There would be guests. Liesel would serve, Johan would get the door. Liesel was quite fond of Ramona, in a subservient materialistic sort of way. They would make a good impression.

They did, actually. The servants provided the comfort of familiarity. The food was rich, and excitingly varied. Something called "Orange Jell-O" for dessert. The house was a glory of technological innovation. These days, lamps were used in the Higgins house and light bulbs were hoarded; but for tonight, the lights were switched on. The cassette recorder provided a large selection of music in various styles. The doll collection managed to surpass its reputation. Not an easy thing to do, for it had grown in the telling.

Finally, there was the welcoming attitude. The Schmidt family found them quite condescending, in the old meaning of the word. They had clearly stepped down from their position of rank to make their guests comfortable. They hadn't, of course, but it seemed that way to the Schmidt family.

Dinner discussion started on the sewing machine company, but wandered far afield, to technology, customs, economics, schooling, fashion and culture. Ramona was somewhat successful in including the Schmidt girls in the conversation. Adolph was particularly interested in the electric lights, and as he learned of them, in the other electronic devices.

Dinner ended, as all things must, and it was time for the show. The television was turned on in time to see the hostess sitting down, but they missed the kiss. It didn't matter much, since of his family only Karl had ever seen TV before.

Rebecca was a wow! For the Schmidt family, it was suddenly like they knew her. Beautiful and gracious, looking them right in the eye, explaining the circumstances within the Ring of Fire, speaking of rationing, but that no one would go hungry. Her comments about Americans needing lots of meat to cook brought an extra delight; tonight's dinner had been rich in meat.

The Buster Keaton movie was a marvel. Made more marvelous for the Higgins clan by the Schmidt clan's wonder. Then Rebecca came back on. She discussed briefly the production projects, not mentioning the sewing machine project. It had for the most part fallen below adult radar. Then she began to discuss the military situation.

"I am Jewish, as you know," she said. But the Schmidt family hadn't known, except for Karl, and not even he had really thought about it. This Royal Lady, with the steady eye, and commanding presence, was a Jew. Well, no wonder she was engaged to the leader of the Americans, Jew or not. This was Uriel Abrabanel's niece, and there was a family resemblance now that he looked for it. Karl's prejudice took another hit that night. It was a fairly big hit, but prejudice takes a lot of chipping away.

Rebecca was still talking, still looking them in the eye. That same sense of involvement that had made Marie Schmidt warn Buster Keaton of impending doom now held Delia and her family silent. Rebecca Abrabanel was not a lady you challenged to her face. By the time the show was over the Jewish princess had more converts to her cause. Tentative converts true, uncertain of what the cause was. Even more uncertain of their place in this new world of magic and miracles, but converts none the less.

September 16, 1631: Schmidt Household

They had talked around it after they got back from the Higgins house. In fact the visit had dominated conversation for several days. They called so much into question, these Americans. They offered so much, but at a price. It was a strange price, and the Schmidt family wasn't sure they could pay it.

Almost, it was a devil's bargain: wealth, power, even glory of a kind, for giving up some certainties. Beliefs are a bit like the soul. They aren't material, they can't be pointed to, but they are part of what makes us what we are. You can't just decide to give them up either, they stick around even when you know better. The Schmidt family didn't think it through like that. Certainly not in those terms. Instead they had an uneasy feeling, like they were about to step off a precipice. Scared and excited. What they talked about by turns, were the marvels and the outrages.

"Music coming out of a box."

"A Jewish woman talking publicly of politics."

"Light at the flick of a switch."

"Dresses above the knee."

"Becky, seemed honest?"

"I've spent my life learning the trade of a smith. I know the making of tools, and little boys are to tell me how to make things."

"No, Adolph, not how to make things—just what things they will buy."

"To be paid for with pieces of paper?"

It went on, but the Schmidts were pragmatic people. So much to be gained.

September 25, 1631: Partow House

The course of business building did not go as smoothly as the dinner with the Schmidts.

"The ceramic cases are deforming," said Trent. "We should have thought of it before. When you make ceramics, you're heating them to the edge of melting and keeping them there for hours. They become plastic at that heat and deform from their own weight."

"Are we going to have to go to wood or cast iron then?" asked Brent.

"That will add a bunch of money per machine. Cast iron is more expensive than clay, and we've already spent a bundle on the ceramic casings. That's money down the drain. Are you sure we can't make them work? Sarah is not going to be happy."

"I don't know enough about ceramics to be sure of anything, that's the problem," Brent admitted. "How much vibration can they take? Will the wood separators really work? Can we redesign the molds so as to compensate for the deformation?"

October 7, 1631: Grantville High School

On the upside of the ledger, they were only one part away from having finished sewing machines. Mr. Marcantonio said he would have the machine to produce that part ready in a couple of days. On the downside, they were going to have to find somewhere for a factory and they were perilously close to broke—past broke if you included the money that Mr. Marcantonio had said they could wait a while to pay.

The Higgins Sewing Machine Company had been

using three storage containers to store parts and blanks. The production machines made by Dave Marcantonio's shop were still in his shop, so to make and finish parts using them, they went there. Final assembly had been moved to the Higgins' garage. This had saved quite a bit in rent, but was far from convenient. Now that would have to change. For one thing, Mr. Marcantonio was being crowded out of his shop. He really didn't have room for all their production machines.

So, with regret, he had insisted that they find somewhere else to set up. He was feeling a bit guilty over throwing them out, and as he was very busy and not at all short of cash, he was willing to wait on payment for the last of the machines.

Which had led to this meeting of the "Sewing Circle." (The kids had adopted the nickname as their own.)

"Grantville is out, till we've sold some sewing machines or gotten more capital from somewhere," Sarah pronounced. "The rents are too high."

"We may be able to use a couple of the storage containers for a while," said David.

"Maybe so, but what we really need is a factory," said Trent. "Over seventy-five percent of our parts are still hand-made. There are a lot of machines that we could make that would decrease the cost of production if we had the money and the room."

"Some of the subcontractors have been asking about buying into the company lately," said David. "It seems some of the other business have started offering profit-sharing and stock options. We don't have any profits to share yet, but some of our suppliers figure we will."

David was thinking mainly of Karl Schmidt. Other suppliers had shown interest, but Mr. Schmidt seemed a bit obsessive. At first he had thought that Mr. Schmidt was cultivating him for his mother's sake; there was probably some of that in it, but that wasn't all of it.

"So have some of the guys from the shop class," added Brent.

"I think we should consider incorporation." Sarah picked up her book bag and removed a notebook. Then handed David, who was closest, a typewritten sheet. "Read it and pass it on. What it is," she said to the others, "is an outline of how I think we could incorporate. We set it up with a couple of hundred thousand shares. The first hundred thousand would be for the original owners. So we would each have ten thousand except for money bags here."

She pointed to David, who buffed his fingernails on his coat and tried to look important. He managed to look silly, which was probably better for all concerned. "Who would have twelve thousand, and Mrs. Higgins would have thirty thousand and so on."

"The other hundred thousand would be owned by the corporation. Which could sell it to raise extra money. Even at a dollar a share, even if we only sell a third of the shares, that's a lot of money."

"What about control?" asked Trent.

"We would probably keep it," said Sarah. "Probably. Let me ask you something though. Why is control important?"

"So the grownups won't take it away from us," said Trent automatically.

"No. What are the grownups going to do? Buy up control so they can stop making sewing machines?"

"Tell us 'Thanks, but we're running things now. Go play with your toys.'"

"Right, and pay us each five percent of the profit," Sarah answered. "David six percent and Mrs. Higgins fifteen percent. Altogether, with everybody, it's fifty percent. It might be worth it to someone, but it's not real likely. I figure we'll probably sell half the hundred thousand shares. Which would still leave us and Mrs. Higgins with more of the stock than any other group, but even if we do lose control, we'll probably get rich from it. So, if they want to tell us to go play with our toys, they are gonna have to buy us some really nice toys.

"There's another reason we should incorporate, or at least, change it to a limited liability company," she continued. "The way we set it up at first we are liable for any debts or damages. What if we get sued? It wouldn't be so bad for us, we don't have much, but what about Mrs. Higgins? One of the things a corporation does, is limit the debt to corporate assets. That would mean they couldn't take the storage lot, or Mrs. Higgins' dolls as payment for the company's debts."

They spent the rest of the lunch hour talking about corporate structure.

October 9, 1631: Delia's Garage

They had removed some of the production machines to the storage lot as a stopgap measure. Mr. Marcantonio had finished the last production machine they absolutely had to have, and they now had parts for several sewing machines. They had spent the entire time from when school let out trying to assemble one. Now it was dinner time, and they still didn't have a working sewing machine.

It was the same trouble they had been having from the beginning. Tolerances. The machined parts were acting as a centerline and the handmade parts could only vary from it so far. Mostly they fell within the limits, but if one part was off a little one way and another part was off in another way the combination meant that the sewing machine didn't work. So they had to go through the parts, find ones that were off in complementary ways and fit them together. It was a painstaking and occasionally painful process. Replete with skinned knuckles, banged fingers and frustration.

October 11, 1631: Delia's Garage

It worked. Five months of hard work, two afternoons, and about fifteen minutes of final assembly, and they had a sewing machine. The important thing was, in another couple of days they would have another; sewing machine production had finally started.

It was time to celebrate. There was a six pack of Coca-Cola that had been sitting in the Higgins pantry since the Ring of Fire and their icebox for the last week. It was about to get drunk.

Trent took over from Brent, and sewed another line of stitches down the folded rag. He then carefully removed it from the machine. From the garage they danced through the kitchen, startling Liesel, and into the living room. They danced around Delia, waving the sewn rag like the flag of a defeated foe, and in a way it was.

David and Johan were in Rudolstadt talking with a supplier, and Sarah was watching Judy the Younger again. Sarah's work could be done at home, and Judy the Younger was proving to be more of a help than the expected hindrance. Which surprised Sarah to no end.

A phone call informed Sarah of the good news.

She would call her parents. Other phone calls followed, to Mr. Marcantonio and Mr. Partow, to Mrs. Partow, to anyone in any way involved that could be reached by phone. Brent took the sewn cloth to show Ramona and the guards. By now there were ways to fairly rapidly get messages to people in Badenburg, Rudolstadt, and other nearby towns. It cost a few dollars and you had to know precisely where the person was. If you had a phone you could have the message which started with the local phone company charged to your phone bill. Which is precisely what Ramona did. She had realized that Karl was interested in the sewing machine project, and Karl was a responsible business man. He would know what to do.

David would have to wait until he got back from Rudolstadt to learn about the completed sewing machine.

By the time David got home, the party was in full swing. Most of the Grantville residents that were in any way involved with the sewing machine project were there. So was Karl Schmidt and his family, and a couple of other suppliers from Badenburg. They had come to see what their parts had made.

The guests circulated between the house proper and the garage. Delia had been the first to actually make something with the sewing machine. She professed to like her Singer better, hiding her pride in the accomplishment. She wasn't really fooling anyone, but the hillbilly version of the stiff upper lip had its rules. Liesel didn't make any such attempt. Liesel was not completely sure she trusted electricity. This could be used anywhere. All the guests had tried it, with Brent and Trent hovering nervously over them.

The Schmidt girls were entranced. Had they had their way, Higgins sewing machine model A serial number One would have been sold then and there.

They did not have their way, however. Higgins A1 would never be sold—though in future years, some collectors would offer truly exorbitant sums trying to buy it.

Karl was, in his staid stolid way, rather entranced himself. He had seen the Singer work. He had known this was coming, but he had not seen the look on his youngest daughter's face when something that would have taken her hours and would still not be done to her sisters' satisfaction was done neatly and evenly, in less than a minute.

There was definitely a market, but how were the tailors going to react? There were none present today. There were guild rules and there were laws about who could make clothes, but no rules about using machines to make clothing. Not yet, anyway. Karl got to meet several people he had wanted to meet for some time. The Wendells, and Dave Marcantonio especially. He needed to know things before he decided what to do.

Food had been cooked, and brought by guests. There was not nearly enough Coca-Cola for all the guests, so it stayed in the fridge. Beer and Kool-Aid were available though. Conversation flowed. Problems were brought up. The cost of the sewing machines was still very high. The value of the company had jumped sharply from what it had been just the day before. Legal questions about children running a company, that had seemed less important when it was a hobby in all but name, were asked. Where would sewing machines be sold? How would they be sold? Sarah Wendell held forth on the subjects of dealerships and "rent with an option to buy."

David Bartley wandered around the party, getting more and more worried as time went on. Aside from Mr. and Mrs. Wendell, there were some other members of the finance committee, and they were busy questioning whether children should be allowed to manage such a potentially valuable export. Mr. Schmidt was asking about the possibility of buying production machines from Mr. Marcantonio. Was he planning on going into competition with them? With the completion of the first working sewing machine, they had reappeared on adult radar, and were in real danger of being shot out of the sky. For their own good, of course.

David didn't trust the motives of those that expressed doubts children could run a company. It seemed to him that many of them were searching for ways to jump onto the gravy train now it looked like it was going to pull out of the station and actually go somewhere. Others appeared to resent their success in the face of adult wisdom.

October 12, 1631: Grantville High School

Sarah had bad news. "I've been checking into the laws regarding corporations. It is illegal in West Virginia for minors to be on the board of a corporation."

"But we're not in West Virginia," insisted Brent. "We're in Germany." He knew better, he was just upset.

"It doesn't matter." Sarah shook her head. "Grantville corporate law is West Virginia corporate law without so much as a period changed. Maybe we should forget about incorporating."

"Maybe not," said David. That moved everyone's stares from Sarah to him. "I was listening to some of the people at the party yesterday. They were worried about leaving the Higgins Sewing Machine Company in our hands. When we actually built a sewing machine, some of the grownups that were never too keen on the kids running a company started paying attention again. Incorporation may be a way to satisfy them, without having them take over. Sarah, are there any other jobs in a corporation that a minor can't hold, like say Chief Engineer, CEO, CFO, any of that stuff?"

"I don't think so. In fact there almost can't be. What jobs there are in a corporation changes from corporation to corporation. How could they make it illegal when all the corporation had to do to get around the law is change the name of the job?"

"Is there a law against a minor owning stock or voting stock?"

"Not owning, I'm pretty sure. Voting I don't know. I think it would be like other stuff kids own. Their parents could probably veto their selling it, and vote the stock for them, or maybe not. It could be something determined in the corporation's bylaws. I can probably find out."

"We can incorporate and select the people on the board of directors, and the people that don't like the idea of kids running a company can look and see that the board of directors is made up of responsible grownups. 'We ain't running things, just doing our jobs the way the board tells us to'." David grinned. "Of course, since the four of us and Grandma hold the biggest chunk of stock, we elect the board. Which will be Grandma, and a few other people. Maybe Mr. Marcantonio, and maybe your parents?"

"I don't know," mused Trent, a bit dubiously. "Mom and Dad are all right, but they take their responsibilities really seriously. So far, they have looked at this as your Grandma's company, with us helping out. We get the occasional lecture about listening to Mrs. Higgins, and the great opportunity she is giving us. I think they have sort of assumed she has been making the decisions right along."

"It's the same with my parents," said Sarah. "There may even be some truth to it. She lets us make the decisions, but she is sorta there. You do the same thing, David. When we get into a fight, you start bringing up stuff that we've forgotten then. I don't know, we're agreeing again, and we have a plan."

This came as a revelation to David. He hadn't realized the others knew what he was doing, and he hadn't realized that Grandma was doing the same thing. He wasn't sure he liked it.

Brent looked at David and started laughing. Then Trent and Sarah joined him. All this time, David had thought he was getting away with something, and all the time, the others had been letting him do it. "Anyway," David said as much to change the subject as anything, "now that we have a sewing machine, what do we do with it? And the next one, and the one after that. How do we sell them?"

"Rent with an option to buy," said Sarah. "Layaway, and in-store credit, first in nearby towns, then through dealerships. If someone wants to pay cash up front we'll take it, but I don't expect that to happen often. They are just too expensive. I figure we're gonna have to charge about four months wages for a journeyman tailor for each machine, or more. I don't think we'll sell many in Grantville. The big plus for our sewing machines is they don't need electricity, that's no big deal here."

"What about the laws restricting who can sew what?" asked Trent.

"Not our problem. If someone wants to buy or rent one, we assume that they are only going to use it to sew in legal ways. Stupid laws anyway."

"I don't know," said David. Then, seeing Sarah's

look, he held up his hands before him; fingers in the sign of the Cross, as if to ward off a vampire. "Not about the 'stupid law' part. About the 'not our problem' part. I figure the tailors' guilds will do everything they can to make it our problem. Making clothing is big business. It employs a lot of people. Some of them are going to lose their jobs. A lot of them, actually. As best as I can tell, it seems to take about a man-week to make one set of clothing. Most of that six-day week is spent just sewing the seams. That is one tailor fully employed for every fifty-two men. For one suit of clothes per-year per-man. It's less than that, but that's because most people don't get a new set of clothing every year. More like every two or three years. I've been talking to some of the German girls."

That announcement brought "woo hoos" from the guys and a haughty sniff from Sarah.

"About their hope chests," corrected David, which only made it worse. "About the sewing in their hope chests."

David tried again to get the conversation back on track. "That's mostly what's in them, you know. Clothing, blankets, bed linen, sewn stuff that they take years making, and it's not because cloth is so expensive. Well, not mostly. Mostly, it's because it takes years to sew the stuff. The women will love the sewing machines, but the tailors won't. Have any of you guys had a run-in with Hans Jorgensen?"

That bought the guffaws to a halt.

They had indeed had run-ins with Hans. In most ways, Hans was a standard down-timer kid trying his best to assimilate, but Hans hated sewing machines and sewing machine makers. It was a fairly convenient hate. He had no direct contact with sewing machines and there were only four sewing machine makers in

Grantville, all teenagers. His father was a master tailor who was now reduced to working in the labor gangs because there was not enough work in the tailor shops. Why wasn't there enough work in the tailor shops? Because the Americans had sewing machines, and aside from fitting and finishing, they didn't need tailors. Clothing, for the moment, cost less in Grantville than it did anywhere else in Europe. The difference between the cost of the fabric in a suit of clothing and the price a tailor could get for a finished suit of clothing was not enough to pay for the labor of the tailor—not without a sewing machine, and Hans' father didn't have one. Also, as the cost of sewing had gone down, the demand for new cloth had gone up and so had its price.

"I know, Hans is an a-hole," David continued, "but I feel a bit sorry for him. He was an apprentice tailor before his village got trashed, worked for his father. They get to the haven of Grantville, and find out that all the sewing machines are rented, and no one is hiring tailors. His dad is in a general labor gang, and Hans goes to school, and what is everyone in school talking about? A bunch of kids making sure that he will never be able to do the work his dad had taught him to do.

"Now that we're up and running, housewives all over Germany will bless the name of Higgins, but tailors will hate our guts. I figure that there is about one tailor for every two hundred people in Germany, and right now, every one of them is needed. Once the sewing machine becomes common, it will be one tailor for every thousand or less. So, in towns where the tailors' guild is strong, we're liable to see laws against sewing machines."

October 13, 1631: Delia Higgins' House

Delia had talked to Dave Marcantonio and Fletcher Wendell, and been lectured by Quinton Underwood. The storage lot was a real waste of resources. Ray had insisted on shed-sized steel containers instead of sheds when they had set up the storage lot. They were more expensive, but with the thick enamel paint they were a maintenance dream. They were also made of great big corrugated steel plates an eighth-inch thick. Grantville needed the steel.

No one was going to just seize them, true. Quinton Underwood gave the impression he'd like to, but that was just Quinton being his usual bossy self. Delia would be paid, and paid a fair price—more than they had originally paid for them. Plenty to put in wooden sheds and make up for the lost rent. They wouldn't force her to sell if she didn't want to. But they were right, Grantville needed the metal.

They were right about something else, too. Grantville didn't really need rows of little sheds for people to store their excess junk. What was really needed was industrial warehousing, big buildings, where raw materials could be stored for later use, and finished products for later sale. The amount of space that Dave and Fletcher were talking about would cost more than storage sheds to build, a lot more, but it would be worth more, too. To her and to Grantville.

It meant the rest of the dolls, or at least most of them, and maybe a bank loan to cover the difference. Fletcher said she could probably get a bank loan to cover the whole thing, but the monthly payment would be a killer. She would be much more likely to go broke if anything went wrong. Besides, Dan Frost had talked to her about the danger of keeping her dolls in the house when everyone knew she had the collection.

Delia knew it was the best course, but the dolls were committed. She had promised them to the kids if they were needed, and they might be yet, in spite of the fact that they were in production now. She almost dropped the idea without mentioning it. But Fletcher Wendell would probably tell Sarah and Dave would tell Kent, who would tell Brent and Trent. She hadn't asked anyone to keep the discussions secret. If she didn't bring it up, the kids would worry about it.

"You've all heard about the storage containers?"

The kids nodded. Delia told them about the possible warehouse, and what it would cost to build. Significantly more than had been invested in the sewing machine company. How long it would take. The rest of the winter and most of the spring. Even if she got use of some of the construction equipment. She told them that she could probably get a loan to cover the whole amount, but the more she could put in up front, the better it would work. "But don't worry, I won't use the dolls, they are promised to you."

Brent, Trent and David looked at Sarah. Sarah was the CFO, and incorporating was her plan.

"Dad likes to quote 'If' by Rudyard Kipling," Sarah said, "The line that goes: 'If you can make one heap of all your winnings and risk it on one turn of pitch and toss.' Then Mom says: 'If you do that I'll divorce you. Even if you win. Diversify!'"

Sarah shook her head. "We all have to gamble now. Since the Ring of Fire, everything we do, every decision we make is a gamble. Maybe they always were and we just didn't notice it before. But we don't have to gamble dumb. Risking it all on one turn of pitch and toss may be very manly. But it's not real smart. We women," she continued with a haughty look at the boys, "say things like 'never put all your eggs in one basket.' The sewing machine company is one basket. It's a good one, I think, but it's only one. The warehouse is another. You've already put some of your dolls in Higgins Sewing Machine Co. Now it's time to put some in Higgins Warehousing Co."

Sarah gave Delia an almost pleading look. "But Mrs. Higgins, please keep some for you. Besides," she continued in a much more practical tone, "the way things worked out, it will be very hard for us to go bankrupt. If we had gotten the loan, then defaulted, the bank could have taken everything we had, but since we didn't get the loan, the sewing machine parts, the production machines we have so far, and one down-time made sewing machine are ours. We have no outstanding debt. Well, except for the money we owe Mr. Marcantonio for the last production machine. We have a plan for that though, and for some other stuff that has come up.

"We think we should turn the company into a corporation. If we convert to a public corporation, with say two hundred thousand shares, we'd take a hundred thousand of them to represent present ownership, and then gradually sell off some of the other hundred thousand as needed. Even at just a dollar or two a share, we should raise enough to handle any problems that come up. Also, I am pretty sure Mr. Marcantonio will be happy to take payment in shares for the last production machine he made.

"Every new part and every new production machine is that much more value the company itself has. So we can use the work we have already done, and the equipment we already have, to get more financing through a corporate loan secured with stock or the sale of stock. We're in a much better position to do that now than we were when we started. Now we can show people working machines, and an inventory of parts."

"What about the possibility of losing control?" Delia wanted to know.

"We've talked about that," said David. "Early on, the thought of losing control really bothered us. We figured that if we showed it to an adult, they would pat us on the head and then ignore us. Or treat it like it wasn't real. Like it was a school project or something. Part of it was that we weren't really sure that it was anything more than a pipe dream. We were afraid that even if it could work, we couldn't get anyone to believe that it would work."

"But you believed in us," said Brent, "and now it's not a pipe dream."

Sarah chimed in. "Between your shares, Johan's, and ours, we would have seventy-seven thousand shares. Even if everyone else that owns a part of the company now voted for the takeover, which they won't, they would still need to buy fifty-four thousand shares. That is a lot of money, and if they spend that much, they will still be leaving us"—Sarah waved to indicate that us include Delia—"and Johan thirty-eight point five percent of the net profit on the business, while they would be doing all the work."

"But if eventually someone is willing to put up that much money to take control," said Trent, "let them have it. With our shares, we'll be able to raise the money to start another company making something else."

What Trent didn't say, but everyone understood, was that, having started one successful company, the kids would be listened to when and if they decided they wanted to start another.

"Besides there are people that want to buy stock,"

said David. "Suppliers from the towns around Grantville and kids at school."

October 14, 1631: Badenburg

There were four tailor shops left in Badenburg. There had been eight before the Ring of Fire, and they had employed sixty-seven people between them, including apprentices. The four that were left were the best and most prosperous, and now, including apprentices, they only employed twenty-three people. It was ridiculously easy for people from Badenburg and the other towns within a day's walk of the Ring of Fire to go to Grantville to buy cheaper clothing. Which is precisely what they had been doing. Several of the tailors from the surrounding towns had moved into Grantville seeking other work. Others had moved away, with a less than glowing view of Grantville.

The tailors' guild in Badenburg heard of the completion of the first locally made sewing machine the day of its completion. They hadn't been at the party, but others had, and they had been told. They called a meeting of guild members, but they could not decide what to do. If they outlawed sewing machines, all it would do was encourage people to go to Grantville to get their clothing. Assuming they could get the town council to agree to it at all, which was not likely. Badenburg's security was now dependent on the Americans in Grantville.

Sewing machines would come into Badenburg, they would do much of the tailor's work, so most of the tailors would be out of jobs. A few would actually do better, the ones who owned the shops that got sewing machines. They would make more profit on their clothing than they ever had. For the rest, it was move away, or find another job. In the middle of a war, where could they go? They couldn't afford to move when they had nowhere to go. There was work in Grantville, but it wouldn't be in the craft they had worked in for years.

Not all members of the tailors' guild were willing to accept that. There was talk of direct action. Of destroying any sewing machine sold in Badenburg and the shop of the buyer. Only talk, however; offending Grantville by destroying its products wouldn't do any good and might well do tremendous harm. No one had forgotten the Battle of the Crapper, nor had they forgotten what Ernst Hoffman and his soldiers had done to Badenburg before the Americans had stopped them. What would the Americans do if offended?

After the meeting had ended, Bruno Schroeder, Guild Master for the tailors' guild in Badenburg, visited Karl Schmidt. Karl had been a long time friend. At the same time, Bruno knew that Karl was providing parts for the sewing machine company. They had discussed it casually a couple of months ago. Karl had mentioned that the company attempting to make the sewing machines was run by children. Bruno had assumed that they were unlikely to succeed. At the time, Karl had not been all that confident in their success either. Bruno wanted to know what Karl thought now that the first sewing machine had been completed. Would they get better at it? Would they eventually be able to turn out a sewing machine a month?

Bruno was a tailor, and a high-end tailor at that, not a manufacturer. He realized that the sewing machine makers had had some set up work to do on the first sewing machine, but Bruno was an artist. Making the second set of clothing was not all that much faster than the first. The same pattern could be used, and you now had experience on the individual's fit, but the time savings were minimal. More important than that, Bruno Schroeder did not realize how quickly the Higgins Sewing Machine Company could make sewing machines because he did not want to. He had closed his eyes and put his hands over his ears. He had come to Karl hoping desperately that he could continue to do so. He couldn't.

When he explained his question, Karl looked at him as if he were an imbecile. Not for long, it took Karl only a moment to get his face back under control, but that look was a shock. Bruno was politically and economically astute, the master of his guild and a political power in his town. It had been a good twenty years since anyone had looked at him that way.

"They will have another sewing machine complete in less than a week," said Karl, as gently as he could. "Then it will get faster. There will be occasional slow-downs, especially at first, but over all it will get faster. Till there is a sewing machine for everyone who wants one, and can afford one."

For Bruno it did not mean that he had to go out of business. A lot of tailors would, but not necessarily Bruno. He had the money to buy a sewing machine; he could remain in business. What it did mean, was that the basis for his political power was dying. His guild was dying. There would be fewer tailors in the future, fewer guild members. As its numbers decreased, so too would its power. Much of the time-consuming work of tailoring would be done by the new machines. People who had worked all their lives to learn a trade would have to start over, and to the best of Bruno's knowledge, no one was taking on fifty-year-old apprentices. Nor was his concern just for the political power, he also cared about the members of his guild.

October 20, 1631: Rudolstadt

Bruno Schroeder had heard that a sewing machine had been sold to the last of the tailor shops in Rudolstadt. There was not much he could do about it and he understood the reasons. With Rudolstadt even closer to Grantville, and a smaller town, it had been hit harder by the new competition. Warner Rudolen had to be hurting. Still, Bruno wanted to see how it was working out. What Warner thought.

What Warner thought, was that he might just stay in business after all. Grantville was becoming a very crowded town. Not everyone wanted to go there. Now he could sell clothing for as little and sometimes less than they sold for in Grantville, and some of his customers had come back. He was saving on cloth because, with sewing so cheap, he cut using up-time patterns. He showed Bruno what he meant. Generally a pair of pants was cut in two sections, one for each leg, which meant you only had to sew the inner seam. But that meant the sections were shaped in such a way that more of the cloth was wasted. The up-timers cut the cloth in four sections, two for each leg, which saved on cloth, but meant more sewing. With the sewing machine he could do it the up-timer way and get an extra pair of pants out of a bolt of cloth.

He didn't have enough work, though. Not nearly enough. He could take a customer's measurements and have a full set of clothing for them the same day. He could do that by himself, and he didn't get a customer a day. He was encouraging his younger apprentices and journeyman to look for work in other trades. Without the sewing machine he would be looking for another trade.

That was when Bruno Schroeder really realized that

he could not win a fight against the sewing machine. Tailors would buy them no matter what he did.

October 22, 1631: Grantville

Bruno discussed it with the rest of the Tailors' Guild. They agreed they didn't have much choice. He then asked Karl to provide him with an introduction to the sewing machine makers. When he met Delia Higgins, he knew that even the last bit he had been hoping for would not be forthcoming. They would not agree to limit their sales to members of the tailors' guild. All that was left was to be first in line to buy one. The Higgins Sewing Machine Company got five orders that day. More than they had the machines in stock to fill. After Bruno left, they wondered why he had given in so easily.

Suddenly it occurred to David that they had been looking at it from the wrong angle. They had all read about the riot that had ruined Barthélemy Thimmonier, the Frenchman who had built the first recorded sewing machine. They had assumed that the rioting tailors who had burned him out and almost killed him had objected to sewing machines. But he now realized that things were more complicated than that.

Barthélemy Thimmonier hadn't been a sewing machine manufacturer, he had been a tailor. Well, a clothing manufacturer. When he built sewing machines, he didn't sell them, he used them. Suddenly other tailors were losing work to Barthélemy Thimmonier, and when he wouldn't sell them the means to compete, of course they were mad. They weren't mad at him for making the machines, they were mad at him for *hogging* the machines. That was the difference between him and Singer. Anyone who wanted one and could pony up the cash could buy a Singer sewing machine, but only Thimmonier could have a Thimmonier. If there was one business that the Higgins Sewing Machine Corporation must never enter into, it was the manufacturing of clothing. That way, if the tailors rioted, it would be against someone's tailor shop. Sweatshop more likely.

They had been worrying about Barthélemy Thimmonier from the beginning, afraid of ending up the victims of an ignorant mob. But Thimmonier wasn't the victim of an ignorant mob, he was the victim of an *informed* mob. A mob he had made himself because of the way he chose to make his money. If he had sold sewing machines he would have gotten rich; instead he was burned out, nearly killed, and finally died a pauper.

October 26, 1631: Grantville

The papers of incorporation had been filed and approved. The production of the first few sewing machines had made it a reasonable move, and apparently no one had looked real closely at the bylaws. At least, no one had commented on the clause that allowed minor children twelve or older to vote their own shares.

The first stockholders' meeting of the new Higgins Sewing Machine Corporation was held in the Higgins' living room. Delia Higgins was voted chairwoman of the board. Dave Marcantonio accepted two thousand shares of stock as payment for the last production machine and was promptly voted onto the board. So was Johan Kipper.

Sarah presented her plans for selling sewing machines. Brent, the plans for several new machines which would decrease the per-unit cost of production, with several interruptions from Trent. David was mostly silent, until the end.

Then he brought up the problem. No money. After they had built the first working sewing machine they had averaged two a week. They had now made five including A1, but they were going to have to stop assembling them for a while to make room in the garage to make new parts. They had sold one sewing machine to a tailor shop in Rudolstadt that had been trying to get someone to convert an up-time machine to treadle power for more than a month. They had had to use Sarah's "rent with an option to buy" plan because the shop could simply not afford to buy it outright. It would be paid off over the next year. It was probable that Mr. Schmidt would buy one for his family sometime soon. But he would probably not pay cash either. The sewing machines were just too expensive for that. Count Guenther of Rudolstadt looked to be interested in buying one and he would probably pay cash.

They had started out looking at storefront property, way too expensive. They had gradually lowered their expectations. They were now looking for a barn somewhere they could rent. As their machines didn't use electricity, the motors adding too much to the cost for the company to afford them, they had considered renting some place in one of the surrounding towns. Their problem was the complex laws about who could and couldn't do what in towns in central Germany looked likely to defeat them.

They were going to sell some stock, but how much? Mr. Marcantonio's two thousand shares had cleared

HSMC's only debt but didn't put any money in the kitty. Sarah's little sister Judy the Younger wanted in and was prepared to pay for the privilege. She had six Barbie dolls and was willing to part with five of them. They were still arguing over how many shares that would buy. Judy the Younger wanted it to be based on the price in Venice. Sarah was pushing for the price paid by Master Vespucci.

October 26, 1631: Fortney House

Judy the Younger had a plan. Judy did not have her sister's economic talent, nor did she know nearly so much about business. In most measurable ways, Judy was not so bright as her studious elder sister.

But Judy was persuasive. While Sarah had focused on, well, money, Judy had focused on people skills. She had loads of friends and somehow, magically, people often ended up doing precisely what she wanted, even her parents and sister. No one, not even Judy, was sure how it happened. She genuinely liked people, even her older sister. She laughed when she was supposed to laugh and even whined when she was supposed to whine. There are times when you're supposed to, since it makes people think they've gotten away with something. You just have to be careful not to keep it up too long. There were times when Sarah made that part difficult.

Judy's plan was amorphous, not really thought out yet. It just seemed to her that it would be great for everyone if the kids at school were stockholders in the Higgins Sewing Machine Corporation. After all, that's what Sarah said corporations were for. To let people that didn't have enough money to start a company get a piece of someone else's, and to let the corporation get enough money to expand.

Everybody wins, everybody's happy, and Judy is the one who arranged it. So everybody is happy with Judy. When Sarah had first mentioned the possibility, Judy had talked about it with some friends. There were a few select eighth graders in Grantville's middle school who had known about the incorporation before even Trent, Brent or David. They called themselves the "Barbie Consortium," but only among themselves. They weren't totally sure what consortium meant, but it sure sounded cool. There were only seven of them, but they were the most popular girls in the eighth grade. It was really quite convenient that just at the age when they were ready to give up their dolls, the dolls had suddenly become very valuable. Judy had told them of their dolls' increased value back in June.

Most of them had hidden their dolls away to escape parental embargoes on sales. All but Vicky Emerson, that is. She had sold hers. That had almost killed the "Barbie Consortium," since it had taken all Judy's persuasiveness to keep the other girls from following Vicky's example, but she had prevailed. When Mrs. Higgins had sold her dolls for so much, Judy had been vindicated. She had full control of the consortium.

Well, not control. Judy never went for control. Judy went for Influence.

Now was the time. Higgins Sewing Machines was going public. They were having the first stockholders' meeting tonight. Which was why Judy was over at Hayley's house. Only three of the "Barbie Consortium" were present but there was still much whispering and giggling. Hayley's mom did not take much notice, comfortably convinced it was about the standard things. Well, some of it was.

October 26, 1631: Schmidt House

Karl Schmidt did not have a plan. He had two plans, and hadn't decided which of them to implement. The first plan, to copy the tools and machines of the Higgins Sewing Machine Corporation and start making his own, had several drawbacks. While Karl had more and better connections outside the Ring of Fire, and in a sense more money, the kids had better connections inside the Ring of Fire, and a head start. They also had, in a sense, Ramona.

Karl really liked Ramona Higgins. Maybe he even loved her. He was no Romeo and he wasn't fourteen so there was no question of abandoning his name and house, but if he could avoid it he would prefer not to hurt her. He would also prefer not to get in a fight with David, not with Johan and his shotgun in the background, although Karl was fairly confident that guns would not come into play over this. If it had been his only option he would have done it. He had even been preparing the ground to do so until a fairly short while ago.

Granted all his preparation so far had been dual use. Not all the machines and tools useful in making the parts of a sewing machine required up-time equipment to make. Forms and tools could be made that in turn could make the production of parts easier and cheaper. Karl Schmidt was quite familiar with tricks of his trade as practiced by the craftsmen of his time, and for the last two months he had been picking up what he could of up-time notions. The combination was useful. By now he was producing most of the parts he sold to the Higgins Sewing Machine Corporation at a good profit.

The second plan had been little more than a wish.

He wished that he could get into the sewing machine business without upsetting Ramona. He even wished he could do it without going into competition with a bunch of kids. Kids that he had come to like. Until recently there had seemed no way to do it, but maybe now there was. Ramona didn't know that much about stock corporations, and neither did Karl, but Uriel Abrabanel did. Karl had learned enough to understand two things. You voted your stock by how much you had, and you did not actually have to own more than half the stock to gain control. You just needed to get a majority to support you.

The incorporation had done something else. It had decreased the chances of competing with them. As they sold stock, they would gain money. Which would eliminate one of his advantages.

November 8, 1631: Higgins House

The stock had sold fairly well. So far they had sold a bit over seventeen thousand shares. Enough for them to rent a wagon shed out on Flat Run Road, and move all the production machines into it. They had gotten their production back up to two days per machine.

One thing David found interesting and a little frightening was Sarah's little sister Judy. She had bought over eight thousand shares, for herself and some of her school friends. He had been peripherally involved because Johan had been asked to find a merchant and help with the negotiating. Johan had asked David who had in turn checked with the Wendells. Only to learn that Judy did indeed have her parents' permission to sell dolls and buy stock. They had even suggested that she ask for Johan's help. He had also learned that Judy had five dolls that she was willing to sell. He had passed on the permission but not the number to Johan.

When he got the report on the deal from Johan he realized that he probably should have passed on the number of dolls. Judy and her friends had had twenty-seven dolls, a Barbie hairstyling head and a few other toys. Johan was impressed with the girls. Aside from translating, they hadn't needed any help. Sad little eyes, crying not quite crocodile tears over having to give up their dolls. Johan's biggest trouble had been keeping a straight face. The merchant hadn't had a chance. The "Barbie Consortium," as they called themselves, had gotten an even better price than Delia had. They had then turned around and spent most of the money on stock in Higgins Sewing Machine Corporation.

Since this was precisely what Johan had been told they had permission to do, he hadn't even thought about it. Acting as an officer of the company he had just taken their money and issued the stock. Besides, they all had parental consent forms signed by their parents. True the parental consent forms didn't specify the number of shares, but then none of the parental consent forms did. It was a detail Sarah, the boys, and her parents had just failed to think would ever be significant. None of the other minors buying shares had ever bought more than a handful.

The rest of the sales to minors had totaled only a couple of thousand shares. They had done better with their down-time suppliers who had bought most of the rest. Only a few shares had been bought by up-time adults.

They needed money from the sale of stock because they weren't selling their sewing machines for cash on the barrel head. Nearly every machine they sold was effectively a loan they made to the buyer. They would get their money back plus some, but not anytime soon. The problem was the bank. Sarah had planned on selling the loans to the bank at a discount, using the contract as collateral for a loan. It was a fairly standard practice up-time, but the bank of Grantville wanted a bigger cut than Sarah wanted to give. So until they worked it out, they weren't receiving nearly as much per machine up front as it cost to make it.

November 13, 1631: Higgins house

"The bank caved; well, mostly anyway." Sarah went on to explain the deal she had reached with the bank, which bored Brent almost to tears. The important point was that they would get paid for the sewing machines when they sold them. That meant they could hire people to do the assembly and make and finish the parts so he and Trent wouldn't have to do it anymore. Figuring out how to make a sewing machine was great fun, even making the first one was fun, but by the time you have made several it's just plain work and boring work at that.

November 23, 1631: Higgins' Sewing Machine Factory

"Look, sir," said Brent excitedly to Samuel Abrabanel, "the neat thing about a sewing machine, well, one of the neat things, is that it's all structured around a two stitch cycle. One complete rotation of the power wheel is two stitches. At any point around in the spin of the power wheel the other parts are all in the same place they would be at the same point in the next rotation. Pretty much all that's in there are cams, levers and a few gears. Then a set of parts that actually do the sewing based on the position of the levers.

"The parts we make ourselves are the parts that would be really hard to make with standard seventeenth-century tools. The other parts we contract out to people like that guy Johan got in the fight with the other day."

"It wasn't a fight, Master Brent," Johan said severely. "It was bargaining." Looking at Samuel Abrabanel: "Begging your pardon, sir, these up-timers have no notion of bargaining. If they weren't so rich they'd all be penniless by now."

Johan shook his head. "It isn't just the kids. All the up-timers are like children in a way."

"Trent and I," said Sarah, with a look at Johan, "have worked it out as well as we could. We figure that making a sewing machine with seventeenth-century techniques could probably be done, but it's just barely within the techniques the very best of your craftsmen have. It would take, we guess, something over five thousand man hours."

"I know that's a lot," Trent interrupted, "but imagine just two parts, each part has dozens of places where they have to fit with the other in exactly the right way. Now add another part and another and they all have to fit together. It's a lot of delicate filing and shaping, and you can't separate the work having one master make one part and another make another. No matter how good they are the parts won't fit.

"With our machines doing the tricky time-consuming parts, we have that down to, we think, around two hundred man hours. The reason it's 'we think' and not 'we know,' is because we really don't know for sure how long it takes the contractors to make the parts we farm out. All we know for sure is how much we are being charged, and we're guessing the hours from that. When you figure labor at eight dollars an hour and add in the cost of materials, it costs us about four thousand dollars to make a sewing machine. Three thousand of that is contracted parts and blanks, another two hundred or so is putting all the pieces together and testing the machine. The rest, the key to producing them at something approaching an affordable price, is the machines you see around you."

"It's very interesting," said Samuel Abrabanel, "but why did you ask me to come here? Are you looking for a loan or an investor?"

"No, sir, not really," said Sarah. "We do sell stock and if you would like to buy some we'll be happy to sell you some, but that's not why we wanted to show you this. What we are really looking for is a distributor. We can sell a few hundred sewing machines locally. To people that come here to buy them, but as production increases we will need to establish markets in other places. To do that we need stores where people can see our sewing machines and try them out before they buy one. We're not quite ready to do that yet but we wanted to offer you the option while you were in town."

Samuel Abrabanel, as was his habit, made no commitments then. But Sarah wasn't expecting any.

December 12, 1631: Higgins House

Karl Schmidt had come to dinner again. This time, he had brought his whole family. He was probably going to formally ask for Mom's hand in marriage.

David didn't really mind. He had been getting along with Karl better the last few months, and Mom seemed happier than she had been in years. From the look on his face Adolph was probably expecting it too.

Officially they were celebrating the sale of the fiftieth sewing machine, which had happened the previous week. They were making a profit on the sewing machines now, but not enough of one. It would take them years at this rate just for the investments Delia and others had made to be paid back.

Karl said, "I would like to talk to you all about a proposal I have. I have already spoken of it to Ramona and Madam Higgins, but without your agreement they will not agree."

Karl hesitated; then: "I wish to take over the Higgins Sewing Machine Corporation. I will put in my foundry to pay for fifty thousand shares of stock. I wish to wed Ramona, and with the wedding, I will control her stock. Together with Mrs. Higgins, I would control over fifty percent of the outstanding stock. If you all agree, she has agreed to give me her support."

"Hear me out," Karl demanded, apparently unaware that no one was in any hurry to interrupt. "You four have done a tremendous thing. Four children have started a company that may someday be worth more than some kingdoms. You have brought wealth into the world, but starting a company is not the same thing as running it. Already there are others interested in producing sewing machines. So there will be competition and alternatives.

"Even if you do everything right, you will be at a disadvantage because people will not want to deal with children if they can deal with an adult. Others will find it easier to buy iron and other materials. People will say 'do you want to trust a sewing machine that was made by children having a lark? Or would you

rather have one made by mature men of consequence.'
Besides, you have schooling yet to complete, so you
will not be able to pay the company the attention it
needs."

Karl talked on. He talked about potential problems,
he talked about what he would like to do, how he
wanted to make the company grow. David looked at
his mother to find her looking at him. Her eyes begged
him not to kill this. She was almost in tears, afraid
of what he would do. He looked at Grandma as she
caught his eye, looked at Ramona, then at Karl, and
nodded. He looked to Sarah, she saw him looking at
her and gave a slight shrug.

Brent and Trent were looking rebellious and
betrayed. David caught their eyes and mouthed the
word "wait." David turned his attention back to Karl,
and the business part of the proposal. It was fair. The
foundry was worth more than twenty-five percent of
the company when you included Karl's connections
with suppliers and customers, and both would increase
in worth with the merger. He looked at Adolph, who
looked like he had bitten a lemon. Apparently he did
not approve.

Karl was running down now. Not quite sure how to
finish. Wanting to come up with something to convince
the kids. David looked back at Grandma. Karl would
take being interrupted by her better.

Delia picked up the signal. "Perhaps we should
give the kids a chance to talk it over?" she suggested. "Why don't you four go out in the garden
and talk it out."

The kids headed for the garden.

They talked it out. Brent and Trent wanted to say
no at first. It wasn't that they found the prospect of
running a sewing machine company all that exciting.
It wasn't.

"Oh, I don't know," said Trent, "I just hate the idea of losing."

"What makes you think you're losing?" David asked. "You're gonna be rich, and Karl's gonna do most of the work to make you that way. You never wanted to be the CEO anyway."

"What about you?" Brent asked "You did want to be the CEO. Don't try to deny it. We were gonna be the chief engineers, Sarah was the chief financial officer and you were gonna be the CEO. The wheeler-dealer. So how come?"

David looked at the ground. He moved a rock with his toe. Then he said quietly: "Mom. She loves the guy and I think he loves her in his way. He'll treat her right."

Then, because mush is not an appropriate emotional state for a fifteen year old boy or a captain of industry: "Besides, it's a good deal. The foundry will really increase production once it's upgraded a bit."

Sarah didn't buy the last part for a moment. Oh it was true enough, but it wasn't what had decided David, and she knew it. David was doing it for his mother. She wouldn't have fought it after that, even if she had cared, but the truth was she didn't much care. She was more concerned now with other things.

Afterword, some time later: Grantville High School

Brent and Trent were arguing as usual when David and Sarah arrived. "I tell you we don't need electricity to make it work," said Brent.

"Maybe not for that, but what is really needed is a household electrical plant."

"What's up?" asked Sarah.

"Huh?" said Brent. "Oh, we got to looking at that list. You know, the one we made up last year, before we decided on the sewing machines. A bunch of stuff on it that seemed impractical at the time might be doable after all. I think a pedal-powered washing machine would be good."

"But what we really need is a home or small business power plant," said Trent. "It opens the way for everything from toasters to TV."

Brent and Trent were off into their argument again. David and Sarah drifted off a ways.

"We're still kids," Sarah pointed out. "The bank probably still won't give us a loan, and I don't want Mrs. Higgins to sell any more dolls."

"True," said David. "But now we have the stock in HSMC, and it's really gone up since Karl took over. I think he was right about the problems people have with kids running businesses. What we need are fronts. People that will nominally be in charge, and won't scare investors away. Uh, Sarah, you wanna go out sometime?"

It just sort of slipped out when he wasn't looking. He had planned and replanned how he was going to ask her out. Then before he realized what was happening, he had opened his mouth and out it popped. That half smile, and the twinkle in her eyes as they figured ways and means of financing the terrible twin's new project. It just happened.

It took Sarah a few moments to assimilate the sudden change in conversational direction. Once upon a time, back when she had been focused on Brent, she had been sort of vaguely aware that David was interested in her. But as they worked together on the sewing machine company she had gradually gotten over her crush on Brent. She had forgotten about David's interest. Apparently he hadn't.

Pretty constant guy, David; not exactly boring, either.

While Sarah was thinking it over, David was sinking into the grim certainty that he had put his foot in it.

Here it comes, he was sure, the dreaded words: *can't we just be friends?*

"Okay," said Sarah. "When?"

The Rudolstadt Colloquy

Virginia DeMarce

April 1633

Ed Piazza squirmed as inconspicuously as possible on the hard bench of the University of Jena's anatomy amphitheater, as the debate on differing Lutheran views of the doctrine of justification by faith alone, both up-time and down-time, flew over and around his head in three different languages. Before he'd made the acquaintance of the different parties that existed among Grantville's new citizenry, he had just been naive in his assumption that only his own Roman Catholic church encompassed communicants with views as divergent as those of Francisco Franco and Dorothy Day.

The brightest idea that anyone—anyone at all—had had last winter had been Samantha Burka's suggestion that the growing tensions among the Lutherans of the United States could be dodged by taking advantage of political geography. Count Ludwig Guenther of Schwarzburg-Rudolstadt had not only built St. Martin's in the Fields Lutheran Church, of currently uncertain orthodoxy, for the benefit of Grantville's huge influx of Lutheran citizens but had also built it on *his own* land. True, Rudolstadt was part of the new little United States; but, on the other hand, the United States was a confederation and that territory was not the responsibility of Grantville itself. Thus, the Grantville government could take the high road, virtuously declaring that it did not interfere in ecclesiastical disputes, and dump the whole squabble into the lap of the Rudolstadt administration.

Consequently the count, with the assistance of his chancellor and consistorial advisors, was presiding over this circus, while Ed was watching. In any station of life, a man can find something to be thankful for.

Somebody made another reference to the *Formula of Concord*. This, Ed had learned in his desperate pre-conference dash through the applicable chapters of the *Schaff-Herzog Encyclopedia of Religious Knowledge*, supplemented by a briefing book that the new Grantville Research Center had pulled together for him from the eleventh edition of the *Encyclopedia Britannica*, had been produced fifty years earlier as part of a major effort to get all the Lutheran theologians on the same wavelength. It still served as a sort of measuring-stick for orthodox Lutheran views in 1633—and had in the twentieth century as well.

Ed glanced down toward the floor as the conscientious young man at the chalkboard, using his one good arm, quickly wrote the page reference for the audience to follow along. Jonas Justinus Muselius had been in Grantville for almost the whole two years since the Ring of Fire and had a pretty swift head and hand when it came to getting around in three languages at once. He now taught at the new Lutheran grade school next to the controversial church just outside Grantville's borders.

In his own copy of the *Concordia Triglotta*, Ed leafed over to the proper page in English. The tome not only had the *Formula of Concord*, Latin and German on the left-hand page and English with a blank column on the right-hand page, but most of the major Reformation documents that had led up to it—the Lutheran catechisms, the *Augsburg Confession*, the *Apology to the Augsburg Confession*, etc. Ed guessed that they were lucky that the Lambert kid was a devout Lutheran. He'd had that book, with the whole thing conveniently lined up in all three languages so the content matched on each pair of pages—all 1,285 of them, index included. Every participant in the Rudolstadt Colloquy now had one, included in the registration packet, which made for a hefty weight in the tote bags.

The publisher in Jena had been happy to get the order. He said cheerfully that if he had any copies left over after the conference, he'd just get someone to smuggle them into England and cause that half-Papist Laud some trouble.

Ed's pencil wiggled. A doodle bloomed on the upper left-hand corner of page 123 (*Apology of the Augsburg Confession, Art. IV. (II.), English version*) and gradually expanded to become an illustrated border all the way around the scholastics, the good works, and the "many great and pernicious errors, which it would be tedious to enumerate." The speaker, clearly, had no problems with tedium. It looked like he was going to enumerate them all. The full sleeve of his gown snagged on a corner of the book; its skirt scrunched up under him, even though he had smoothed it out before he sat down.

"What *is* a colloquy?" Ed remembered asking that question when the project of having a colloquy in Rudolstadt to smooth over the differences among and between the various factions of Grantville's up-time and down-time Lutherans was first brought up. Innocence, blessed innocence! Now he knew. Colloquies were events whereby someone put dissenting parties of theologians and their adherents into a room with spectators and insisted that they keep talking until they reached some sort of a resolution on the controversial issues.

Colloquies did not have time clocks.

This colloquy involved the Flacians, orthodox Lutherans on the model of Matthaeus Flacius Illyricus, and the Philippists, slightly less stringently orthodox Lutherans on the model of Philip Melanchthon—from the 1633 here and now. The two factions had been disputing since Luther's death, and they were disputing still. In addition to these by-now classic components, it had as a plus factor those interesting up-time equivalents, the Missouri Synod, a largely German-heritage and theologically orthodox organization of Lutherans in the up-time USA, and the ELCA, or Evangelical Lutheran Church in America, which appeared to Ed to be pretty much the outcome of a multi-stage amalgamation of the descendants of Swedish, Norwegian, Finnish, Danish, and some portion of German Lutheran immigrant churches.

The colloquy was thus providing an excuse for half the academics on the continent, plus a few from the British Isles, to see the Americans for themselves while billing the trip to their employers. As a result, it had grown to the point that no place in Rudolstadt, a county seat that had a population of slightly over a thousand residents two years ago and only half again that many now, could cope with the attendance. Therefore, they were having the Rudolstadt Colloquy some twenty miles down the Saale River to the north, in the university town of Jena, whose permanent population regarded it as a great financial boon. A rousing theological colloquy was an event which attracted not only theologians, but politicians, visitors who came for the entertainment, souvenir salesmen, and food vendors. Outside, in Jena's market square, beverage booths were vying with street musicians, while booksellers displayed their wares next to pretzel bakers. Almost every house in the town was crammed to the rafters with temporary boarders.

Ed thought idly that if the debate should degenerate into a riot, anyone with a strong right arm and the three and a half pounds of the *Concordia Triglotta* in a tote bag could do a lot of damage to an opponent—though, luckily, it was a paperback. In the seventeenth century, book printing and book binding were separate trades, and anyone who wanted a cover on his book usually took it to a binder after he had bought it. True, Count Ludwig Guenther had assured him that any riot was more likely to take place outside in the streets rather than among the participants themselves, but half the people outside—farmers and artisans, students and merchants, journeymen and apprentices, male and female—had bought a copy of the book, too. It was by far the most popular souvenir for visitors to take home.

The man next to him shifted restlessly. Ed looked over and saw that his Latin text had acquired an even more elaborate decoration than his own, in pen rather than pencil. The thin-faced little man returned the glance, with a surreptitious grin, and penned a question in the margin of page 122.

You American?

Yes. Ed Piazza. Grantville.

Leopold Cavriani. Geneva. Beer when they stop?

The two men came out of the university grounds into what Ed still couldn't help thinking of as a picturesque, old-fashioned, German town that would delight any right-thinking tourist. It was, he reminded himself, a picturesque contemporary German town in which dozens of people who lived in what *they* considered to be modern times were standing around an old-time West Virginia fiddler. He was sitting on an upside-down keg that had once held imported Norwegian salted herring and playing "Will the Circle Be Unbroken?" A skinny teenaged German girl was selling the sheet music.

Ed chalked up one more "Benny sighting." Old Benny Pierce, a childless widower, had been 79 at the time of the Event. *He must be 81 now*, Ed thought. Benny kept wandering around south central Thuringia with the single-minded focus of preventing the legacy of Mother Maybelle Carter from being lost. Some people—especially his nephew's wife Doreen—worried that he was going to get himself into trouble. But, after all, even Doreen admitted, you couldn't keep a grown man pinned down. Still, Ed did sort of try to keep track of him. There was no predicting where, when, or if he might someday need to be bailed out, since the grandly-named Department of International Affairs was still doing double duty as the Consular Service.

The weather was nice: that is, it wasn't actively raining. Yet. Ed and Cavriani took their beers to an outdoor table behind the restaurant. "Ahh," Ed said, as he sat down.

"Do you prefer 'Signor' Cavriani?" The Italian that Ed had learned from his grandparents was rusty, but serviceable.

"Not for a long time," Cavriani replied in German. "My first language is French. Seventy years or so ago, my grandfather was a university student, thinking modern thoughts. Seventy years ago, those thoughts were about Protestantism, naturally, but he was in Naples. So he found it prudent to leave. Of course, it's much easier to leave Naples than to leave a lot of these inland places—he just took a boat to Marseilles and from there went over to Geneva. He wrote home, telling his family that if they would send him enough money to buy citizenship, he would open up a branch of the firm. They did, he did, and we're still there—*Cavriani Frères de Genève*. Neapolitan politics are fun, of course. I still keep my hand in, a bit. Just as a hobby, you know."

"And *Cavriani Frères* deals in . . . ?"

Cavriani waved his hand. "Oh, a little of this, a little of that. You could think of us as brokers, I suppose. I rather like your up-time word—facilitators. Smoothers of paths. Those who make the rougher places plain."

Ed's mouth quirked. "You're in road construction?"

"We can ensure that a road is constructed. Or that a boat is built and crewed. That an enterprise is financed. Or even, sometimes, that an idea is spread. As the fiddler whom you watched is ensuring that an idea is spread."

Ed cocked his head. "Would it be indiscreet to ask just whom, or what, you have been facilitating in or near Grantville?"

"Ah," said Cavriani. "Not at all. My meetings with Count August von Sommersburg, if not public as to their specific content, have not been concealed. Nor has their general purpose, which is financing the expansion of his slate quarries southwest of Grantville. I assure you that my presence is known to your Saale Development Authority. I paid Mr. Bolender at the Department of Economic Resources a courtesy call as well."

Ed thought privately that if Count August was slick, his backer was likely to be even slicker. Nonetheless, Cavriani was a pleasant man to have as a new acquaintance. But "facilitators" usually were pleasant. Amiable. Courteous and easy to talk to. It was part of their stock in trade.

Cavriani was continuing. "If we could meet for dinner, I would be happy to explain the proposals we will be presenting."

But Ed had an out, at least temporarily. "Unfortunately, Monsieur Cavriani, I have a prior commitment." Ed dangled a tidbit of information to gauge Cavriani's reaction. "Margrave George of Baden-Durlach—who, as you know, is here as King Gustavus Adolphus' personal observer—has invited several gentlemen to a private supper this evening."

Ed was gratified to see Cavriani's eyes brighten, ever so slightly. He thought that, undoubtedly, the man would make it his business to find out just which among the "several gentlemen" in attendance at the colloquy would be meeting with the margrave, and equally undoubtedly would know the answer before the dinner even took place. And why not? Information would certainly be one of the major trade items purveyed by Cavriani Brothers of Geneva (not to mention by Cavriani cousins, current Cavriani in-laws, and potential husbands of Cavriani daughters, sisters, and nieces, wherever they might be found). It would be very surprising if the firm didn't have permanent correspondents at every major Imperial and CPE post office, picking up the news as fast as it came in.

Ed glanced down at his watch. "But our break is over. Back to the discussions."

They returned their beer mugs to the vendor. Ed noticed that, under the stern eye of Jena's new Public Health Security Force, the booth actually had a couple of pans of dishwater in the rear, and a boy who was washing the mugs before the owner re-used them. He refrained from commenting that the practice would be even more helpful if they occasionally changed the dishwater. One step at a time. Apparently the sanitation squad hadn't gotten to Chapter Two.

Knowing I'm on the street where you live . . .

Ed Piazza's attendance at the Rudolstadt Colloquy had not been uncontroversial within the Grantville administration. To quote Mike Stearns' explosion of the previous December: "Damn it, Ed. We've got six to a dozen major projects going and all of them need you more than we need to have you sitting in on an academic debate and listening to a bunch of guys argue about who's going to be the minister of one single Lutheran church."

Ed hadn't kept on top of every turn of the kaleidoscope for the past twenty years, watching Grantville High School's cliques and allegiances shift on the basis of both current interests and longstanding family feuds, for nothing. If any occupation could have prepared a resident of Grantville to conduct early modern diplomacy, it was experience as a social studies teacher and high school principal.

"Look, Mike," he said patiently, "we can't just do things according to our own priorities. We have to factor in the priorities of our allies. Yes, they're arguing about who's going to be minister at St. Martin's. Okay.

Point One. Specifically, they're talking about whether the minister, whoever Count Ludwig Guenther's appointee turns out to be, will be a Matthaeus Flacius Illyricus-style Lutheran or a Philip Melanchthon-style Lutheran. Point Two. Even more important for us, they're arguing about whether, if he's a Flacian, he can exclude all of the followers of Philippist-style teachings who are now living in Grantville from taking communion. And, I suppose, *vice versa*. I'm still not sure on that one."

"That still doesn't mean that you can afford to spend a week listening to them. Much less two weeks. Or three. Or a month!"

Ed continued unperturbed. "Point Three. More generally, the result of this specific decision about this church just outside of Grantville is going to be a weather vane about the overall direction that the Schwarzburg-Rudolstadt consistory is going to take. If they *do* make an exception from strict Flacian orthodoxy for the church serving Grantville—or the church*es*, since Count Ludwig Guenther is building another one on the other side of town to take up some of the overflow—then he'll be getting requests for exemption from other congregations in the county, and he knows it. If the theology faculty at Jena swallows hard and accepts an exemption in this county, they know that similar requests will be coming in from every other little city, county, and dukedom in Thuringia. What's more . . ."

Mike groaned. "There can't be more."

"Yes, there can be more. There is more. Point Four. Every Lutheran ruler in the CPE is sending a 'personal observer.' Which means that they're sending their chancellors. Gustavus Adolphus is sending a 'personal observer,' for Chrissakes! He's sending Margrave George of Baden-Durlach, and even if the man is old and getting very, very, tired, he's still been one of the most consistent defenders of the Protestant cause from the very beginning of this war. Don't count him out just because he lost a battle in 1622. He's never given up and he's taken exile rather than compromise with the Imperials."

Ed paused, then started again. "Listen, Mike. This colloquy is a *big deal*. Colloquies are academic debates, in a way, but they're academic debates on steroids. They're academic debates that affect the real world. If this war wasn't on, they wouldn't be sending 'personal observers.' They would be coming themselves: John George of Saxony, Wilhelm of Hessen-Kassel—even though he's a Calvinist himself—George of Hessen-Darmstadt, the Anhalt mini-princes, all of the Saxe-Whatever dukes. Reuss. Probably Brandenburg, even though the elector himself has turned Calvinist like Hessen-Kassel, because he's taken the unusual measure of not imposing his faith on anyone but the court personnel. Most of his subjects are Lutheran. Maybe even Prussia. The Prussian duke will be sending an observer if he has someone suitable on retainer who can get here in time. Count Anton Guenther of Oldenburg *is* coming in person, but there has to be something else behind that. If it weren't for the war, Gustavus Adolphus himself might have come. When the Reformation got started, the Holy Roman Emperor sat in on some of the religious debates."

Mike looked sour. "It didn't do the Holy Roman Emperor a lot of good, either. They've been having religious wars ever since."

Ed sighed. "Sometimes, a smaller scale can be more effective. The theologians will debate and discuss. The 'personal observers' will listen and report back. And, Point Five. At some point, while the public debate goes on and on, the 'personal observers' will get together and pool the collective wisdom of the 'patrons' of German Lutheranism about the way to go. If the 'way to go' turns out to be maintaining orthodox exclusionism, the different Lutheran parties will be back at each other's throats and the CPE will fall apart. If it turns out to be enforced mutual coexistence, no matter how much the theologians argue, we've maybe got the lever in place with which we can move the rest of Germany when it comes to religious tolerance. Capisce?"

"So the Lutheran princes will tell the Lutheran churches what to do." Mike pulled a sour face. He knew that he would have to live with the "established church" phenomenon, but he didn't have to like it.

"For the time being." Ed leaned back, touching his fingertips to one another in a reflective manner. "There really have been quite a lot of changes in the past century. Lay patrons still appoint ministers to the Lutheran churches—that's true enough. Connections still help in getting an appointment—that's true, too. But they can't appoint just any ne'er-do-well cousin who needs a sinecure. Not anymore. They pick off a list of church-approved candidates who've finished a theological course, sometimes at a university and sometimes at a seminary, and who have been examined and approved by their own church board for the principality—the consistory, it's called, mainly, or sometimes the general synod. There's no rule about what it's called. It works pretty much the same in the Calvinist principalities. Actually, a lot of it has rubbed off on us Catholics, as well. Compared to the middle ages, one thing that Europe has now is a clergy that's a lot more literate, a lot more educated, and a lot more committed to the job."

Ed grinned. "Of course, all of those things mean that as a general rule they spend a lot more time reading and arguing about fine theological points than back in the days when quite a few rural priests could barely stumble their way through the liturgy. Not to mention that the fashion for long sermons means that the parishioners hear a lot more about points of theological controversy, too. A fair number of homilies seem to encapsulate the major points that the local pastor intends to make in his next letter to a neighboring minister with whom he disagrees about the nature of the Real Presence or the significance of Christ's Descent into Hell."

Mike's eyebrows were still raised—high.

Ed persisted. "Shall I go over it again? We can't just do things according to our own priorities. We have to factor in the priorities of our allies. Mike, we're living on their street. They're our neighbors. They *care* about this. They really, really, do. Therefore, *we* care about this. Whether you want us to or not. And we *will* send a delegate of equal status to the chancellors of all those allied territories. That's me."

"So everything else gets dropped for a month?"

"No. I'll just make Arnold Bellamy 'acting.' He's perfectly capable of keeping everything else on track. If I die of the plague or get thrown off a damned horse and break my neck, he will be doing the job. That's why there's a Deputy Secretary of State."

Mike frowned a little, thinking that almost a year ago, when Grantville's delegates first met with Gustavus Adolphus, Ed hadn't been anything like this assertive. He had stood there looking very behind-the-scenes, very advice-but-not-policy, very subordinate-in-a-clear-hierarchy-of-authority. He'd had a lot of on-the-job experience as Secretary of State since then, of course, but still, how had he changed so much?

Then Mike reconsidered, and decided that it was last April that was the aberration. Ed's whole career track had been aimed at being a principal: not a vice-principal or a deputy principal. He'd run the high school with a fair amount of input—there was a faculty senate and a student council. He'd run it with good cheer, common sense, and an even temperament. But somehow no one, neither teachers nor kids nor even the county superintendent of schools, had doubted that the hand that directed Grantville High School belonged to Ed Piazza. Before the RoF, after the mine had closed, Ed had managed the single largest enterprise in Grantville, from the standpoint of budget and personnel, and he'd never been afraid to make a decision once he had the data on which to base it.

"What if I directly order you not to go?" he asked.

"If you directly order me not to go, I will stay here. But I will continue to think that you are wrong." Ed leaned forward in his chair. "Don't just take it from me. Ask the rest of the cabinet, if you want to. Bring it up for debate. But I *should* go. From beginning to end. That's where I stand."

They also serve who only sit and sit.

Ed had only brought the essentials for this stay in Jena. In his view, the essentials included an old aluminum Drip-o-lator and a thermos bottle with the kind of top that nested six different sizes of plastic cup. He could remind himself a thousand times that this was not a quaint Renaissance Faire staffed by costumed reenactors but rather the modern world—insofar as there was a modern world. Nonetheless, the thought of beer for breakfast turned his stomach. His wife Annabelle had concocted some reusable filters out of an ancient roll of gauze she had turned up somewhere. Turkish coffee arrived in beans rather than pre-ground, but he'd managed to modify a peppermill to deal with that problem. He stood in the public room of the Black Bear Inn the next morning, brewing coffee with a dramatic flourish for the benefit of his entourage.

Since the secretary of state's support staff in Jena consisted entirely of kids who had gone to high school since he joined the staff, they expected the flourish—even early in the morning. They would have been disappointed not to have it. Before he became principal, Mr. P.'s "extracurricular" had been directing all the school plays—usually teaching by doing. Ed could drop into any role. His students never quite understood how, when a demonstration was called for, a burly man of about five and a half feet, wearing a yellow polo shirt, could turn into an imaginary six-foot-tall rabbit (*Harvey*), a psychopathic killer (*Night Must Fall*), a Russian empress (*Anastasia*), or a ditzy spinster (*Arsenic and Old Lace*)—without even putting on a costume. When he became principal, his first addition to the staff had been Amber Higham as a full-time drama teacher, but he had still dropped in on the rehearsals whenever he could find a minute.

But they all knew his favorite role. "Hey, Mr. Piazza," said Tanya the radio operator, as Ed poured boiling water into the Drip-o-lator, "Give us the serenade."

The serenade was Ed's glory. Six times, during his life, he had been called to this acme of thespian desires—in high school already; in college; while he was in the army, during an R&R in Guam; three times for community theaters. He had met Annabelle during the first community theater version. It was never enough. There couldn't be too many productions. So as Leopold Cavriani came in, hoping to extract data about the previous evening's conclave of chancellors, he found the odor of coffee, six apprentice diplomats (only one of whom officially worked for the Department of International Affairs) sitting around their breakfast table wearing borrowed St. Mary's second-best choir robes that they tried to pretend were seventeenth century academic gowns, enthusiastic applause, and the secretary of state, garbed in a matching choir robe, throwing himself into a glorious basso rendition of "Some Enchanted Evening" as the sun rose.

That was another thing that Ed had learned about colloquies. They started early. The participants were not inclined to waste daylight.

"Ah, M'sieu Cavriani, good morning. Do join us. My staff—Tanya Newcomb, our tech. She's based in Grantville, in my department. I've borrowed two of them from our administrative delegations assigned to the cities of the U.S., just for the conference, to broaden their perspective a bit. Peter Chehab, Suhl; Joel Matowski, Fulda. Zack Carroll—he's in the army and will be sent to Erfurt in the fall. By the way, his sister Sara just graduated from our high school this spring and joined the army, too. Jamie Lee Swisher—she's been working as a page at our National Library, but she did such a good job getting stuff together for this conference that I've borrowed her—and if I can, I'll steal her for my permanent staff. Staci Matowski—she's taking teacher training and we hope to have her in the social studies department at the high school in a few more years. Right now, her folks said that she could come along because she's Joel's sister and he could keep an eye on her."

Cavriani recognized them—not the individual young people, but the type. He had been one, at their age. His son had recently become one. Trainees: the pool from which the designated successors would someday emerge. The only really, ah, *interesting* thing about the American staff was that half of them were girls. He stashed this in his mental file, for future consideration. Obviously, he couldn't put his daughters—*four girls to one boy! What had Potentiana been thinking of as she conceived?*—as assistant factors in most of their branch offices. It just wasn't feasible in the environment of European business. But, in a couple of years—maybe in this Grantville . . . If daughters could become contributing members of the firm, it would far more than double their personnel. In this generation, the Cavriani Frères were very short on Cavriani Fils. He would think about it. Idelette was fifteen now . . .

As soon as they were sufficiently fortified with coffee and hard rolls, Ed collected his tote bag and joined Cavriani for the walk over to the medical school. Cavriani was clearly pumping for information, but at least Ed had something to offer that was both news and would shortly be public anyway. He said solemnly, "No, Margrave George's guests found that the situation is not yet opportune to move the colloquy toward a conclusion. Late yesterday afternoon, the delegation from the University of Tuebingen theological school arrived. Nothing will be decided until they have had their chance to speak. Anything else would be gravely discourteous."

Cavriani nodded with equal gravity. Both men knew what this meant in terms of hard-bench-days.

The delegation from the University of Tuebingen theological school included all of the faculty and most of the students. Down toward the southwest, in Swabia, Bernhard of Saxe-Weimar (theoretically on behalf of the French component of the League of Ostend, but mainly for himself) and Gustav Horn (for Gustavus Adolphus and the CPE) had spent the past six months campaigning with a lot more energy than generals usually brought to the late autumn, winter, and spring seasons. Both of them were young men—Horn just turned forty and Bernhard a good decade younger. Both were energetic; both were ambitious; both had funds. They both regarded war as a combination of job and sport.

The results had been rather hard on the civilian population of the Duchy of Wuerttemberg. Among other consequences, the University of Tuebingen had closed down for the spring semester. Since staying in Tuebingen did not appear to be the best of options, any theologian who could get out of town had prudently withdrawn to Darmstadt. With a colloquy on the spring schedule, the Tuebingen Ensemble had just relocated again. After three months of exile from their classrooms, they would certainly be prepared to speak. At length.

Andreas Osiander had been a rather heterodox theologian—the Flacians had hated him. His grandson, Professor Lukas Osiander Jr., was one of the most vociferous spokesmen in favor of strict orthodoxy. He was a controversialist. He was a polemicist. He was willing to take on the Catholics and he did. He was willing to take on the Calvinists and he did. It was to be anticipated that he would relish a chance to confront not just the concept of open communion among different schools of Lutheranism, which was technically the subject of the colloquy, but more generally the dangerous underlying ideas of religious tolerance and separation of church and state. Professor Lukas Osiander Jr. was able to recognize the thin edge of a wedge when he saw one.

Cavriani winced—at the prospect of another two weeks of non-stop quotations, Ed presumed. "And, I suppose, the Jena faculty has welcomed these reinforcements with open arms?"

Ed shook his head. "Not so entirely as one might think. They're orthodox here, of course, very orthodox. But, generally, their approach isn't as confrontational as the Tuebingen style. Additionally, along the way, Osiander has attacked the works of Johann Arndt. He's proclaimed that Arndt's 'True Christianity' is contrary to the proper Lutheran doctrine of justification. Arndt was the pastor who inspired the dean of the Jena faculty to enter the ministry. . . ."

"Ah." Cavriani's hand circumscribed a spiral in front of him. "Indeed, so much of life is like that. It's not what you know, but whom you know."

The colloquy came to order.

There could be no doubt about it: the theologians of Tuebingen knew really a lot about the doctrine of ubiquity. They appeared to know even more about the supposed or alleged errors that Philip Melanchthon had made in regard to the doctrine of ubiquity. They were prepared to pursue every detail of how these errors had been maintained by Melanchthon's successors and followers since 1560.

It was not as if the communion question that was now plaguing St. Martin's in the Fields in the County of Schwarzburg-Rudolstadt was new. The Tuebingen delegation was prepared. As far as its members were concerned, they already had the answers, fully worked out. Wuerttemberg's consistory in Stuttgart, which was basically the Tuebingen theological faculty wearing different hats, had been through this only a few years ago before—with a lot of publicity—in the case of that irritating, arrogant, hard-headed, and (God be praised) recently deceased native son of the duchy, the astronomer and mathematician Johannes Kepler.

Professor Osiander was loaded for bear, Ed thought.

"No minister of the church, who wants to be a true caretaker of God's secrets, may admit a person in communion who outwardly boasts of the true evangelical religion, but in the articles of faith is not exact in all things."

Ed looked for Gary Lambert, who was in his place on the bench, far enough around the curve of the anatomy theater from Ed to be visible. He was nodding solemnly, as if to say, "Of course!" Gary was the sole representative in Grantville of the Missouri Synod, the conservative American up-time branch of the Lutheran church.

"No one who maintains a formal membership in the Lutheran church, but who privately deviates from sound doctrine, obscuring it with dubious meanings and absurd speculations, both being confused and confusing others, may be admitted to communion."

Ed frowned and penned a note to Cavriani. *How do they know whether or not he's deviating, if he does it privately?*

Cavriani cocked his head, then scribbled. *I suppose when they go to the pastor to make confession and pre-register for communion, he asks them.*

Ed frowned again, grateful for the comparatively large blank spaces in the *Concordia Triglotta* that had resulted when the three different languages used more or fewer words to say the same thing. *Catholics go to confession. Protestants don't go to confession.*

Cavriani scribbled another response: *Lutherans do. Maybe not where you came from. Or when you came from. But they do here. Or now. Whatever.*

Cavriani flipped over to a largely empty page. *It's the old "laudable custom" maneuver. Luther threw out five of the seven Catholic sacraments in*

*the sense that he defined them as "not sacraments."
But since the people were attached to them, they
turned into "laudable customs" and kept hanging
around. That's why we proper Calvinists think
they're still half Catholic. Confession is a laudable
custom; marriage ceremonies are a laudable custom;
ordination of ministers is a laudable custom; confirmation is a laudable custom. I think some of them
still perform last rites.*

Professor Osiander, at the podium, was not showing any sign of winding down. "Anyone who does not
wish to commit to the definite form of pure doctrine,
and shrinks from subscribing to the Formula of Concord as the symbol of the orthodox Lutheran church
founded in the Holy Scriptures, may not be admitted
to holy communion. Unless such a person drops his
erroneous opinion and harmonizes his beliefs with
those of the church, he must and shall be excluded.
A minister who so excludes a person who denies the
omnipresence of the Body of Christ—as the Calvinists
do and as these crypto-Calvinists who are a malignant
growth within Lutheranism do—acts in a manner that
is clearly pleasing to God."

Dramatically, Ed thought, this would be a fine conclusion, and a really good place for Professor Osiander
to stop and let everybody else get some lunch.

Professor Osiander, however, was drawing another
breath. He clearly did not approve of people who
thought for themselves in matters of religious doctrine,
"being carried away according to their own judgment
in matters of faith."

Ed thought that this was a distinctly peculiar opinion
on the part of someone who claimed to be a successor
of the man who started the Protestant Reformation by
insisting that he had to rely on the conclusions of his
own conscience and not on what someone else told

him. Evidently, for Professor Osiander, the "priesthood of all believers" didn't have room for all of "all."

Gary Lambert, again, was nodding solemnly. His up-time opponent Carol Koch, Grantville's ELCA representative to the colloquy, on the other hand, was scribbling madly, trying to keep notes.

Ed thought for a moment. He didn't think that Grantville's ELCA Lutherans had deliberately chosen Carol as their delegate in order to "make a statement" about the role of women in the church. There just weren't many up-time Lutherans in Grantville. None of them were natives of the town. It hadn't been a Lutheran kind of place before the Ring of Fire. Gary was the only one who had belonged to the Missouri Synod except for his wife, who had been at work at the hospital in Morgantown when it happened. The ELCA—Evangelical Lutheran Church in America, to use the full title—had had a grand total of ten members. Ten adults, anyway, and three teenagers who had to be pretty close to eighteen by now, if the Kochs' two weren't already older than that.

According to the story Ed had heard, the ELCA bunch, however many, had met at the Sutters' house. Billy Nelson and Melvin Sutter had declined the honor of presenting their case—before the Ring of Fire, Billy had been a truck driver and Melvin had run a filling station. Ron Koch, the only mining safety engineer in town, clearly couldn't be spared for a week or a month—he didn't have a deputy. Those three were the ELCA's sum total of adult men. There really was only one person who could take the time. Ron's wife.

"You'll just have to do it," Roberta Sutter had said. The victim—um, nominee for the honor—had been looking appalled. Roberta had reached into the armory that was available to her in her secondary role as

president of Grantville's genealogy club. "Your mother's
father was a minister. Your mom was an organist. You're
bound to have inherited some kind of a knack for it.
You'll have to do it, Carol."

When the colloquy finally—finally!—broke for lunch,
Ed saw that Benny Pierce was once more established
on his herring keg in the market square. The girl who
had been selling the sheet music yesterday was singing.
She had a high soprano, a little reedy, but with good
carrying quality—a mountain kind of voice. Ed waved
Cavriani to go on to the beer stand and wandered over.
She was singing "Lorena"—not the soupy Civil War
ballad, but Mother Maybelle's "The Sun Shines No
More on Lorena," in which a slave, taken to Kentucky
when his master moved, hears many years later that
his wife has died back in Virginia. She was singing it
in German: *"Und man sagt mir, Lorena, Du bist tot."*
The more sentimental members of the audience had
tears dripping from their eyes. Ed never ceased to
be astonished at how smoothly a lot of English verse,
such as, "And they tell me, Lorena, you are dead,"
went into German, and vice versa.

Benny stopped playing, leaned back, and stretched
his arms. "Hi'ya, Ed. Meet Minnie Hugelmair. Minnie, this guy here is Ed Piazza. If anything happens
to me, head for Grantville and ask for him. Play
something—keep 'em entertained." He handed his
fiddle over to the girl.

As Minnie started a skipping rendition of "Wild-
wood Flower," Benny said, "Y'know, Ed, if you felt
like it, you could radio down to Grantville and ask
someone to bring me up my autoharp when they're
coming. Dave and Doreen have got the key to my
bedroom. It's in there. I rented out the rest of the
place. We're doing pretty good here. I think we'll stay

to the end of this foofara, so there'll be time for it to catch up with me."

"Sure, Benny, I can do that. People go back and forth every day, so it won't take long."

"Minnie should do real good on the autoharp." Benny studied his calluses. "It might be that you'll be hearing from her ex-boss. I helped her run away."

"Might be?"

Benny grinned. "I don't guarantee he'll figure out that I'm the one who helped her. He didn't seem to be the sharpest knife in the drawer. I expect he's more likely to think it was a young guy who wanted to put his hand up her skirts than an old guy who wanted to put her hand on a fiddle bow. But anyway, he was as mean as a generous skunk and she's better off working for me, even if she was indentured to him for another three years."

"Where were you when you, ah, provided this assistance to a damsel in distress?"

"Minnie wasn't distressed. Minnie was mad. He'd promised to pay out her wages yearly and went back on the bargain—said that according to the law, he didn't have to pay until her indenture was up. She only stole what he owed her—not a *pfennig* more. Well, I watched to make sure that's all she took. Left to herself, she can be a lying little sneak, but what can you expect? She's the first real, live, foundling I've ever come across. I thought that was real interesting. She's going to be the best fiddler I've ever taught. Oh, the other? Somewhere up around Halle, on the other side of the river. I'd hitched a ride on a barge."

Somewhere up around Halle, on the other side of the river equaled Saxony. Mentally, Ed moved the concept of *possibly needing to bail Benny out* to a slightly higher rung on his ladder of priority items for the Department of International Affairs.

Waving to them both, he picked up his beer and joined Cavriani, who had acquired two bratwurst as well as a beer, plus two of Ed's staffers for company. Ed joined them happily. Among the advantages of being a Roman Catholic "personal observer" at a Lutheran conference was that he never had to sit among the head table guys when the topic was theology. They only needed him when the subject veered into politics. Behind him, he could hear that Benny was handling the fiddle again. Minnie started to sing "Coal Miner's Blues." By the time the lunch break was over, they'd made it through "Bury Me Beneath the Willow" and a bilingual version of "When the Roses Bloom in Dixie Land."

They had also attracted a new audience that Ed recognized—the delegation of Tuebingen theology students. Minnie started to sell music again, while Benny treated them to "San Antonio Rose."

It was hard, hard, hard to go back to Professor Osiander, who, when they slid into their seats a few minutes late, was announcing that: "Christ, who is the purest bridegroom of His church, does not share His love, as expressed in the sacrament, with those who have vain and blasphemous opinions."

Osiander explained the rationale which had led the Tuebingen faculty to this conclusion in the most minute detail, with frequent references to the *Concordia Triglotta*, throughout the afternoon. He defined "church" and he defined "sacrament." He defined "vain" and he defined "blasphemous." He advanced comparative instances of usage of the words in the Bible, both in Hebrew and in Greek, along with variant translations into Latin and German.

Then he defined "opinions."

Ed had picked up a rumor that there had once

been an attempt to assassinate Professor Osiander during one of his sermons. Now *if I had been on the jury . . .* he thought. On his right, Leopold Cavriani was sleeping quietly.

Cavriani, in fact, had not been sleeping. He had been pondering the question of who had been doing the German translations for Benny Pierce. He thought that Secretary of State Piazza must be so familiar with the words of Benny's songs in English that he really hadn't paid any attention to the German lyrics. Cavriani had paid attention and he knew enough of both languages to catch that, "When the roses bloom in Dixieland, I'll be coming home to you" bore a reasonable relationship to *"Als die Rosen naechst im Suden bluh'n, kehr ich ein, mein Schatz, bei dir."*

But the next verse of the English, which talked about birds singing music to the sweetest girl that the boy ever knew, bore no relation at all to: *"Wenn wir endlich von dem Kriege ruh'n, kehr ich ein, mein Schatz, bei dir!"*

The English words said nothing at all about finally resting from this war. There was a reason why he had made that "ensure that an idea spreads" comment to the American. He'd been vaguely disappointed that Piazza hadn't picked up on it. This evening, he thought, he would see where the old man and the girl went after they packed up in the market square. It would be interesting to find out who their associates were.

"My life hasn't been much, really," Benny said to Cavriani. "I graduated from eighth grade, but that's as far as it went. Fought in the Second World War. Down in Italy, it was—your name sort of rings a bell, but we've got a lot of Italians in Grantville, too. Got married. Mary Ann's family came from Lebanon. She was Catholic. I've got to say that bothered me a bit—we were Methodist teetotal at home and I was really brought up on the 'no popery' line. But she switched over, so it was fine. I used to play 'The Romish Lady' in her honor. Hmm . . . haven't played that one in quite a while. Maybe I can polish it up tonight. If you come by the market tomorrow, I'll play it for you."

Benny stopped talking for a moment to eat before his grilled cheese sandwich got cold. "These aren't bad, are they, Mr. Cavriani? They aren't burgers, but they aren't bad. Do you really want to hear more? Well, I worked in the mines most of my life. After the mine exploded at Farmington in sixty-eight—that was bad, seventy-eight men killed; only four got out—Mary Ann carried on 'til I gave in and quit. I was forty-seven then and went to driving the trucks; did that for twenty-three years. I'd figured on keeping on 'til she could collect her social security, but she died in ninety-two, before she'd even applied. I'd fiddled all my life, but after I lost her, I started fiddling pretty much full time. Galax; other competitions. Even did a few gigs at the big Tamarack tourist center down by Beckley. Wish you could have seen that place—it had quilts, jams, hand-carved duck decoys. You'd have liked it, I think. A marketplace with a roof over the top."

Benny looked at his new friend, who nodded solemnly. Cavriani wasn't able to identify half the references, but they weren't going past him. He was storing them in his mind, to be written down later in the evening and checked out as soon as he had a chance.

Cavriani glanced at Minnie, who quite obviously didn't understand what Benny was talking about either.

But, right now, she didn't care. Cavriani had ordered two whole sandwiches and a large glass of milk for her. Minnie was apparently a focused woman: she was definitely going to finish eating it all before the men stopped talking and left the Freedom Arches. For a minute, Cavriani was afraid that she'd try to cram that last half-sandwich into her mouth all at once and try to wash it down with the rest of the milk, but Benny started talking again.

"Well, anyway. Then we landed here. Sort of cramped my style, at first, but then I figured that I could hitch a ride on the carts going off to markets and I started bumming. In the beginning, all I could do was instrumentals. A guy can't sing with a fiddle under his chin. Sometimes, I'd put the fiddle down for a couple of minutes and do a verse. That went over okay, I guess. But I knew it would be better if folks could understand the words."

The old man had ordered a kettle of boiling water for a beverage, and had dropped some odd dried roots into it. He poured some of it out into a mug and rinsed his mouth.

"Sassafras tea, if you're wondering. I told you I was brought up teetotal. Still am. Want to try some?"

Cavriani had consumed stranger things when he was doing his training in the firm's various branch offices. His digestive system still remembered Aleppo well. "*Aendere Laender, aendere Sitten,*" he murmured. "How did the Americans say it? 'When in Rome, do as the Romans do.'"

He nodded. Benny poured three mugs and gave the third to Minnie before continuing.

"At first, I just did the towns and villages around Grantville. After about a year, I guess, I worked myself all the way up to Magdeburg, mostly playing one night stands—stayed a little longer in Erfurt when I passed through. Well, anyway. In Magdeburg, I met this kid who's a friend of Jeff Higgins' wife. He writes poetry in German, and said that if I sang my stuff for them, he had a friend who would copy it into sheet music. I could sell that, and make a bit more. And he'd translate the words of some of them into German for me, free. Real nice of him, I thought. He did three that first trip, but every time I run across him, he's done a couple more."

Cavriani nodded. His face showed genuine interest. Benny loved an audience.

"I didn't do so good at singing the German words, but most people didn't care. At least, they got the idea. Then I found Minnie. She can really sing them. He brought four new ones for me when he came down for this foofara. So he's the one you want to talk to, I guess. Name's Joachim. Let me write it down—they spell it like that, but they say it just like Yokum in the L'il Abner cartoons."

Benny was starting to wind down. His hands met behind his neck and he pushed his elbows and shoulders back.

"Well, Mr. Cavriani, I must say that it's been a pleasure. I do thank you for the invitation. But I'm getting to be old bones. If I'm going to polish up 'The Romish Lady' before tomorrow, we'd better be going."

"The pleasure was all mine," said Leopold Cavriani. He meant it. Sincerely.

It was Benny's favorite hymnbook. His grandma had a whole stack of them, bound in red oilcloth covers. *Apostolic Hymns. A Collection of Hymns and Tunes for all Occasions of Religious Worship and Social Singing. Containing Selections of Upward of Fifty Ministers, Music Teachers, and Singers. And a*

Comprehensive Gamut by Prof. Blackburn, Pilot Oak, Ky., edited by Elds. J. V. And R. S. Kirkland, Fulton, Ky., Assisted by Prof. A. M. Kirkland, Como, Tenn. J. V. & R. S. Kirkland, Fulton, Ky. Copyright 1898. It was thin enough to fit in the larger bib pocket of his overalls. Whenever he felt like Mother Maybelle's "Lonesome Homesick Blues" were going to take him over, he pulled it out to remember the sing-alongs they used to have.

Funny how things worked out. He had a brother and two sisters. He and Mary Ann never had any kids. Emmie and Lester never had any kids; Lester had been dead for years and he didn't think that Emmie would last much longer—she was the oldest. Homer and Hattie's kids had been left up-time; Hattie had died in ninety-eight and Homer sure wasn't well. Betty and Fletcher had a boy and a girl, but then of those two, Louise and Bill didn't have any kids and she wasn't likely to have any now, being forty-three. One little baby. Betty's great-grandson, Dave and Doreen's grandson, born in February. Benny had been back to see him once, already. Suddenly, he decided. He was going back to Grantville to see that little buster again before he started his summer tour.

Well. Back to the hymnal. He'd already taught the whole "Rudiments" to Minnie. What is a lyric? What is a tune? What is pitch? Treble clef. Base clef. Whole, half, quarter, eighth, and sixteenth notes, with how to draw them. The most frequently used times, such as 2/4, 3/4, and 4/4, with how to accent them. Rests, measures, bars; how to draw them. It was only six pages. The kid who had turned his vocal music into sheet music had acted like it was manna from heaven.

No. 35. "The Romish Lady." Benny loved "The

Romish Lady." Political correctness had never advanced very far into the life he lived. He loved all eleven verses of it.

So, it turned out the next day, did the members of the Lutheran theological faculties of the universities of Jena, Wittenberg, and Tuebingen, with assorted associates and accompanying students.

> *There was a Romish lady brought up in
>   popery,*
> *Her mother always taught her the priest she
>   must obey.*
> *O pardon me dear mother, I humbly pray
>   thee now,*
> *For unto these false idols I can no longer
>   bow.*

Professor Osiander cast a rather apprehensive glance in the direction of the U.S. Secretary of State. Herr Piazza was known to be a Roman Catholic.

> *Assisted by her handmaid, a Bible she
>   concealed,*
> *And there she gain'd instruction, till God his
>   love revealed.*
> *No more she prostrates herself to pictures
>   deck'd with gold,*
> *But soon she was betray'd, and her Bible
>   from her stold.*

But Herr Piazza was calmly drinking his beer and grinning. "Just wait," he said to Cavriani. "It gets better."

As Benny proceeded through the verses, the issue of whether it got better or worse was probably a matter of interpretation. The comparatively few English speakers in the square summarized the plot development for their friends:

> With grief and great vexation, her mother
>   straight did go,
> T'inform the Roman clergy the cause of all
>   her woe.
> The priests were soon assembled, and for the
>   maid did call,
> And forced her in the dungeon, to fright her
>   soul withal.

"I've got to have him sing this for Spee and Heinzerling," Piazza said to Cavriani. "In it's own way, it's a classic."

> Before the pope they brought her, in hopes
>   of her return,
> And there she was condem-ned in horrid
>   flames to burn.
> Before this place of torment, they brought
>   her speedily,
> With lifted hands to heaven, she then agreed
>   to die.

"You've got to admit," Ed was saying, "that it goes a long way toward explaining why two-thirds of the people in Grantville are expecting a man as civilized as Urban VIII to burn Galileo any day now. Even if they've never sung it themselves, their grandparents did. It's part of their cultural heritage."

Benny kept merrily on, as the maids-in-waiting commiserated, the victim's gold jewelry was confiscated by the avaricious inquisitors, and the raging mother reappeared:

O take from me these idols, remove them
*   from my sight;*
Restore to me my Bible, wherein I take
*   delight.*
Alas, my aged mother, why on my ruin
*   bent?*
'Twas you that did betray me, but I am
*   innocent.*

So the tormenters proceeded to light the fire. With her dying breath, the Romish Lady asked God to pardon the priest and the people, "and so I bid farewell."

About ninety-nine percent of the people in the marketplace in Jena broke into a mad storm of applause. If ever there was a song with the Right Stuff, this was it.

Benny didn't have any sheet music copies of it.

Crisis. Until Ed volunteered that if Benny would lend him the hymnal, he would take it down to the printer, stay there while he copied it off, and bring the book right back. There would be sheet music tomorrow, even if some unfortunate apprentice had to stay up with a candle all night carving out a woodcut of the musical score.

Professor Lukas Osiander, Jr., really did not understand what was happening here.

Benny segued into an encore. "Mother's Bible" was always a good one.

As Ed headed for the printer's, Benny's voice called after him: "Ed, get him to copy 'Standing on the Promises,' too. And No. 261. 'Deliverance Will Come.'"

The colloquy came to order.

Maybe Grantville's ELCA members should have

thought again before they elected a delegate whose maiden name was Unruh. Her responses to the colloquy discussions had been—disturbing. "Unrest" was a pretty mild description of the reactions that Carol's contributions to the dialogue at the Rudolstadt Colloquy had caused.

As in the matter of what she now presented as the ELCA response to Professor Osiander's exposition of the doctrine of ubiquity. The ELCA delegate's response was, as usual, brief. Carol Koch's maternal grandfather had been a pastor, but her father had been a newspaperman.

"We thank Professor Osiander for his extensive explanation of the doctrine of ubiquity. Jesus said, 'Unless you become again as a little child, you shall not enter into the Kingdom of Heaven.' I'm pretty sure that no little child has ever understood all the fine points that are so important to Professor Osiander. I'm pretty sure that no little child ever will. Talk about making a mountain out of a molehill!"

Carol sat down.

Joachim von Thalheim's eyes were glittering with enthusiasm. He had thrown himself into Committee of Correspondence politics wholeheartedly—but even among his colleagues, there were so few who really appreciated what he was trying to do. Most of them just didn't see political propaganda as an art form. Not even Gretchen. He looked across the breakfast table at the guy Benny Pierce had sent over to his room the evening before.

"So, you see, just look here." Joachim pulled out the English and German words to "When the Roses Bloom in Dixieland" and placed them side by side. "Down here."

*I've been saving all my money, to buy a little cabin
home for two.*

"Now," he said, "I've translated it as, *'Ich werde
all mein Geld ersparen.'* That's good, in itself. Most
people will understand it that way, literally, just like
the original words. But for a mercenary, his pay is his
'Gelt' and they sound exactly alike. If we're lucky, he'll
hear the song somewhere and start thinking that he
can save up, and then when he's discharged, he can
go home and see if there's a girl for him to marry
instead of turning to banditry."

"Isn't that expecting a bit of deep thought from your
average mercenary?" Cavriani asked sardonically.

"Oh, I don't expect that it will have any effect on
most of them. But, nothing ventured, nothing gained.
It's not as if it costs us anything. And every mercenary
who does go home and settle down after the war will
be one less problem for Gustavus Adolphus. One less
problem for Grantville. One less problem for all the
rest of us."

Joachim, clearly, would have been more than happy
to explain all the ramifications and potential multiple
subliminal levels of meaning, allegorical and anagogi-
cal, of every single line. He was a product of the
same educational system that had produced Professor
Osiander.

"I'd love to talk about it again," said Cavriani.
"But I have to get over to the meeting. Perhaps this
evening?"

"That's fine. I've got some people to talk to this
afternoon, and that could run into supper. Eight-ish
to nine-ish, at my place?"

"I'll be there," said Cavriani. "Probably closer
to nine-ish." He started to leave; then turned back
as if something had just casually crossed his mind.
"*'Geld'* versus *'Gelt'* may not cost your organization

anything. But you and your friends still have to eat. I know some people who might be willing to pay a fee for Italian translations of your German versions of these songs. If you're interested, I'll be glad to put you in touch."

Count Anton Guenther of Oldenburg called upon Count Ludwig Guenther of Schwarzburg-Rudolstadt. Upon behalf of his cousin Emelie of Oldenburg-Delmenhorst, who freely consented, he announced that she was delighted to accept Count Ludwig's marriage proposal.

With the foundation of the long-standing ties of blood between the two families reinforced and renewed for another generation, the two counts were able to proceed to further discussions. Each realized that the other had a problem; each realized that the other had something to offer in the way of a solution.

In spite of its strategic geographical placement *vis-a-vis* Denmark and the Netherlands, Count Anton Guenther's prudent management had kept Oldenburg neutral throughout the war. Well—he'd bribed Tilly to stay out of his lands with a gift of lots of the famous Oldenburg horses. It had been worth the cost. He had added Varel and Knyphausen to his domains. He had obtained an Imperial grant for the Weser River tolls that added substantially to his income.

There was some suspicion by orthodox Lutherans that he harbored crypto-Calvinist tendencies. Not just plain crypto-Calvinist tendencies, but Arminian, Remonstrant, crypto-Calvinist tendencies. Over the past three generations, Oldenburg had repeatedly offered sanctuary to men tossed out of the Netherlands by the stricter Calvinists. Justus Lipsius had thanked his host by complaining that the town "stank of brown coal and bacon." Count Anton Guenther's grandfather had replied calmly that this smell only signified that all of his subjects were prosperous enough to have a warm fire and meat for supper every night. Within the last few years, Hugo Grotius had enjoyed full run of the count's library while he was temporarily between employers (or, depending how one looked at it, on the lam). Oldenburg's sympathy for those in religious difficulties was sometimes extended even more widely. Jan Amos Comenius had spent some time in the library of Anton Guenther's neat little Renaissance-style residence.

Or, in other words, the counts of Oldenburg were Philippists. Tolerant Philippists. Lax, even as Philippists went.

The Count of Oldenburg's problem was a longstanding attachment to a woman of unequal birth. Elizabeth von Ungnad was scarcely a kitchen maid—her grandfather had served as Imperial ambassador to Turkey. But she was not of the higher nobility. Ferdinand II's uncompromising introduction of the Counter-Reformation had driven her family out of Austria and they had found refuge in Oldenburg. By this relationship with Elizabeth, he had a dearly-beloved namesake son, very promising, who was not entitled to inherit Oldenburg. He foresaw that his snug, well-governed, little corner of Germany would some day be torn apart by feuding cousins from Denmark and Holstein, as Juelich and Cleves had been by cousins from Brandenburg and the Palatinate.

The Count of Rudolstadt's problem, obviously, was how to resolve the quarrels among the disputatious groups of Lutherans encamped upon his doorstep.

Surely, the two of them thought, something could be arranged.

Count Anton Guenther proffered the first hypothetical suggestion. *If Ludwig Guenther could see his*

*way to granting the exemption to let Grantville's Philip-
pists take communion at St. Martin's near Grantville,*
he suggested, *then, in view of the upcoming marriage
alliance, he himself might extend feelers through his
new cousin-in-law that could possibly lead to an
alliance of Oldenburg with the CPE.*

If Anton Guenther were interested in an alliance,
Ludwig Guenther replied, *he was sure that Gustavus
Adolphus would be happy to discuss terms.* He cleared
his throat. *It was possible, of course, that such terms
might include support for young Anton's succession
to his father. There might be ways for an interested
ruler to legitimate his status, since neither of his
parents had ever been married to anyone else. If it
should be found that the mother's family were to have
been raised into the higher nobility prior to the boy's
birth, but that somehow this had been inadvertently
overlooked . . . ?*

Once the hypotheses were out in the open, more or
less, the conversation advanced to procedural concerns.
Count Ludwig Guenther commented that he would be
willing to invite the King of Sweden's personal observer,
Margrave George of Baden-Durlach to dinner the next
evening. If Margrave George proved to be open to
further discussion, the American secretary of state, Mr.
Piazza had a radio operator from Grantville here in
Jena. There was a radio operator from Grantville with
the King of Sweden. With a judicious use of these
marvelous radio communications, one might . . .

The conversation continued for several hours, every
sentence carefully kept in the subjunctive. It never
referenced the doctrine of ubiquity. Not even once.

Both men were, in their own ways, very sincere,
faithful, practicing Lutherans. Ludwig Guenther, to be
sure, was considerably more pious, but, still, Anton
Guenther was also. The doctrine of ubiquity had

never played a large role in either of their religious lives, any more than it did in the religious life of Carol Koch.

If men are from Mars, then Carol is from . . . some planet outside the solar system. (Attributed to her husband, Ron Koch.)

Privately, Ron did think that she might be from Venus. But also, as a good Lutheran, he thought that the Venus aspect of her life wasn't anyone's business except her husband's. Besides, it didn't have anything to do with the way she conducted a debate.

Ron never argued with Carol. Over the past twenty years, he had realized that there wasn't any point in it. It wasn't that she pouted. It wasn't that she sulked, or screamed, or threw things. It wasn't that she didn't fight fair.

She just didn't follow the argument script. A proper argument was like a minuet. The first speaker performed a step. The second speaker responded with the appropriate riposte. The first speaker took the next step in the dance. The second responded with the expected answer. In Ron's view, a proper argument was almost liturgical in form.

It didn't work with Carol. If he advanced with the first minuet step, she offered a mental pirouette. If, disconcerted but persistent, he nevertheless performed the second step in the minuet, Carol did a bit of a tango and added some cha-cha-cha as a codicil.

Just because they were on opposite sides of the official debate, Gary, Jonas, and Carol didn't see any reason why they shouldn't eat supper together. It was a relief just to speak plain American English for a change. While the two counts were dining with one another, the three of them occupied a corner bench at the Freedom Arches.

"They're going at it all backwards," said Carol with annoyance. "If the confirmation class mothers had taken this, 'I won't give an inch' sort of attitude, we'd never have agreed on a class time that everyone could make."

"I think," said Jonas cautiously, "that the schedule for a confirmation class really is adiaphoral. Possibly even from Professor Osiander's perspective."

"Not if one person digs in her heels and says it will be nine A.M. on Saturday or else and four of the kids can't make it then. Men! They go in and toss all these demands on a table. 'This we've got to have.' Well, they can't both eat the whole cake, so even when they negotiate a compromise, they all go home with a grudge, thinking that they've lost something."

If Dickens had been writing Carol's dialogue, she would have added, "Bah!" *Bah!* was inherent in her tone of voice.

"Er," Gary said. "That's the way negotiations are done. It's laid out in all the business textbooks."

"No." Carol was firm. "Yelling, 'it was at 9:00 on Saturday morning when I was growing up' or 'we always had it on Tuesday in our church' just causes fights. The way to do it is to make up a paper with squares, right at the beginning. The days of the week and the hours of the day. Then you take a red hi-liter and mark out what's impossible—like school hours, or when the pastor holds services at the retirement home. Everybody gets a copy of that. Then, at the first meeting, all the mothers say what's impossible for them—like Kevin's sports practice or Alyssa's flute lesson. Mark those out in orange. Then everyone says what would just be a little difficult—like, 'We might be ten minutes late some days if the traffic gets tied up.' Mark that in yellow. When you finish, you look at the white spaces that are left and you know what you have to work with. It might be that nobody in the whole room would have suggested 'after supper on Thursdays,' but if everyone can make it then, it'll do. You're down to what everyone can agree on, or at least work with. And nobody goes home mad."

Both Gary and Jonas looked deeply saddened. There had to be something wrong with that, philosophically. Politically. Somehow, such a procedure reflected a lack of strong convictions. A guy who thought that confirmation classes ought to be at nine A.M. would stick with it, come hell or high water—a firm ideological commitment. If Carol Koch was a reasonable specimen of the workings of the female mind, they could only reach one conclusion. Women were frighteningly, terrifyingly, pragmatic.

Gary had started to suspect that already, during the eighteen months of his marriage to Sheila. The all-too-short eighteen months—Sheila had been left behind by the Ring of Fire.

Jonas leaned forward, resting his chin on his good hand. "Have you guys noticed that we've got a problem?"

"Yeah," said Gary. "That's why we're here."

"No," said Jonas. "A new problem. The Tuebingen people weren't here yet when the conference started. They missed the opening statements. They had heard that Carol spoke before she delivered the ELCA response today—that I guarantee. But they hadn't seen it. They hadn't sat there when it was happening. We could get a rerun of the first couple of days of the colloquy."

Gary rested his chin on both hands. "Well, I don't care what the Saxon chancellor said, Carol, they can't have you beheaded. Two swords or no two swords. I went down to Rudolstadt last Saturday and looked it all up in the count's library. According to the law, they beheaded those crypto-Calvinists in Saxony for treason, not for heresy. You can't commit treason to the Elector of Saxony or even to the Duke of Wuerttemberg. You're not one of their subjects. He's just blowing smoke. And I'm inclined to tell him so."

"Oh, I never really thought that he would have me beheaded here." Carol looked a little reflective. "But if I ever went up there, I think he might actually try. His mouth was pretty frothy. And the professors from Wittenberg were just egging him on. But these guys from Tuebingen are even more so."

"It was the 'Philip had four daughters who prophesied' reference that really got to him." Jonas grinned. "Especially since Melanchthon's name was Philip."

Carol looked injured. "He annoyed me with the 'women should keep silence in the church' bit. I still don't understand, though, why he slammed that baton on the table so hard when I pointed out that we were in a lecture hall and not a church."

"Um," said Jonas. "Carol, has it ever occurred to you that you have a rather literal mind?"

Gary referred back to her earlier comment. "The guys from Tuebingen are 'even more so,' in a way. But they didn't ever try to behead Kepler. They just excommunicated him and wrote lots of letters. It really wasn't even them that were involved with having his mother tried for witchcraft—that was accusations from her neighbors and a local judge who didn't like their family. It's not as if *these guys* were out to get her . . ."

His voice trailed off. "I think, maybe, I'm getting an idea. Give me a couple of days to work it out."

As the colloquy droned on the next morning, Gary sat quietly at his place on the bench, fingers laced in front of him with his thumbs going around one another in circles, first clockwise and then counterclockwise, closing out the speeches and examining his idea. Gary didn't come up with a lot of ideas. He didn't have one of those sparkling, scintillating minds that threw out innovative concepts right and left. Consequently, when he did have an idea, he tended to react with a certain amount of apprehension. He was looking at this one very carefully—sort of the way that Red Riding Hood would have examined the wolf if she'd been on high alert.

The weekend came. Ed, who had conscientiously refrained from asking Tanya why the counts of Oldenburg and Schwarzburg-Rudolstadt had needed four hours of private, uninterrupted, radio communications with Magdeburg, nevertheless rode home for a long talk with Mike.

The weekend went. Ed dutifully returned to Jena. With every day that passed, those benches got harder.

Monday evening, the "personal observers" again met for supper with Margrave George. Later, Ed would describe the conversation to Mike as "acrimonious," although, in fact, as the representative of the state that had dumped the problem in the lap of the others, he had rather enjoyed it. The German word was *Schadenfreude:* delight in the tribulations of others.

It ran late. In seventeenth-century Germany and Scandinavia, religion was a matter of doctrine, but for the rulers, it was more. From the perspective of the princes, religion was important in the "here and now" because religion here and now was a way of making the population behave. In Lutheran countries the church was, if not simply, at least also, a branch of the executive government. Any change in church practice would affect the maintenance of public order—which was the reason, for example, that Christian IV of Denmark promoted orthodox Lutheranism although he privately favored Calvinism. The chancellor of Hessen-Kassel had made more than a few pithy remarks about the unsettling effects of religious change—he had lived through Kassel's switch from Lutheranism to Calvinism.

On Tuesday morning, Count Ludwig Guenther opened the colloquy with the bland statement that since all views had now been given a sufficiently full and fair hearing, the morning would be free. He carefully failed to look at the Tuebingen delegation as he made the statement about a full hearing, for fear of observing any signs that there might be a contrary opinion. The afternoon, he stated, would be devoted to short summaries. He would permit four summaries only—each of the plaintiffs, the Philippists and the ELCA, might have one representative speak. Each of the opponents, the Flacians and the Missouri Synod, might have one representative speak. He would announce his decision in regard to St. Martin's Wednesday morning. Wednesday afternoon and evening would be devoted to the closing ceremonies and a state dinner. Any delegates who lived near enough to Jena were encouraged to bring their gracious wives to the banquet. Please notify his steward of the number of attendees from each delegation. He smiled and rose.

The down-time delegations started to buzz. Who would snag the prestigious opportunity to serve as closing speaker for each position? They adjourned to squabble.

The up-time delegations didn't have to wonder who would be speaking, since each delegation consisted of one person. Within ten minutes of the count's rising, the only occupants of the anatomy theater were

Carol, Gary, and Jonas, who was leaning against the chalk board, looking a little deprived at not having a full morning of multilingual page references ahead of him.

"What now?" he asked. He dropped his chalk into the holder and sat down.

"I sure wish that I had some idea what the count's going to decide," said Carol.

"Me, too," said Gary. "But we don't."

Jonas looked at his pupils sternly. "Write! You've each got two hours to get down the basics of what you want to say. Then I've got one hour apiece to turn your English into German that says what you probably intended for it to say. Move it, guys."

"I've already got mine written." Gary started poking around in his pockets. "I knew this thing had to end some time." He fished out a sheet of paper, neatly hand-printed on both sides. "The points are in order, and I've numbered them." He handed it over to Jonas. "You can work on this now, while Carol's writing, and then you'll have more time for hers. I've got to go down to the printer's."

Gary Lambert believed, very sincerely, that he did not have the right words. If he had ever heard the maxim, "We are dwarfs, standing on the shoulders of giants," he would have subscribed to it on the spot. For the time being, he would be content if he could just achieve one goal—to sound as much like his grandfather in the pulpit as possible.

Gesturing toward the door, he said: "I have brought printed copies of the speech upon which my words are based. There are enough copies for everyone here. If you need more copies, you are certainly all welcome to have it reprinted. It was made by a far greater man than I—by the first president of the Lutheran synod that it is my honor to represent here. His name was C.F.W. Walther and he spoke these words in 1848. He spoke them just over a century and a half before the intervention of God transported Grantville to this place and time."

Gary glanced up at Count Ludwig Guenther a little nervously. The man had been good to him and had done many fine and commendable things for Grantville's refugees.

"These words are also mine, and I'm glad that I can say them before the honorable Count of Schwarzburg-Rudolstadt announces the outcome of the colloquy. We don't know, yet, what his decision will be in regard to the church of St. Martin's. Yet, there is one thing that we do know. Whatever the decision is, it will have been taken by a secular prince—a Lutheran prince, but still, a secular prince. Because of that, whatever the decision may be, we must fear that it will not have been taken entirely upon the basis of Scriptural teaching. We must fear that it will have been influenced by considerations of political expediency and pragmatic necessity. That is the very nature of civil government."

In the chair, Count Ludwig Guenther kept his face very stiff. If the young American had been speaking defiantly, the count might have reacted otherwise. But Gary's words were said more in sorrow than in anger.

"The views expressed by Professor Osiander here," Gary continued, "are in great part the views of Synodical President Walther. The church must not compromise its doctrinal stance. It cannot accept being forced to grant communion to people who hold heterodox opinions."

He paused, straightened his shoulders, and drew a deep breath. "However, the Church has no proper authority but that of the Word of God. It must not try to use the State as a tool to force the consciences of others. The position of my Synod is that there is one proper remedy for the orthodox Lutherans—a remedy that will avoid the parallel danger that the State will try to use the Church as a tool.

"Gentlemen, it is the position of the Missouri Synod"—*all one of us, you arrogant, stupid, idiot; what do you think you are doing?* a niggling little voice in the back of his mind screeched at him—"after careful and conscientious consideration of the argumentation presented here, that the orthodox Lutherans of Germany should withdraw from the State churches and form an independent synod, neither funded nor controlled by the princes."

The assembled authorities of German Lutheranism looked down from their elevated benches. From the podium that had been set up on the floor of the operating theater, a not very tall, slightly stocky, prematurely balding, dishwater-blond man with a round face, thick glasses, and a very worried expression looked back at them, all the way around the circle.

"I've also brought copies of Synodical President Walther's manual about how to set up an independent synod. The title is, *The Proper Form of an Evangelical Lutheran Congregation Independent of the State*. There are copies of that over by the door, too. I'm not a theology professor. I'm not even a pastor. My college major was in business administration and I'm the business manager for the hospital in Grantville. I'm not saying this to you from me, the person, because I have any authority. I'm saying it to you because Lutherans had tried out a lot of ways of governing their churches between the seventeenth century and the twentieth century. This—which was worked out by your descendants, who were also my ancestors—was the only one that let them hold to pure doctrine. When the Ring of Fire happened, I lost my wife and my parents. I lost all my friends and my job. But I didn't lose my faith. So I'm not going to give you any more of my words. This is how Synodical President Walther ended his speech."

Gary lifted his head.

"'Even though we possess no power, but that of the Word, we nevertheless can and should carry on our work joyfully. Let us, therefore, esteemed sirs and brethren, use this power properly. Let us above all and in all matters be concerned about this, that the pure doctrine of our dear Evangelical Lutheran Church may become known more and more completely among us, that it may be in vogue in all of our congregations, and that it may be preserved from all adulteration and held fast as the most precious treasure. Let us not surrender one iota of the demands of the Word. Let us bring about its complete rule in our congregations and set aside nothing of it, even though for this reason things may happen to us, as God wills. Here let us be inflexible, here let us be adamant. If we do this, we need not worry about the success of our labor. Even though it should seem to be in vain, it cannot then be in vain, for the Word does not return void but prospers in the thing whereto the Lord sent it. By the Word alone, without any other power, the church was founded; by the Word alone all the great deeds recorded in church history were accomplished; by the Word alone the church will most assuredly stand also in these last days of sore distress, to the end of days. Even the gates of hell will not prevail against it. "For all flesh is as grass, and all the glory of man as the flower of grass. The grass withereth, and the flower thereof falleth away; but the Word of the Lord endureth forever.'"

"Amen," Gary said.

Gary Lambert had just achieved something that no one else in human memory had achieved. Professor Lukas Osiander, Jr. was temporarily speechless.

He recovered quickly, but he realized that he was also going to have to rewrite his carefully prepared summary statement. It seemed a little . . . irrelevant.

He called for an overnight break. Count Ludwig Guenther gave him two hours.

It was possible, of course, that if Count Ludwig Guenther had granted the full overnight break that Osiander requested, the world would have turned on a different axis. But there was no way to peer into time and find out the *what ifs* and the *might have beens* of history. The count, like many others, was getting very tired of those hard benches. His secretary was writing up a draft of the decision he had already taken after his supper with the "personal representatives" at Margrave George's rooms, even as the summary statements were being publicly presented. He was fifty-two years old and he was feeling every one of them. He wanted to go back to his own quarters and sit on a comfortable chair. He definitely did not want to stretch this meeting out for another day, especially since the provisions for the scheduled closing banquet were being delivered to all the contributing—and unrefrigerated—kitchens of Jena at this very moment.

Professor Osiander spent very little of the two hour break looking at the Walther material. His colleagues and associates were alternately reading random sentences from it out loud and shouting at one another. There was no chance that they would reach agreement on a modified summary statement within the allotted time. Osiander suddenly thought that no secular ruler *should* have the right to prevent the church from making a full and conscientious examination of a crucial issue before it.

He ended up presenting his original summary. With one more sentence at the end.

"If the decision of the count should be to require an orthodox minister to extend communion to lay persons who claim to be members of his congregation, but who are not in full doctrinal agreement with the teachings of the *Formula of Concord*, then the defenders of Lutheran orthodoxy feel that they must take the step of consulting with their brethren of the Missouri Synod on possible changes in the constitution and structure of the visible church."

Wednesday morning, the chancellor of Saxony and his entourage left Jena at first light, riding hard for Dresden. The Wittenberg theologians, however, stayed behind.

Cavriani, who just happened to be leaning against the city gate when it was opened, took down a list of those departing. He and his list made it back to the Black Bear in time to have breakfast with Ed Piazza. "The distinction between Saxony's politicians and theologians is, to say the least, an ambivalent signal," he mused out loud.

Tanya promptly roused up the people napping next to other radio sets and relayed a copy of the list to Magdeburg and Grantville.

In the matter of the ministerial appointment at St. Martin's in the Fields, near Grantville, United States.

In the matter of the associated appointments of the teaching staff at Countess Katherina the Heroic Lutheran Elementary School, near Grantville, United States.

In the matter of the anticipated ministerial appointment at St. Thomas the Apostle, near Grantville, United States.

In the matter of the associated appointments of the teaching staff at the yet-unnamed Lutheran Elementary School to be constructed in connection with the church of St. Thomas the Apostle.

Count Ludwig Guenther rechecked the heading to make sure that his secretary had included everything. He didn't want to go through another one of these in the foreseeable future. Schwarzburg-Rudolstadt was a small county, only about 35,000 in total population. It had a limited budget. This colloquy had been a big financial drain, coming on top of the mandatory war contributions. He would, once it was over, have to call his Estates—the county's legislature—and request a special tax levy to cover the debts that he had incurred.

Count Ludwig Guenther had a well-known streak of financial prudence, two miles wide and two miles deep. He loathed asking for special tax levies. The Estates always wanted some kind of a *quid pro quo*. It was much better for a man to live within his means.

His announcement of the decision proceeded at a measured pace. In addition to the actual decision itself, which would come at the end, his presentation covered all the possible approaches, as his consistory saw them and upon which it had advised him, as well as the points debated in the colloquy.

There was the option of appointing an orthodox minister to both churches, allowing them to exclude those unwilling to subscribe, without reservation, to the Formula of Concord and unaltered Augsburg Confession, from communion;

There was the option of appointing an orthodox minister to both churches, but requiring them to admit such persons to communion;

There was the option of appointing an orthodox minister to one of the churches and a Philippist to the other;

There was the option of establishing a parity arrangement, in which one group used the church facility for part of the time and the other group used the church the remainder of the time, each group having its own minister;

There was the option of appointing Philippist ministers to both of the churches—who would, it was assumed, be willing to admit Lutherans of all theological views to communion.

The count evaluated the advantages of each option—carefully. Ed Piazza was a little surprised by some of the analysis. Nobody else who had spoken at the whole colloquy thus far had, for instance, addressed the question of just how far any given arrangement would require the Grantville parishioners to walk in order to attend church.

Clearly, the count said, the first option would be preferred by the theologians from Tuebingen and Wittenberg and, indeed, by those of Jena, as well as by the clerical members of the consistory of Schwarzburg-Rudolstadt. However, in his capacity as *Landesvater*, advised also by the lay members of his consistory, he found that his duty to ensure the provision of religious services to so many Lutheran immigrants, displaced from their former homes by this tragic war, was more important than the maintenance of the strictest orthodoxy. He did not feel that he could agree to an arrangement by which St. Martin's and St. Thomas would not be open to them.

Steadily, Count Ludwig Guenther moved through the points. He had, he said, concluded that on the basis of experience with applying parity between Catholics and

Lutherans for using the churches in certain German Imperial cities, the arrangement was most inconvenient for all concerned and led to ongoing, persistent, disputes and ceaseless controversies. Such an arrangement would be very difficult to administer.

The whole parity idea was new to Ed. He'd never heard of any such thing. But once more he pulled to the front of his mind the general maxim that in the 1,000-plus little political entities that made up the Holy Roman Empire, any imaginable arrangement probably existed somewhere.

Yeah, Ed thought, contemplating Tino Nobili's probable reaction to any such proposal if it were instituted at St. Mary's. *I can see how it might cause ceaseless controversies.*

Tino was one of the crosses he had to bear. If Opus Dei had ever invited Tino to join, he would have been honored to accept. Tino's kids had already finished CCD classes by the time Ed took over as chairman of the parish education committee; his grandchildren hadn't been old enough yet. Ed breathed a short prayer of thanks for God's infinite mercies and brought his attention back to the count.

Who, clearly, had moved on quite a space while Ed's mind was wandering.

"Thus, in the matter of the faculty appointments at both of the Grantville schools that our consistory is currently subsidizing, given that the teaching of religion to children prior to the age of confirmation rarely demands more than a good knowledge of the *Shorter Catechism*, we will not require more than a willingness to subscribe to the Augsburg Confession, with no specification as to altered or unaltered."

Ed looked around the room and saw young Muselius smiling brilliantly. And, why not? He had just been told that he was going to keep his job. Carol Koch had formed her thumb and forefinger into a circle. Gary Lambert's face was completely impassive.

"In regard to the ministerial appointments . . ." The count paused.

"While we do not believe that it would be feasible to institute simultaneous parity, we have decided that the ministers appointed to each parish shall be, alternately, of the Flacian and Philippist persuasions. There is sufficient legal precedent for this in the arrangements for some of the North German dioceses, whereby the administrator is alternately Catholic and Lutheran. No candidate for the ministry will be required to accept an appointment to these parishes. Therefore, any man of the orthodox persuasion who has qualms of conscience about extending communion to all of his parishioners may simply refuse the post. This, we believe, should be an adequate reservation in cases of conscience."

When Ed looked at the Tuebingen theologians, the expressions on their faces gave him the distinct impression that they did *not* regard it as an adequate reservation in cases of conscience.

But the count was not finished. Switching from the formal "we," he continued: "I specifically wish to avoid the problem that the northern dioceses have encountered, of both Catholic and Lutheran rulers appointing young, untried, untested, and insufficiently mature men to the dioceses in hopes that they will be long-lived and extend either Protestant or Catholic control for as long as possible. Such pursuit of purely political advantage is unconscionable among those who claim to hold a divinely entrusted responsibility for the spiritual welfare of their subjects."

He looked rather firmly at the "personal observer" from the Duchy of Brunswick, who had almost single-handedly caused the Monday evening meeting at Margrave George's quarters to run so late by insistently demanding that Ludwig Guenther remove this comment.

"We have decided to apply, in these cases, a concept that is not entirely strange to our own law, and which was well established in the law of the ancient Romans, but is in practice much more frequently applied by our American friends." He bowed toward Ed—the first official recognition of his presence inside the lecture hall since the first day, when all the "personal observers" had been introduced. "The appointments to these parishes shall be five-year terms, alternating. If one incumbent dies during his term of office, another candidate of the same opinion shall be nominated by the consistory to complete the term."

"This decision shall stand." The count publicly signed and sealed about two dozen copies of it that were neatly stacked on the table next to him.

"The County of Schwarzburg-Rudolstadt extends its most sincere thanks to all who have contributed to its deliberations on this important matter. The colloquy is adjourned."

To the work! To the work! There is labor for all . . .

None of the university students, whether Jena's own or the visitors, would be attending the state dinner, of course. Now that the formal closing ceremonies were over, they were milling around, somewhat at loose ends—and, in the case of those from Tuebingen and Wittenberg, bitterly disappointed with Count Ludwig Guenther's decision. Most of them decided to have another beer, since the booths that sold beer weren't even starting their close-out.

None of the ordinary visitors who had come to Jena to have a look at colloquy would be going to the state dinner, either, but those who hadn't already started for home were still wandering around, hoping to pick up bargains from some vendor who would rather not carry his stuff home. The marketplace was also full of apprentices and day-laborers who were packing up unsold merchandise, dismantling booths, and loading carts and wagons, trying to get things out of the way before the late-afternoon formal procession from the medical school to the city hall, which was where the banquet would be held.

Aside from them, as the booths were removed, the center of the square, beyond the cordoned-off route, was gradually filling up again, mostly with people from Jena itself who wanted to see the parade. Along the sides of the square, there was an unscheduled procession of maidservants and errand boys, delivering to the city hall, which had no kitchen of its own, all the dishes that the housewives of Jena had devoted their day to preparing from the provisions brought in by Count Ludwig Guenther. After they handed the roasts and pies in, at least half of them, whether with or without permission from their employers, were not returning home, but augmenting the group of spectators.

The procession was forming up, Count Ludwig Guenther's steward ensuring that all diplomatic representatives and their guests were in their proper places—that always minimized protocol disputes. It should be coming into the marketplace in just a few minutes.

Since Benny Pierce didn't have a booth, but just an upside down keg and an old backpack, he kept on performing. The sheet music sales of "The Romish Lady" had been really good. He wanted to pick up any last-minute loose change that might be flying around.

After the wild success of the week before, he'd decided to add more old-time Gospel to his Mother Maybelle mix. In spite of the fact that any thinking seventeenth-century theologian would ask a lot of questions in regard to doctrinal issues pertaining to "certainty of salvation," he'd gotten away with:

Let us labor for the Master from the dawn
    till set of sun,
Let us talk of all His wondrous love and
    care.
Then when all of life is over and our work
    on earth is done,
And the roll is called up yonder, I'll be
    there.

Even "Work, for the Night is Coming" hadn't caused any catastrophe.

Alas! Joachim had just given him a quickly translated German version of "Toiling On." Joachim hadn't stopped to think about the theological implications—it had just struck him as a rousing call to action, usable as a song for the Committees of Correspondence meetings with only minor modifications.

He had, unfortunately, left out the line about *Salvation is free.*

As the formal procession to the state dinner rounded the corner and the heralds in front entered the marketplace, Minnie sang:
Schaffe nun, schaffe nun!
Es gibt noch viel zu tun!

The town was tense enough, as it was. One of the apprentices, more than half-drunk, and obviously not having been present during the rendition of "The Romish Lady," suddenly yelled:

"Work Righteousness! The Americans are secretly teaching Popery! Right here in Jena!"

Minnie reacted fast when she saw the first cobblestone coming. "Save the fiddle!" she shrieked, pushing Benny to the ground and snatching up the herring keg, which she proceeded to wield as a three dimensional shield above his body.

Benny saw nothing wrong with her priorities. He scrabbled around the ground with his right hand until he located the violin case, pulled it over, tucked in the instrument and bow, and covered them both with his body.

Minnie's past life experiences had not been such as to give her much confidence in the civil authorities. However, Benny had firmly told her that if there was trouble, she should call, "Help! Police!" Minnie's voice really did have carrying quality. On general principles, she switched to, *"Hilfe! Polizei!"* Under the hail of cobblestones, the keg was coming apart in her hands. She started throwing the staves.

Tanya and Jamie Lee were back at the inn with the radio, which was never left unattended, but the other four kids who had come to Jena with Ed were at one of the picnic tables behind the brewery booth. Pete, Joel, and Zack headed over toward Benny Pierce at a dead run. Staci grabbed a tub of very dirty dishwater from the back of the booth and dumped it over the head of the guy who had started it.

The police had been positioned to guard the procession of notables. To get to the scene of the fight, they had to go through the crowd on the south side of the parade route, toward the booths lining the edge—since these weren't in the way of the procession, they were the last ones that would be taken down.

It was slow going. The crowd was starting to turn

to see what was going on. Parents with children were trying to go at a perpendicular angle to the police movement, to get them out to safety.

Somebody yelled, "What's going on?"

At the edge of the crowd, the reply came. "Papist spies! Somebody found a nest of Papist spies!"

Several dozen day laborers who had been working on dismantling the booths on the west side didn't have the obstacle that faced the movement of the police. They came around the edge of the crowd, not sure what was happening but anxious not to miss it, whatever it might be. One of them took a look and added another cry. "That girl's a thief! She stole money from my uncle in Dieskau. I recognize her. Thief! Thief! Thief!"

Then, to add to the general confusion, he shouted: "*Hilfe! Polizei!*"

Loudly.

Somehow, "Papist spies" had become "Imperial spies." The cry was spreading through the crowd, rapidly mutating into, "Imperial assassins! There are assassins here!"

The Tuebingen students, however, kept the original focus: "Work righteousness! Popery!" They threw themselves into the melee, swinging canvas tote bags that, by now, were weighted down not only with the *Concordia Triglotta* but with two treatises by C.F.W. Walther and any other miscellaneous books and merchandise they had bought in the marketplace. The Wittenberg students regarded this as an omen: they followed.

The two counts and the "personal observers" from the other principalities all had military experience. So did most of their invited guests. Who were, of course, wearing their dress swords. Which they drew, coming

to the assistance of law and order by following the
path that the police had blazed through the crowd and
yelling for the spectators to get out of their way.

Most of the august and dignified theologians had
participated in at least one riot during their student
days. Additionally, they felt a certain responsibility
for their current students who appeared to be, given
the number of academic gowns being worn by those
involved in the fracas, right in the middle of things.
They plunged through the crowd after the swords-
men.

All in all, it took Count Ludwig Guenther's steward
quite a while to get the procession re-formed. Dinner
was delayed by three hours.

"Well, Mike, that's the way things ended up." Ed
was finishing his debriefing. "The colloquy was about
the dangers that orthodox Lutherans perceive coming at them from creeping Calvinism. That's what
this 'crypto-Calvinism' is, when you get right down
to it—Calvinist ideas sneaking into Lutheranism. The
riot—well, it wasn't. So don't haul Erika and the others
who are in Jena to train their police over the coals.
We'd warned them, German and American alike, to
be on the alert for anti-Calvinist slogans that might
precede an outbreak of violence. There just wasn't any
logical reason for them to have their ears open for, 'No
Popery.' Not even though it's a good, all-purpose call
to an urban riot in most Protestant cities in the here
and now. If anything did break out that evening, we
expected it to be aimed at someone in the procession,
so they were all sort of looking that way, over toward
the far side, where they could hear the trumpets. It
was just a perfectly ordinary riot, as far as anyone can
tell. Conspiracy theories to the contrary."

"Give me the body count again." Mike sighed.

"Not as bad as it might have been. All things considered. Quite a few bruises and broken bones, but those heal. The bad thing is that most of them are little kids who just got trampled. It would have been worse in a closed area, but that market square is pretty open, with lots of exits. My boys got Benny off the scene and behind one of the buildings. He was a bit shaken up, but not hurt. The fiddle's okay. Minnie has a concussion—we think she got that from a cobblestone. At best, she'll have a scar from her hairline down into her left eyebrow. At worst, she may lose that left eye—Doc Adams says that it's too soon to tell. Those things make mean weapons—it sort of makes you realize why city fathers in this day and age aren't fully convinced of the merits of street paving."

"Tell me," said Mike, "just how Minnie became a citizen of Grantville. As far as I know, she'd never set foot in this town."

"Oh, that." Ed looked a little abashed. "I didn't think of it myself, I'm sorry to say. It was a great idea, though."

"What idea?"

"Benny adopted her. Right there in the alley. Things had quieted down a bit, but the 'Thief! Thief!' guy was standing over her and the Jena police were going to arrest her and send her back to Saxony to be tried. Cavriani suggested it—he thinks fast. He asked whether, since Americans had so many other Roman laws, like public offices with terms, they also had the Roman ability to do adoptions that put the adopted child on the same footing as a natural one. Carol Koch looked at him and said, 'Sure.' He's a notary—apparently it comes in handy for a guy who does a lot of procurement. He wrote out the papers then and there. Then the boys witnessed it."

"And how did the, um, 'Thief! Thief! guy' take this development?"

"Not very well. The Jena police seemed more or less inclined to take his side. That was when Carol bent over, took a running start, and rammed him in the balls with the top of her head. It distracted him—and them—long enough that we were able to toss Benny and Minnie into the government truck that had brought you and your guests up to Jena to attend the state dinner. Sorry about that, by the way. But we figured that those two needed fast transportation more than you did. Right then and there, anyway. You'll probably be hearing from the guy's uncle. I bailed Carol out. She's feeling rather smug that she finally got to use one of the techniques she learned in the self-defense for women class that Ron sort of made her take. Not that I'd really classify the way that she used it as 'defensive,' but she says that she was defending Minnie, 'so it counts.'"

Ed stretched. "How was the dinner, by the way?" The exigencies of his post-riot diplomatic activity had caused him to miss it.

"Pretty stiff. The seating was according to protocol, which meant that half of those who were seated next to one another weren't on speaking terms. Since I was the only head of state there besides the two counts, I got to talk to the Oldenburg guy. He seemed pretty pleased with the outcome."

"He ought to be pleased," Ed said. "He engineered it."

"You know," Mike commented, "this isn't the way that the story is supposed to turn out."

"What do you mean?"

"It's backwards from what we expect. It's the liberals and the progressives who are supposed to revolt against the forces of princely tyranny, ally with enlightened ideas, and forge onward toward future progress. Melissa calls it 'the Whig interpretation of history.'"

He leaned back, smiling slyly. "I wish that Melissa was here, actually. I'd really love to see her face when she gets the news that the theological liberals are still happily in bed with the established-church guys and the ultra-orthodox are showing every sign of running with 'separation of church and state.'"

Ed frowned. "That's not quite right, Mike."

"What's not quite right?"

"Theological liberals." Ed thought a few seconds; then said: "The word 'liberals' is wrong. Really, the Philippists—the 'crypto-Calvinists' that the orthodox Lutherans are so opposed to—or at least a lot of them—aren't any more 'liberal' than the orthodox. They don't believe their doctrines any less. They just think that fewer of them are essential. They'll be just as stubborn about the ones that they do consider essential."

"Oh, grief!" said Mike. "Well, 'it's a great life, if you don't weaken.' Let's get back to work."

Ed went back to his office. Sitting on a bench outside the door was Leopold Cavriani, who smiled pleasantly and asked, "Would you be interested in talking about Naples, now?"

Ed studied him for a moment. *Cavriani Frères de Genève—facilitators.*

"I'd ask who you were working for, at the moment," he said dryly, "but I'm sure the answer would confuse me even more than the fine points of theological doctrine argued at the colloquy."

Cavriani's smile now bore a remarkable resemblance to that of a cherub.

Ed shrugged. "Sure, why not? Let's talk about Naples. 'O brave new world, that hath such people in it.'"

Radio in the 1632 Universe

Rick Boatright

Introduction

The military and diplomatic radio situation in Europe at the end of the novel *1633* is a result of a unique combination of the authors' needs in the story line, the limitations imposed by the authors' choice of town to base Grantville on, and other historical accidents which left us with a wealth of some technologies and a dearth of others.

There are four important elements to the radio background of the 163x series: the environment that the planet and solar system provide due to Eric Flint choosing to start the series in the year 1632, the people of Grantville, the physical resources they have available, and the goals of their government.

The Radio Environment

From a political perspective, 1632 occurs during the Thirty Years War. From a social perspective, 1632 occurs during the "Early Modern Era." From a biographical perspective, 1632 features players who are still household names, such as Cardinal Richelieu, Galileo, King Charles the First, Oliver Cromwell, etc. It's a fascinating time and a critical point in the development of western culture. When Eric contacted me and asked that I help brief him on the possibilities for radio in 1632, it became quickly clear that from a radio specialist's perspective, Eric could not have chosen a worse time to drop a town into than 1632. Just at the beginning of the period where there are telescopic observations of the heavens, approximately simultaneous with the trial of Galileo, 1632 drops Grantville into the beginning of a time best known to science as the "Maunder Minimum."

At about the same time as Galileo published his description of his construction of the Dutch invention of the telescope, natural philosophers throughout Europe began noting that the sun had imperfections, "spots" on it. This was far easier to watch with a lens, since you could project an image of the sun onto a white sheet, and observe it without destroying your eyes. The novelty led several natural philosophers to begin a program of noting the sunspots on a regular basis. Therefore, we have an excellent European record of the number of sunspots starting with Galileo's first such observation in 1610.

This notion of the imperfection of the sun would have come as no great surprise to the court astronomers of China and Korea. In the court logs of the observations of those staff astronomers, there are sunspot records made with the naked eye going back another millennium and a half. Using those records, we can trace the sunspot number from about 28 BCE, using a reasonable relationship between the capabilities of naked-eye astronomers and those using projections and lenses.

For all of this two thousand year period of recorded observations, the number of sunspots on the surface of the sun has varied in an eleven-year cycle. As of this writing, in 2003, we are near the falling side of the peak of the current cycle with sunspots near the historic high of over 200. This extreme activity has resulted in spectacular auroras being seen as far south as 30 degrees north (Oklahoma City). At the other end of the measure, the lows have had sunspot numbers in the low teens to the mid-20s. The "average" low is between 20 and 30.

For reasons that no one understands, starting in about 1610, the number of sunspots plummeted. By 1632, which should have been a peak year, the sunspots were down to the mid-teens, and by 1640, had dropped to zero. (There is an anomalous high data point in 1639.) The 11-year cycle did continue, with peaks as high as 8 or 9 between 1645 and 1700. Then, again for reasons that no one understands, starting in 1710, the numbers went back up, and have continued quite regularly for the last three hundred years. This is *not* a "lack of observations" artifact, since the court observations in China and Korea correlate quite well with the western records. This is real.

Recent work by observational astronomers using a combination of new techniques by really really smart people on type G2V stars like our sun have figured out a way to measure the sunspot number of a star even though we cannot "image" the star. This work indicates that G2 stars may typically spend as much as

20% of their time in this "quiescent" mode. It could start again tomorrow. No one has any models for why it happens, or what causes it, or why it stopped. It's all quite confusing.

So what, you say? Well, it turns out that the number of sunspots is very highly correlated with the thickness of the upper layers of the ionosphere. There are several "layers" in the upper atmosphere, which get ionized for different reasons. These are labeled, from the inside out: D, E, F and "topside."

It turns out that the number of sunspots is very highly correlated with ability of the atmosphere to reflect radio waves back to the earth. There are several "layers" in the upper atmosphere, which get ionized for different reasons and have different effects on radio waves.

The layers are caused each day by the action of solar X-rays, ultraviolet light, and charged particles streaming out from the sun on the earth's upper atmosphere. This is the same action that splits O_2 apart and gets the free oxygen that can combine into O_3, to form the "ozone" layer. Ionization increases in the sunlit atmosphere and decreases on the shadowed side. Although the Sun is the largest contributor toward the ionization, cosmic rays make a small contribution. Any atmospheric disturbance effects the distribution of the ionization. These ionization layers form every morning at sunrise, thicken throughout the day, and then begin to fade at sunset. The combination of their chemistry and their electrical properties causes them to absorb and reflect radio waves. The amount of the ionization in each layer controls the absorption and reflection of radio waves. High frequency radio waves are absorbed by the weakly ionized D region.

Further out, the topside and F2 layers are ionized not only by UV light, but also by the action of the solar wind on the outer layers of the earth's atmosphere and its interaction with the earth's magnetic fields. During periods when there are lots of sunspots, the sun puts out a lot of particles, and these ionization layers are quite thick and robust. Without the solar action, during sunspot minima, the F2 layers are thinner and weaker.

The thicker and more robust the outer layers are, the shorter the wavelength they can refract or reflect. During sunspot maxima, the maximum usable frequency (MUF) can get as high as 30 or even 50 MHz (six meters). That is, 30 MHz signals can bounce right off the ionosphere, or be trapped between two upper layers and ducted around the world before breaking out and coming down most anywhere. That's how CB radio "skip" works, when folks listening to the radio in their cars on the highway in Kansas hear the chat between boats working the shrimps in the gulf of Mexico. Normally a CB radio is good for 5 miles, but when the sunspots are high, all bets are off.

During a normal sunspot minimum, when the sunspot count is down around 20 or 30, the MUF stays up around 14 MHz for at least part of the day, and seldom goes below 7 Mhz.

Frequency and wavelength are related. The higher the MUF, the shorter the wavelength and the smaller the antenna that is needed to send and receive radio signals. In general, one wants to use as short a wavelength as possible, because the higher the frequency, the smaller the antenna needed. A 30 MHz transmitter uses a "natural" antenna that is only three meters long. But a 7 MHz transmitter uses a natural antenna that is about twenty meters long.[§] Thus, the higher

---

[§] Wavelength in meters = 300 / Frequency in MHz. A "natural" vertical antenna is one quarter wavelength long. A "natural" horizontal antenna is a half-wavelength long.

the MUF, the more convenient it is to build radio installations. Most Hams therefore work the 20-meter bands, and the 40-meter bands are not uncommon. But it's the rare Ham who works 80 or 160 meters, since the natural antenna for 80 meters is 40 meters long, and 80 meters long for the lowest common Ham band of 160 meters.

However, remember the missing sunspots? During the Maunder Minimum, during the period that Eric has set the 1632 series in the middle of, the F2 layers of the ionosphere go away to a great extent. Of course, there is always *some* solar wind, some extreme UV, and some ionization by solar X-rays and cosmic rays. Thus there will be some ionization and some reflection. But for the purposes of the story, the tech team and the authors have decided that the MUF keeps dropping and dropping toward the lowest usable frequency (LUF) until, by the year 1640, to do long-distance communications without relays you would need to be using 2 MHz for much of the day, and can get up to 4 MHz only late at night.

And remember that the D layer *absorbs* the radio waves, so the low MUF means that you have little if any ability to do long distance communication during the day at all. The absorption of the layers defines a lowest usable frequency, an LUF. It is possible for the LUF to be higher than the MUF. Then, nothing much reflects.

No one really knows what the effect of the Maunder Minimum was on the radio characteristics of the atmosphere. Some contributors have suggested that the poor ionosphere is balanced by the low amount of interference due to the low number of radios on the air. Nevertheless, based on some reasonable guesses, the tech team and the authors have decided that *for the purposes of the 163x stories* short wave above 80 meters is pretty much useless from 1630 to 1710.

As a result of the long wavelengths, the radio installations in 1632 universe end up using *very* large antennas. The most common antenna for a diplomatic mission will be an 80M inverted V two-element beam installed this way:

Take a piece of wire, forty meters long, and cut it in the middle. Put a glass insulator in the center of it, and hook another piece of wire to each of those twenty-meter-long pieces. The "hookup" wires are held apart every few inches by a hunk of glass or plastic or wood, like a little ladder two inches wide. This ladder leads back to the transmitter. Meanwhile, take your center insulator and haul it up to the top of a tower as high as you can get. One hundred and fifty feet is really a good height. Attach the glass insulator to the tower, and then draw a line on the ground, in the direction of the city you want to talk to the most. Stretch each of the twenty-meter-long legs away from the tower at 60 degrees up from vertical, 30 degrees down from horizontal, and perpendicular to the line you drew (crossing it). Then hook the end of each wire to a rope with another glass insulator, and pull the ropes taut so that the wire is as straight as you can get it.

Now, remember how you drew a line towards the radio you want to reach, that you want to "beam" at? Build another tower, 20 feet back away from your destination, on that line. Now, do the exact same thing with another piece of wire on that tower. (You do not need hookup wires on this one.)

So, two 150-foot towers, two 40-meter long hunks of wire, suspended in the air, and lots of rope. If you want to use 1.7 MHz (160 meters) instead of the 3.5 MHz we designed this for, double all the numbers above. (Well, you can keep the tower height the same, but taller is better.)

Repeat this, as often as necessary to build a beam pointing at each city you want to talk to. A big central diplomatic radio installation will have a cluster of these beams pointing in a variety of directions and will require a clear level space a quarter of a mile on a side.

You begin see the problem. . . .

As the characters in the series approach 1640, the electronic situation in the atmosphere worsens. The MUF drops towards 1.7 MHz, and the antennas and such get bigger as above, and harder to build. It's not fun. That's why Gayle and Jeff kept muttering about the bad timing of the radio situation in *1633*. From the perspective of a Ham, they were dropped straight into hell.

What can be done about it? Several things:

1) You use a lot of power to overcome the fact that not much bounces.
2) You experiment to find the best frequencies available and use them.
3) You build good antennas.
4) You send your messages at the right time of day (generally a window about four hours long starting at sunset called the "gray line").
5) You set up relays, i.e., you send the message as far as you can, and then relay it. Thus, in *1633* the mission in Amsterdam relays to London and to Scotland.
6) You maximize the use of the power you have, by using CW (Morse code) instead of voice. Voice requires *far* better signals than CW does.

Very awkward, yes. But that's the situation until the newly emerging society can get satellites back up, which will be a long time yet—in fact, at least as long as the year 1700, which is about the same time that the short-wave bands will reopen.

In short, no matter how you slice it, long-distance radio communications will be a very different thing in the 1632 universe than what we've experienced in our own timeline. And as tube production comes on line, and high power radios go into production around the world, bandwidth for long distance communications will be a precious and rare resource. The pressure to build cables across the ocean will be even higher in the 1632 universe than it is in ours.

The Physical Resources

In addition to the physical world around them, the radio situation in Grantville is shaped by the technological world they brought with them. What radio technology does Grantville posses? What just won't work? Let's examine each of the common up-time radio technologies and consider its place in Grantville after the Ring of Fire. When Eric began writing *1632* he did a very clever thing. He decided that with a few exceptions which he has carefully limited, Grantville is based on the real-world town of Mannington, West Virginia. In general, and with a few specific exceptions (the main one being the power plant), it's safe to assume that if something was in Mannington in late 1999 or early 2000, it's in Grantville; and if something was not in Mannington then, it is not in Grantville. That presumption drives the following discussion.

Stores

There is not a Radio Shack store in town, there is no electronics store, there is no radio dealer of any kind. Some CB radios will be available at a few stores. There is one TV repair shop.

Cell Phones

Sadly, while there was a cell phone antenna and cell in Mannington and thus, in Grantville (an analogue one—no CDMA or TDMA digital cells were operating in Mannington in late '99 or early '00), the cell was not linked to the local phone switch. It was operated by a different company. And while one of the short stories from the *Ring of Fire* anthology explains that there is an excellent phone tech in town, he's not a cell phone guy. It may be possible eventually to cross connect that cell to the phone system, but in the first two years, no one has had any success at it. The manuals for the cell weren't in town, no one knows the computer passwords, and the cell was not set up for autonomous operation. The cell phones themselves are useless without the cell being attached to a billing and authorization computer system and to a phone switch. For all practical purposes, you may regard cell phones as a source for small high energy density rechargeable batteries and other electronics parts, but not as radios.

Commercial Radios

Pre-Ring of Fire handheld and base station commercial FM radios were used by the coal mine, by the electric company, the police, the school district, the city water department, etc., etc. The presumption of the 1632 authors is that these radios remain dedicated to their pre-RoF use. One radio from each incompatible frequency set was placed in the Grantville emergency Operations Center to provide cross\network links.

CB Radios

CB radios are featured in *1632* because they were owned by Mike Stearns and his friends, as well as many other residents of Grantville. CB radios are common in the U.S., particularly among rural populations prior to the wide spread of cell towers. They provided unlicensed, free, simple radio communications for a variety of purposes. It was automatic that the Stearns administration began to use the CBs to coordinate the new military actions that Grantville found itself engaged in. By the end of *1632*, CB radios are primarily used by the military for tactical coordination.

CB radios operate at 21 MHz (11 meters) and are well above the MUF described above. Without relays, they are good for one to five miles on level open ground. The signals are blocked by hills or mountains. CB radios in airplanes, or situated on mountain tops can generally talk about 20 miles line of sight. Of course, we can relay over-and-over and go any distance.

Four types of Pre-RoF CB radios exist:

1) Children's toy walkie talkies. These are useful for small-area crowd control type operations. They would have been gathered up where possible and parsed out as needed—except some kids refused to give

them over and . . . it's a free countrylet.
There are probably twenty to a hundred
total in the town.

2) "Base" stations designed to operate off the
110V mains. There are probably between
twenty and forty in the Ring of Fire
area.

3) "Walkie-talkies" that are "full power" 5-watt
mobiles, generally with cigarette lighter
power take-offs for use in cars when not
using internal batteries. This is the most
common style radio produced in the last
six years. We estimate that there are one to
two hundred of this and other high-powered
mobiles (see type 4) in the RoF.

4) High-power mobiles, 5-watt mobile radios
designed for use in cars. These and the
high-powered walkie-talkies exist in two
sub-types:

   a. AM only. Older CB radios only sup-
      ported AM modulation.

   b. Single Side Band capable. SSB gives you
      basically double the range for the same
      power. Newer CB radios have a switch
      that allows them to run SSB.

SSB radios have a second advantage in addition
to range. They can not be overheard with a crystal
radio. AM radios can be eavesdropped on with 17th
century built radios. SSB radios have built-in signals
security. SSB signals are not understandable without a
BFO (Beat Frequency Oscillator) capable receiver, and
so SSB is secure except against stolen radios capable
of tuning into the 27 MHz band. Having said that,
stealing a CB is a possibility, but they also need to
steal a battery charger, a generator, a set of batteries,

and so on. The on-ship radios for the air force and the on-ship radios for the navy are the newer SSB models.

CB Radio Use Outside the Ring of Fire Area

Managing radio outside of Grantville for tactical use by the military is non-trivial. Batteries die, there are no power lines to plug chargers into. Cars with cigarette lighter outlets don't exist. If you and your army buddies go outside the RoF and you want radios to chat among yourself for battle coordination, you have to figure out how to power them. This is tricky.

First, just forget solar power; we have no supply of solar cells in Grantville and cannot make any. The Lindsey publications book "Make your own working solar cell" aside, the copper oxide cells that are described produce so little power that a CB radio would require the entire roof of a house papered with them. High output solar cells are many decades in Grantville's future. Wind, water, steam, and cranks are how we must power electronics outside Grantville.

If someone manages to steal an up-time radio, even if they steal a set of batteries and a generator, they will still need to have a person with pretty good electronics knowledge to manage the care and maintenance of that radio and battery and generator. Destroying radios and batteries is just as likely as charging them if you are not *very* careful.

For those taking radios away from Grantville and from Gustavus Adolphus' Europe, away from steam engines and windmills, the radio heads looked to Australia's native genius Alfred Traeger for a hint. We'll be taking a page from Traeger's book. Traeger

was tasked with the problem of providing radios for
the Royal Australian Flying Doctor Service, providing medical service throughout the vast Australian
outback. No electrical generators existed. No batteries existed. Few if any of the outback stations had
electric motors or lights. Traeger developed a small,
lightweight generator with a set of pedals attached
that could be screwed down to the floor of a wooden
building in front of the table that the radio was set
on. No batteries were needed. When you wanted to
run the radio, you sat down and pedaled, and the
radio ran. This was a major benefit.

Battery management is difficult. A car battery lasts
about three thousand charge cycles. Even with careful use, the best will die within the next six years.
Once we've used up the supply of car batteries, we
will be down to wet cells of some sort. Danielle
cells, or hand-built lead-acid cells with *much* lower
efficiency than what we brought along with us can
be made. Danielle cells (wet cells) were used to
power the first radios and telegraphs and telephones.
They are well documented and simple to make, once
Grantville begins importing and refining zinc, but
they have transport and reliability problems. The
Traeger pedals solve the problem. Anywhere we
can take a radio, we can take a six-pound pedal
generator. That's not to say that our fixed installations won't also have batteries, and windmills and
steam generators. They will. But the first choice is
the Traeger pedals.

Hand-held radios will slowly become man-portable
and then fixed base operation as the supply of rechargeable batteries declines and Grantville lacks the tech
base to make new compact batteries for them. Over
the course of the first few years down-time, the battery to run a walkie talkie turns from a few C cells

into a couple of three-gallon buckets of blue goo and sulphuric acid.

FRS Handheld Radios

There will also be a small number of FRS (Family Radio Service) 49 Mhz handhelds which are FM. Gayle used one pair in *1633* to chat with Oliver Cromwell in his dungeon. Range is *very* limited (less than one mile). Plus, see the battery problem above. Less than 20 FRS radios exist in the RoF, since in 1999 they were not yet popular.

Ham Radios

You can't talk about Ham Radios without talking about Hams. The 1632 authors are blessed with a good selection of people in Grantville who know about radios, who build, operate, and collect radios as a hobby, and who have the material needed to set up a functioning communications system for the new United States (which, by the end of *1633*, is now the United States of Europe).

In late 1999, there were eighteen amateur radio operators in Mannington, and thus in Grantville. There are three Extra class (the highest), two Advanced class Hams, five General class and one Tech-plus. All those have shown Morse code proficiency. There are five Technician class Hams who have shown general class knowledge of radio operation and design. There are two Novices. One of the Extra class Hams is female.

The FCC database does not give information on original date of issue of licenses, but a number of those licensed have licenses dating back ten years, which is the expiration period. Two of the three "extras" must have studied and tested together, because their call signs are sequential.

These individuals—not them, of course, but the characters who reflect their skills in the 1632 universe—have a large variety of radios available. Several of those have been sent out with the various diplomatic missions along with antennas and antenna parts to London, to Amsterdam, and (in the upcoming novel *1634: The Galileo Affair*) to Venice. As follows:

Julie and Alex Mackay have a portable Radio Shack DX-398 and a supply of six-volt lantern batteries to power it. This is a middle range portable transister radio, designed for the mobile short wave listener. It weighs less than three pounds.

Gayle Mason has three FRS handhelds described above, a Radio Shack DX-394 receiver, and a hand-built CW transmitter and amplifier powered by a set of Traeger pedals. She has an isotron 80b antenna which she hangs out the window of the tower to use. An isotron is a very odd antenna. It looks like a six-sided aluminum box with a coil suspended in the middle. It is about 32 inches tall, 16 inches wide and 15 inches deep. It is very very different from typical "wire" antennas and is refered to by the Grantville away teams as "modern art."

Rebecca Stearns and her mission were supplied with the best radios of any team in *1633*, which makes sense, as she *is* Mike Stearns' wife. (And, leaving aside nepotism, her Holland mission is likely to bear the brunt of the relaying work for all the diplomatic missions.)

Becky has a Kenwood TS520 transceiver. It is simple to operate, plug and play, 12 V ready, 160M to 10M all band transmitter, SSB, CW, AM capable of operating at either 20 watts or 100 watts. It will "punch through" to Grantville with no problem. In the same box integrated is an excellent receiver, better than the one sent with Gayle for our purposes. Original cost was around $600. Good stuff, two revisions back from the current state of the art. It's bulletproof. It pulls 20 amps at 12V for power, exactly on target for our power budget. It was chosen from the radios available in Grantville because its tube finals will tolerate poorly matched antennas better than an all-solid-state radio would. The Holland team also has an isotron 80b antenna and wire to make a big "beam" antenna if they get a place and the time.

Radios have been assigned to the mission headed for Venice also, but as of the time this article was written those stories had not been published and a discussion of their capabilities would give away story elements currently not for publication.

Meanwhile, as of *1633*, large antenna installations are in place in Grantville, Magdeburg and Luebeck with up-time designed and built "Ham" radios for long-distance use. Due to the Maunder Minimum and the sunspot issues, long distance communications is done via Morse code at 3.5 MHz, and sometimes at 1.2 MHz.

Grantville will be building more "Ham" style radios for use by the army, the diplomatic corps, and the banking system. Using recycled parts, and arranging a relay network, Grantville can build between one hundred and several hundred CW (Morse code) radios for this purpose until they get tubes on line.

It is expected that Grantville can start tube production sometime in the late 1630s or early 1640s. (Radio tubes are very hard to make. The characters will have to reinvent a few industries to make tubes. Radio tubes are not light bulbs. They are much harder to make than light bulbs.)

Using these down-time-built but up-time-parts radios, Grantville and the USE can have world-wide communications as soon as they can train operators and send them out. The limiting factor on building down-time-built radios is the availability of high power transistors and tubes salvaged from radios and old TVs. It is unclear how many such high-power parts will be available. Transistors have a "top frequency" beyond which they become mostly useless. In order to build high-powered radio transmitters, the techs will need high-power high-frequency transistors and/or tubes. The salvaging of power supplies of dead equipment will be a booming business for a while. *Every* tube will be cherished.

If Grantville was really good at putting its junk into the dump—which, alas, was not within the Ring of Fire and remained behind in the old universe—then there will be substantially fewer high-power radios built, and spark-gap radios will become far more important than is described here.

Strategic radio, long-distance diplomatic and military communications will be CW-only (Morse code). This is due to the Maunder Minimum.

Additionally, it is presumed that we are not transmitting CW in clear, and that either one-time-pad ciphers generated off the computer screens, or reasonably sophisticated codes beyond manual cracking will be used.

However, the number of up-time parts is limited. What can they do, until they get to building down-time tubes, to make new down-time radios?

The obvious answer is "spark" radios. Spark existed long before tubes did, and they can and will build spark transmitters and crystal radios.

Details about the design and operation of spark transmitters and crystal radios will have to wait for another article. Spark transmitters and crystal radio receivers can be built with 17th century ("down-time") resources.

Broadcast Radio & TV

1632 and *1633* depict the existence of TV in Grantville. No commercial radio or TV broadcast facility existed in Mannington in 1999/2000, so it does not exist in Grantville at the time of the RoF. The high school had a TV production studio, but no transmitter. No one had a commercial TV or radio transmitter.

The TV "broadcasts" that Rebecca Stearns gave in *1632*, and which continue in *1633*, are not "over the air" but are rather "cablecast." A link was made from the TV studio in the high school to the "head end" of the cable TV system in Grantville, and shows and movies were distributed over the cable system. There was no "transmitter," no tower, and no antennas were needed.

The people participating in the 1632 Tech Manual conference in Baen's Bar discussed for a long time how to resolve the lack of a commercial radio station in Grantville. The FCC antenna tower database made it clear that no appropriate towers existed in Grantville for an AM radio station. While it would have been possible to build an FM radio station simply enough, you can not hear an FM station on a crystal radio. Since the authors of the 1632 series wanted a supply of down-time radios to be available to listen to the broadcasts of the Voice of America, it was necessary to figure out how to build a radio station.

Gayle Mason's Ham radio station could be rebuilt to provide a modestly powered AM radio transmitter, but what to use for an antenna? A natural antenna for an AM radio station is 140 feet tall. The folks in Grantville did not have such a tower, nor did they have the free steel to build one. The available steel was going into the ironclad ships and into railroad track.

Additionally, the government of the new U.S. wished to conceal its ability to talk to its remote diplomatic staff as long as possible. After months of discussion on Baen's Bar by the "Barflies," the concept of the Great Stone Radio Tower was born. Many European cathedral towers exceeded the height needed for the Voice of America transmitter tower. By building a stone antenna tower (and running copper wires down the outside to act as the active antenna elements), Grantville solved both the technical problem of building the tower, and the political problem of distracting the French and the English from the ability of Grantville to talk to its diplomats. Somehow the idea that long-distance radio requires huge massive antennas became commonplace.

By early 1634, the Voice of America will be on the air with a transmitter rebuilt from Gayle Mason's high powered Ham radio transmitter, and the Great Stone Radio Tower. Prior to the Great Stone Radio Tower's construction, the Voice of America was on the air with a variety of makeshift antennas.

The Barflies have long discussed, but no "official" author has yet mentioned, the idea that Gustavus Adolphus will not be satisfied with the Voice of America and will push for a second AM broadcast radio station to promote the concord of his nation and his faith. The Barflies refer to Gustav's station as the Voice of Luther.

The Voice of Luther will go on the air in late 1634 or early 1635 using an all-down-time built transmitter using the same style transmitter as the first broadcast AM radio station. The details of the construction of a Fessenden Alternator are beyond the scope of this article, but suffice it to say that operating this station will involve speaking into a microphone *directly* inserted into the feed line from the transmitter to the antenna while it is carrying up to 10,000 watts of power. This is *very* dangerous. Operating broadcast radio stations in 1632 is not for the faint of heart. A wrong move will result in a fried DJ.

Acknowledgement and personal note:

The technical and historic background in the 1632 series is the result of the work of a huge number of participants in the "1632 Tech Manual" conference at the Baen's Bar website.

This article attempts to summarize information from two sources: the background briefing documents prepared for Eric Flint and David Weber, and the collective wisdom of the Baen Barflies. The mistakes, of course, are my own.

The combination of people, material, and environment presented by 1632 results in a rich playing field for people who want to work on alternate history. Certainly I have enjoyed the experience. I strongly invite any of you interested to join us. There is still a lot of work to do.

End Notes:

NASA site on sunspot numbers:
  http://science.msfc.nasa.gov/ssl/pad/solar/
    sunspots.htm

Visual Large Sunspot record:
  http://alpha.uni-sw.gwdg.de/~wittmann/
    awittmann-Dateien/navbar-Dateien/
    Largespotscatalog.pdf

Extra Solar sunspots:
  http://www.ucar.edu/communications/lasers/sun/
    stars.html
  http://www.owlnet.rice.edu/~echollet/
    solcon.html

For more than you want to know about the Ionosphere see:
  http://www.ngdc.noaa.gov/stp/IONO/
    home.html

Isotron antennas:
  http://www.rayfield.net/isotron/

The Traeger pedal radio:
  http://www.antiqueradio.com/traeger_pedal_07-
    99.html

They've Got Bread Mold, So Why Can't They Make Penicillin?

Bob Gottlieb

The above is one of the more common questions asked by readers following the 1632 series, especially those who are interested in the subject of disease and medicine. Unfortunately, there is no simple answer to the question. There are thousands and thousands of different kinds of mold. True, a few of them produce various effective medicines, like penicillin. But many are useless, even leaving aside those which produce hallucinogens like LSD, or which are outright poisons. The process of isolating a *specific* mold that produces an antibiotic is expensive, time consuming, and severely constrained by the availability of resources.

The purpose of this article is to give readers who lack technical education in the subject a general overview of the problem. Let's begin by reviewing the major diseases which the characters in the 1632 series have to deal with.

Disease

There were a number of frequently fatal diseases sweeping across Europe during the Thirty Years War. The two most devastating were bubonic plague and typhus. In addition, there was smallpox, syphilis, influenza, tuberculosis, and any number of infections caused by wounds, badly stored food, and general unsanitary conditions.

The most devastating disease during the second half of the war was bubonic plague, which is often simply called "the plague." There are three forms of the disease:

- Bubonic itself, the most common form, is not usually transmitted from one person to another, and is frequently fatal;
- Septicemic, which is usually quickly fatal, often before plague symptoms even show, and is easily spread if it reaches the lungs;
- Pneumonic, in which the infection starts in the lungs and spreads to anyone breathing nearby. This version is almost always fatal, the sort of thing that gives Dr. James Nichols nightmares in the series.

Plague is caused by the *Yersinia pestis* bacterium.

It is usually spread by fleas, especially those found on rats. Plague can be treated by many antibiotics, including sulfa drugs, but it is not affected by penicillin. Modern vaccines are good for only about six months. (It is interesting to note a recent discovery that a genetic mutation in some people that makes them resistant to plague also makes them resistant to AIDS.)

Prior to 1630, the most devastating disease during the Thirty Years War was probably typhus, also called "gaol fever," "camp fever," and "the Hungarian disease." Typhus was spread from person to person by body lice, common especially with armies. The disease probably caused far more deaths during the Thirty Years War than the armies caused directly in the course of fighting battles. It devastated many German cities.

Typhus is caused by a rickettsiae, a small kind of bacteria, with the specific name *Rickettsia prowazekii*. It is fatal about one-third of the time, and more so in the sick and elderly. It is rapidly and effectively treated by the antibiotics tetracycline or chloramphenicol, but not penicillin or sulfa drugs. It can be prevented by getting rid of body lice, i.e., by sterilizing clothes, using insecticides, and bathing.

Smallpox was also endemic during this time period. It is caused by the *Variola* virus, and is spread only by breath at close contact. It did not tend to spread as rapidly as the plague or typhus. Still, it was frequently fatal, with no known treatment until Edward Jenner discovered that vaccinating with cowpox, a very mild infection caused by the *Vaccinia* virus, prevented the spread of the disease. It is not treatable by antibiotics. Many of the people in Grantville who are over the age of forty will have some resistance to smallpox due to childhood vaccination. They probably won't have enough resistance to prevent the disease, but are likely to have enough to reduce its severity.

Syphilis was apparently a much more lethal disease several centuries ago than it is today. Spread mainly by sexual contact, it killed half its victims after several years, many of them going insane before they died. Syphilis is treatable at an early stage with penicillin and other antibiotics, but not sulfa drugs. The first effective drug was called salvarsan, a fairly toxic mercury-based compound.

Tuberculosis, commonly referred to today as TB, is an infection that usually starts in the lungs. It is bacterial in nature, and the airborne version mainly infects those who are sick or elderly. A different version is spread from unpasteurized milk, and effects mostly children. Also called consumption, it weakens its victims over time before often killing them. It is difficult to treat, but can be treated with streptomycin, as well as some TB-specific drugs, such as isonazid.

Fortunately, the childhood version of the disease can be prevented by pasteurizing milk, a process which will be rather quickly available in the 1632 context given the modern knowledge of the characters. But an even simpler method which can be applied immediately is just to boil milk before using it. This is one of those diseases which can be prevented by the application of simple prophylactic measures known to modern medical science.

Staphylococcal bacteria often caused infections in wounds, as well as food poisoning. They are usually treatable with antibiotics. Streptococcal bacteria cause strep throat, as well as scarlet fever, in which the infection reaches the blood stream and often infects the heart. It is also treatable by antibiotics.

Antibiotics

Today, there are a large number of antibiotics available to treat various kinds of infections. The reason so many different antibiotics are needed is that the bacteria that cause the diseases mutate, or change, to better survive in their environment. So while in the 1950s there were originally only half a dozen different kinds—such as penicillin, tetracycline, and streptomycin—now there are many dozens, some of which are no longer used because they don't work as well against today's mutated versions.

Almost all the antibiotics used today are initially grown from pure cultures of some mold or other microorganism, and then slightly modified chemically to be more effective against newly resistant bacteria. However, the first antibiotics were synthesized, chemically produced from simpler compounds. These include sulfa drugs and chloramphenicol.

Equipment

It takes many steps to develop a usable antibiotic. This is called the "drug discovery process," and is long, expensive, and labor-intensive.

As a start, consider the equipment needed for isolating a drug. This is probably the biggest problem in finding an antibiotic in the setting of the 1632 series. Large quantities of supplies and equipment are needed—and there are no laboratory supply stores in Germany in the 1630s.

First, the characters in the series need something in which to grow cultures. Lots and lots of cultures:

thousands of them. They need something with a relatively flat bottom, because it will be filled with a material that the samples grow on. The material, called a growth medium, is poured in as a liquid and then gels to a solid, and so a container that is not flat requires more growth medium. Also, it is harder to handle things that don't have a flat bottom. It is important that the sample grow without being affected by other mold or bacteria, so it needs to be covered. The container shouldn't kill or grow the cultures, so metal and wood are not suitable. To process many samples, it is best if all the containers are the same size and shape. The containers need to be reusable, so the medical industry doesn't have to make more and more of them. Finally, it is best if they don't break easily, so that lab workers handling them are not exposed to dangerous germs.

We currently use something called a "petri dish" to do that. It is a pair of round glass dishes, one slightly larger than the other, with flat bottoms and straight sides. It requires only a little growth medium, has a top to prevent dust and spores from landing on it, and can be baked in steam and reused. It is made of pressed glass, a technology that wasn't well known in the 17th century. This involves making metal molds, taking a measured glob of molten glass, putting it into the mold, and then pushing a top to the mold to shape it before the glass has a chance to cool. Molten glass is very hot, and very dangerous. This will take a lot of work to develop, and a lot of time.

They also need large flasks and small flasks, as well as test tubes, for growing the possible antibiotics and for growing the germs to be attacked by them. It is convenient that the plug on the top come in standard sizes. The plug will probably be a wax-impregnated cork, because that is far more available than rubber in 17th century Europe. Flat bottoms are better, because the flasks need to stand up. Narrow tops are also probably better. The same safety factors apply as with petri dishes. For medium size flasks, wine bottles will probably do well. Gallon jugs are probably suitable for large flasks. There should be no problem obtaining empty wine bottles from the Germans (as well as the people of Grantville).

Growing the molds and bacteria presents another problem: food. Surprisingly, molds and bacteria can be very picky about what they eat. For mold, potato glucose should work. For bacteria, it really depends on the bacteria. Some will probably like an extract based on blood. Others will like glucose or other things. Figuring out the right foods will require some trial-and-error.

A gelling agent is needed to provide a solid surface for some of the steps in the process. This is the most difficult ingredient to obtain. While gelatin can be used, it still has to be wet when the mold or bacteria is put on the dish, and larger quantities of samples are needed. The best gelling agent is agar, which is made from red seaweed. Since seaweed will rot, it will need to be boiled and dried where it is found, on the coast, and transported to the lab from there. That means that someone with the needed knowledge will have to make a trip to the coast—in a continent torn by war—locate the seaweed, and figure out a way to make it into agar. Then they will need to hire and teach some people how to make it, and arrange for transport and payment.

Discovering an Antibiotic

Once the equipment and supplies are there, the work itself can be started. First, a large number of samples of molds and other microorganisms need to be collected. This is a lot of work, as each sample is collected from a different source, often from dirt. Penicillin was originally collected from mold from an overripe cantaloupe, by the way, not from bread or an orange.

As each sample is collected, it is placed in a test tube and transported back to the lab. The sample is swabbed onto the petri dish and placed in an incubator at body temperature. It is grown until cultures appear on the plate, which usually takes two or three days. From there, individual molds are selected and swabbed into test tubes containing diluted food for the mold. This gives pure samples which are grown for several days. Some of a given sample is taken and spun very rapidly in a centrifuge, causing the denser cells to go to the bottom of the tube, leaving what chemicals are produced by the mold in the top of the tube with water. The liquid at the top is removed very carefully with a long glass straw. This can be concentrated further in the same way that sugar is produced, by heating the mixture in a vacuum chamber. A low-tech vacuum pump can be made from the same kind of piston used on a steam locomotive, but in reverse; instead of having steam push the piston to drive the wheels, an engine pushes the piston, sucking air out through the cylinder. Another dish is swabbed with the bacteria, and then a large drop of the extract is placed in a spot in the center of the dish, and this is grown. If a circle containing no bacteria appears in the center of the culture, then this makes a possible drug. (The identification, isolation and pure culture of disease-causing bacteria to test with is yet another challenge, by the way. But that's beyond the scope of this article.)

That's the easy part—just lots and lots of repetition.

But it is not without risk! If the people doing the work get sloppy, they could get one of the diseases they are testing against, and kill themselves and their co-workers as well. A cut from a broken test tube or petri dish, a spill of germs, and there could be trouble.

Once a mold is chosen, it needs to be grown in greater quantity, in larger bottles. A lot more extract is made and purified. It will probably be made into a powder so that it is at a consistent dosage. This is carefully measured out, and a small amount is fed to a lab mouse. If it dies, this probably isn't a good drug. Larger amounts are fed to mice, until they figure out how much is safe for the mouse to take. Then, they infect mice with bacteria. Some are given doses of the drug by injection, with a few other mice given no drug for comparison. If the dosed mice live when the undosed mice don't, then you have a drug that will cure mice of the disease.

A promising start. But it's risky, because if the sick mice bite or scratch anyone, they run a very real risk of getting the disease. This process is repeated with larger animals, such as pigs or dogs. Again, if it cures the disease, it increases the likelihood that people can benefit from it.

Next is the really scary part: trying it out on people. It would be nice if the drug could be initially tested to see if it was penicillin or tetracycline, but that is beyond the Grantville high school chem lab's capability. To start with, you need healthy people, and they must be volunteers. This is important, for both practical and moral reasons. People must know what you are doing, and what risks they are running. You start by giving a few volunteers single small doses of the drug, and see if it makes them sick. If not, then the process is continued with larger and more doses until you reach the level that it worked (per weight) in animals. At this stage, it is easily possible that they could become quite sick or even die. If it does not make the volunteers sick, then it has passed the first step in testing the drug.

Next, you need to find a sick volunteer. This is risky to the volunteer if there is an alternative treatment that works. It could waste valuable time if the drug doesn't work, making them more sick. In some cases, using both an alternative treatment (like sulfa drugs) together with a possible antibiotic is a good idea, because sulfa drugs work more slowly. The idea is to see if the drug works to slow or stop the disease. If so, then it has passed the second step in testing the drug.

Finally, the drug is tested against any alternative treatments to see if it does as well or better than any alternatives. If it does, then you have an antibiotic.

But don't celebrate yet!

Drug Production

Making flasks of the antibiotic for testing has been done. But translating that into mass production is a far more difficult problem. First, they will need larger equipment that can be sterilized, so it doesn't get contaminated. Stainless steel vats are probably required. Large quantities of food for what is grown required. Because it only grows where there is air present, on the surface, lots of sterilized air will need to be bubbled thru the vat, and the contents of the vat agitated, like a giant bread mixer. The fluid will need to be drawn off, either continuously or in a batch process, and the drug isolated from the fluid and purified.

There is then one last step. Many antibiotics produced in this manner have problems being administered to people. Penicillin produced this way needs to be injected, because it breaks down in stomach acid. In this form, the body removes about 95% of it through urine. Modifying it chemically into a slightly different drug can permit it to survive in the stomach, be retained in the bloodstream, and generally be more effective. This will require figuring out what they have actually made, so that it can be modified into a known form by following some steps similar to drug synthesis.

Synthesized Drugs

Synthesized drugs are those that are made by taking other, more easily made chemicals, and processing them to produce the desired drug. In one way, this is better than hunting for an antibiotic, in that there is a specific process to produce the drug. If the source chemicals are pure, and the processes are not done in a faulty manner, then by doing step one, then step two, then step three, and so on, the drug can be consistently produced. But there are lots of steps, and each one needs to be done correctly, with the right ingredients, at the right temperature, and in the correct order.

The source chemicals are limited to what can be obtained or made by Grantville in the early 1630s. As all these drugs require variants of a chemical called benzene, that is one starting point. The easiest way to produce benzene in quantity is from coal tar. This is made by baking coal to a very high temperature. A number of flammable gases are produced, and these gases are captured, cooled, and carefully separated. Benzene is one of the products. Roughly ten pounds of benzene can be extracted from every ton of coal. This is then processed through a series of steps, along with other chemicals made by Grantville, until the desired drugs are produced.

Some of these chemicals are difficult to make, and can be quite dangerous if misused. Exposure to benzene, for example, can cause liver cancer. Again, another critical factor is purity. If another chemical is present with the one that is required, it could contaminate the process. This makes the results of all the previous steps worthless, and requires starting over again.

One example of a chemical that is difficult and dangerous to make is a special acid, produced by cooking sulfuric acid and chlorine gas under moderate pressure. Both ingredients are highly corrosive and poisonous. (Chlorine was used as a poison gas during World War I.) That means that stainless steel is almost a necessity to safely produce the acid.

Many other chemicals are similarly dangerous in a variety of ways, some exploding when mixed with water, a few burning when simply combined with air. Almost all are poisonous in one way or another.

Sulfa Drugs

The very first antibiotic was called Sulfanilamide, a member of a family of drugs called *sulfa drugs*. You may have seen it in a World War II movie, where a medic sprinkles a white powder over a wound. The ability of sulfa drugs to stop infections and allow people to heal was miraculous for its time. It was discovered by accident, when people found that a red fabric dye stopped infections. This took a while to figure out, because the dye itself didn't stop disease in the lab, but rather broke down in the body to make the antibiotic.

Sulfanilamide is fairly toxic, and there is not a lot of difference between a dose that has little effect and one that makes a person sick. It's not an ideal drug, but still one which in many ways deserves the term "miraculous."

Once scientists figured out what the drug was, and how to produce it, they tried a variety of chemical variations to see what might work better or be less toxic. They found a couple of dozen varieties, with differing ability to stop different diseases with more or less toxic effects.

Today, sulfanilamide is not used anymore as a medicine, but it is often made as an exercise in sophomore organic chemistry lab. It is the easiest antibiotic to synthesize. Sulfa drugs are less effective than penicillin and other drugs commonly used today. That's because they do not actually kill bacteria, but rather stop them from growing, requiring the immune system to do the killing. They are also limited in what they work against: they have no affect on typhus, syphilis, or smallpox, and only some effect on plague. But they are fairly effective on wounds and skin infections.

Chloramphenicol

Chloramphenicol was originally grown from microorganisms, as were penicillin, tetracycline, streptomycin, and the other half dozen or so antibiotics available in the 1940s and 1950s. Once the structure of the drug was determined, a method of making it from chemicals proved cheaper than growing it. This gave it a large competitive edge over the others in terms of price. In the context of the 1632 series and the resources available to the characters, it is the only powerful antibiotic that can be synthesized. Its chemical formula is even listed in *Encyclopedia Britannica*, as well as the *Physician's Desk Reference*, or PDR.

In some ways chloramphenicol is ideal, in that it can treat a wide variety of infections. Unfortunately, it has a couple of disadvantages as well, which is why most people today have never heard of it:

First, it is often not properly processed by newborns, leading to something called "Gray Baby Syndrome." Fortunately, this syndrome usually reverses itself when the newborn is taken off the drug. But, obviously, it limits chloramphenicol's effectiveness for very young children.

Secondly, and more damning, is the fact that in about 1 in 25,000 people, it causes aplastic anemia. This is a disorder in which some blood cells are no longer produced, resulting, about two weeks later, in the patient suffering a very unpleasant death.

As documented in the book *Adverse Reactions*, a number of cases of this were allegedly reported shortly after its introduction, and yet the manufacturer continued an aggressive marketing campaign. It was over a decade before Congressional committee hearings and lawsuits revealed the very real dangers to the public and stopped the deaths of many patients. Because of the danger, chloramphenicol is no longer used today in the United States or other wealthy industrialized nations. But it is still a drug of choice in Africa, where its cost effectiveness overrides the occasional fatal side effects.

In the context of the 1632 series, however, chloramphenicol is an ideal drug. The drug can effectively treat typhus and syphilis, which sulfa drugs cannot. It is far more effective at treating plague and most other bacterial infections than sulfa drugs. And when the death rate from the drug—1 in 25,000, or .004%—is compared to a 33% fatality rate for typhus, and a higher one for plague and syphilis, it is easy to see the advantages. If someone has one of these diseases, chloramphenicol is the only treatment available, and is arguably the most valuable man-made product in the 1632 context. Obviously—as was already touched on in the novel *1633*—there will be many issues needing to be dealt with regarding fairness and the cost of the drug. But that's true of the availability of up-time medicine in general.

While it will not be easy to produce chloramphenicol with the resources at hand, it *can* be done—with a lot of Grantville's money and skilled people. Early production would probably be limited to bucket quantities, however, enough to treat perhaps a hundred people per month. Only with the advent of stainless steel and chemical plants will production on a larger scale become likely. And for some time, the people capable of manufacturing the drug will be limited to a small number of the up-timers with a pharmaceutical or chemical background.

Conclusion

I'm afraid there isn't an easy answer to the development of penicillin or other grown antibiotics. It will take time, effort, expense, and some risk. Ultimately, in a decade or so, the characters in the 1632 series will succeed. In the interim, chloramphenicol and sulfa drugs will have to fill the void, and save as many lives as possible.

Chemical Engineering in 1632:
It's not just a job, it's an adventure.

My thanks go to Rick Boatright, Drew Clark, Laura Runkle, and other members of the 1632 chem group for their contributions to this article, as well as to my wife, Marla, for editing it.

End Notes:

History of Chloramphicol: *Adverse Reactions*, by Thomas Maeder, Harper Collins: 1994.

Synthesis of Sulfanilamide: *Experimental Organic Chemistry, a miniscale and microscale approach*, second edition, by John C. Gilbert and Stephen F. Martin, International Thomson Publishing: 1998; pp. 545-559.

Horse Power

Karen Bergstralh

The people of Grantville have been plunged into a world where horsepower literally means horse power.

In the 17th century muscle, water, and air provided power. Water wheels provide power for mills but their use is limited by location. Water is also subject to seasonal variations. Air-driven power always comes to mind with the Dutch windmills; but, again, air-powered windmills are limited by location and subject to variations. The ability of boats to move down rivers with the currents and back upstream with wind power again depends upon variations in the water and wind.

For dependable and portable power, that leaves muscles. The muscles involved might be human, canine, bovine, or equine. Horses, mules, and oxen provided the heavy muscle power.

The major categories that horses are used for are:

- Draft—pulling carts, wagons, plows, harrows, canal barges, and such;
- Transportation—riding;
- War—cavalry, officers' mounts, pulling artillery;
- Power—hitched to sweeps to provide rotary power for machinery;
- Food—do I have to explain this one?

Each category has different physical and mental requirements. A horse that is well suited to be a cavalry mount would not be suited to pull a wagon or plow. Each job requires a different combination of body type and personality. Also, each of these broad categories can be broken down into more specific uses, all with their own body type requirements. Within each category there will be a wide range of horses from the few, very good, very expensive, to the many solid, medium priced, to the poor quality, very cheap.

Draft horses may be light, medium, or heavy. Light draft would be pulling two wheeled carts to haul produce or people from the farm or around the city. Small placid horses and ponies are suited to these jobs. A new wrinkle, starting in the 16th century and continuing in our timeline (OTL) until well into the 20th, is the development of fancy carriage horses. These fancy carriage horses fall between the light and medium draft categories. Medium draft horses would be used in teams of two to eight to pull plows, harrows, and wagons on the farms. Heavy draft horses, also used in teams, are needed to pull the mechanized farm equipment Grantville will be building.

Light and medium draft horses abound; heavy draft

horses do not. A major change, one that is just starting in the 17th century, is the development of the heavy draft horse. As road systems get better between towns the larger draft breeds also begin to show up. They are the heavy trucks of the day. Oxen are still the animals of choice for plowing because the plows are so big, heavy, and awkward and horses are expensive. Slowly, in OTL, several heavy horse breeds developed and others were remodeled from medium to heavy draft. The early introduction of mechanized farm equipment will speed the demand for these heavy horses and in this area, the Grantviller with the Belgians may have something to offer his down-time farmer friends.

Horses used for transportation can be generally assigned to two categories—speed and comfort. The speedsters are bred for just that. They are used to speed mail and messages and for the man in a hurry. The comfort horses are the amblers. Another major change that occurs in OTL is the almost complete disappearance of amblers or gaited horses from Europe. The ambler has a soft, easy to ride gait much appreciated by those who ride long distances. Modern examples of amblers would be such as the Peruvian Paso, Paso Fino, Icelandic, and Missouri Foxtrotters. The ambling gait is a natural gait and is known today by a number of names such as singlefoot, shuffle, amble, Paso Llano, Paso Fino, or Tolt.

Warhorses also come in several types. There is the heavy cavalry horse, the light cavalry horse, the officer's horse, and the artillery horse. Again, those horses best suited to each category differ in body type and personality. All warhorses, regardless of use, must be able to learn to tolerate the battlefield or they have a very short career.

The medieval knight's destrier or Great Horse has disappeared from the battlefield along with the full suits of armor, victims of changes in warfare. The destrier type still hangs on, but is now seen mostly in the grand equestrian schools such as the Spanish Riding School. Some officers, to prove they are true gentlemen, will use the 17th-century version of the destrier as their mount. The various movements, such as the Airs Above the Ground, once used in battle, now are reduced to equestrian exercises.

The heavy cavalry horse is a sturdy animal, similar to today's Irish Draft horse. This troop horse can carry the heavier armored soldier in grand charges against the enemy line invoking terror in those facing his charge. This is the horse of close order formations and close quarter engagements. He has to be strong enough to cart his soldier to and from battle as well.

The light cavalry horse is more of a speedster; his soldier has less armor, and the tactics used are more hit and run or pursuit of broken (routed) troops. In Poland, they have been breeding Arabians since the 12th century and intermixing them with native light horses to produce the ideal light cavalry horse. All across Europe horse breeders are mixing various types in efforts to attain these ideal cavalry horses. In OTL, one result of this will be the English Thoroughbred.

Artillery horses are somewhere between the heavy cavalry and medium draft horses, or will be with Grantville's improvements to the Swedish artillery. Artillery in the 17th century was heavy and it moved slowly. Oxen were preferred for artillery draft animals. This will change and a medium-sized, strong, and quick artillery horse will be in demand.

All types of horses can provide power and food and often the sweeps were the last stop before the larder for aged and broken-down horses.

Grantville's impact on the horse population will come mainly in the demand for new types of horses. In leapfrogging three hundred years of gradual improvements to farm machinery they will quickly create demand for the heavy draft horses.

Changing horse types takes time. Gestation in horses takes eleven months. The foal is dependent on its dam for roughly six to seven months. At two years the horse may be developed enough to start training but two is when they lose their baby teeth. A sore mouth is not a good place for a bit. By the time they are four the growth plates in the knees are mature and the legs can withstand heavy work. Some breeds are not considered fully mature until six or even later. Starting a horse working too early can lead to physical problems. Training can add anywhere from six weeks to six or more years, depending on what the horse is being trained for. Adding it up, from breeding to useful animal is five years at a minimum (for those needing only the most basic training) to ten years or more for the highly trained.

One example of new horse types being developed is the Oldenburg. Bred in Lower Saxony, near the city of Oldenburg, they were based on the Friesians with a mix of Spanish, Neapolitan, and Barb blood. Early on they were known for consistency of type (conformation) and for being powerful animals with a kind character and a willingness to work under saddle, pulling a carriage, or in the fields. The Oldenburgs were started as a breed by Graf Johann XVI von Oldenburg (1573–1603) who set up breeding farms to produce warhorses. His son, Count Anton Günther von Oldenburg (1603–1667), also a renowned horseman, continued to breed these animals for riding and carriage pulling, warhorses being no longer at a premium.

Of the medium-sized draft breeds existing in the 17th century, one is the Percheron. They developed in the province of Le Perche in France. This breed's history is not well documented. What is known is that the breed began as a warhorse. Their size, 15 to 16 hands high, is documented from the 1600s although at that time they were still mixed use—riding and carriage—animals. While substantial, they were not as heavy as today. As with all European warhorses, they probably have some Spanish and possibly some Arabian blood. In the 17th century the breed began to be used as a carriage horse. Once relegated to draft roles, the breed changed conformation and size to suit its new role.

Breeds and Types

In the 17th century the term "breed" did not mean what it does today. What they called breeds were really types. As an example, a "Flemish" horse normally meant that it came from Flanders, not that it was a particular breed. On the other hand, if a horse was called "Spanish" or "Friesian" certain body and temperament characteristics were expected regardless of where the horse was actually bred. These body characteristics are what horse folks call "conformation."

Most 17th century breeders carefully selected both sire and dam and kept records as to the animals used. The breeders had a specific conformation and temperament in mind as they selected and bred. They did not place as great an importance on the origins of a horse as they did on its physical and mental suitability. If the object was to breed large draft horses with feathers then they selected the largest horses with draft type builds and feathers and bred them together until they achieved a strain that bred true.

An Oldenburg horse was a horse bred by Graf Johann XVI von Oldenburg or his son, Graf Anton Günther von Oldenburg. Graf Johann and Graf Anton Günther were breeding fancy carriage horses that could also be ridden. They selected those horses that most closely matched what they intended the end product to be and bred them together. These horses were known as "Oldenburgs." However, as Graf Anton Günther allowed tenants and others to breed their mares to his stallions, the term "Oldenburg" might also apply to animals that did not come from the Graf's breeding program. The upshot was if the horse met the criteria of an Oldenburg, it was acceptable to almost everyone as an Oldenburg. Naturally those horses sold from the Graf's stables commanded the higher price and some people undoubtedly got taken by smooth talking horse traders into thinking that the Oldenburg they purchase had come directly out of Graf Anton Günther's stables instead of Bauer Schmidt's pasture.

Today, what we know as breeds have studbooks and registries to control which animals can be called by the breed name. A studbook is a list of horses meeting the standards of the breed and being registered as that breed. Some breeds have closed studbooks; others run open studbooks.

The Thoroughbred is an example of a closed studbook. No Thoroughbred can be registered unless both of its parents are also registered Thoroughbreds. A Thoroughbred must be able to trace its ancestry back to the horses found in the General Stud Book (GSB). The GSB was established and first printed in 1808. The GSB used private records to attempt to detail all the horses that deserved the name Thoroughbred. At the beginning, in the late 17th century and early 18th century, there was no such thing as a Thoroughbred and those developing the breed had no controls on

what animals could be bred. The Thoroughbred was
developed in England as a light cavalry and racehorse.
Reading the GSB you find horses listed as Turks, Barbs,
Arabians, Royal mares (no breed specified) and others
with only a descriptive name such as Old Bald Peg.
At its beginnings, the Thoroughbred was a type. When
that type had reached a point where it was breeding
true the studbook was established and closed.

With a closed studbook the horse still has to meet
the breed standards to be accepted and registered.
Many closed breed books only allow certain coat
colors. With Andalusians, only Gray (which ages to
white), Black, and Bay are allowable colors. Closed
books usually require an examination by a breed judge
before the horse can be registered.

The other option is an open studbook. In most
breeds today with an open studbook the term "open"
is a bit of a misnomer as the registry only allows
breeding to certain other registered breeds. Taking
the Quarterhorse Stud Book as an example, to register
a horse as a Quarterhorse both of its parents must
be registered Quarterhorses or one parent must be a
registered Quarterhorse and the other must be registered as one of the other acceptable breeds, such
as Thoroughbred. A racing Quarterhorse may actually
be 7/8ths Thoroughbred. One result of this style of
open studbook that Quarterhorse confirmation has
divided into racing, ranch, and show types. There
is an ongoing debate among QH breeders as to the
physical standards of the breed.

Perhaps a better example of an open studbook can
be found today in the various Warmblood registries.
In most, one parent must be registered as a Warmblood, the other should preferably be from a recognized
breed, but if the horse meets the confirmation and
performance standards it can be registered.

Some of the color breeds, such as Paint Horse, allow almost any animal displaying the appropriate color to be registered. It is preferred that an animal have parents registered in one of the recognized breeds. With the concentration being on color one finds a wide range of conformation in these breeds.

Open or Closed Studbooks do have breed standards. Even when both the parents were registered members of the breed, if the offspring does not exhibit the desired traits it can not be registered. I offer an example of one such here: A very well known and respected Arabian breeder had set up a mating that should have resulted in a dream horse. The foal was a nightmare. While not deformed, it certainly did not meet the breed standards and was an embarrassment to the breeder. Some foals do grow out of their problems, so the breeder stuck this one in a far pasture and let him mature. At two years of age, the colt looked no better. The breeder called his vet and told him to destroy the colt. Instead the vet convinced the breeder to give him the colt and he would find it a home where no one would know his bloodlines. Many people learned to ride on the back of this gelding, little guessing what Arabian blue blood ran in its ugly body. He was never registered and the record for his dam the year of his birth lists "foal died."

Except for a couple of breeds there were no studbooks prior to the 1800s. The idea of studbooks seems to have developed late and it is only in the latter part of the 19th century that the idea of closed studbooks appear. This does not mean there were no records, only that what records existed were kept by the individual breeders. The early studbooks consisted of careful notes by the breeders of matings and the results. There was no central registry, no control over what could or could not be called by a breed name.

Even these early versions of studbooks were striving to breed a type of horse.

There is a specific meaning for the term "type." A type is a collection of desired traits including conformation, abilities, coloration, personality, and such that are determined by the breeder or breeders to be what they want in their animals. There is no dependence on the sire or dam being listed in a studbook, only on what the actual animal is like. Today there are many grade horses (unregistered) that meet the physical standards for various breeds. Because one or both of their parents were not registered they cannot be registered and none of their offspring can be registered. In the past this would not have mattered in considering them for breeding.

What does the above have to do with Grantville? After all, by the 17th-century, horse breeders in Europe have been breeding types of horses literally for millennia. In breeding, the guideline has always been: "Breed the best to the best hope for the best and cull the rest." This was well understood by the horse breeders of the time.

The Impact of Up-time Horses

I've consulted with Cheryl Daetwyler, who lives in and is familiar with the area upon which Grantville was modeled (the real town of Mannington and its immediate surroundings), and we've come to the conclusion that a lot of up-time horses came through the RoF. While we do not have an actual nose count, of course, it should be at least 1,000 and perhaps as many as 1,700. Many people have a horse or three tucked away on the odd acre of grass. The heaviest breed concentrations seem to be Quarterhorse and Appaloosa with smatterings of every other breed found in the U.S.

If we start with the low end of the number of horses in the RoF, we have a thousand horses. How does this break down into mares, geldings, and stallions? With all these horses, I could identify only three stallions within the RoF area, one Quarterhorse, one Appaloosa, and one Belgian. That leaves us with 997 horses to account for. At a guess based on my horse experiences, the majority are geldings. Geldings are the most popular for just plain general riding. Assuming that 600 of the remaining horses are geldings, that leaves us with 367 mares and foals. There are people in the Mannington area breeding horses, so we have to assume a percentage of the remaining horses are foals. Arbitrarily, let's say that 67 of the 367 are foals between newborn and two years old. This leaves us with 300 mares.

Now the question becomes: how many of the mares are of A) breeding quality; and B) breeding age?

At a guesstimate again based on experience, we have around 1/3 or 100 mares that are too old for breeding. Some mares are successfully bred into their twenties but as the years pile on the chances of a successful breeding starts going down. If a mare has never been bred, something common with riding stock, the chances of successfully breeding her over the age of 17–18 approaches zero. Note, this comment is for mares that have never been bred only. While successful breeding difficulties do increase with the mare's age they do not rule out breeding entirely. Secretariat's dam was 18 when she dropped him and I don't know anyone who will argue about his quality. Mind, breeding older never-before-bred mares has been done, and it can be done, but the risk of losing both mare and foal are very high even when you can get the mare bred in the first place.

This leaves us with 200 mares, a goodly number, but . . .

Another guesstimate gives us 50 of these remaining mares as being under four years old. They can be bred, but as with the older mares, this is risky. Better let them grow up a bit.

Now we've got 150 mares to breed. How many are worth breeding? Some have conformation faults so great that no breeder seeking usable horses would think of breeding them. Some have temperament problems and should not be bred. The general rate of successful breeding—i.e., the mare is bred, carries, and delivers a live foal—runs around 75%. (I'm being generous here—the more normal rate for estimating is 60%). If we breed all 150 despite confirmation questions, we could expect 112 live births. By the time they are one year old, this number will be reduced to 100 or less due to birth defects, accidents, infections, and injuries Grantville's vets can no longer control. Remember also, these mares are of many different breeds and the immediately available up-time stallions are of just three breeds. This is not a good case for most of these mares breeding true to their own type. The reestablishment of any up-time breed is therefore chancy due to the lack of numbers.

Another wet blanket is the problem of several of the up-time breeds having multiple, distinct body types. As mentioned above, the Quarterhorse has divided into three body types. I've heard endless lectures from a friend on "old-type" vs. "new type" Morgans and even I can see the differences. One would think that Thoroughbreds would not change body type much, as they have continued to be used for racing. Not so. On a long, warm afternoon several years ago I had the privilege to be seated amongst a group of elderly Thoroughbred breeders while watching Grand Prix

Jumping. What interested me was their agreement—and agreement among two or more breeders on anything is rare—that today's Thoroughbreds do not resemble those of forty or more years ago. This sent me off to look up some old pictures. The Thoroughbreds that most closely resembled the old horses were those bred for jumping and dressage, not for racing.

We also have to take a very long and hard look at what our up-time horses have to offer in improvements over the existing European stock. Unfortunately the answer to that is "Not much." Europe at this time is full of horses well suited to their uses.

Please remember: *in the 17th century horses were not a hobby*. Life and death could and did ride on their backs. A moderate quality riding horse would be expected to do forty miles a day for several days. Many of today's horses are physically unable to cover twenty miles a day without a day or so of rest. And before I have all the horse folks on my neck, yes, it can be strictly a matter of conditioning. Unfortunately I've seen and dealt with a lot of stock that physically could not be conditioned to even that level. Go out and look at your horses and try to see them through the eyes of a 17th-century horseman. What does your horse offer that he cannot find among his own down-time horses?

The answer to our question comes down to: *What impact will these foals have on the horses of the 17th century?* Except in the case of HyPP in descendants of Impressive and the possibility of there being an X-Factor Thoroughbred mare in Grantville, the answer sadly has to be: *little or none*.

If any of the breeding stock is carrying the HyPP gene (Hyperkalemic Periodic Paralysis), using them for breeding would be stupid and in the long term, dangerous. HyPP makes itself known by shaking, trembling, weakness (especially in the hind end), unexplained lameness and collapse. Horses with the gene may die suddenly at any age, apparently from heart failure or respiratory paralysis. HyPP has been called the equine AIDS. This is not something you want in horses that are necessary for transportation, farming, or cavalry. Today it can be tested for and, to some extent, managed. Unfortunately vets send their specimens out to specialized labs for testing. Grantville does not have such a lab and so the ability to test is lost.

Even if there is a Thoroughbred mare carrying the X-Factor gene, the beneficial results (a greatly improved cardiovascular system through a larger heart) will take a very long time to show up. Also, unless she is a double X mare, we would again be reduced to waiting until her offspring are dead to determine which of them inherited the gene. A better gift than HyPP, but one that will not make its impact for generations.

Fear not, there is one area where Grantville has a head start. We've identified a small farm breeding Belgians (heavy draft horses) within the RoF. As best I can determine the OTL family that owns them breeds for show and sale. It appears that they have one stallion and about eight to ten mares. They also seem to have frozen semen from at least one other Belgian stallion on hand. As discussed elsewhere, the true heavy draft horses came into being in the 18th, 19th, and 20th centuries. Down-time breeders, once they understand the new demand for heavy draft horses, will begin to develop and remold their medium draft breeds but the process can take from thirty to one hundred years before the down-timers will have true breeding heavy draft horses.

What Grantville can offer is mostly an understanding

of basic genetics, veterinary help, better parasite control, small improvements to draft harnesses, major improvements to saddle building, and four hundred additional years of general horse knowledge. Whether or not the horse breeders of the 17th century embrace these gifts is a different question.

Horses of the 17th Century

So, what horses are available to Grantville and the surrounding area?

Grantville found itself in the middle of both the Thirty Years War and a devastated area, repeatedly fought and picked over. Within this area the immediately available equine resources were primarily limited to those brought along by the Ring of Fire (RoF). There were very few useful down-time horses, mules, or oxen available locally. Within the RoF there are lots of riding horses but few suited to draft purposes. To insure survival, Grantville and the local down-time farmers need to find suitable draft animals.

Horses are available elsewhere in Europe. The prices have gone up, especially close to the devastated area. Horse dealers have to travel further to buy stock. They have to move their stock safely past armies that are always in need of fresh animals. This costs money in the form of additional guards and/or bribes. The added costs go into the end price of the horses. On the other hand, from the horse traders' point of view, it is definitely a seller's market. Horses are so desperately needed that animals rejected elsewhere command premium prices within the devastated area. In the end, the horses and mules are out there, but they cost more and your choices are not all first quality animals.

What follows below is a survey of draft horse breeds of Europe. Included are some modern breeds as well as those that existed in the 17th century. A few breeds for which there is very little information are excluded. These breeds may be extinct or the name has changed. Breed names do change and one breed may be known under several names or by different names at different times or in different places.

Breeds change more than their names. They change in size, type, natural gaits, and usage, also. Present day examples of any horse breed may have little resemblance to their ancestors. Horses have been molded to fit the requirements and fashions of every age. Few pictures exist that identify breeds so we cannot say with any certainty what most breeds looked like in the 17th century.

Many European breeds saw the introduction of Arabian, Turkish, and Barb blood when the Crusaders returned with their equine prizes. Poland became a major breeding area of Arabians but the fashion for mixing Oriental horses with native stock began as early as the 1300s and continues through today.

A Note on Terminology:

Where possible, the century of development is given; otherwise the terms Modern, Ancient, and Old are used to indicate the relative development period. Some breeds have gone through various periods of development.

"Modern" indicates the breed was developed in the 18th, 19th, or 20th century.

"Ancient" is used for breeds whose development can be traced to before the Middle Ages (12th century or earlier).

"Old" is used for breeds that can be shown to have existed prior to the 17th century, but not as far back as "Ancient."

"Draft" indicates use for pulling wagons, carriages, plows, canal barges, etc.

"Saddle" indicates use for riding.

"Warhorse" indicates a horse used for war. This might be an armsman's horse or a destrier (knight's horse).

"Pack" indicates use as a pack animal, which was quite common in areas with bad roads.

European Horses

Austria:

Avelignese. Italian Alps region. Small saddle, pack, & light draft horse. Old breed.

Lipizzan. Vienna. Warhorse, saddle horse. 16th century, established in 1580 by Archduke Charles II.

Noric. Also known as Noriker or Norisches Kaltbult (German), Pinzgauer—see below.

Noriker. Four main bloodlines: South German Coldblood (also called the Bavarian), the Steier, the Tiroler and the Karntner. Draft horse. Ancient breed.

Balkans:

Albanian Mountain. Small saddle horse, warhorse & pack horse. Ancient breed with a 14th-century infusion of Arab blood.

Albanian Myzeqea. Pony sized saddle & pack horse. Ancient breed with a 14th century infusion of Arab blood.

Danube. Light saddle and draft horse from Bulgaria. Modern (19th century).

Belgium:

Ardennais, aka Cheval de Trait Ardennais or Ardennais (French), Belgian Ardennes. Heavy draft horse. Ancient breed, much altered in the early 19th century and again in the early to mid 20th century.

Belgian Draft Horse, aka Brabant. Draft horse. Ancient breed that may have been used as a warhorse by the Romans before being bred up in size for draft.

Flemish. Draft horse and possibly warhorse, considered the rootstock for the Belgians. Ancient breed, much altered in the early 19th century and again in the early to mid 20th century. It is rare today.

Bulgaria:

Danube, aka Dunavska, Danubian, Dunav. Saddle & light draft. Modern (20th century).

Czech Republic:

Kladruber, aka Kladruby. Carriage horse, possibly a warhorse. 15th- & 16th-century roots with Spanish and Italian ancestors, especially the Alpine western horse. Rudolf II, the son of Maximilian II, established the Bohemian court stud farm in the year 1579 at Kladruby by the river Elbe.

Denmark:

Frederiksborg. Saddle, carriage, and cavalry horse. Stud farm founded in 1560s by King Frederick II with Spanish and Neapolitan stock with large infusions of Thoroughbreds in the 19th century.

Jutland. Draft horse, possibly a warhorse. Old breed, updated in the 19th & 20th centuries.

Knabstrup. Saddle and carriage horse. Old breed.

Estonia:

Toric, aka Tori. Light draft, saddle, carriage horse. Modern (19th century).

Estonian Native, aka Mestnaya estonskaya, Estonskaya loshad, Estonian Klepper, Estonian Pony. Saddle & light draft horse. Ancient breed.

Finland:

Finnish Horse. Saddle horse. Modern (19th century?).

Finnish Draft. Draft horse. Modern (19th & 20th centuries).

France:

Ardennes, aka Cheval de Trait Ardennais or Ardennais (French), Belgian Ardennes. Draft horse. Ancient breed.

Auxois. Draft horse. Old breed updated in the 19th century.

Breton. Draft horse. Ancient breed with three distinct branches—Heavy Draft Breton, the Postier Breton and the Corlay or Central Mountain Breton.

Corlay or **Central Mountain Breton.** Draft horse, crossed heavily with Arab and Thoroughbred in the 18th, 19th & 20th centuries.

Postier Breton. Coach horse crossed with English Norfolk Trotter and Hackney in the 19th century.

Heavy Draft Breton. Draft horse crossed with Ardennes and Percheron stock in the 19th & 20th centuries.

Boulonnais. Draft horse. An ancient breed (1st–2nd century A.D.) which may have been lightened up for use as a jousting horse. There are two distinct branches. The "fish cart" Boulonnais was a light draft horse with good endurance developed in the 17th and

18th centuries. The Large Boulonnais or **Maree** was a heavy draft horse—a true "heavy" developed in the 19th century. This version is very rare today.

Camarque. Saddle horse. Old breed.

Comtois. Draft horse; may have seen use as a heavy warhorse. Old breed.

Mulassier. Draft breed, now very rare. Horse half of the **Poitou Mule**. Old breed, possibly ancient breed. Mulassier means "mule breeder."

Percheron. Draft horse, may have been used as a heavy warhorse. Old breed, reputed to be crossed with Arabians in the 14th–15th centuries.

Poitevin. Draft horse—see Mulassier.

Selle Francais. Saddle horse. Modern (19th & 20th centuries).

Poitou donkey. Donkey half of Poitou Mule. Ancient breed—large, hairy, and very rare. Breed has remained pure (no outcrossings to other types of donkeys) because it breeds such good mules.

Germany:

Hanoverian. Saddle horse. Origins may be 17th century; 20th century infusion of Thoroughbred.

Holsteiner, aka Schleswig-Holstein. Saddle, draft, carriage, cavalry horse. Old breed (12th–13th centuries) with much use of Spanish, Neapolitan, and Oriental stock. Much updated with other breeds in the 19th and 20th centuries.

Oldenburg. Saddle horse. 16th-century breed,

Trakehner. Saddle horse, cavalry horse. 18th-century breed; 19th- & 20th-century infusions of Thoroughbred.

Rhenish German Coldblood. Draft horse. 20th-century breed, rare today.

Schleswiger Heavy Draft. Heavy draft version of Schleswig-Holstein draft horse. 19th-century breed.

Schleswig-Holstein. Draft horse, carriage horse. 19th-century breed.

South German Horse. Heavy draft horse. 19th-century breed.

Britain, Scotland & Ireland:

Cleveland Bay. Saddle, pack, draft, carriage horse. 17th-century breed.

Clydesdale. Heavy draft horse. Breed's beginnings trace to late 16th century.

Hackney horse. Saddle & carriage horse. 18th-century breed.

Irish Draught. Saddle & light draft. 19th-century breed.

Shire. Heavy draft, possibly a warhorse. Old breed (pre-15th century) whose size may have increased in the 18th century.

Suffolk Punch. Heavy draft. Old breed (13th century).

Hungary:

Gidran. Saddle horse. 19th-century breed.

Nonius. Draft, carriage, & saddle horse. 9th century, originally a draft horse, lightened for riding in the 19th century.

Kisber Felver. Saddle horse. 19th-century breed.

Shagya. Saddle horse. 18th- & 19th-century breed.

Iceland:

Icelandic, aka Islenzki hesturinn, Icelandic toelter horse, Iceland Tolter. Saddle & light draft. Very ancient breed. Closely related to the Norwegian Fjord horse.

Italy:

Haflinger. Saddle & light work horse. Old breed.

Italian Heavy Draft. Draft horse. Late 19th-century breed.

Murgese. Light draft & saddle horse. The breed origins are unclear.

Lithuania:

Lithuanian Heavy Draft. Draft horse. Breed origins are unclear.

Zhemaichu, aka Zhmudka. Saddle, pack, & draft horse. There are 16th-century references to the breed.

Netherlands:

Dutch Draft Horse. Draft horse. Modern breed (20th century).

Dutch Warmblood. Sport horse, saddle horse. Modern breed (20th century).

Friesian. Saddle & carriage horse. Ancient breed, stud farms date back to 12th century.

Gelderland. Saddle & carriage horse. 17th-century breed.

Groningen. Draft & carriage horse. Old breed? Origins are unclear.

Norway:

The **Dole Gudbrandsday,** aka Dolehest, Gudbrandsdahl. Small draft horse, saddle horse. Old breed.

Norwegian Fjord Horse. Small saddle & light draft horse, Viking warhorse. Ancient, bred in Norway for 2,000 years.

Nordland. Pony, light draft, saddle. Origins unclear, probably ancient.

Poland:

Hucul, aka Carpathian pony. Saddle & light draft. Old to ancient breed with the earliest written records from 1606.

Konik. Small saddle, pack, and light draft horse. Ancient breed later updated with Arabian blood.

Polish Draft. There are five different types of draft horses, all called Polish Draft, bred in different regions for different purposes. The five main types are the Lowicz, the Sztum, the Sololka, the Gravolin and the Lidzbark. The origins are unclear.

Malopolski. Light saddle and draft horse. Modern (20th century).

Arabian. Saddle horse. Ancient breed, brought to Poland throughout the Middle Ages.

Portugal:

Lusitano (see Andalusian). Warhorse. Very ancient breed, mentioned by the Romans.

Russia:

Alti. Saddle horse. Ancient mountain horse breed.

Bashkir. Light draft and utility horse. Origins unclear but definitely old.

Byelorussian Harness. Draft & harness. Origin not clear, apparently modern (19th century).

Budenny, aka Budyonny, Budonny or Budennovsky. Saddle horse. Modern (20th century).

Don Horse. Saddle horse & cavalry horse. Developed by the Cossacks in the 16th and 17th centuries.

Kabarda. Saddle horse. Origins unclear.

Karabair. Saddle horse from the steppes. Date of origin unclear. Probably very old.

Karabakh. Saddle horse from Azerbaijan. Ancient mountain horse.

Kazakh. Saddle horses from the steppes. Ancient breed (5th century B.C.).

Kustanai, aka Kustanaiskaya. Saddle horse from Kazakhstan. Modern (19th century).

Orlov Trotter. Light harness horse with great endurance. Modern (18th century).

Russian Heavy Draft. Heavy draft horse. Modern (19th century).

Russian Saddle Horse, aka Orlov-Rostopchin Horse. Saddle horse. Modern (19th & 20th centuries) descendant of the Orlov saddle horse.

Russian Trakehner. Saddle horse. Stud farms established in the 13th century by the Order of Teutonic Knights. From 18th century on Arabian and English Thoroughbred blood was added.

Russian Trotter. Trotting horse. Modern (19th century).

Tersky & Strelesky. Light cavalry horse. Modern (19th century).

Vladimir. Heavy draft horse. Modern (19th century).

Vyatka, aka Vyatskata. Saddle, pack, light draft horse. Old (14th century).

Spain:

Andalusian, aka "Spanish Horse," in Portugal known as Lusitano. Saddle & warhorse. Very ancient breed known to the Romans. The **Carthusian** (aka Carthusian-Andalusian) is a side branch of the Andalusian.

Astrurian, aka Asturcon. Small saddle horse, pacers or amblers. Ancient breed—Pliny mentions them.

Galiceño. Small saddle & harness horse. Ancient breed.

Losino. Small saddle & harness horse. Ancient breed.

Pottok, aka Basque, Vasca (Spanish). Small saddle, pack, & light draft horse. Origins unclear, may be ancient.

Sorraia, aka Marismeño. Prehistoric breed, wild horse in Spain, foundation stock for many European saddle breeds.

Spanish Barb. Saddle horse, warhorse. Ancient breed.

Tiger, aka Spanish Jennet, Caballo Tigre. Saddle horse. Ancient breed, very popular in Europe from 15th through the 18th centuries, an ambler.

Sweden:

Gotland, aka Skogsruss, Russ, Gotlandsruss, Skogsbaggar, Skogshäst. Small saddle, light draft horse/pony. Records exist from the 13th century.

North Swedish horse. Draft horse, carriage horse, cavalry horse. Old breed.

Swedish Warmblood. Saddle horse; original was 12–14 hands high, bred up in size from 16th century.

Switzerland:

Freiberger, aka Swiss Mountain Horse. Saddle, pack, light harness. 19th-century breed?

Ukraine:

Russian Heavy Horse, aka Russian Heavy Draft Horse—see above.

Turkmenistan:

Akhal-Teke. Saddle horse, warhorse. Ancient breed.

Iomud, aka Iomudskaya (Russian), Yamud (Iran). Saddle horse. Ancient breed.

Web sites for further reading:

http://www.ansi.okstate.edu/breeds/horses/
Good site with descriptions of breeds and pictures—some descriptions are spotty.

http://www.imh.org/imh/bw/eur.html
International Museum of the Horse—breeds of Europe. Provides good descriptions and photos.

All the descriptions above are based on my interpretation of the information available. Anyone with further information on any of the above mentioned breeds or breeds I've left out is welcome to contact me at Baen's Bar in the "1632 Tech Manual" conference.

Afterword

Eric Flint

There was an "Images" section in the electronic edition of the magazine which contained portraits of prominent historical figures of the time, along with my commentary. Retaining print rights to and reproducing those portraits in a paper edition would have made the volume too expensive, so they're not included here. However, if you'd like to see that section of the electronic edition, you can find it—free of charge—by going online. As follows:

1) Go online and type (without quotes): "http://www.baen.com" into the Address/ Location bar in your web browser.
2) Select "About the Free Library" from the menu on the top.
3) Once in the Free Library, select "The Authors" from the menu on the left.
4) Select "Eric Flint."
5) Select "Grantville Gazette Image Archive."

⊷ Grantville Gazette ⊷

An electronic-only magazine of stories and fact articles based on
Eric Flint's 1632 "Ring of Fire" universe.

Volumes 1, 2 and 3 are already available,
with Volume 4 on the way.

◈

In Volume 1, one story recounts a religious conference called in
Rudolstadt which will determine doctrine for all the Lutherans in
the new United States. In Volume 2, stories recount the first air raid
launched by the United States of Europe against Paris, among others.
In Volume 3, among other stories, the same teenagers who appear in
the short story "The Sewing Circle" (in the paperback book, *Grantville
Gazette*) move on to conquer the financial world. These magazine
volumes also contain factual articles exploring such topics as 17th-
century swordmanship, iron, agriculture, telecommunications, and
the logic behind the adoption of the Struve-Reardon Gun as the basic
weapon of the USE's infantry.

Grantville Gazette magazine can be purchased through Baen Books'
Webscriptions service at www.baen.com. (Then select Webscriptions.)
Volumes 1, 2 and 3 of the *Gazette* can be purchased as single copies for
$6 each, or you can purchase Volumes 2-4 as part of a $15 package.